Coattail Karma

by

Verlin Darrow

Coattail Karma

Cover Art by *Kim Mendoza*

The Wild Rose Press, Inc.
PO Box 708
Adams Basin, NY 14410-0708
Visit us at www.thewildrosepress.com

Publishing History
First Mainstream Fantasy Rose Edition, 2019
Print ISBN 978-1-5092-2374-9
Digital ISBN 978-1-5092-2375-6

Published in the United States of America

"I've been expecting whoever it is that thinks he's Buddha's clone."

I stared at him. "How do you know about that?"

"I'll tell you about it later," he said as he continued rowing. "But first put on my hat."

"Why?"

"So the men in the boat won't see you. It's easier than your diving back into the bay."

"It's bright red. They're much more likely to see me in your cap."

"They won't see you if you wear the hat," Marco said.

"That doesn't make any sense."

"Fuck sense," he said.

I just lay there. *This guy is crazy.*

"I'll tell you what," he said. "As a gesture of good faith, I'll give you some idea of who I am, so you'll put on the hat."

"Okay."

"Think about something that's completely immaterial—something I couldn't possibly know."

"Okay." None of this seemed as ridiculous as it would've the week before. I took a moment and recalled an incident at the San Francisco zoo in which a gorilla had signed to me from his enclosure.

"Interspecies contact can be powerful, can't it?" Marco said amiably. "And it's always available on some level. Animals are much more aware than we give them credit for."

He took off his hat and held it out to me. I immediately sat up and jammed it on my head.

Praise for *COATTAIL KARMA*

"*COATTAIL KARMA* isn't just a book. True, it's an exciting, fine piece of writing with plot twists galore, peopled with characters that behave like villains and metaphysical superheroes. And it's certainly fun to read. But it's so much more than that.

"In other words, Verlin Darrow's outrageous fantasy masquerades as something that readers can easily grasp and be wildly entertained by, but along the way he also shares wisdom and his own quirky take on the meaning of life in mind-blowing fashion.

"Well, if it isn't a book in the ordinary sense of the word, what is it? An experience? Yes, that's closer.

"Who can write such stuff and get away with it? Verlin Darrow can...and did. I can't recommend this book more highly. I love it."

~Richard House, MD,
author of Between Now and When

Dedication

This book is dedicated to everyone who's
learning to thrive in free fall,
or beleaguered by thoughts like science fiction stories
written by drunk monkeys,
or trying to stuff awareness back into
the benign Pandora's box it arrived in,
or trying to arm wrestle life into submission,
or struggling to give yourself permission
to be where you're at,
or trying to waltz with a badger,
or unfolding yourself and trying to return
to the simple, blank sheet of paper that you once were
before you became the complex, completed origami
that is reading this dedication.
In other words,
I dedicate this book to all of us walking around
in these outlandish human disguises.

Chapter One

I wasn't sure who was who in my shared waiting room since our receptionist had quit the week before. On the phone, Paul Arthur's baritone voice had sounded adult, poised, and not at all crazy. I ruled out the older woman in a rainbow tie-dyed dress and the teenaged boy texting at breakneck speed. This left three likely candidates.

My task would have been easier if anyone had glanced up from their reading material or cell phone. If I were a new client waiting for my first counseling appointment, I'd look up. I probably should've just called out Paul's first name, but what sort of psychotherapist can't solve a match-the-telephone-voice-to-the-person puzzle? As usual, my pride got in the way of taking care of business.

A giant, muscular Samoan man shifted in his might-not-be-strong-enough chair at that point, so I examined him first. Despite the chilly early April weather, he wore khaki shorts and a voluminous black polo shirt. He probably didn't realize the Monterey Bay kept Santa Cruz from warming up for a few more weeks. The guy could've been a pro football player or a sumo wrestler on a diet. He scowled as he read an *Oprah* magazine.

Candidate number two was a rat-faced guy in his fifties who looked as though he'd stepped out of a

1940s film noir. He'd have been the super in some seedy New York—no, make that Chicago—apartment building who told the cops the guy they were looking for had lit out and owed him a couple of sawbucks. Rat-Face was reading a fat Saab car-repair manual, of all things. I moved on to possible Paul number three without further ado.

Although he still hadn't glanced up, I sensed that Number Three was aware of me. After seven years at my job, I trusted whatever intuition popped up about clients. Sometimes this didn't work out, but I hadn't mustered anything more reliable yet.

Perhaps Number Three was demonstrating his presenting issue—ignoring people he should've glanced up at. What diagnosis could I invent for that? Glancephobia? Ignoritis?

In the Danish film this guy would star in, he'd be torn between his love for a sickly cellist and a lusty barmaid who was really a philosophy graduate student. He'd be so chock full of sensitive Danish love, it just wouldn't make sense to squander it all on one woman. But others wouldn't understand.

He was about forty—a few years older than I—his graying hair buzzed down low. An indigo fatigue sweater spilled down over ironed black jeans.

All in all, I was rooting for the big guy. I'd never worked with a Pacific Islander before—if he even was one, of course. Just then, Danish Guy turned over the shiny white tablet on his lap and peered up at me. "I had to finish reading an email," he said as he placed his iPad in a black nylon backpack. His alert blue eyes clashed with his sweater. They were his best feature, I decided.

"No problem," I said. "I presume you're Paul. I'm Sid Menk."

"Yes, I'm me," he said, standing and holding his hand out.

As I touched him to shake, a huge spark flew—I could actually see it.

"Whoa," Paul said. "It must be the carpet." He grinned as though he liked surprises.

I was taken aback and had no words for a moment. I'd never experienced any static electricity on that scale before. Heat spread up my arm, dissipating at shoulder level. *What the hell,* I thought.

"Why don't we go back into my office?" I suggested once I'd regained my poise.

I gave Paul his choice of chairs, and he made a beeline for my favorite, a dark green wingback. Then he took the time to thoroughly survey my office and told me that he liked it. I did too. It was spacious and well lit, with a second-story bay window overlooking a tree-lined street. I'd displayed my own photographs on the pale-yellow walls—mostly landscapes, with a few dogs mixed in. And every piece of furniture was just as comfortable as it looked. People fell asleep on my loveseat; clients ran from the office to go buy chairs like mine.

"Thank you," I said. "So what concerns bring you in?" This was my standard opening gambit. I'd been taught to sit there like an idiot and wait for clients to speak first, but that just annoyed people. And it was no fun feeling like an idiot once an hour, either.

"I'd rather not say, actually." Paul spoke so affably that at first it didn't register that he'd declined to answer.

"Oh? Would you rather start some other way?" I asked. A certain percentage of clients needed to assure themselves that I was qualified to help them before they decided to trust me with anything personal. This was more prevalent among men, I'd noticed, but it had never led to anything out of the ordinary before.

"Yes. Thank you," Paul said. "I'd like to ask you a series of questions. Some of them may seem strange. Are you willing to answer them?" He cocked his head and stared, which felt like a challenge. Was he testing me?

"Probably. Let's see what they are," I said, meeting his gaze and smiling. On the inside, my impatience gathered itself, and I hoped it wouldn't direct me to say something unprofessional. Clients playing these types of games irritated me, and I seemed to get more than my share of them.

"Fair enough." Paul retrieved his iPad from the bag at his feet and tapped it several times. "Question number one. Why do you do what you do?" He didn't look up, and his smooth delivery hinted at rehearsal.

"You mean why do I work as a therapist?" My confusion nudged me into stall mode.

"Whatever the question means to you. None of this is valid if I specify more," he told me, looking up briefly.

"Valid for what? To whom?" These words shot out of me without thought.

He smiled half a smile, moving just the very corners of his mouth ever so slightly upward. "I know this isn't how it usually goes in here. Can you bear with me? It really wouldn't be a good idea to go into that right now."

A sigh leaked out of me. A very unprofessional sigh. Then I told myself that maybe he wouldn't be a major pain in the ass. *Give the guy a break.* I was aware for the millionth time that I needed to work on my judgmentalism. If I hadn't just weathered a six-month stint of therapy with a manipulative policewoman client, I'd have felt more kindly disposed at this point.

"All right," I said. "I'll try to explain why I'm a therapist. I guess the short answer is that it's the only thing that's real enough now." I paused. "Let me try again." A new thought formed, and after a moment I tried to organize it aloud. "I think that my life experience—my curriculum, if you will—forced me to abandon unreal things like ideals and fantasies and thinking I'm in charge of much of anything. After that, being in service is what was left. It's like it's my default setting. We're really all in this together, aren't we?"

Paul studied me carefully as he assessed my alarmingly candid response. Then he began taking notes on his tablet. What was I thinking? Why would I let myself muse that way in a session? This was my deepest, most closely held life philosophy, developed after brief participation in a shamanic cult, a decade of meditation, and copious reading. Suppose he had come to therapy to work on his ideals or his fantasies. I would've just accused him of being full of crap.

"Next question," Paul said, giving no indication of any reaction to my answer. "What is your ethnic heritage?"

I pondered the inappropriateness of this line of inquiry before deciding to answer. For some people, it was relevant. I am Asian. Perhaps a given client's father had been killed in Vietnam or his mother had muttered Chinese epithets while she beat him. Who could work with the enemy?

"I honestly don't know," I told him, crossing my legs and fidgeting with my hands. "I was adopted under odd circumstances. Obviously, I'm Asian. Probably not East Asian—Chinese, Korean, or Japanese. Beyond that…beats me. An Indian minority? Tibetan? Hmong?"

I knew I could get a DNA test to find out, but so far I'd preferred not to. I don't know why. I did know that just thinking about it made me nervous. What if it was something really unpalatable? Would that make me a racist?

Paul nodded and read off the next question. "Were you raised in a wealthy enclave?" he asked.

"Well, yes," I muttered. This was not something he could have known. My brows drew together, joining my frown.

"Next," Paul said, averting his eyes. "Are you an only child?"

In fact, I am. Or at least I'm the only one my Caucasian parents adopted. "May I ask again why you feel the need to know these types of things?" I tried. "How could the fact that I'm an only child be relevant to our work?"

My stomach clenched, and I told myself that I was overreacting. It didn't help. I'd made a serious effort to keep a low online profile. What was Paul up to? Was he corroborating information that a private investigator had uncovered? Why? My mind sped up, seeking an answer on its own.

It was one thing to eyeball me and wonder about my nationality. I understood that. And perhaps a client could read me well enough to guess that I'd grown up quite wealthy, despite all my efforts to distance myself from that world. Likewise, the only child deal. But Paul wasn't asking me things based on any in-the-moment experience. When he'd momentarily tilted his tablet down, I'd seen a list on there—it looked like some sort of form.

"If this is going anywhere, you'll have an opportunity to have all your questions answered. Not by me—I only know part of it." He blushed, which made him look like a schoolgirl caught passing a note about a boy.

I decided to take a more direct approach. "Paul, each time you answer a question—or evade answering, I should say—I feel even more confused. Are you saying you're not a client? That you're here for some other reason?" I locked eyes with him and tried a smile—a patently insincere smile, as it turned out. For a moment, I wondered how a better therapist would've handled the situation.

"That's right," he said, nodding with relief. Apparently, he wasn't happy about the deception, either. "I'm paying for your time as a counseling client would, but the help I need is getting answers to these wildly inappropriate questions, and I'm not supposed to say why." He leaned back in his chair and smiled his half smile, and I realized I kind of liked this guy. This had snuck up on me while I'd been busy feeling annoyed.

He continued. "In fact, I've already disclosed more to you than to any of the others."

That was interesting. There were others. "Other therapists?" I asked, leaning forward, closing the gap between us.

"No, no. That's why the protocol is awkward here. It's one thing to interview a baker or an architect. It's something else entirely with a therapist. You're all so secretive," he said, shaking his head.

Secretive, huh? I nodded warily. "So you're paying to interview me after misrepresenting yourself as someone in need of psychological help? Is that what you're saying?" All things considered, I couldn't help but give him a dose of grief.

"Essentially. If I'd been forthcoming on the phone," he said, "I don't think we'd be here. And I do need help—it's just a different kind of help than I led you to believe."

I started to respond, but he lifted his hand to stop me. His stubby, inelegant fingers caught my eye. "Here's the bottom line," Paul said. "Are you willing to continue under these circumstances?"

"I need a little more to go on," I told him, sinking back into my chair. I'd been leaning so far forward that I'd almost toppled. "If you don't feel you can reveal whatever this is about, at least tell me why not. What's the general nature of this that makes it 'not a good idea' to tell me what's going on?" I needed to hear a benign explanation for his uncanny questions.

It was his turn to ponder. I studied him again. Paul's hands weren't his only physical flaw. His substantial unibrow perched above his clear blue eyes, although it was light brown and not nearly as caterpillar-like as some.

"All right," he said. "If that's what it takes. There's an organization—I only know their initials—that's looking for a man with some sort of special birthright or legacy. I don't know the details. They hired me to help find him."

"It's an inheritance? Is that what you're saying?" I embraced this idea; it warded off the less palatable alternatives.

"I don't know. Maybe it's not about money," Paul offered. "Maybe you're the next king of France—or make that Nepal. I do know that it's something profoundly important to impressive people. And I hope you appreciate what I'm doing here. I haven't broken the rules for anyone else."

"Impressive?" I was stalling again. As a kid, I'd yearned for amazing birth parents to show up and claim me, but this wasn't something I wanted to resurrect without a damned good reason. I focused on his breaking his own rules. Why was he doing it? I had no idea.

"They're balanced people," he told me. "Kind people that I admire and respect. I've had limited contact, but these women are some of the most evolved souls I've ever met." His blue eyes reflected exactly what he'd said. He really was a beautiful guy. If I were gay, he'd have been my type, which was probably a form of self-loathing since his ethnicity was pretty much the opposite of mine.

It was women? This surprised me for some reason. *Maybe I'm a sexist too.* "What are the group's initials?" I asked, ready to jump out of my head back into the conversation.

"RGP."

"Hmm. Really Good People? Royal Group Promoters?" I could think of several scatological possibilities as well.

"It might not even be in English," Paul offered.

"Why do you say that?"

"I know they're conducting interviews in at least a dozen other countries," he told me, leaning forward again.

The forward and back thing we were both doing was disconcerting. I held myself still, which for some reason was a major effort.

"At first," he continued, "we were only using photographs to find people. Now there's so much more to it—it's a big operation."

"All right," I said. "I'm intrigued. Go ahead and ask the rest of your questions." I felt my gut relax. Apparently, some part of me wanted to get on with this.

"What's your favorite color?"

"Blue." I didn't think. I just answered.

"Which do you like better—water buffaloes or parrots?"

"Water buffaloes."

"Do your hands ever tingle for no reason?"

"Yes."

"Do you crave for life to be other than it is?"

"All the time, but I'm working on it." I was almost in a trance now—only answering questions.

"Dogs or cats?"

"Dogs." I gestured at a few of the photographs on my walls. I felt more present for a few seconds while Paul perused the photos. Then we were back into it.

"Are you allergic to anything?" he asked.

"Yes."

"Mangoes?"

"Yes."

"What else?"

"Grapes. And various pollen."

"What about alcohol?"

"What about it?" I asked back.

"I mean, do you drink?"

"Rarely. On special occasions."

"Are you a vegetarian?"

"Mostly."

"Do you dream in color?"

"Yes."

"Have you ever had a dream that a man who looked like you but was older told you something important?"

"Yes."

"Was it about being patient?"

"Yes."

"What else was it about?"

"Courage."

For the last stretch, the rapid-fire interrogation had kept me focused on my answers, but I was beginning to feel overwhelmed by the surreal quality of the experience. How could anyone know about my allergy to mangoes, let alone a dream I'd had? What the hell was going on? This was way beyond the scope of a private investigator. Was Paul working for psychics?

A part of me was dying to get answers instead of providing them, but if I let my curiosity sidetrack whatever Paul's protocol was, I probably wouldn't find out.

"I'm going to show you some objects now," Paul said. He was in teacher mode, modulating his voice and speaking more slowly. Maybe he taught when he wasn't roaming the planet looking for allergic dreamers.

He reached into the black backpack at his feet and pulled out a red velvet sack. It looked like it ought to hold a two-hundred-dollar bottle of brandy. "I want you to pick your favorite item from each grouping," he said as he untied the bag's drawstring.

"Favorite?" I had no idea what he meant. How could I have a favorite if I'd never seen the things before?

"They'll be three objects at a time. You decide what 'favorite' means. Just point to the one you pick. Don't describe it or explain anything."

Paul flipped over his white tablet and adeptly lined up a pebble, a piece of bone, and a fragment of pottery on the back of it.

I wasn't thinking again—just responding. I pointed to the bone. I don't know why.

The next grouping was another bone fragment, a threadbare shred of brown fabric, and a triangular metal shard.

"I don't like any of those," I told him. The words fell out of me. While maintaining a rigid posture—no more leaning—I nonetheless scooted my chair back a couple of feet. Perhaps my body knew something I didn't about whether I should be in the room with this man.

There were two more groupings of similar nondescript items. In each of these, I picked one without employing any conscious criteria.

Finally, Paul repacked his collection and spoke. "Well, it's not up to me. But I think you're the guy."

"So you know what stuff I was supposed to pick?" I asked, eager to get answers. So far, the only thing that had occurred to me was that I might be the next Dalai

Lama, even though I wasn't a little kid. I'd watched three-year-olds in movies select things from past lives. Sometimes they were white kids instead of Tibetans, which pissed me off. I was only Asian on the outside, but still…

"No. I have no idea," he told me. "It's the way you picked, and your answers to the other questions. You had a lot of yeses to very specific questions. Either you're a great liar, or there's a match here." He smiled. Clearly, he was rooting for the latter.

"So what happens next?" I asked, a bit scared of what I might hear. Whatever part of me had shut down to answer Paul's questions was coming back online. My hands shook, and my throat was tight.

"I'll submit these results, and then I guess you'll hear from the RGP people if I'm right. If not, some other lucky guy gets to be king of wherever—or whatever the hell else is going on," he said with mild bitterness.

"I gather you're sick of this gig?" I asked. If I focused on Paul's experience, I wouldn't have to endure mine.

He ran a hand through his hair and sighed. "Absolutely. I've been thrown out of offices all over the West. And I'm down to just a few names. It's been a long haul." The fatigue on his face reflected his words.

"I'm sorry, but are you ready for the proverbial 'I see we're out of time'? Because we are," I told him.

"Gee, I was just starting to sound like a client, too."

"It's a shame. I'll tell you what. I won't charge you for the session we didn't have."

"Are you sure?" he asked.

"Yes," I said, and it felt right.

By now we were both standing, ready to shake hands. I hesitated, remembering the disturbing static spark when we'd first shook, and Paul spoke.

"Different carpet, different result, I'm thinking."

"Let's hope."

We shook, and this time it was completely ordinary.

I watched from my second-story window as Paul departed the building and strode in the direction of the bay. The watching-from-the-window trick was a ritual that helped me shift mental gears before my next session, which in this case was an extremely anxious woman with terminal cancer.

A moment later, the Samoan man from the waiting room left the building and also turned right on the sidewalk. He was even more imposing standing up—about six foot six inches tall and as wide as two men. When Paul paused just short of the next street corner to help a woman untangle her Chihuahua's leash, the Samoan halted as well. Suddenly, he was very interested in the tree beside him.

Paul was being followed.

Chapter Two

The rest of the afternoon was filled with a series of clients and their problems. They paid me to listen and respond, so I did, which gave me very little chance to assimilate or process the hour with Paul. I couldn't warn him about being followed, either. There'd been no receptionist to request contact information, and I'd never gotten around to asking him for any myself.

As soon as I'd walked my last client to the door, I flopped back down in my chair and called my best friend Chris. I was unnaturally exhausted, as though I'd run a 10K with an ex alongside me, belittling me with every step.

"I need to talk something over," I said. "Are you around?"

"Sure. Come on down. But stop and get a pizza."

"If you order one, I'll pay the delivery guy," I said. "I really need to deal with this right away." I found myself twirling a lock of my straight black hair, which was a regressive coping strategy that I'd been mocked for in middle school.

"Whoa. Are you pregnant?"

"Maybe. In a broader sense."

I hung up on him and headed over on my bicycle. Unless I was traveling out of town, I preferred to stay on two wheels—my stealth bomber of a bike—a carbon-fiber frame with full Campy that I'd spray-painted black to make it look less theft-worthy. Unfortunately, the paint job also made it look as though it had already been stolen and repainted, so I met quite a few police officers while I was out and about.

On the bridge across the San Lorenzo River, I almost ran over an unleashed corgi. Then an elderly pickup truck nearly took me out at the next corner. Both near accidents were my fault. I tried to pay better attention as I pedaled over to my friend's house.

Chris lived in the Seabright neighborhood near Castle Beach, where everyone should've bought a place ten years ago. Especially me. He perched on the railing of his front porch, holding a beer bottle in one hand and Karma's leash in the other. He lived in a modern one-story house he'd had built on the site of a 1940s beach cottage. Then, dissatisfied with the look of it, he'd added an old-fashioned, wooden front porch. Karma was a rowdy Border collie who loved to herd me—on my bike—into the bushes alongside the porch. I was grateful that for once Chris was acting as though he were a responsible dog owner. Which he wasn't.

"Come on in," he said. "I ordered the pizza, and I even decided to bankroll it since you're so troubled and all. Of course, I got it with weasel heads and human body parts, but you can always pick those off."

I smiled wanly, marched by him into his funky living room, and sat on the purple upholstered couch his grandmother had left him. Every piece of furniture in the house was mismatched to every other piece, as well as to the house itself. Chris and Karma followed.

She jumped up next to me and laid her head on my lap. This tended to be endearing at first and then increasingly uncomfortable as my crotch roasted underneath her thick fur. It was clear that Karma didn't always consider the effects of her actions on others. (I don't mean this in the philosophical sense of the word karma. I know now that Fate always stays focused on consequences while it's busy kicking free will's ass).

Chris disappeared into a giant black recliner and swigged his beer. Weather permitting, he wore the most hideous Hawaiian shirts he could find. Since he was overweight, his torso served as an expansive canvas. At the moment, he sported a green and orange pattern of hula girls and, inexplicably, tractors.

"You like my new shirt?" he asked.

"Of course not. What kind of question is that?"

He was only a bit taller than I, as opposed to pretty much everyone else over the age of thirteen. Apart from being short, we had little else in common physically. Where I'm slim, brownish, and somewhat androgynous-looking, Chris was round, very dark-skinned—East African parents—and bearded. His bushy beard ought to have rendered him somewhat hip, but it didn't. He just looked like an African nerd with a big black beard and an unfortunate acquaintanceship with a passive-aggressive shirt salesperson.

I loved Chris. Women had come and gone in my life, but Chris had always been there. His perspective on my relationship failures was helpful, too: "It's a personnel issue, Sid. You can't waltz with a badger. Pick someone normal, for God's sake."

"So?" he said. "What's up?"

"I had a very weird session today."

"I thought you couldn't talk about your work," Chris said as he raised his beer bottle to his lips. He always drank Mexican beer, since he'd turned twenty-one while on an epic road trip in Baja.

"I can't. That was part of it. He wasn't a client, it turns out."

I told Chris what had happened, including as many details as I remembered. I could tell he was taking mental notes. Blessed with a brilliant mind and an almost photographic memory, he'd earned bushels of money designing tech devices, but he also employed these traits to generate a running smart-ass commentary. For me, as his audience, funny usually trumped annoying. At the moment, I hoped I could evoke his serious side.

When I'd finished, he asked a few questions. "Do you believe this Paul guy?"

"Yes." I hadn't realized this until I answered. At the time, it hadn't occurred to me that he may have been lying.

"Could you picture the Samoan dude playing on the offensive line for the Packers?" Chris liked to envision people doing things.

"That would be about right," I said, stroking Karma's head. If a dog was within range, I always petted it. It seemed like the least I could do after all they did for us.

"Any long-term effects from the handshake spark?" he asked, tilting his head in a dog-like way.

"No, I don't think so." I suddenly felt even more exhausted. It was seven thirty by now, which certainly didn't explain it.

"Do you think this is about your birth parents?" he asked next. "I do. Maybe your mom was in a goddess cult or something. That would explain the evolved women and all the hocus-pocus."

"What about the little objects?" I asked, sinking deeper into the sofa's cushions.

"They could be sacred dealies that only a cool guy would know about—like what they do to find the next Dalai Lama," he said.

"Yeah, I thought of that too. So you think I might somehow know which item was special and which was just ordinary crud?" I wished I had a drink too. Chris hadn't offered me a beer or one of the black cherry sodas he kept in his fridge for me because he knew I'd just go get one if I wanted it. I was more tired than thirsty, though, and I would've had to displace Karma.

"Exactly," Chris said.

"That sounds pretty far-fetched. I mean, we have to go way past logic to consider something like that. What do you make of Paul being followed?" Karma decided to reposition herself at this point. My lap was grateful. Now she lay with her head away from me, trying to tempt me into scratching her just above her butt.

Chris frowned. "It's alarming. Nice people don't follow one another. And I think it indicates there's real money in this. You don't hire humongous people to follow other people if you haven't got deep pockets."

"Let's get to the really weird part," I said, leaning forward. "What's up with someone knowing my dream?" A flash of fear surged in my gut and my forehead tightened, which Chris noticed, narrowing his eyes and nodding.

"Ask me if I ever had a dream like that," Chris said, softening his tone.

"Have you?"

"No. Really ask me, I mean."

"Fine. Have you ever dreamt that an older version

of you told you stuff?" Here was annoying Chris. He was never too far away, even when the rest of him was trying to help.

"Yes. I'll bet a lot of people have. But most of them probably don't remember."

"We do…because?"

"You're a therapist. I'm me. Enough said." He tilted his head back and finished his beer. "This is my least alarming theory, bro. Why not go for it?"

"I'm trying, believe me. But this guy Paul knew— well, his iPad knew—that the dream was about patience," I said.

"Yeah, okay. That's weird."

"Any ideas? How is that possible?"

"Let me think a minute," Chris said.

A knock on the door announced the pizza delivery. I struggled to my feet, answered the door, and paid with the wad of bills that Chris tossed to me. Then I had to wait another fifteen minutes while Chris scarfed down the pizza. He never talked while he ate. Food was a priority for him—a passion. Karma begged continuously until Chris gave her the last piece.

"That's why she begs," I said. "Because it works."

"So? I like begging. It's cute." He shrugged.

"Fine. Why don't we get back to your theories?"

"Sure." Chris flicked pizza crust crumbs from his shirt. "Here's one. Do you know the racetrack tout scam?"

"I don't even know what a tout is. Why would you?"

"I considered a career as a con man when I was fifteen. It seemed like it might be a viable alternative to a real job. So anyway, a tout purports to be an expert at picking horses, and he sells a tout sheet to clueless bettors."

"That sounds like a doomed scam," I said, shaking my head. "Once his horses don't win, he loses his customers. And if he really did know the winners, he'd just bet on them himself, right?"

"I haven't told you the scam yet," Chris said. "That's just the standard tout deal. Now suppose there was a race with ten horses running and the tout gives out ten different sheets, each with a different winner."

"One guy gets a winner and thinks the tout knows something, right?" I nodded and felt pleased with myself for the first time all day.

"Exactly," Chris said, gesturing with both hands to form an expansive circle. "Now expand the scope. Suppose he handed out various sheets to a hundred people—or emailed a hundred thousand—using multiple races with seemingly impossible odds."

"I get it. Someone gets a series of winners and gets his mind blown like me."

"Yeah, that's my first theory." He looked up and to the right. I'd learned what that meant in graduate school, but I could never remember what. Recalling something? Having a feeling? "They could've interviewed such a shitload of people," Chris continued, "that statistically they were bound to be dead-on with someone. And it was you. What do you think?"

"I'm not sure. It does explain some of it." I liked the theory because it was so normal—so much a product of human nature. We were a greedy, selfish species, weren't we? I was rooting for Chris to clear the whole thing up with something along these lines.

"Con men are convincing," Chris said. "That's why

cons work. Well, that and general idiocy on the part of the patsies. In this case, all Paul's people had to do was compile a list of iconic dreams and ask about different ones in their interviews. Statistically, there are only so many."

"I don't have a lot of money or anything else they'd want," I pointed out. "You know about my parents' estate, right?"

"Yeah, I don't know why the hell they gave away all those millions instead of leaving it to you. Frankly, I'd like you better if you were richer. But back to the RGP people. Maybe *they* don't know what happened to the money. Or they might be signing up whoever matched their tout sheet to be a pawn in a bigger game—with bigger fish. I picture a marlin or one of those giant tunas that sell for a fortune in Japan."

"How would that work?" I asked, resisting the temptation to vote for the marlin. My mind couldn't jump around like Chris's and still get the job done. "I can't imagine how anyone could use an ordinary guy like me in some grand scheme," I added.

"I don't know. Maybe you're the Judas goat that could lead wealthy fat cats into their scheme. And Paul could be honest. He could be a puppet of the women—*they* could be the scammers," he said. "That way, you'd believe him because *he* believes him."

"Okay. We're starting to verge on paranoia here. What's theory number two?"

"Psychics." He stared at me, knowing I would find his answer unsatisfying.

"That's it? It's a one-word theory?"

"Well, they're real. They exist. One reason the deal might seem bizarre to you is you're not used to dealing with psychics."

"And you are?" It was my turn to stare. Chris could be so full of himself, so self-satisfied.

"There was Carla," he said. "And I'm more open-minded than you, anyway."

"Carla was the worst girlfriend ever."

"True. But she always knew when I was thinking about Anne." He smiled ruefully. "It was uncanny."

"The second worst girlfriend ever." I'd kind of liked Anne, but I wouldn't have dated her if you'd paid me. She liked to yell, then cry, then curl into a ball and not say anything. She'd do this in a restaurant with other people around.

"Don't make me play the Susan card, bro."

"Okay, I won't." She'd been my most recent and possibly my most tumultuous ex, which was saying something. Between the two of us, Chris and I had put in our time in Crazyville. "So what would you do if you were me?" I asked. "I feel like the ball is in their court. Do I need to do anything on my end?"

"I don't think so." He shook his big, round head.

"So if they contact me, I guess I'll just have to play it by ear, huh?" I felt like a kid asking his dad what to do. It was uncomfortable, but I felt I needed direction.

"Yeah. Just stay in the moment, and do whatever seems sensible. Isn't that what you do all day long as a therapist?"

"Yes."

"And isn't therapy supposed to be a microcosm of life?"

"Yes."

"And aren't you good at both?"

"Mostly," I conceded.

"You just got knocked off balance by the weirdness, right?"

"I guess so."

"It'll all work out, bro. Everything does," Chris said.

He hopped up to get another beer, and I sat with that.

****

I slept well that night. It helped that I no longer shared my small condo with a partner. Susan had left me nine months earlier for a woman. I'd really thought she was the one for the first few months. After that, I was just too chickenshit to pull the plug from my end. Susan could be vengeful.

My workday was slated to begin early, so I hustled through my morning routine and hopped on my bike. The mostly uphill ride to my office from my not-so-great neighborhood required me to keep a change of clothes in the office for when I worked up a sweat on the way in, but I didn't need them that day. The fog saw to that; it was probably forty-six degrees.

My key wouldn't turn in the front door of my building—a two-story white Victorian home at one time—and I was momentarily confused until I discovered it was already unlocked. Only rarely did one of my suitemates start her day before me, and never this early.

My heart raced as I carried my bike in on my shoulder and entered the waiting room from the street side. *What if I catch a burglar rifling through our stuff? Worse yet, will the Samoan ambush me in there?* Then I took charge of my mind and told myself it was probably just Janet seeing someone new. My paranoid first patient didn't need a comrade in arms.

I discovered one of the most beautiful women I'd ever seen. She sat in the waiting room with the posture of a dancer or a yoga instructor. I guessed she was my age or a bit older. Her simple white top and brown pants accentuated her slim build, and her porcelain skin gleamed as if lit from within. She'd tied her blond hair in a long ponytail.

She also had a presence—a weight to her—which took my breath away. I just stood there staring. The New Age movie that would feature this woman would also star a curvaceous redhead who would look way hot until this angelic being showed up to do some altruistic thing, at which point the entire audience would wonder why they'd ever thought the first woman had been attractive at all.

"Sid?" she asked. Her voice was lower than I would've expected.

I regained my composure. "You're from RGP, aren't you?" I asked. I felt relieved and curious.

"Yes. Can we meet for a few minutes before your first client?" She rose and towered over me. Surprisingly, my short-guy syndrome didn't kick in. It tended to show up at very inconvenient moments.

"Sure. Give me a minute." I released my bike from my shoulder, and it landed awkwardly, threatening to roll away and mow down an end table. I felt like a flustered teen as I wrestled it into submission and then wheeled it into the closet. "Come on into my office," I said as I emerged. I didn't make eye contact. I'd always been intimidated by magnificent women. Whatever happened with them mattered more; they were a litmus test of my desirability. Throughout all this, it never occurred to me to wonder how she'd gained entry into the building.

"I'm Sid Menk," I told her as we began walking. "You are?"

"Call me Sam." She strode beside me, as though walking behind me would've fulfilled an unpalatable gender role. I knew this was probably more projection, but as usual I bought into it anyway. My mind took comfort in pretending to know things about people.

"How much time do we have?" Sam asked, her voice lilting up at the end of the sentence. It charmed me. I had a strong urge to do whatever she wanted—to influence the litmus test in my favor.

"About fifteen minutes," I said. "I like to have space between things."

"Me too," she agreed. Clearly, we were a great match.

She chose the same chair as Paul, reminding me of something important. "Listen, when Paul left yesterday, somebody followed him," I told her. It came out faster than I'd intended. And my voice was higher pitched than usual.

Sam's face tightened. "What did he look like?" she asked, leaning forward.

"A giant Samoan."

She nodded. "He's a Maori—from New Zealand. Did you see his partner? He looks like a—"

"Rat?" I finished.

"That's him."

I waited while Sam gazed directly into my eyes and thought about this new development. Her blue eyes held mine for what would have been an uncomfortable duration with someone else. They were remarkably clear and present, like Paul's on steroids.

She finally spoke. "We don't have time to do much more than meet and arrange to talk later," she said. "But you may be in danger. I'll wait in your lobby today while you work."

"And do what? Stare at bad guys with those beautiful eyes of yours?" My compliment produced a brief smile, but I could see that she took it as an insult.

"I'm a martial artist. I can pretty much kick anyone's ass." She said this matter-of-factly with no trace of ego.

I flinched and then felt embarrassed that mere words had triggered such a response. "You'll get bored," I tried, mostly just to have something to say.

She shook her head, which stayed perfectly level throughout the maneuver. "I don't get bored."

"Ever?"

She shook her head again. I was developing a strong crush on Sam, partly because I was becoming aware there was something uncannily familiar about her. I knew I'd never met her before—I could scarcely forget someone who looked like her—yet I felt a kinship that was independent of her striking appearance. At least it seemed that way. I'd learned to mistrust my early take on the attractive women I met.

"Well, let's get you set up, then," I said. "Unless this is something we should bring to the police?"

"No, there's no crime here. Yet."

I didn't like that "yet." What did she know that I didn't? "I'll show you around," I said, leading the way back into the waiting room while she scrambled to keep up. "We can meet for lunch. You definitely owe me some explanations."

The Maori stood in the middle of the room, his dark eyes gleaming in the fluorescent light. "Hello, Samavati," he said in a New Zealand accent. "I was hoping we'd meet again."

Chapter Three

He moved onto the balls of his feet, pivoted slightly to one side, and curled his huge hands into fists. Sam shoved me to the side and slid forward. Were they planning to brawl right there?

"Why don't we let the council settle this, Jason?" she said. "There's no need for conflict."

Jason? His name is Jason?

"Frank's here too," he said. "And he's armed. Just let us have the shrink, and we'll be on our way."

Frank. Now that name fit the other guy. I was aware I wasn't focusing on the matter at hand, but I couldn't seem to. Would Sam kick Jason's ass? That seemed very unlikely despite what she'd said. The guy was not only gigantic, he moved like an athlete. Even cocking his head demonstrated a fluid grace. He wore the same outfit as the day before, and this time I saw a long, black braid snaking down his back.

All of a sudden, Jason came at her. God, he was quick. I scrambled farther out of the way as Sam swept a lithe leg out and caught him on the side of his knee. It didn't slow him down. She slid to the other side of him and leapt into the air. I'd never seen anything like the acrobatic kick she aimed at his head, but he dodged it and came back punching. He was like a mixed martial arts fighter, and she was some sort of kung fu goddess.

Sam blocked the big man's strikes blow by blow as

she backpedaled smoothly. Then, as suddenly as he'd come at her, she attacked. Her initial side kick caught Jason in the solar plexus, and he bent forward momentarily. Almost in the same motion, Sam knifed the edge of her hand at his neck, but he ducked to the side and then blocked her follow-up straight left with his forearm.

It was all happening faster than anything I'd ever seen, even in a movie. The moment one of them moved, the other one was countering and launching something else back. It was like an intense dance with no music, just a staccato series of grunts and thuds.

Sam landed far more strikes, but when Jason caught her off-guard, he rocked her. Once, she fell to her knees following a kick to her ribs. Twice more, his punches seemed to stagger her.

I pressed my back against a built-in bookcase and simply watched. Perhaps I could've helped—hit Jason over the head with a book or called the cops—but it didn't occur to me.

Sam began to wear him down. Gradually, his balance suffered, aided by her peppering him with compact, quick punches to his hips. Then he failed to recover from a complex series of kicks that seemed to be choreographed. Sam moved in and backfisted his temple from close range. A nanosecond later, she swept his legs out from under him, and he went down hard. The floor shook, and the bookcase rattled. He didn't get up. At first I thought he was dead, but he shook his head and moaned. His ass had definitely been kicked.

Before I had a chance to ask Sam if she was okay—she could've broken a few ribs at the least—a gravelly voice rang out from across the waiting room.

"I have a gun," Rat-Face said from the doorway. "And I like shooting it. Especially at people." His posture was cocky, and the revolver looked alarmingly comfortable in his hand.

All of this was very hard to absorb. *Has my life turned into an action movie?* And the next thought was about as useless. *Where is my client? She should be here by now.* A moment later, panic replaced all that. Adrenaline pumped through me, and I was ready for fight or flight, neither of which made much sense, given the circumstances. My heart raced, and my legs shook. I focused on breathing deeply and tried to return my attention to the very moment I was embedded in. No one was currently hurting me. The present was an antidote to anticipatory fear.

Once Jason managed to get to his feet, Frank herded us from the waiting room into the back seat of an old car. I didn't even notice what model. My mindfulness practice had failed me again.

Jason had gathered himself well enough to drive, apparently, which worried me. He could have a brain injury from the fight. I think I seized on this to keep from freaking out about all the rest. Frank sat up front with Jason and trained his old-fashioned revolver on us. It was huge.

Sam seemed very calm for someone who'd just weathered an all-out battle and was now being kidnapped at gunpoint. She was breathing deeply, though—playing catch-up, I guess—and sweat had soaked through the front of her white cotton top.

I tried to calm down, continuing to concentrate on my own breath. "What's going on?" I asked Frank. The breathing was no longer helping. Panic welled up again.

"You're a special guy," he told me. Everything he said was a growl.

"In what way?" I struggled to keep my tone normal. I didn't want these guys to know how scared I was. For that matter, *I* didn't want to know how scared I was, either. I focused on the surreal quality of the situation, avoiding facing what might come next. *Will they kill me when they're through?* I shivered, wriggling like a fish in shallow water.

"That remains to be seen." Frank wouldn't answer any more questions, and he told Sam that he'd shoot me if she spoke at all.

In a few minutes, we were on Highway One heading south. Traffic was light; we mingled with reverse commuters, most of whom seemed to be illegally talking on cell phones instead of noticing the guy aiming a gun at us. In fairness, he held his weapon low between the front seats.

It was clear that forces beyond me were in charge—more explicitly than usual, I mean—and that my internal reactions were irrelevant to the outcome. I told myself this, and it helped me settle down a bit. A bit was better than nothing.

As the car continued south toward Monterey, I wondered what in God's name was going on. Was I an heir of some sort as Paul had suggested? Were Jason and Frank hired thugs or members of some gang or organization? Was Sam—Samavati—a spiritual person or some sort of hired hand herself? That name sounded Sanskrit, but why would spiritual people be mixed up in something like this? Nothing that Paul had asked or shown me back in my cozy office helped me decipher things.

The weather stayed gloomy, but Frank turned on the radio, and it blared cheery Mexican polkas. Jason sang along to several in heavily accented Spanish. You haven't really been kidnapped until you've been serenaded in fractured Spanish by a giant Maori, while another guy with a rat face laughs and waves a revolver around.

They were having fun. For some reason, this struck me as the most absurd aspect of the entire situation. *Fun? Now?*

Then another thought occurred to me. I'd seen Sam in action; she could move incredibly fast. Surely she could have kicked the gun out of Frank's hand while he carried on. So why didn't she? She seemed to be on standby or something. Maybe she wanted to go wherever they were taking us.

We ended up on a runway at the Monterey airport, where a good-sized charter jet waited. There was no ticketing, no security, no baggage, and no opportunity to escape. I tried speaking up.

"Hey, what's the deal here? Where are you taking me? What the hell is going on?"

Frank told me to shut up, and I gathered myself to push back. Then I remembered the last time someone had barked at me like that. It had been a court-ordered client with antisocial personality disorder who'd fired me after two sessions. The guy had raped and killed the woman therapist he'd seen next.

I shut up. What were *these* maniacs capable of?

They separated Sam and me on the empty plane. I sat on an aisle near Jason while she sat with Frank and Frank's gun. The window curtains stayed closed, and I never saw a pilot or a flight attendant. The cabin sported wide, black leather seats—two per side—and dark wood trim on the walls. It looked like something a bond trader in a Wall Street movie would own.

Our flight consisted of eight hours of boring, noisy isolation with one break for handmade peanut-butter sandwiches from a plastic cooler that had been stashed under one of the seats. My mood gradually morphed from terrified to apprehensive to outraged to curious to bored to numb. I liked numb the best.

We landed eventually—rather poorly—and our plane taxied up alongside a much smaller black jet. We were hustled onto it, but in the dimming light, I could still see a palm-strewn beach and several low-slung resorts. The heat and moisture felt good after the plane's dry, cool air. Looking at Jason, I figured we were more likely in the South Pacific than the Caribbean, but it could have been anywhere. In the movie featuring this island, giant zombies would roam around and attack slutty teenagers. Or maybe a honeymooning couple would fall off a cliff and have to crawl back to civilization, but only the woman would make it, so she'd cry a lot.

The new plane seated eight—less comfortably. The seats were smaller and harder, with less headroom and legroom. I took some satisfaction in watching my giant kidnapper squirm in his. The jet engines shrieked as we took off.

Again, Sam and I were kept apart, and no one talked. This time I meditated. Six hours later, calmer than hell but no more enlightened, we landed—perfectly—at night at a private airport in what seemed to be the middle of nowhere.

My guts gurgled. Rain spattered against the

fuselage. My knees screamed at me. And suddenly, my meditative calm vanished, and I didn't miss it. *Fuck this!* It felt good to be mad. My brain shut down, and the feeling took over.

As soon as we stumbled down a portable staircase, I began striding toward what looked like a small terminal. The anger was driving me. It didn't want to take orders from anyone.

"Hold it," Frank called in his gravelly voice.

"Shoot me if you want," I said. "I'm hungry, and I'm eating." I kept walking. I could've run, but that would've showed fear. I was shooting for defiance.

Jason ran over, grabbed me from behind, and pinned my arms. It was like being held by a bear—a bear wearing cologne. He smelled like cinnamon and leather.

"Let's get takeout," Sam suggested calmly as Jason effortlessly dragged me back. "What's good in New Zealand?" she added. This time I could hear the disguised tension in her voice.

"New Zealand?" I said when Jason released me from his embrace.

"North Island," Jason said. "Home."

Without a word, Frank handed the gun to his partner and scuttled off. Jason gestured for us to hunker down on the plane's stairway. He stood a few feet in front of us in the light rain, holding the gun uneasily. I could see that like most martial artists, he didn't like guns. It probably felt like cheating to him.

"Have you been here before?" I asked Sam, turning to look at her. Her pale face gleamed in the plane's landing lights, and she tried to smile.

"Once."

"You guys better shut up before Frank gets back," Jason said.

"Or what?" Sam asked. "I know you wouldn't use that gun."

"Why not?"

"Your vows."

"What about yours?" he asked, raising his voice.

I flinched. "Vows?" I asked.

The two of them just stared at one another. Sam was icy; Jason glared. Would they fight again?

Just then, a short white guy in a navy-blue uniform trotted toward us, and Jason held the gun out of view alongside his massive hip.

"Are you a cop?" I shouted when he came into range. I stood and launched myself in his direction, banging into the muscular arm that Jason thrust in front of me. It was like getting hit by a metal baseball bat.

"Mind yourself," Jason whispered, flashing the gun.

"Good evening," the uniformed man called back in a slightly different accent from Jason's. "I'm the airport manager and have a few questions I need to—" He broke off as he got closer. "Hey, aren't you Jason Patariki?" he asked, his face lighting up.

"I am," Jason told him.

"Oh my God. What an honor. Right here at our little airport."

"What's your name?" Jason asked, smiling like a politician.

"John. I'm John. Oh man, this is really something."

"Well, John. I'd like to visit with you, but we're right in the middle of something here."

John finally turned his attention to me and Sam.

"Oh, of course. I'm sorry. Please carry on." He jogged away, and that was that.

"What happened to his questions?" I asked. "Who are you?"

Sam supplied the answer. "Rugby. He was the king. And they're mad for it here."

"Oh." I thought that over and decided to try a psychological approach. Since I knew how to do therapy, surely I could flip things around and do anti-therapy.

I forced myself to smile and mustered a passably sincere-sounding tone as I addressed Jason. "I guess it was hard to make the transition to civilian life, huh? It's kind of sad, really." Then I switched gears, adding an edge to my words. "You're a national hero one day, then you're following people, trying to beat up women—unsuccessfully, I might add—and finally you even kidnap us. That's the worst. Did you know in the US you can get the death penalty for kidnapping? What's next? Are you going to molest some kids?"

The gun was back. "Why don't we all just shut the hell up until Frank gets here?" he barked.

His jaw clenched, and his eyes blazed. I'd gotten to him.

"Is that a rhetorical question, Jason?" Sam asked. "Because I can think of several good reasons why we ought to talk without Frank. You know he's crazy."

"Shut the fuck up!" he roared. "That's an order from the guy holding the gun. Enough!" With each word, his volume and intensity increased. He radiated palpable energy and power. It was easy to picture him dominating a rugby match.

Somehow, I managed not to flinch, and I felt a

flash of satisfaction from this inconsequential triumph. Then I wondered if my baiting Jason was making things worse or if I was investing in a riling-up account that would come due later in some useful way. I wasn't interested in pushing my luck to find out, so I followed orders and shut up.

Ten minutes later, Frank jogged back to the steps by the plane, where we sat in the light rain. He nodded at Jason. "He's on his way," he said.

"What's next?" I asked.

"We find out if you're a clone or not," Frank said.

Chapter Four

A clone? Seriously? That's what this was about? If no one had publicly cloned anyone yet, how could it have happened thirty-seven years ago? It was unimaginable—at least to me. Clearly, looking at the others' faces, all three of them could imagine it. Were they privy to some backstory I didn't know about?

By this time, we were thoroughly soaked. What was wrong with sitting in the plane, anyway? Then a much smaller Maori man drove up in an oversized silver SUV. Sam and I were blindfolded and shepherded into the third row of the vehicle. This was harrowing on one level, but on the other hand, I was now sitting in proximity to the most beautiful woman I'd ever met. And wherever she was going, I was going there too.

I decided to focus on something useful. What did I know about New Zealand? Not a lot. I thought about what I knew instead of brooding about the possibility of being a clone, or being killed, or whatever else awaited me at the end of the car ride.

The two main islands were supposed to be very green and unspoiled, with more sheep than people. Most of it was rural, with thousands of miles of rugged coastline. All sorts of flora and fauna had developed independently on the islands—tree ferns, kiwi birds, and... My list ran out there, and I couldn't remember anything else about New Zealand. This left me with cloning again. And what might happen to me. Thank God Sam began whispering to me at this point.

"Don't worry," she said.

"Don't worry?"

"We'll be fine. They need us. And to my knowledge, they've never murdered anyone."

"That's faint praise, don't you think?"

"It certainly is," Sam agreed.

"Who is this 'they'?" I asked.

"Shut up!" Frank shouted. This seemed to constitute about eighty percent of his working vocabulary.

The answers would have to wait. After a few more minutes of worrying, the effects of sitting hip to hip with Sam penetrated my preoccupation. Much as Jason had radiated energy, Sam did too. Hers was gentle and a little buzzy, like a mild electric charge. It washed over me in slow, calming waves.

I slipped my blindfold up and glanced at her, puzzled. Hers was around her neck. Other than Paul's handshake, I'd never felt anything like this before. Sam nodded her acknowledgement of the phenomenon. She was doing it on purpose—sending me positive energy. I raised my eyebrows. *What the hell,* I tried to say without words.

Sam smiled a sweet half smile—like a feminized Buddha statue. Her face was completely relaxed, and her skin glowed with light.

As weird as all this was, I was comforted when she put her arm around me and pulled my head onto her muscular shoulder. Frank noticed we weren't wearing our blindfolds; we slipped them back in place.

Eventually, I fell asleep.

Sometime later, the SUV slowed to a halt. At this point, I lay with my head on Sam's lap, and her hand rested on my head. After a brief moment of peace, my gut tightened and my mind slipped back into frenetic thinking in a futile attempt to escape the fear and confusion that arose.

Just before we were led out, Sam whispered, "I'm on your side." This time, her attempt to shore me up sounded insincere. The comfort I'd found evaporated. All I knew about her was that she was beautiful, seemed oddly familiar, and could transmit energy. Were we really allies? Why? Who the hell was she?

After stumbling along, still blindfolded, on a dirt road or a dirt trail or a dirt something, our footsteps landed on a more substantial, smooth surface underfoot, and unseen hands maneuvered us onto a wooden bench. It had stopped raining or maybe it had never rained here. I had no idea how far or how long we'd driven. I heard feet shuffling and a slight echo of that sound as well. Were we indoors? It didn't feel like it. The air was quite cool, and it smelled damp. Could the echo be from a canyon? A few minutes later, while I strained to hear a whispered conversation somewhere off to the right, at least this small mystery was solved.

"You can take off your blindfolds," said a male voice with an Asian accent.

An elderly man stood before us in the antechamber of a large cavern, dressed in a cobalt blue robe with a black belt. I couldn't tell his ethnicity—Indian maybe? Pakistani? The cavern was unremarkable—no stalactites or other formations. The movie that would feature it would have intrepid spelunkers getting lost, but then a dog saved them, but then the dog died. My film plots had certainly taken a turn for the negative.

"Bhante," Sam said, standing and bowing to him with her hands clasped.

"Samavati," he said, bowing back. "It's a pleasure to see you." He turned and bowed to me as well. "Sid, thank you for coming." He was bald and large-featured, with especially oversized, droopy ears.

I stood, my fists clenched. "Are you serious?" I asked. "We were kidnapped at gunpoint on the other side of the planet, for God's sake." My voice trembled, terse and raw.

He smiled, and his warmth tried to thaw me. "I assure you that in Christian terms, it was very much for God's sake. And I asked Jason to invite you here. I'm afraid when he encountered his old nemesis—Samavati—he reacted from a primitive ego level. The rest followed. And Frank will no longer be working with us. We cannot tolerate weapons. So I apologize for everything. I'm very sorry."

"You're sorry? Sorry?" I shouted. "You think that makes it all right?"

"No, of course not." Bhante tilted his head down, his eyes on his own feet.

"So we're free to go?" I asked.

"Of course." His head snapped up, and he looked me in the eye. "But as long as you're here, perhaps you'll honor us with your company for a few hours." He smiled again. He seemed to have a lot of confidence in its ability to influence people.

"No, thanks," I said, turning to leave. Standing behind us were two exact duplicates of me. They both smiled at me with my face.

"There are more of us," one said.

"Can't we persuade you to stay?" the other one added.

My knees went weak. My limbs felt dead, and I couldn't speak. My face flushed hot too, and my chest tightened so much, it was hard to breathe.

At least my doppelgangers didn't have my voice. The first one spoke with a Spanish accent. The other one sounded like he was from New York. They walked around us and stood beside the Bhante guy. One wore a black robe, one wore a green one.

Sam bowed to them as well and then studied me as I struggled and failed to accommodate yet another extremely unpalatable slice of reality.

"Well?" said Bhante. "I can offer you a shower, a cup of tea, and as you can see, a change of clothes in your exact size."

Now, stuck in neutral, I couldn't form thoughts, let alone words. Being a clone was like finding out I was adopted times a thousand. *Were clones even real people? How long did clones live? Maybe I'm a triplet.* Finally I mustered, "Sure. Whatever. But let Sam go. She doesn't need to be here, does she?"

"I want to be here," she said. "It's time RGP found out the truth as well. And if Bhante is here, we're safe. My concern was that Jason and Frank might be operating on their own."

"Thank you," Bhante said. "You're very welcome to stay, although as you can imagine we have no spare women's clothes here."

"Is this a monastery?" I asked.

"Of sorts." He gestured to a downward set of stone stairs off to our left.

As I followed the trio of Bhante and the two other versions of me, Sam sidled up beside me and held my hand. Hers was quite callused, which must've been a martial arts thing. I appreciated the support in that moment. And her energy snaked up my arm as well.

In hindsight, descending that long staircase represented some sort of profound sign-up—a willingness to move toward that which terrified me. And it was downward, too—underneath the world I knew.

At the bottom of the stairs, a long hallway carved out of the limestone cave's walls stretched ahead. Bright red wooden doors marked a series of rooms along the hall. Bhante gestured to the second open doorway on the left, and Sam and I walked through it hand in hand while our host and the other Sids remained in the hallway. This room was also carved out of stone; axe and chisel marks scored the rough walls. In a moment, two more versions of me came out of the bathroom adjoining the small, simple bedroom.

"Everything is ready for you, Sid," one of them said. He spoke in an English accent and wore jeans and a black T-shirt.

"There's a towel and toiletries laid out on the counter," the other me told me. He didn't have an accent. His hair spiked up, punk-style.

Unlike a mirror, these images of myself moved independently in three dimensions. For the first time, I could see how I truly appeared to others—striking-looking, handsome even. My Asian features fit together on my face in a pleasingly exotic way. And my arresting eyes were dark and piercing. I would've bet money that if I ever had an opportunity to see myself more clearly, I'd move myself down on the one-to-ten hotness scale. As it was, I decided I was an eight.

Another part of me watched myself go sideways again to avoid my emotional experience. "How many of you—of us—are there?" I asked. Another surge of adrenaline kicked in, despite the lack of a physical threat. At this rate, I'd deplete my endocrine system and be unprepared for any future emergencies.

"We don't know," they said in unison. The second one continued. "When the first seven or eight found their way here and we were all in the Great Cave together, it was too overwhelming for some of them. Two are still struggling psychologically—maybe you can help them. So now there's a rule that we never have more than three in a room at the same time. Identical triplets don't go crazy, right?"

"So give me a ballpark figure," I said. "Ten, Twenty? A hundred?"

They looked at one another. Sam squeezed my hand. For some reason, the number mattered to me. "Maybe twenty or twenty-five," the first one said. "By the way, I'm Norm. This is Jim."

We all shook hands, an extremely strange experience. *So that's what my hand feels like.* It was smaller than I expected.

"You're not asking the sixty-four-million-dollar question," Sam said to me.

"Which is?"

"If you're clones—and I'm not sure you are—who are you a clone of?"

I was floored by this. I hadn't thought of it at all. I'd been focused on the copies, but who were we a copy of?

"We don't know," Norm and Allen said in unison again. The hairs on the back of my neck rose as a unit, as well. This was like a scene in a science fiction movie. *People can't speak in unison.*

"Why don't we clean up?" I said to Sam, happy to change the subject. "And then we'll have a chat with Mr. Bhante about that." I wasn't in a rush to find out who "Dad" was. It mattered too much. What if he were a despicable historical figure like Pol Pot or Ho Chi Minh? After all, who had the resources to manage something like this?

"The word 'Bhante' is an honorific," Norm told me. "Like Lama or Monsignor. It's not his name."

"What tradition is this?"

"Sri Lankan Buddhism," Sam answered. "With a twist. I'll see you soon."

She left with the others, and I headed for the shower.

****

I considered the new information under a stream of hot water. Buddhists, huh? They weren't acting like any Buddhists I'd ever heard of. And what did Sam mean when she said she wasn't sure I was a clone?

Maybe it was all a hoax. Maybe these lookalikes had undergone plastic surgery to resemble me so I'd think we were clones. But this brought me back to the discussion I'd had with my friend Chris. Why would anyone go to all this trouble to con me? I wished I could've called Chris and recruited him to research the crap out of all of it. But not only had Jason confiscated my cell phone early on, there'd be no service in a cavern anyway.

And what was with the cave dwelling? Was this a

secret cult that hid out underground? Maybe the cave was a deprivation deal so the monks could meditate without distractions.

Next, I wondered why Sam trusted Bhante. And what did she know about all this? What sort of group was RGP? Another branch of Buddhism—feminist Buddhists? Finally, I decided to just focus on the shampoo in my hand. Mindfulness was my go-to remedy for pretty much everything, despite its inability to help me since Bhante's goons had shown up.

When I'd finished cleaning up and dressing in well-worn jeans, a white T-shirt, and a brown hooded sweatshirt with a gold rocket logo across the chest, I explored the room more thoroughly. The walls were solid all the way around, which felt a bit claustrophobic. Also, they conveyed a timeworn quality. It's hard to describe, but it was more than just the hand-tool marks or the antiquity of the stone itself. Somehow, I knew these walls had been here a very long time. I also knew that New Zealand itself hadn't been. If it hadn't been the last large settled land mass on the planet, it was close to it. Of course it was possible I wasn't even in New Zealand. I only had other people's word for that.

I ventured out into the hallway, expecting to find an escort, but I was alone. So I wandered several doors down, where I found yet another me sitting cross-legged, looking at a hot rod magazine on a purple yoga mat on the floor.

"Is that a new kind of meditation?" I asked.

He answered me in an unfamiliar language and shrugged. Maybe it was something Slavic. It sounded odd coming out of an Asian mouth—my mouth.

"He just got here," a voice called from down the hall. "He doesn't speak English yet."

I pivoted and spied yet another me. This one was wearing a navy-blue warm-up suit. He tilted to the right as though he were about to steal second base in a softball game.

"I'm Ken," he said. "You must be Sid."

"That's right."

I waved goodbye to hot-rodder me and walked down the hall toward Ken with my hand extended.

"I'm getting over a cold," he said. "I'd better not. Where are you from?"

"California. You?" I listened to myself. My voice was poised and steady. Maybe I was adapting.

"Florida, sort of. Air Force brat. Adopted, obviously." Now he rocked back and forth on the balls of his feet. He reminded me of a fireman client who'd suffered from unmedicated attention-deficit hyperactivity disorder. I'd liked the guy, but the sessions had been exhausting.

"Do you know where the others are?"

"It's teatime. Follow me," Ken said.

He practically ran down the long corridor, so I did too. At the end of it, just around a sharp corner, another set of steps were carved into the limestone. They led up to a large, surprisingly well-lit room that seemed to be a library, with several floor-to-ceiling bookcases on three of the four walls. I looked up to find the light source. Wall-to-wall banks of fluorescent lights clung to the ceiling.

"It's full spectrum," Ken told me, grinning like he'd just won something. "You miss the sun down here after a while."

That was worrisome. Was Ken a cheerful underground prisoner? Would I be one soon?

At the far end of the room, Bhante, Sam, Jason, and another clone sat in an ensemble of antique teak chairs grouped around a low wooden table. I strode toward the empty seat next to Sam. Ken peeled off and headed back.

"Jason is here to apologize," Bhante began, nodding his head amiably.

"Oh?" I felt my gut tighten a bit.

"I'm sorry," Jason said.

Other than the words, I saw no evidence of this on his face or in his body language. "Well, that was short and sweet, wasn't it?" I said. "What are you sorry about?" *I'll be damned if I make this easy for him.*

"Everything. I allowed my personal feelings to keep me from cooperating with how things needed to be."

"That's really vague, and it sounds like a hand-me-down aphorism," I said. It felt great to be back in my power. I found myself sitting up straighter.

"I'm very sorry my apology isn't better," Jason said. Again, his declaration struck me as insincere.

"Here's what I want," I said, swiveling to address Bhante. "Answers. Forget the apologies, the fluffy towels in the bathroom, and the tea you're pouring right now. I want answers."

"I agree," he said. "It's time for answers." He gestured to Jason and the unnamed clone. "Would you two leave us, please?"

They rose and walked away through a doorway in the side wall. The contrast between my clone's frame and the Maori's was startling.

"Let me explain as best I can," Bhante said, fussing with the blue ceramic teapot.

Sam leaned forward; she seemed at least as interested as I was in what was coming next. This was the first time I'd even glanced at her, which said something about my focus. Her face glowed with life force, well worthy of my attention.

"In the Buddha's time—the Buddha most people are familiar with—things were very different," Bhante began.

I directed myself to face him again. It took some effort. "Wait a minute," I said. "There was more than one Buddha?"

"The one you know—Siddhartha Gautama—was not unique." Bhante gestured elegantly with both hands. The smooth, measured movements looked like part of a formalized dance, but I didn't see how they related to his words. "He was simply a man—an incarnation of consciousness—who became enlightened," he continued. "Others came before him in like fashion. Who knows if Buddhist history is true in the ordinary sense? But do you think, amongst the multitudes of people who have ever lived on this planet, only one person has ever fully awakened?"

"I suppose not." In spite of enjoying my one-up position a minute before, I found myself intrigued enough by Bhante's words to enjoy my current role as a student.

"We are all sleepwalking our way through illusion. Periodically, we need someone to remind us there is another way," Bhante said.

"Okay, I'm with you so far. I can accept there were other Buddhas before the one I've heard of."

"Excellent." Bhante paused and sipped his tea. Once again, his movements were ritualistic. "You know, they grow this a few kilometers from where I was born."

"Where is that?" Sam asked.

"Kandy, Sri Lanka."

He sipped his tea again, and I tried mine. It was by far the best tea I'd ever had. Even the temperature seemed perfect.

"Have a scone," Sam said. "They're delicious."

"Maybe later."

"So the Buddha's story is well-known," Bhante continued, studying me, perhaps to ascertain if I knew it.

"Born a prince," I said. "Never saw suffering, finally did, wanted to understand, left, became an ascetic, got enlightened, went around teaching?"

"Yes!" Bhante clapped his hands together. Clearly, he was delighted by my one sentence synopsis. "But less well known are such things as his teachings to his inner circle, his prophecies, and various secret texts in Magahi Prakit, his birth language."

"Which may or may not exist," Sam said. "Every other early Buddhist text in the world is in Pali. Magahi Prakit may not have been a written language at all. Certainly, it has no trustworthy translation if it was."

"We have corroborating texts in Pali, Sanskrit, and modern Magahi, which is still spoken in parts of northeast India," Bhante told her. His hands were wrapped around his teacup, but his bald head bobbed from side to side. He seemed excited, but it was hard to tell with these spiritual types.

"So is this like finding more books of the Bible?" I

asked.

"No, that would not be accurate," Bhante said. "Let me explain. Buddha had a keen sense of what would be helpful for students—or anyone—to know. And also what might impede their progress, however true."

"So he knew more than he was willing to tell?" Did we really need all this background crap? *Get on with it.*

"Exactly. When people asked him esoteric questions about the nature of the universe—the meaning of life and all that—he'd tell them it didn't matter. If they were worried about what would happen after they died, he'd tell them to sit quietly and be with their worry. He wasn't interested in dispensing answers. He was showing people how to live so they might arrive at things themselves. Always, it was practical—nuts and bolts. What worked, what didn't work."

"But he knew all the esoteric stuff. That's what you're saying?" I asked. It was clear Bhante was a born teacher who wasn't going to let an opportunity to teach slip by. Perhaps I could move things along by demonstrating that I understood.

"Most assuredly. Buddha knew whatever there is to know. That is enlightenment."

"So what's this about special teachings and prophecies?" I said. "That doesn't sound like him." I kicked myself for expressing an interest. Now another history lesson would be coming my way.

"There is one widely known prophecy that belies his general message of self-reliance. He said another Buddha will appear when the world needs a great teacher again—when Buddha's message has become lost. He said it might not be himself per se, and it might be either a man or woman."

"Like a messiah? Like Jesus?" I thought I knew quite a bit about Buddhism, but this was news to me. I was more familiar with the spiritual practices and general principles, as opposed to the literature or history.

He shook his head, and his torso moved with it. "Oh, no. It will not herald the end of the world or be on the television news. It would just help everyone. A great teacher just helps."

"So you're saying, in all this time, there hasn't been a Buddha since Buddha?" I asked. "Surely there's been a need lots of times." I felt caught up in Bhante's words now.

"This is a subject of great debate," Bhante said, steepling his hands together. "Various historical figures have proclaimed themselves to be Buddhas. And various eras have seen Buddhism on the decline. But there has never been a consensus about these things in terms of Buddha's prophecy."

"So Buddhists have been squabbling about this for a long time?" I asked.

"I wouldn't care to describe it in that fashion. But certainly there has never been a unifying figure since Siddartha." He frowned as if he suddenly remembered something unpleasant.

"A unifying figure?" I asked. "That makes it sound like a politician or a war hero. Eisenhower as Buddha. Is there something wrong with having a variety of religious leaders? A variety of Buddhists?"

"Of course, there is never anything right or wrong about the way things are," Bhante said. "It is arrogance to judge reality. Let me say it this way. One of Buddha's realizations was that everything is connected—no, everything is One. So separation is an illusion. His message was so simple, the variety of perspectives you speak of merely represent a variety of misunderstandings. There is no need for all these separate Buddhist organizations. There are not even separate people within these groups. This is all a misunderstanding." He smiled broadly, and I saw his teeth, which were a jumbled mess.

"So a new Buddha would reunite Buddhists?" I asked. "And unity is a major part of his message?" I felt pleased with myself for this.

"Yes. An incontrovertible Buddha—a consensus Buddha—would become the focus of all the groups. Even non-Buddhists would listen to a great teacher. A modern Buddha could retell the message using modern language that could speak to modern people." He smiled and beamed his hope across the table to me.

"So why now?" I asked. I sipped my tea, and he paused to sip his. Sam watched us both.

"Theravadan Buddhism, which is pure, original Buddhism," Bhante began, "moved to Sri Lanka from India when invaders arrived, and then spread to Southeast Asia." He peered at me. I would've been wondering if my involuntary student was still interested. Bhante seemed to be looking past that—into me somewhere. "This could've been an era that invoked the prophecy," he continued, " 'when the world needs a great teacher,' but the message stayed strong in these new lands. So for all these years, no Buddha has been needed."

"And now?" I still didn't know where we going with all this. What sort of payoff could justify such an extended preamble?

"We had bloody civil war in Sri Lanka for decades and military rule in Myanmar—Burma. Pol Pot committed genocide far worse than the Nazis in Cambodia, and we all endured the sadness of the Vietnam War, not to mention the rampant sex trade in Thailand. Our Theravada bastions of Buddha's message are no longer living true to it. Southeast Asia has regressed."

"But Buddhism is popular in America and Europe," I said. "I know lots of people who read and meditate and try to be loving and kind. Especially in California."

"That's well and good, but most of it is not real Buddhism. The Western versions of Zen and Tibetan Buddhism, for example, are watered down to make them palatable. At best, they are distortions." He frowned, forming wrinkles below the corners of his mouth where none had been.

"So what do your 'secret' texts say about this?" Sam asked, her passion animating her face. "You say you have access to esoteric teachings?"

"Much as RGP does, Samavati. We are both caretakers of vital information, and I think neither of us would be interested in sharing it unwisely. Keeping secrets can be habit-forming, but we both know how our organizations came to be. Some secrets need to be secrets—at least for now. The Buddha taught us that." He seemed tired now, as though he was no more accustomed to all this talking than he was to frowning.

Sam nodded. I was struck again by her beauty. In that moment, the symmetry of her features was like a soft, mobile sculpture of a Scandinavian goddess. Some women exuded warmth through their eyes or their smile. Some stunned you with their raw sexiness or their model-like elegance. But best yet, the intelligence and awareness that rested in Sam's eyes told me that she knew how to connect at the deepest level. It took my breath away.

"But I will say this," Bhante said. "We have a text that is more specific about when and how the next Buddha will appear. We have kept it in a buried reliquary, along with several of the Buddha's toe bones. These were retrieved by his brother from his cremated ashes. The Buddha told his inner circle that he will come back 'when his body reappears.' "

He leaned back as though he were done expounding. Then Bhante looked at me expectantly. I'd more or less forgotten that all this applied to me somehow, which amazed me. Did Bhante have some special ability to hold people's attention?

"And?" I said.

"Think about it," Sam said. She smiled gently, as if she were waiting for a third grader to work through an arithmetic problem.

I did. It didn't help.

"How does a body reappear?" Bhante asked.

I shook my head.

"How do they duplicate animals?" Sam added.

Suddenly, I understood. "You think I'm a clone of the Buddha? From a bone relic?"

"I know you are," Bhante said. "The question is: are you Buddha himself? He has reincarnated in only one of the clones."

He studied me again as I absorbed this. *Holy shit.* My face froze, and my chest tightened. "Wouldn't I be a lot nicer?" I said. "Or wiser? Or just an all-around better person?" I floundered, not even sure what I'd said. I'd been expecting intensely distressing news. Instead, his words overwhelmed me in a different way. *Could it be true? Am I Buddha?*

"Perhaps," he conceded. "But Buddha was only a man, not a god. He was much like you or me before his realization."

Sam spoke up. "Your answers to Paul's questions show you're the strongest candidate the RGP has found," Sam said. "By far. There's an uncanny correlation between your life and Siddhartha's in terms of early life circumstances, personal preferences, and of course, your affinity for items associated with the Buddha."

Sam was in on this, too? Did that add weight to the idea or lessen it? I had no idea. "So it was the same kind of deal as when they show some little Tibetan boy a bunch of stuff to see if he's the next Dalai Lama?" I asked. I knew that if I kept talking, I could get through this. Words were a refuge from the maelstrom of my emotions. My gut churned, the vise of my chest muscles strangled my ragged breath, and my heart pounded as if to split at the seams with each new beat.

"Yes," Sam said, her eyes soft. "I'm sorry we couldn't reveal any of this to you."

"I think it's time I heard about this 'we' that you keep talking about," I said.

"I don't mean Bhante and I," Sam said, turning to face me. Tingling energy flowed out of her, and I felt marginally calmer. I also felt oddly connected to her. Was her energy merging with mine? Gluing us together?

Sam continued. "RGP has been interviewing

potential Buddhas for years. We didn't know about the clones, of course, because Bhante here has apparently been gathering and hiding them. I guess our organizations have been coming at this from different angles."

Bhante smiled. "The potential Buddhas are a fine group of men," he said. "It's been my joy."

"Did they all sign up to live in this cave and work for you?" I asked. That seemed unlikely, but Bhante's lure of Buddhahood was certainly seductive. I'd already pictured myself sitting under a tree answering questions from a bevy of gorgeous women. Now I visualized myself leading a meditation at the UN.

"Oh no. We've visited many candidates who chose not to leave their life situations," Bhante said, bringing his teacup up to his lips although there was no tea left in it. "And no one does any work here that they don't wish to do. Most feel a certain obligation when they learn of their heritage."

"Heritage, huh? You know that no one has cloned a human, right?" I said. "Aside from the ethics of it, the science hasn't been there. How could someone have done it thirty-seven years ago?" I glared at him. In that moment, the whole deal felt like a hoax.

"I am not a technically oriented person," Bhante said. "But people in my organization have been working on this since shortly after World War II. In fact, some of the early pioneers were German scientists who'd become persona non grata."

"What *is* your organization?" I asked. "What's its name?" It was time to get some practical answers.

He looked down, and his face reddened. "It's a secret," he said. "I can't tell you."

"That sounds like some kid's TV show," I said. "Are you the head of it?"

"Oh, no."

"Who is?"

"I can't tell you." This time Bhante held his head up and looked me in the eyes. Apparently, he felt embarrassed about keeping the name a secret, but hiding who was the leader didn't bother him.

I looked at Sam. "I don't know," she said. "I wish I did." She looked away, the first time I'd seen her space out.

"Hold on," I said. "I need to slow down." I was enjoying my grandiose fantasies of leading the world into the Light with my saintliness, but this was also patently ridiculous. I lived in Santa Cruz, a hotbed of New Age and Eastern practices, but I was no saint. Most of my spiritual seeking had led to dates with nutty women instead of bliss or enlightenment.

"So Sam," I said, "if you didn't know I was a clone, what led you—or Paul, rather—to my door? Do you have some other criteria besides Bhante's prophecy that helps you find people? What do *your* texts say about all this?"

"RGP is an organization that formed shortly after Buddha left his body," Sam began, sounding like a teacher now herself. She'd ceased transmitting energy, but I still felt it in my chest as a warmth—no, a glow. "That was twenty-five hundred years ago," Sam continued. "We've preserved teachings no one else knows. Even Bhante here would be surprised to learn much of it. But it wouldn't be helpful to make any of it public—not yet. So revealing the reason we sought you out in particular would cause more harm than good."

"In other words, it's all a big secret, and neither of you are going to tell me shit," I said, glaring at both of them in turn. Bhante flinched at my profanity. Sam smiled. "So where do we go from here, Bhante? Do I get to pick which group to join? Because I like the one that doesn't kidnap people better. For that matter, the hell with both of you. Send me home. I've got to think all this over."

Just then, an alarm bell went off, echoing loudly against the limestone walls.

"What the hell is that?" I asked.

"We're under attack," Bhante said.

Chapter Five

Bhante sprang to his feet and led us to one of the imposing bookcases to our right. He seemed quite calm. And very spry for an old man.

"We're prepared for this," he said. "Just keep following me, no matter what happens."

Reaching up to the corner of a shelf, he swung the bookcase open, revealing a dimly lit passageway cut into stone. Jason waited there.

"We need to hurry," he said. "They're armed, and they've got helicopters. It's probably Jackson's people. Someone's betrayed us, and my bet's on Frank."

Fear raced up my gut and tightened my chest. It was hard to breathe again. *More guns? Helicopters? Who is Jackson?*

Bhante swung the hidden doorway closed, and we ran down the passageway. Jason led the way but soon outdistanced us. That guy could really move. Even in the dim light—low wattage bulbs lined the side wall—it was beautiful to watch.

At the end of a long straightaway, we rounded a curve and found ourselves facing yet another flight of stairs. These were cut more roughly on a steeper upward angle than the others. Bhante led the way; Jason was no longer in sight.

The older man shoved open the spring-loaded door at the top and slithered through. I took a deep breath and followed. We entered the back of a low-ceilinged, shallow cave with bright daylight in sight ahead of us. I traced my fingers over a series of cave paintings unlike any I'd ever seen in books. Various flightless birds in faded greens and blues stood in a meadow, their wings spread. Another mural depicted a rocky beach in the foreground with a limestone cliff behind it.

"Bhante," Sam said, peering at the birds. "Those are prehistoric, aren't they?"

"Not quite," he answered.

Our guide urged us forward. In a few moments, I found myself back in the world, standing on a wide rock ledge several hundred yards above an expansive turquoise bay. It was my first sight of New Zealand in daylight, and as my eyes grew accustomed to the glare, a scattering of small, very green islands came into focus, and a flatter, larger one sat a few miles beyond them. The scene stretched even farther than that, and a white lighthouse gleamed at the neck of the irregularly shaped bay where it met the sea. What sea, I had no idea. Steeply sloped limestone bluffs like the one in the cave painting surrounded most of the bay. To complete the panorama, a few sailboats zipped along the glimmering surface of the water, propelled by a strong, chilly wind.

Gunshots sounded back in the cavern complex, and someone screamed—a male voice. *Is it one of my clone brothers? Oh my God. Things are getting worse and worse.*

Bhante locked eyes with me. "Yes, these people are ruthless. Make no mistake about it."

Sam moved closer to me and took my hand again. This time it felt softer. When I glanced at her, she winked, which seemed out of character, or at least the character I'd projected onto her. The wink served as a good distraction, though, which was perhaps what she'd intended.

"We're probably safe here," Bhante said. "This side of the property isn't accessible to intruders, and soon we'll be hidden from the view of any helicopters."

As if on cue, we heard a helicopter approaching. All three of us ducked back into the cave. I found my hand was still entwined with Sam's as we stood three abreast and peered at the slice of sky ahead of us.

Bhante continued. "The danger now is the perilous climb down. There will be a path for part of the way, but there is a considerable amount of climbing."

The sound of the helicopter receded. As we waited a bit more to let it get out of visual range, my agitation built, and I spoke up. "Who's attacking us? What's going on?" I shouted this without meaning to, and the older Sri Lankan held a finger to his lips.

"We can't waste time talking," he whispered. "We need to begin our descent. Jason will be waiting at the bottom with a boat. But he'll be vulnerable there."

Bhante strode back onto the ledge, and we followed. He then sidled to its left edge, where there was a gap in the adjoining cliff side.

"The very first part of our short journey is a bit intimidating," he said as he grabbed a handful of rock and levered himself down and out of sight.

He'd definitely understated things, but Sam and I managed to follow him. After a quarter mile or so, Bhante leading the way and Sam bringing up the rear, the older man stopped short, and I almost ran into him.

"This is the tricky bit," Bhante said, his Sri Lankan

accent asserting itself. "Oh, my," he added.

I didn't like the sound of that.

"It's much worse than the last time I was here," he said. "The final section resembled steps before. Now it looks almost smooth."

"Can we go back?" I asked. "Maybe all the fuss is over now." I turned and faced Sam, who stood just behind me, looking grim. Her lips were tight, and a frown turned down the corners of her generous mouth.

"That's not an option," she said. *Does she know more about all this than she's letting on?* "Let me through, and I'll take a look," she continued. "I've done a lot of climbing."

I turned sideways on the narrow trail, and she worked her way past me, choosing to face me so her breasts rubbed against my chest. She turned the other way to pass Bhante. Sam surveyed the thirty-foot stretch of limestone cliff for longer than I would've liked. *A simple, safe solution would be easy to notice.*

"It's doable," she pronounced. "And Jason's already been through here, right?"

"Yes," Bhante said.

Just then, we heard a helicopter again. We dropped to the ground and flattened. After a few minutes, the racket subsided.

"As I was saying," Sam continued once we resumed our positions, "it's doable. We'll need to hand traverse for a short stretch at the end. See the *huecos* up at eye level? Sorry, the little pockets—holes—in the rock?"

"Yes," Bhante said.

"We should be able to get a few fingers in them and swing across that section without any footholds.

It's going to be more about nerve than finger strength. As your tendons and ligaments overstretch and the pain mounts, you have to stay centered."

I turned to Bhante. "Are you sure you can do this? Sam seems to be assuming you're some sort of expert like her."

"To be honest, I have no idea if I can or not. It'll be interesting to find out," he answered cheerily.

"Finding out might entail dying," I pointed out.

"That's fine. Dying is just another thing to find out about," Bhante said, smiling.

I was too nervous to think about that. My mind was racing with negative scenarios.

"Okay," Sam said. "I'm going to reach out and grab that dark-colored *arête*—corner—and then I'll step over to that…let's call it a triangular thingy, okay?"

She smoothly stepped off solid ground and gracefully accomplished exactly what she'd described. It looked fairly easy if you forgot about the two-hundred-yard drop underneath her. She proceeded step by step to the hands-only part at the end. It really did look doable so far, as long as I could stay calm.

Then she stuck her right hand into a small hole up above her and swung out over a whole lot of nothing. Even she couldn't make that look easy. Her legs dangled as she reached across herself and tucked a few fingers of her other hand into an even higher indentation in the rock. When she let go of her first hold a moment later, all of her weight was on just those fingers as her body swung under her.

She performed this maneuver three more times, each time feeling for the next indentation—and they were all over the place. But it didn't take her long to get to a safe patch of trail beyond the pitted rock, where she stood and rubbed her hands together.

I let out my breath, which I'd been holding for quite some time. Sweat dripped off the tip of my nose, and my hands shook.

"Sid," she called. "Don't think. Your mind isn't your friend right now. Just reach out and touch the corner of the first rock—the dark one at two o'clock. Can you do that?"

I nodded and extended my right arm, placing my hand on the rough rock. The texture would make it easier to grip.

"Okay," she continued. "When I say 'go ahead,' you're going to hold tight onto that corner and put your right foot on the triangle thingy—remember that? It's not hard at all, Sid. Once you get going, you'll be fine. Are you ready?"

I nodded. She gave me the go-ahead, and I did it without thinking. Step by step, I followed her directions and made my way across the cliff.

Until I got to the hand-traverse section. My body balked first, and then I began to think about all the reasons why it wasn't a good idea to proceed any farther. Some of these were rational, but others were ridiculous—I didn't want to show off, I still owed Chris $850, I'd never been to the NFL Hall of Fame, etc. I didn't even like football.

Sam could tell she'd lost me. What happened next froze my mind and pulled me back into the moment.

"Close your eyes, Bhante," she said, and then pulled off her top and peeled off her black sports bra.

Her milky white breasts were medium-sized, well formed, and freckled, her rose-pink nipples erect in the cool breeze. Sam stood still and let me examine her.

"Now don't think," she said after a moment. "Just stretch up with your right hand and put three fingers in that first hole."

I did it, tearing my eyes away from her.

"Now grab with all your strength and let gravity bring you over to the next hole."

I did it. And I swung. I held on, the pain almost unbearable. Then I locked my other hand into the next crevice and let go of the first one.

"Can I open my eyes?" Bhante asked.

"No," Sam answered.

From there, I managed to execute the maneuver several more times. I remained terrified, but it no longer interfered with my ability to do what I needed to do.

Shortly before Sam fished my leg out of the air and pulled it toward her, Bhante called to her. "I'm peeking."

I almost laughed. Perhaps he knew what I shortly found out. My incentive program had become purely conceptual; Sam was fully clothed again.

"Hey!" I said once I was back on the ground. "You tricked me."

She whispered her reply. "They're still here, Sid. And there'll be other opportunities to get more acquainted."

"I hope so," I said. Like her wink, this seemed out of character, but I was happy to adjust to a flirtier Sam.

"Okay!" she called back to Bhante. "Your turn, Mr. Peeker."

His robe slapped around his wiry brown legs as he swung like a gibbon. All was well until the last hold. His left hand gave way just shy of his goal, and he began to fall. Instinctively, I leaned forward and grabbed him around his waist. Gravity would've pulled us both down, but Sam, in turn, grabbed me from behind, and our combined weight served as sufficient ballast to haul the older man in.

The rest of the way down to the bottom, while tricky in a few spots, was anticlimactic. I paused to enjoy the view several times, eventually spying Jason standing in a long, sleek speedboat directly below us. I wasn't sure he was really going to be there.

A few minutes later, we waded through chilly water and climbed into the boat. The slippery teak deck contrasted with the black fiberglass hull and the high-tech console that Jason stood behind. The boat had no downstairs or upstairs, or whatever the correct nautical terms would've been.

"I was just beginning to worry about you," Jason called, shoving the dual handles beside the steering wheel. We roared off, and the boat's long, narrow prow nearly stood up from the hard acceleration. I had no idea where we were going, but this beautiful boat was built for speed, and we were going to get there in a hurry.

Chapter Six

White built-in bench seats lined the edges of the rear deck, and Jason's abrupt maneuver threw me back onto one. Blue cushions kept me from bruising my butt.

The Maori man's long hair hung loose, and the wind created a wake of black locks behind his huge head as we tore into the bay. It was exhilarating, or maybe I was just excited to be off the cliff in one piece. Sam and Bhante ended up in seats near each other on the other side of the deck. Sam tried to talk to the older man, but for now the engines and the prow slapping against the water were just too loud.

If anything, the bay was even prettier from the water. When Jason slowed down, I truly appreciated the scale of the topography. The bluff we'd survived comprised a section of a half-mile-long expanse of towering rock, and the mouth of a river fed the bay beside it. Just beyond that, a marshy estuary wandered along the shore; seabirds dive-bombed its shallows. The bay was ringed by a variety of other water sources, as well—and even a few waterfalls. Clearly, it rained a lot in New Zealand.

We headed toward a small town almost directly across the water from Bhante's cave. With that minor mystery solved, I felt free to close my eyes. I needed to think, and the magnificent scenery was just too distracting.

So I guess I am a clone. That was hard to deny. But the idea that Buddha had been my original blueprint still seemed crazy. Could you really get good DNA from an old bone? I'd read somewhere it didn't work that way. And who could be sure after all these years that a given relic truly belonged to Buddha?

My jaw tightened, and now nausea welled up. The emptiness in my chest reminded me of when I'd heard the news of my parents dying. I guess I was scared to fully feel whatever was lurking back there.

I was open to the idea of reincarnation. Whether the phenomenon was literally true or not, it was certainly a good metaphor to live by—life as curriculum, replete with consequences for ignoring our customized lessons. That all fit for me. But even if reincarnation and Buddha's prophecy were real, accepting that Buddha's next incarnation was in his own clone was another matter entirely. *Did souls really have nothing better to do than just hang around for centuries, waiting to go back into particular bodies?*

Regardless of all that, I was profoundly alarmed by what I'd just endured. Who wouldn't be? As I thought about it, I revved up my outrage. I'd been kidnapped, for God's sake. And if Frank and Jason were working for Bhante, then he was responsible for what they did. Why hire a creep like Frank or a hothead like Jason unless you wanted dirty work done? He could've sent a dutiful monk or even contacted me himself. I couldn't trust these people—any of them.

Sam may have been trying to ally with me, but she'd sent Paul, and everything had stemmed from that. Her organization probably wanted to exploit me in some way, too. If any of them had just asked me if I wanted to participate in their deal, it could've all been so different.

My chest tightened again, and I clutched the rail beside me so hard, the pain woke me up to the full magnitude of my anger. None of this was okay with me, to say the least. I fantasized sneaking up behind Jason and punching him in the back of the head. I also had an urge to yell at Bhante and ask Sam who the fuck she really was. With my eyes still closed, it was easy to picture all this, but I knew it would fade away in the light of day. It always did. I was just too reasonable to pursue my rage fantasies in the real world.

After some deep breathing, I wondered why everyone was in such a big hurry. Sam showed up the morning following Paul's visit. Then Jason and Frank whisked us away a few minutes later, and we were only in the cave a short while before somebody else named Jackson attacked us. Next, we were hustled down a cliff and out onto the bay. Why? If I was Buddha, then I'd been him my whole life and I'd be him next week too.

Perhaps the fast pace had been designed to keep me off-balance. I liked this theory better than the idea that my life was now completely out of control, careening like a billiard ball from one crazy scenario to the next.

The real question was, how did I want to respond to all this? Could I just go back to my life in Santa Cruz and forget about it all? I could contact the police and report the slew of crimes that had been committed. Or I could hang around and find out more about my potential role in modern Buddhism, despite the drama.

I realized that if I could press a reset button and just return to my life before I met Paul, I wouldn't do it. I just didn't know enough yet to make a call about anything. If I walked away or had everyone locked up, I probably wouldn't find out who I really was.

As usual, I'd managed to overwhelm myself with a flurry of unanswerable questions. I opened my eyes and found Bhante sitting next to me.

"Jason called ahead and made hotel reservations," Bhante told me. "I think you'll enjoy Tuaranoa. It's a lovely town."

The ordinariness of this confused me. Weren't we on the run from some armed force? "Uh, okay," I said.

"I'm sure you're very tired," Bhante continued. "By the time we get in, it will be past nightfall here, but very late for a world traveler such as yourself. We'll just leave you to your sleep, and we can talk in the morning if you wish. Or of course, we can arrange transportation for you if you still wish to leave."

"Okay," I said again. It seemed pointless to argue or express my anger.

"I owe you my life," Bhante continued. "I would have fallen off the cliff but for you. I hope you'll afford me the opportunity to repay you in some way." He put his hands together and bowed. Then he walked carefully to Jason's side, where he stood with his hand on the big man's shoulder as he spoke to him.

I moved across to Sam's side of the boat and sat next to her on a wet, cold cushion. "Have you heard the plan?" I asked.

"Yes. It's kind of them to make arrangements."

I didn't respond to that. Sam sensed my mood. She put her arm around my shoulder and leaned into me. I hadn't noticed before, but my wet butt clued me in that it was getting cooler by the minute as the sun sank lower. Our legs were still wet from wading to the boat, too.

Sam was wonderfully warm. "You're a furnace," I said.

"I run hot. Is that a complaint?"

"Oh no."

I leaned into her too, and we just huddled together wordlessly for the remainder of the boat ride.

****

The hotel wasn't a hotel; it was more of a sprawling bed-and-breakfast—a wooden, one-story building that had apparently been a boat works at one time. Its own weathered wharf snaked out into the bay, and an attractive young woman met us there to help with the luggage we didn't have.

"Oh my God!" she said when she spotted Jason. This seemed to be the standard New Zealand reaction to the guy. I guess it was akin to running into Michael Jordan or Tiger Woods. Jason was gracious—even kind—to her, and needless to say we were treated like royalty.

"How do you know Mr. Patariki?" the front desk clerk whispered to me. He could've been the gay best friend of a film protagonist—maybe a set designer or a gossip columnist. His pink polo shirt clashed with his red cardigan sweater.

"He kidnapped me," I whispered back.

"Ha, ha. Very good."

Bhante insisted Sam and I each take a bay-view room, while he and Jason shared a small suite near the lobby. Once I used the bathroom and showered, I discovered an internal door between my room and Sam's. I unlocked my side of it. *You never know.*

I fell asleep almost as soon as I'd taken my clothes

off and climbed into bed.

Some hours later, I rolled onto my side and stretched out an arm to scratch an itch on my calf. *Oh God, I ache all over.* I lifted my head and winced. *At least I'm still alive.* That was as positive as I could manage in that moment. I wasn't looking forward to becoming vertical.

Then I saw Sam! She lay next to me, naked, the covers completely off her. I stopped breathing for a moment and then gasped. One creamy white breast rested by her arm; the other tilted toward me. Her belly was flat. Underneath that, her blond pubic hair trailed down between her open thighs, allowing me a glimpse of what lay underneath. Her lips there matched the color of her small, light pink nipples.

My morning erection throbbed. In repose, no wrinkles marred her dreamy, serene face—*lo and behold, she has a face, too.* The sight of her—so near, so vulnerable—moved me at some deep level. Half of me was now in my heart; the other half was still residing in my penis. It was confusing. I didn't even know this woman. What did my heart have to do with finding a beautiful, naked woman in my bed? Had her energy from the day before had yet another effect on me?

Sam's strong Scandinavian features complemented each other, and the sum was much greater than the parts. In isolation, her nose, her mouth, and all the rest were pretty enough, but it was the synergy of them that was so harmonious.

Eventually, I reached down and pulled up the covers, hovering near her to manage the task. Without opening her eyes, Sam slowly reached up, encircled my torso, and then gently brought me down onto her. She opened her eyes, and she was right there—right behind her eyes. Perhaps she'd been awake for a while; there was no sleep in her at all. Her sky-blue eyes held flecks of gray.

We held our poses, just gazing at one another. It was peaceful, even soothing for a moment, and then my erection asserted itself against her belly.

"Oh my," she said softly. Her sweet breath wafted across to me—a contrast to mine, I was sure.

"I'm sorry," I said.

"Don't be," Sam replied, moving out from under me and reaching down to hold me. A moment later, she'd slithered down, and her mouth encircled my cock. I closed my eyes as waves of exquisite sensation came at me. It had been a long time.

Sam wasn't about to end our lovemaking there. After bringing me tantalizingly close to coming several times, she slid up my body and kissed me as she repositioned herself. Moments later, she held eye contact as she slowly lowered herself onto me. We fit together perfectly. Despite her increasingly furious rocking, we remained locked together as our pleasure mounted.

The end was spectacular. My explosion and her spasms arrived mere seconds apart.

Utterly spent—I'd never felt more relaxed—my mind floated away as I lay entangled with Sam. Dreamy images came unbidden—the night sky, the ocean, Sam's exquisite face hovering above me while we made love. Then I felt her energy again, stronger now. Or was it hers? It seemed to be emanating from me—from my heart. I basked in its warmth, its love. That's what it was—it was love. Somehow I knew this.

We hadn't spoken for the last half hour, and I wasn't inclined to return to the world of words. My bladder yammered at me, though, so I gently disengaged myself and padded off.

On the way back, my stomach emitted a startling yowl. "Are you hungry?" I asked.

Sam stretched and smiled, glistening with sweat. I was tempted to leap back into bed, but she answered me before the impulse translated itself into action. "I'm famished. Do you think the kitchen is open yet?"

"Let's find out."

We hustled into our filthy clothes and headed for the dining room. It was a larger space than I would've imagined, with a massive limestone fireplace and picture windows overlooking the water. Yellowish wood planks lined the walls and also formed the floor. Another couple and an older Hispanic man were the only other diners. The man was a long way from home. But so were we.

"Do you think Bhante's picking up the tab?" I asked Sam after we'd seated ourselves.

"I'm sure he is." She reached across the wooden table and took my hand. Once again, hers felt softer than the last time I'd held it. *How is that possible?*

I relinquished my hand and ordered eggs Benedict and a plate of local, fresh fruit from the quiet young man who waited on us. Sam requested "whatever you like the best and lots of it," which animated our server, who bustled off to surprise her.

"Why don't we get to know each other?" I suggested, playing with my fork.

"I know a great deal about you already, Sid," Sam

pointed out.

"So I'll play catch up. Where are you from?" I switched to my spoon.

"DC, until I was twelve. Then New Jersey."

"That's a tough age to move. What exit?"

"Eightish—Princeton."

I smiled, and Sam smiled back. "That's hardly New Jersey at all. I've been there. Tell me about your family," I said. The knife needed adjusting next. Maybe after that, I'd keep my hands still.

She sighed. "My mother was abusive—mostly verbal but sometimes physical. My father was largely absent—a workaholic. I had an older brother who died from a nurse's mistake in the hospital—an overdose of painkiller."

"God, that's awful. How old were you when it happened?"

"Twenty-seven. I drank." Sam grimaced and shrugged.

"You?"

Sam nodded. "I hadn't been to therapy yet. And I still thought the world was only random chaos. I had no way to hold a tragedy—to make sense out of it."

"You can now?"

"Yes, but let me ask you something I've been wondering about. How are you doing with all this? You're hard to read, Sid."

"No one's ever told me that before," I said. In fact, I thought of myself as rather transparent.

"Oh, I see what's on the surface—the fear, the confusion, the anger." She smiled gently, but I felt insulted that she'd only listed negative emotions. "And your thoughts are evident sometimes," she continued, "but you're a complicated guy. I sense layers below the Sid the world sees. Your energy signature reflects that, too. It's as if there are three or four beings built on top of one another inside of you—the way modern cities use ancient ones as their foundations."

"Well, that's an interesting way to put it. At the risk of dodging your original question and demonstrating my opaqueness, what do you mean by 'energy'? I've been having some new experiences along those lines."

"Tell me about them."

I did, although I had to struggle to describe what I'd felt. As I spoke, a continuous warmth in my chest somehow enhanced my sense of connection to the world, and I brought that up, too.

"What I thought was sexual afterglow now seems to be a shift at a more basic level," I told Sam. I stopped and looked closely at her face. "Were you doing some sort of tantric thing in bed—sending me energy? Rearranging me?"

She smiled. "Maybe it's love," she said. Then she frowned.

Does she regret saying that? My heart seemed to stutter for a moment. "That's not much of an answer."

"For now," Sam said, "let's call it *chi*—life force. We all have it. And it's exchanged during lovemaking. I'm enjoying yours, too."

"What's mine like?" I leaned forward, my eyes locked with hers.

She pondered this, tilting her head charmingly. "It's ineffable."

"I don't know that word."

"Indescribable. I have a feeling you're soon going

to be using it quite a bit."

"Why am I suddenly feeling this energy if it's always been around? I never felt it before."

"I'm not sure."

"What about RGP? I know you didn't want to talk about your organization with Bante there, but it's just us now."

Sam gently shook her head. "I'm sorry," she said.

Our food arrived. Cold eggs might've discouraged me on another day, but I was starving. And the variety of unfamiliar fruit was a delight. I especially liked the feijoa, which resembled a guava (if you squinted real hard).

Sam hit the jackpot—blue moki soft tacos with hash browns and a fruit plate twice as big as mine.

"Our moki's from the deep waters off Three Kings Island," our server explained to Sam.

I tried a few more mundane questions and discovered Sam had worked in HR for several years before her calling, which she described as a spiritual awakening that came with an AAA-style roadmap—one with a highlighted route. She'd been married once for four years, had never had children, and now lived in Los Gatos, California, which was only a half hour's drive from Santa Cruz. I smiled; she wouldn't be flying back to Timbuktu or wherever when all this was through. Whatever *this* was.

As Sam talked, she pulled me deeper and deeper into the moment. I felt markedly calmer, and everything became radiantly beautiful. Life was exactly the way it should be. All of it. I suddenly knew this in my bones.

Jason strode in as Sam and I finished our leisurely breakfast, and all that immediately vanished. By now, the sun was fighting through the mist, occasionally sending a column of morning light into the room, and one illuminated his broad torso as he approached our table. I surprised myself by offering Jason a seat.

"Is Bhante still asleep?" Sam asked as he lowered himself onto his chair.

One of these days, a piece of furniture is going to disintegrate under him.

"He's been up for hours. He's out walking," the Maori said.

"He certainly is active, isn't he?" I said. "How old is he, anyway?"

"I have no idea. In his eighties, maybe. Was he whizzing around on that hill yesterday?" His New Zealand accent made "whizzing" a bit difficult to decipher.

"He certainly was," Sam said.

"He's a marvel," Jason said. "I want to be like him when I grow up." He smiled a huge, warm smile.

"*If* you grow up is more like it," I said.

"Aw, don't be like that, man. I'm talking about Bhante here, not me. Everybody should be more like him. He's a really great guy. And how about the way he keeps his cool when all hell's breaking loose?"

I was struck by the rhythm and pattern of his speech. It was a cross between African-American and Hawaiian. At this point, the other guests departed, and we were alone in the room. The couple had gawked at Sam's beauty on the way out, while the Hispanic man had studied my face as he passed.

I decided to test the waters with Jason. "So Bhante told me I was free to go if I wanted to—that your strong-arm tactics were against his orders. So what if I got up right now and walked away? What would you do?"

"I'm sorry," Jason replied. "He didn't say anything about that to me. I can't let you go."

"Sam can kick your ass," I said.

He smiled. "You can't get in my head today. Maybe she can, and maybe she can't. But why have a big fight here in this nice place? What's your hurry? If we wait for Bhante, he can tell me it's okay, and then you can do whatever you want. What do you say? Can we be friends this morning?"

Bhante appeared in the doorway behind him before I had a chance to answer. "Namaste," he called.

"Good morning," Jason and I said simultaneously.

"May I join you?" he asked.

"Of course," I answered.

He wore his recently dirtied blue robe. Dark semicircles drooped under his eyes. He lowered himself gingerly onto the seat beside me. Almost immediately, the waiter served him tea.

"How are the clones?" I asked. "Is everyone okay? Did they escape, too?" I was back to playing with my fork. This time I twirled it as quickly as I could.

"I've been able to reach several of your brothers, and they report all is well. The attackers had some way of distinguishing you from the others. When they realized you and I and Jason were no longer there, they became angry and destroyed some items of value, but then they withdrew."

"And the gunshots?" Sam asked.

"To get everyone's attention," Bhante answered, "but a shot ricocheted off the wall and hit one of the attackers in the arm."

"Instant karma gonna get you," Jason said, chuckling.

"They didn't discover the back door?" I asked.

"Apparently they did, but the helicopter didn't spot us, and it didn't seem plausible to them that we could have escaped down the cliff. I am a bit more agile than a casual observer might think."

"Wait a minute," I said. "You said that they destroyed things, Bhante. What about the relics—the Buddha bones? Is that what you meant?"

"Oh no. They're safe in another location. But I fear if the cave's secret has become known, perhaps the relics are not as secure as I would like to believe. We must journey there. It is essential that they not fall into the wrong hands."

"Why? And whose hands are wrong?" I asked. "Who is Jackson?"

Jason's breakfast arrived at that point. He'd ordered twice as much food as we had. A pink note with a hand-drawn heart and a phone number sat on top of a stack of pancakes.

"These women," he said, shaking his head.

"Jackson is a rival of sorts," Bhante said, waving away the menu the waiter offered. "He is a very powerful spiritual being whose interests collide with ours."

"A spiritual being?" I asked. "What you mean by that? And by definition, isn't deploying troops and helicopters an unspiritual mode of problem solving?"

Bhante threw his hands in the air, startling me. "None of us can escape our basic nature. We are human." He brought his arms down gradually, as if to counterbalance his sudden movement.

Sam repeated the other part of my question. "So why are the relics so important?"

"Well, of course, they're sacred and have healing powers," he said, "but their value to our organization goes beyond that. With the DNA from the relics, we can prove that Sid is truly a clone of the Buddha."

"Who is it that we need to prove this to?" I asked. "And why? What's the big deal about who I might be?"

"The entire world needs to know," Bhante said, spreading his arms. "You came into human form with an imperative destiny, Sid. Unless you fulfill your mission, the physical universe may perish."

"Perish?"

"Disappear. Cease to be."

"That's ridiculous," I said. I glanced at Sam, expecting to see incredulity on her face, too. But her face remained impassive. And it didn't look as though this took effort.

"Is it? You know very little about these things, don't you? What if I told a medieval man about an atom bomb?"

I shook my head at this analogy. *Is Bhante claiming to be a millennium ahead of me in his understanding?* "Why don't you try to make your case with more logical arguments?" I suggested.

"Very well," he said. "If you don't accompany us on a boat ride to where the relics are stored, your life will be in great danger."

"From Jackson?"

Bhante nodded. "And others."

"Thanks to you." My head hurt. "I'll need to think this over," I told him.

"Am I welcome on this relic-gathering trip?" Sam

asked cheerily.

"Oh yes," Bhante said. "Please join us. We were planning to contact RGP when we were a bit further along." He clambered to his feet. "I need to make a few phone calls before our transportation arrives," he said. "Jason will provide you with funds and take you to buy clothes and other necessities."

"We'll talk again," I said. "I'm not necessarily signed up for any plan of yours, so don't count on me."

"I understand," he said and ambled back toward his room. He definitely wasn't as spry as the day before.

I visited the spotlessly clean restroom while Jason paid. Then I met Sam and the Maori in the cozy lobby, and we strode out onto a narrow sidewalk. In a souvenir shop a few doors down, we managed to find toiletries and several articles of clothing that were neither T-shirts nor wool sweaters. The store hadn't been open, but when the girl vacuuming inside saw Jason through the glass front door, she'd rushed over to let us in. She threw in a nylon duffel bag for free since we were with him. Unfortunately, it was bright orange with turquoise lettering proclaiming I was the "World's Best Fisherman!"

When we returned to the B&B, Bhante met us in the lobby. He stood at attention with his hands behind his back. "We need to board our benefactor's yacht soon," he said. "It's at the hotel dock taking on supplies for our journey."

"I need some alone time to think things over," I said. "I'm not willing to be rushed onto a boat or anywhere else."

"Certainly," Bhante said. "But I can grant you no more than an hour. The ship must sail by then."

"Uh…okay." I looked at Sam.

"I'm fine either way," she said. "It's up to you, Sid. I think I'll take a stroll on my own." She marched away without waiting for a response, which I found odd. And hurtful. Maybe she needed to call her RGP bosses for further orders.

"When you've decided," Bhante said, "come knock on my door. It's number eleven."

"Sure."

I walked to my room and lay on my back on the bed, propping my head up with both arms. With the bed aimed at the window fronting the bay, I couldn't help but spy a huge boat tied to the dock. It looked like a photograph I'd seen of a presidential yacht from the twenties or thirties. Clad in dark wood, two stories tall, it sported a wraparound deck and railing. An unfamiliar flag flew at its stern, which looked to be about eighty feet from the bow. Beyond it in the patchy mist of the bay, a host of small sailboats sliced through the azure water, and a distant sunlit dot looked to be a rowboat.

Letting my head fall back to stare at the ceiling, I got to work. Sam was first and foremost on my mind, despite Bhante's urgency about leaving soon. I didn't flatter myself that I was so attractive or endearing, any beautiful woman would be smitten by two days of exposure to my irresistible charms. And while I'd been traumatized at times by our adventures together, I didn't think we'd bonded through shared trauma. Sam hadn't seemed unduly upset by any of it, which was strange.

Perhaps she was drawn to me because of my purported role as a future messiah. By the time she met me, she must've already believed I was—or at least could be—Buddha. This might be an aphrodisiac of sorts to a serious Buddhist.

I vowed to pay attention to how my future experiences with Sam supported this hypothesis. I felt tempted to sign up for one of the I-still-get-to-have-sex-with-her versions of reality, but clearly I was in way over my head with these people already. It would be wise be wary.

I had no empirical evidence that Bhante was trustworthy. His air of authenticity and the trappings of a Buddhist leader pulled for this, but what he said was often so fantastic, I felt gullible for having gone along with so much. For all I knew, he could've been an actor or a well-disguised criminal. Certainly, some of his underlings' actions had been villainous. And one of them had apparently betrayed his own people, since Jackson could only have known about the cave if there was a traitor.

Jason seemed sincere, and everyone we met confirmed he wasn't merely an actor, but clearly he had anger-management issues and was willing to compromise his values to promote his organization's goals. He was a convert, I assumed, and converts usually embodied a problematic zealotry.

The clones—my brothers?—were another matter entirely. I'd been avoiding thinking about them from the moment I'd spied two of them in the mouth of the cavern. It was time to approach my fear.

Did we share a common personality? I hadn't noticed that in the cave. Were they all on board with Bhante's program? It had seemed so, but how could I know from my brief exposure to something so surreal?

Once again, a strong feeling snuck up on me, this

time with almost no physical manifestation. I was more scared than I realized. Deep down, I was close to terror again. I couldn't find my center—my psychological security. My sense of self had been so destabilized that, if I wasn't careful, I might clutch at whatever straw came my way to feel solid again. I retreated up into my head in an effort to regulate the dosage of all this. For better or worse, this was how I'd been coping for decades.

Clones represented a different class of personhood—a lower-class, it felt like. We were cookie-cutter people who'd been manufactured, not born. And our supposed seed person—Buddha—lived 2500 years ago. Were we way behind everyone else in terms of evolution?

My fists clenched and a surge of anger overcame me, directed not at Bhante or some anonymous scientist—but at my adopted parents. They either knew the deal and didn't tell me, or they didn't bother to investigate my birth circumstances. Whatever the story, they'd set me up to suffer. My life felt like a hoax—a scam perpetrated against me. In fact, my so-called father had been German-American. Perhaps his father—whom he never talked about—had been a Nazi geneticist.

I'd lost my parents in a plane wreck when I was twenty-one. They were celebrating their thirtieth wedding anniversary by zipping around South America in a friend's small jet. Somewhere between Cartagena, Columbia, and Cusco, Peru, their plane went down.

I'd been angry then, too. They'd abandoned me—by dying—because, as usual, they'd been pursuing their extravagant, pleasure-seeking lifestyle. I was busy grinding away in school while they were taking foolish risks. Flying over interminable jungle in bad weather was just stupid. It took me years to begin to forgive them. And it didn't help that they'd left most of their fortune to a nonprofit foundation instead of me.

Despite the emotional roller coaster I was currently riding, something I trusted floated up from somewhere. Whatever the risks, whoever the involuntary bedfellows, I genuinely felt a strong need to follow things through. I couldn't be happy in my old life knowing I was a clone and maybe even Buddha's reincarnation, so what choice did I have? I didn't have to push all my chips in the pot, after all. The only pressing decision was whether to go for another boat ride.

Relief swept through me, relaxing my painfully tight muscles. I liked boats. Maybe it would be fun. This was the kind of convenient thinking that had gotten me into trouble with the cult I'd joined, and with my first crazy girlfriend. What was the harm in trying an Amazonian herbal drink? I liked herbs, right? And Earline was so cute. How could someone like that have a prison record for aggravated assault? Sure, she seemed a bit wild and passionate, but that didn't mean her ex was right about her when he called me early on and told me to run as fast as I could.

A few minutes later, when I knocked on Bhante's door with my bag in hand, Jason opened it and ushered me in.

"I'll go with you," I told the two of them.

Jason immediately hugged me so tightly, I dropped my duffel bag and wondered if he could completely compress someone if he tried. I pictured police detectives puzzling over a two-dimensional corpse.

"That's great!" he boomed. "All systems go!"

Bhante bowed deeply. "I'm honored. May I suggest we board the yacht without further delay?"

"Is Sam back?"

"I'm sure Samavati will rejoin us soon. You can meet our host while we wait for her. He's an extraordinary man."

"Ah," I said, holding up my gaudy bag with the inane fishing boast embossed on it. "But can he fish like me?"

Chapter Seven

The yacht was even more impressive close-up. Its gleaming wooden hull proclaimed its name—the *Silent Love*—which I assumed had a backstory. A deaf-mute wife? A pair of star-crossed lovers who'd been barred from expressing their feelings?

Two solicitous, khaki-uniformed crew members met us at the gangway. "Welcome," the beefier of the two said crisply in a broad Australian accent.

"Thank you," I said and then asked, "How could a ship this big dock here?"

"We have eight feet to spare," the other crewman told me in a by-now-familiar New Zealand accent. "The town is here because this is a deepwater harbor. From glaciers or whatever." He took my bag. "Watch your step," he told us as we began to board the yacht.

Belatedly, I glanced at Bhante and Jason's empty hands—no luggage. Why was this?

"We have things here on the ship," Bhante said. The guy certainly paid attention. "It is our home away from home. Ram has been very generous."

Ram? Wasn't that a Hindu god? Was Bhante expressing his gratitude toward God's bounty? I didn't have to wait long to find out.

"Call me Ram," a very elderly, slim Indian man said as he emerged from a nearby doorway. His maroon shirt and brown paisley ascot set off the white of his linen suit. He was completely bald and so clean-shaven, I doubted he had a beard at all. Actually, it looked as though his sparse eyebrows were tattoos. *Maybe he suffers from alopecia.*

He moved slowly, but with precision. As he shook each of our hands, he looked us squarely in the eye. His hand was tiny and very dry. It was like holding the hand of a papier-mâché puppet.

I found his small-featured face hard to read. On the one hand, he displayed a superficial deference, exhibiting a warm smile, but his dark brown eyes belied this by projecting an aura of great authority. It was easy to believe he was rich and powerful. He seemed genuinely glad to meet me, but he also studied my face as though he were searching for the presence of something quite specific. I pretended I was Santa Claus and tried to beam good cheer. I'd had some practice with this as a therapist.

"Come," Ram said once he'd shaken everyone's hand. "Let's sit in my parlor and chat." His English was very English—impeccably so.

"Do boats have parlors?" I asked no one in particular.

"This one does," Jason said. I'd forgotten he was standing behind me.

Truly, the room looked as though it had been lifted from a nineteenth-century English manor house, replete with an array of antique pieces of furniture, including a massive wooden bookcase that held autographed cricket bats, blue and white Chinese vases, and a collection of glassware—decorative plates, pitchers, and even a few snow globes. I couldn't imagine keeping things like this on a boat. I hoped they were glued down, at least.

In the historical film that might unfold in a stuffy Northumberland parlor like this, Sam would be drawn to the forbidden love that our various ethnicities represented. But unfortunately, she'd be the only one white enough to be allowed upstairs in the main house. End of film.

We seated ourselves on various upholstered chairs and loveseats, and Ram spoke. "I've been looking forward to meeting you, Sid," he said. "Is that short for Siddhartha? Were your parents aware of your status?"

"I have no idea. And it's just Sid—not even Sidney. It was a tough name for a little boy."

"Perhaps it better suits an old Jewish man," Ram said. "I have known several."

"Exactly. Now what about you? Who are you?" I asked.

"I was a physician. Then I discovered the power of love—of spirit—and things came my way. It began with an invention—an early stent that was less expensive to make than what was on the market." His simple gestures and pursed lips somehow conveyed the pride that underlay his supposed spiritual transformation. "Eventually, I came to own hospitals and resorts and extremely large tracts of land," he continued. "Much of the land has water, and water will be the new international currency."

"Isn't owning and doling out water a rather ruthless enterprise?" I asked. "Are you really living true to your spiritual values when you hold people's health for ransom to make even more money?"

"Well-argued," Ram said, flashing bright white teeth. "I am not in the water business. All who live on my land have free water for life. But the value of the

92

land—the financial leverage it affords me—is based on water. More specifically, on vast aquifers. I tell you this because there are many inaccuracies about my business online. If you Google my name, you may read things that sound monstrous. I am not a monster." He gestured elaborately to the ornate tea set on the low table. "Tea?" He seemed to be trying to demonstrate whatever goodwill a monster wouldn't have.

We nodded our assent as Ram focused on each of us individually as he poured us the fragrant tea. I was struck by how he never dealt with us as a group but always as individuals. Perhaps this was a technique in the Indian version of *How to Win Friends and Influence People*.

"There is nothing quite like tea," Ram said.

"Certainly not," Bhante agreed. The Sri Lankan sat to my right and beamed at our host. Perhaps he was always happy.

I spoke up again while several fit young men in blue jumpsuits brought in trays with shortbread cookies and fruit tarts. They looked like they belonged in a children's movie—Hollywood's idea of what a billionaire's servants would wear.

"So your answer to my question seems to be centered on your career," I said to Ram. "Is that how you define yourself?"

He cocked an index finger at me. "You are a pistol," he said. "There are no flies on you." He paused and thought for a moment, looking upward. "You ask me who I am. There is no more basic question. Sri Ramana Maharshi taught that if all one does is ask this question of oneself, always delving deeper into its meaning, one eventually finds there is no one. So in one sense I am a rich man in retirement, trying to better the world. In a deeper sense, I do not exist."

"What do you mean?" Jason asked. "Did Buddha teach this?"

"Am I this body?" Ram asked. "Am I this role I have in the world? Am I my feelings? My thoughts? Who am I?"

Jason still looked puzzled.

"There is no 'I,' my friend," Ram continued. "There is no one who exists as a separate individual. It just seems so. Certainly the Buddha taught this—in his own way."

"Are you a Buddhist?" I asked, shifting in my cushy chair. I was ready to get this show on the road.

"I am not," Ram said, his voice thin but strong. "But I have a perspective that is compatible with Buddhism, as well as several other faiths. I support whatever and whoever can help transform this era of spiritual and social decadence."

"This is a dark age," Bhante agreed affably. "But the wheel will turn."

Sam strode into the room, and Ram arose and met her. She moved so gracefully and embodied my idea of beauty so perfectly, I found myself briefly holding my breath as I watched her.

"You are a wonder," Ram told her. "I am merely Ram Jessawalla. Welcome aboard."

Sam was equally gracious. "You are kind to help us," she said. "And your yacht is a work of art." After several more flowery interchanges, she sat and Ram served her tea.

"Would it meet everyone's approval if we set sail now?" Ram asked. "I understand that time is of the essence."

We all nodded. Then he pressed a button under the edge of a small tabletop beside him, and within moments, I felt the deep vibration and heard the low hum of the yacht's engines. Shortly after that, we moved smoothly away from the dock.

Sam asked questions about the boat, which Ram answered thoroughly, occasionally asking her something about herself. She carefully crafted her answers to sound forthcoming, but didn't reveal anything substantive.

We were only out in the bay for about twenty minutes when a gunshot rang out across the water. Before anyone could react, there were several more shots, including at least one from our boat. Jason scrambled to his feet and sprinted out of the room.

"Get down!" Sam called, and we all hit the floor— in the nick of time, as it happened. A moment later, a bullet shattered one of the room's windows and embedded itself in the chair in which I'd been sitting.

We lay as flat as we could manage. My heart pounded against my tight chest, and I shook uncontrollably. Could we run? Where to? We were trapped on a goddamned boat, weren't we? And would my jellified legs even obey me?

After a minute or two, we heard more gunfire and a lot of shouting, some of it through a bullhorn or loudspeaker. I couldn't make out any words, but clearly the demanding electronic voice originated from another boat.

More gunfire followed, and I could hear the high-pitched staccato of the other craft's engine as it approached us. It must've been a smaller, faster boat. It seemed alarmingly close, and the shouting outside our room grew in volume and intensity.

Then we were rammed. It was incredibly loud, as though a bomb had gone off. I slid across the polished mahogany floor, along with the others. We were like sausages on a tilted, greasy skillet.

I gathered myself and found the sharp prow of the attacking boat had speared the hull and pierced the parlor wall. It was a gleaming blue wedge, embedded in the dark wood paneling. Waves of salt water surged in with it, and we were already starting to sink from damage below the waterline. Broken crockery and glass were strewn everywhere.

Events were happening so fast, it was hard to process. Footsteps pounded overhead and on the deck outside us, but I didn't hear any more gunshots.

We clambered wordlessly to our feet. Everyone seemed to be intact, although Ram was quite pale and may have been in shock. In a moment, the door to the parlor banged open, and Frank strolled in with several Maori men. All of them brandished handguns.

"Ahoy!" he called in his gravelly voice. "Hide the women and children. The pirates have boarded."

"Where the fuck is Jason?" a skinny, goateed Maori barked. His western-style black shirt with pearl snaps, faded jeans, and green lizard-skin cowboy boots created a weird juxtaposition of cultures. And I realized I expected all Maoris to be built like sumo wrestlers. The other men were. There were five of them altogether.

Since no one responded to the cowboy, I spoke up. It seemed like a good idea to cooperate with anyone aiming a gun at us, let alone someone crazy enough to ram a yacht.

"He ran out of the room when we heard the shots," I said. "I assumed you'd captured him."

"Are you the Buddha guy?" he asked. He turned to Frank before I could answer. "Is this him?"

Frank nodded. He still looked like a particularly unattractive rat.

"So nobody knows where he is?" The cowboy glanced around the room, although we were all standing bunched together in the middle of it.

Everyone shook their heads and Sam said, "No."

The Maori, who seemed to be in charge, glared at her. "You try any kung fu shit and Frank'll shoot you. He likes to shoot people."

"Yes," Sam said. "He made us aware of that earlier. Who are you?"

"Tommy T. I run things north of Auckland. Now everybody shut up, and let me think."

The boat lurched and slid sideways. Maybe we'd all drown before he decided what to do.

"Okay," he finally said. "Frank, take these people over to the fishing boat. The rest of you"—he turned to his henchmen—"come with me. And stay alert. My cousin Jason can whip all your asses with one hand tied behind his back."

He said this with an interesting combination of pride and bitterness. The Maoris left, and Frank gestured with his matte-black, squared-off pistol.

"Let's move it, people. You old farts go in front."

He herded us out of the parlor onto the far deck of the listing yacht, where the mist had drifted in. I didn't see any of Ram's men or, for that matter, any of the pirates. A third boat—not the speedboat that had rammed us—bobbed in the water beside the rail. A large, well-worn commercial fishing vessel, it smelled hellaciously fishy, even from where we stood. Long, vertical poles were spaced across the back of it, and several oversized fiberglass boxes overflowed with netting. Every surface of the wooden boat was either filthy with black soot or covered in slick fish scales. It was disgusting. On the other hand, it wasn't sinking.

They'd lashed a thick two-foot-wide plank from one boat to the other, and it rocked back and forth over the water. We were in a bay, not a lake, and the water was far from placid. How would this work? Could Ram really get across that thing? The board was about six feet long. I watched him as he eyed the contraption. He didn't look scared, but he certainly didn't look confident, either.

Another big Maori appeared on the expansive back deck of the fishing boat. "Send 'em over," he called.

"I don't know about the old one," Frank called back. "Maybe we should leave him on the yacht for now."

"Save him for last," the man said. "We'll check with Tommy."

"I've been kidnapped before," Ram told Frank. "My directors will cooperate. And the yacht is insured."

"Shut up," Frank said. "I don't know who you are, and I don't care. By the way, you look like a major doofus in that fucking ascot."

Sam walked across the plank first. The most challenging part seemed to be climbing over the rail and establishing a solid footing on the lashed end of the plank. The rope they'd used was thick and unevenly shredded. Sam placed her feet carefully and then waltzed across. Two gunmen on the other side of the watery gap trained guns on Sam.

Bhante crossed next; the yacht shifted abruptly just before he reached the fishing boat. He had to scoot to reach the end of it, landing awkwardly on the slippery deck.

It was my turn, and I surprised myself by how easily I traversed the plank. Prior to my cliff experience, I might have struggled with my nerve. Falling into the water itself wouldn't have been a big deal—I'm a very strong swimmer—but the boats were so close to one another, it would've been easy to be crushed between them. Somehow, I managed to not think about that and just keep moving.

At that point, Tommy T. and his men came around the corner of the yacht's wraparound deck, prodding Jason from behind.

"Where is my crew?" Ram called to them. "Are my people safe?"

"They're in lifeboats on the other side," Jason told him. "We got everyone on board." He stood tall on the balls of his feet.

"What's the holdup?" Tommy T. asked Frank. His sharp, commanding voice cut through the sea air.

"The old fart—you think he can make it across? He acts like he's important—I think it's his yacht—so I didn't know how you wanted us to handle it."

Jason spoke up. "I'll carry him."

Without waiting for his cousin's permission, he strode forward, curled an arm around Ram's waist, and hoisted him under his arm like a human baguette. It was as if the old man didn't weigh anything at all. Then Jason scampered across the makeshift bridge.

When they reached the fishing boat, he gently deposited Ram beside him and called to Tommy T. "I'm telling your mother about this," he said. "It's not too late to back off, you know."

"Fuck you, Patariki," Tommy growled, climbing over the yacht's railing and heading our way.

Once everyone had switched boats, two of the men unlashed the plank and pushed against the sinking ship's hull with metal poles. We began drifting away, and someone in the wheelhouse started the diesel engines. Across the water, the *Silent Love* tipped all the way over. Perhaps the plank had held it in place, although it was hard to believe that a plank could keep a huge yacht from tipping over. The sinking boat generated waves that rocked ours.

We stood on the slippery back deck as the fishing boat pulled away from the yacht and headed toward a flat expanse of the shoreline where a small river joined the bay.

"You'll never get away with this," Ram said. "We're within sight of land. The volunteer rescue fleet will be out here soon. You can't just—"

Frank stepped forward and slapped him. Ram was rocked but kept his feet. For a guy who had to have been in his late eighties at least, he was pretty durable.

"Let's go inside and talk," Tommy said to us. "Frank, you and Trevor and Robert come with me. The rest of you put on that fisherman crap in the bins and try not to look like gangsters."

The square room at the front of the boat's interior was stark. Peeling white paint revealed the pea green color underneath. It was considerably less filthy than the deck. Wooden bench seats lined both sides, and a long metal table was bolted to the middle of the floor. At the front end of the room in a glassed-in porch—the wheelhouse—another Maori man steered the boat. He wore shiny yellow rain gear.

"Sit," Tommy barked, gesturing to the bench on the left side wall. He and Frank parked themselves on the edge of the table facing us, and we shuffled to the seats. Tommy played with the hems of his jeans to display his green boots. The two other thugs stationed themselves by the back door, guns in their hands. One held a sawed-off shotgun; the other, a shiny revolver.

I ended up seated in the middle of our group. Sam sat next to me on my right, and Jason was next to her. Bhante and Ram perched on the ends. What an odd assortment we were. A Sri Lankan monk, an Indian businessman, a New Zealand athlete, a female American martial artist, and a fucking clone. Hell, I was an odd assortment all by myself.

"So what is it you want?" Bhante asked as Tommy gathered his thoughts again. I was struck by the fact that this was the first time Bhante had spoken since we'd been attacked. His voice was clear and strong.

"The bones, of course," Frank answered. Tommy frowned; Frank didn't notice. "You know as well as I do," he continued, "that religious relics with a good provenance will bring millions of US dollars. And then there's Sid."

"What do you mean?" I asked.

Tommy spoke up. Everything he said had an edge to it. "That's enough, Frank," he told him. "I'll do the talking."

"Sure, Tommy. No problem," Frank said, fear leaking out in his tone.

Jason spoke next. "You steered me to Frank for help in the States because you already knew him? He was working for you all along? How do you know an asshole like Frank? You can't trust him, you know."

"Jason," Tommy said, "I know you're not a bad guy, but I still don't like you. I never have. So if you don't shut the fuck up, I'm going to let Trevor pistol-whip you. He'd like that. Guess who his sister is—Eva Mahinarangi. Ring a bell? Wellington? 2009?"

Jason turned and faced one of the men by the door. "Sorry, man," he said. "I feel bad about how I treated women back then."

"Fuck you," Trevor growled. He was about three-quarters the size of Jason, with tribal tattoos covering almost all of his exposed skin—even half his face. He scowled and maintained an athletic stance—ready to move quickly. On an energy level, he radiated menace. If this guy got off his leash, people were going to get hurt.

"I know the relics aren't in the cave, and they weren't on the yacht, either," Tommy said. "What I don't know is where they are instead." He glared at Bhante. It was a world-class glare.

"I have been entrusted with them," Bhante said. "I can no more tell you than fly to the moon."

Tommy nodded at Frank, who slid off the table, stepped forward, and decked Bhante with a right cross to his upper cheek. The Sri Lankan toppled against me and then fell to the floor.

Somehow, despite all the threats and the earlier slap Frank had delivered, I'd been in denial about our situation. Now I was shocked into reality. They were going to beat up an old man to get what they wanted.

My heart raced, and I shrank back against the dirty wall.

Sam sprang into action. Moving even faster than she had back in my office, she lunged forward and dropped Frank with a kick to the side of his head. A split second later, she launched herself at Trevor, who failed to aim his revolver in time. It went off as he went down, and I heard the thud of the guy steering the boat hitting the floor.

Meanwhile, Jason attacked the other thug who'd been brandishing a shotgun. Tommy shrank back to the far side of the room, and several gunmen dressed in raincoats poured through the back door.

I decided in a split second to gamble that they needed me alive. I leapt to my feet and ran toward the wheelhouse. The man on the floor had definitely been shot, and I had to step on him to hurl myself out the open window on the side of the small room. It was a crappy dive—my feet hit the window frame as I knifed through—but I made it into the water.

The cold, salty bay shocked my nervous system. Adrenaline—my new friend—drove me, and I immediately changed direction underwater and swam under the boat. I'd seen this maneuver in a spy movie. Unfortunately, the boat in the movie hadn't sported external propellers like this one. Partway across the expanse of the wider-than-expected ship's keel, I realized I was about to be chopped to bits as the big boat lumbered over me. I dove straight down for dear life, hoping I'd have enough breath to make it back up again. I barely made it, despite all those long hours on my bike and in the pool. When I finally came up for air, I didn't hear anything before I dove again and headed back toward where Ram's yacht had sunk.

The shore may have been reachable, but a swim that long gave Tommy T. too much time to find me. I figured my best chance was to get picked up by one of the yacht's lifeboats back at the site of the collision. And I didn't think Tommy was stupid or desperate enough to return to the scene of his crime. Wouldn't he be satisfied with making Bhante tell him where the relics were?

After some hard underwater swimming and a dozen more gasps for air, I popped my head up to fully oxygenate and survey the situation. I was a good distance away from the fishing boat now. I couldn't spy anything else in the other direction; my low-in-the-water vantage point was limited and it was still a bit misty. Had both the *Silent Love* and the speed boat completely sunk already? Maybe I'd headed the wrong way.

I swam hard for another quarter mile or so, before I paused again to rest and take another look at things.

"Need a lift?" a male voice called from behind me.

This seemed so unlikely, I wondered if I'd imagined it. I turned around in the water and saw the older Hispanic man from the B&B dining room in a rowboat, of all things. An old wooden rowboat.

"I guess I do," I called, still very out of breath.

"Hop in," he said, pulling in his oars.

I swam over and discovered this was easier said than done. My soggy, heavy clothes had been challenging enough in the rough water. In the air, I had to fight for every inch. The man just waited calmly for me to manage it. Why didn't he help? And surely he'd been privy to all the mayhem out on the bay. Why did he look so serene?

"Where to?" he asked once I'd levered myself aboard and lay on the floor of the boat at his feet.

"Uh, I have no idea. I don't even really know where I am, let alone where I ought to be," I said.

"Why don't we go to my island, then?" he said. "I was heading there anyway—I just came into town for breakfast."

"Sure. You own your own island?"

"Yes," he said. "I won the lottery, so I bought one. You can sort through things there. I have a nice dog, too."

"Okay." He spoke with a complex accent—not local—and an easy, casual manner.

The man began to row again. He wore old khaki pants, a red windbreaker, and a red ski cap. He certainly wouldn't be hard to spot if anyone was pursuing us or even just scanning the water with binoculars.

His face was leathery and wrinkled from the sun, but he didn't have worry wrinkles or any other evidence of emotional stress. In my experience, this was unusual in anyone past the age of thirty. He could've been a character actor in a 1950s Western—maybe the retired, half-breed gunfighter who'd had to strap on his guns again for some implausible reason.

I heard a speedboat in the water behind us. It may have been Tommy's people—perhaps the boat that had rammed us hadn't sunk—or rescuers. I'd begun to pull myself up onto the other seat in the rowboat, but now I lay back down. I wasn't eager to find out who it was.

"They'll probably see you there," he said. "Why not sit up? I'll take care of this."

"You don't know who these people are. They're

dangerous—violent."

"Oh, I'm sure we'll be fine. By the way, call me Marco." Again, I was struck by his breezy demeanor. *Is he developmentally disabled? Who wouldn't be alarmed?* The speedboat drew closer.

"I'm Sid," I told him.

"Of course you are," he said. "I've been expecting you."

Chapter Eight

"I beg your pardon?" I said.

"Oh, don't misunderstand. I don't mean you in particular. I've been expecting whoever it is that thinks he's Buddha's clone."

I stared at him. "How do you know about that?"

"I'll tell you about it later," he said as he continued rowing. "But first put on my hat."

"Why?"

"So the men in the boat won't see you. It's easier than your diving back into the bay."

"It's bright red. They're much more likely to see me in your cap."

"They won't see you if you wear the hat," Marco said.

"That doesn't make any sense."

"Fuck sense," he said.

I just lay there. *This guy is crazy.*

"I'll tell you what," he said. "As a gesture of good faith, I'll give you some idea of who I am, so you'll put on the hat."

"Okay."

"Think about something that's completely immaterial—something I couldn't possibly know."

"Okay." None of this seemed as ridiculous as it would've the week before. I took a moment and recalled an incident at the San Francisco zoo in which a gorilla had signed to me from his enclosure.

"Interspecies contact can be powerful, can't it?" Marco said amiably. "And it's always available on some level. Animals are much more aware than we give them credit for."

He took off his hat and held it out to me. I immediately sat up and jammed it on my head.

Holy shit, I thought. But I didn't seem to be feeling much of anything else. Why wasn't I scared?

"I don't want you to be," Marco said. "But enough of that. Now that I've established my credentials, I'll save all the showing off for any pretty mermaids we might meet." He laughed at his own joke, and his laugh was beautifully liquid—a flow of round, bubbling sound. It was unlike any laugh I'd ever heard.

The speedboat had veered away and bombed around in the bay past us, but now it circled back. The mist had almost completely dissipated, but I still couldn't see the fishing boat or the yacht. We were about to test the magic red hat. When the launch reached us—the same one Jason had piloted the day before, actually—one of the mastiff-like Maoris throttled back, and Frank called across the water to Marco. I held my breath.

"Hey, old man! Have you seen a guy in the water?"

"What kind of a guy?"

"He's Asian. Maybe mid-thirties," Frank said.

"No, I haven't seen anybody like that. Did he have a red hat on?"

"What the fuck are you talking about? Did you see anyone or not?"

"I don't like your tone," Marco said.

Frank swore at him, and the speedboat roared

away.

"Wow," I said.

"So if I say or do something that doesn't make sense to you," Marco told me, "try not to pay attention to that."

"You got it."

I was completely baffled by what I'd witnessed. Once again, though, I wasn't having any sort of emotional reaction to it.

"Let's be silent for the rest of the trip," Marco suggested.

"Okay. Is there some special reason?"

"It'll help me keep you invisible," he said. "The same part of my brain that does words does that, too."

"Just tell me this," I said. "How far is your island? I kind of need to pee."

Marco held up one finger.

"One mile?"

He shook his head.

"One more minute?"

He shook it again.

This was absurd. I was in a rowboat in some obscure corner of New Zealand with a magician or a psychic or God knew who, and now we were playing charades.

I gave it one last try. "One hour?"

Marco nodded.

"You row over an hour each way to go out for breakfast?"

He nodded and smiled.

I shut up and peed over the side. I was very wet, very cold, and very confused.

****

It turned out I'd seen Marco's island on the trip across the bay the day before. It was only a few acres across—maybe five or six—with a modest tin-roofed home perched on a hillock in the middle of it. Several small sheds were scattered around the property, and all the buildings were painted black.

"Black?" I asked as we drew close to our destination.

"It's an easy color to make disappear," Marco said, his first words in an hour.

"But I can see them," I said.

"Some people can, some people can't."

"Oh."

A beagle came racing down to the rock ledge we seemed to be heading toward. There wasn't a dock or a beach.

"That's Lucy," Marco told me. "She'll like you."

"Dogs do tend to like me," I said, shooting for modesty with my tone of voice.

"She likes everybody."

"Oh." I felt embarrassed—my first emotion in a while. "Hey, I'm feeling stuff again," I said.

He smiled. "Your emotions are no longer likely to endanger us," he told me. "So feel away, my friend."

Lucy did like me, and I liked her. She ran in figure eights between our legs as we walked up an impeccably landscaped path to the house. Or the back patio of the house, actually, which was a simple array of irregular slices of limestone, topped by a wooden pergola. Two aluminum-framed beach chairs sat on the patio facing the water, and a blue plastic cooler served as a low table between them.

Marco gestured to one of the chairs and ambled

into the house, so I sat. In a moment, he returned with a brown comforter, which he draped around me. I kept wearing the magic hat. Then he sat as well. Lucy lay beside Marco, her front feet splayed forward and her head on the cool stone.

"Would you like to ask me questions?" Marco said.

"Yes, I certainly would." That was a massive understatement. "Is English a second language for you?" I thought I'd start with something easy.

"Fourth. I grew up speaking Italian in Argentina."

"Oh."

I examined him more closely. Argentina fit. I could see that he was as much Italian as Hispanic. Overall, there was nothing remarkable about Marco's looks. He could've been a gardener in a movie, or maybe a bail bondsman. He definitely had charisma, though— something powerful behind his looks.

"How did you recognize me as the clone person?" I asked. "Have you seen the others around?"

"The cavern you were in holds a strong energetic charge, and it's in you now," Marco said.

"How can a cave hold energy? What do you mean?"

He leaned over to scratch behind Lucy's ear just as she wriggled sideways to try to scratch it herself. She sank back down with a grunt. "The man-made part of the cavern predates modern migration to New Zealand," Marco said. "It goes back thousands of years, so the energy in there has had more time to build up than elsewhere on these islands."

I considered this. Maybe places embodied energy, and maybe they didn't. What did I know? "So that told you where I'd been," I said. "But how did you know I was Buddha's clone? Isn't that a big secret?"

"You're not."

"What do you mean I'm not?"

"You're not a clone. You're not Buddha. He's done."

"Done? Wait a minute. Who were all those guys in the cave?"

"They looked like you?"

"Yes," I said.

"Your brothers."

"Dozens of them?"

"You're one of a set of identical triplets from Nepal who were separated soon after birth and adopted internationally." Marco's impassive face and relaxed posture revealed little about him. Clearly, none of this represented a big deal to him. That much I could tell. *Does he have great boundaries—a strong awareness that my problems are mine, not his? Or maybe he's just world weary and nothing matters anymore.* He continued in his even tone. "Bhante found the other two and trained them in accents and quick costume changes—you can buy breakaway outfits to use onstage. The cavern is riddled with hidden passages, so they could keep appearing from room to room. I'm sure you never saw more than two at a time."

I was stunned by this information. Was it true? On balance, it certainly seemed more likely than the clone story. And it was true that I'd never seen more than two duplicates at any one time.

Marco spoke again. "You may be a Buddha. I'm just telling you that you're not *the* Buddha—Siddhartha Gautama."

"But what's the point? Why would they go to all

that trouble?" I asked.

"I'm sure Bhante explained it to you." He smiled—just a little. *He's enjoying remaining an enigma despite all the opportunities in our conversation to show me something—anything—that revealed who the hell he was.* "Except for the clone business," he continued, "he tends to be fairly straightforward. They want you and everyone else to believe there's a fabulous new teacher on the scene. Someone with impeccable credentials. Buddha."

"Why?"

"His organization believes that unless more people wake up to the truth, the world will end. Through the centuries, apocalyptic thinking has justified all sorts of unprincipled means."

Does Marco actually understand the metaphysics behind Bhante's belief? "Is there any truth to it? Does the world need me?"

"Yes, but not in the way you think. We'll discuss this after your enlightenment." Now he straightened in his beach chair, reminding me of a professor at UCSC who'd shifted into schoolmarm mode right before sharing any information she was planning to use on a test.

Enlightenment is something theoretical you read about in biographies of saints. Is he serious? Me?

Marco smiled as he watched me wrestle with this.

"Are you Bhante's boss or something? Is that how you know about this?" I asked.

"Oh, no. He only knows me as a rumor." Marco held his hands unnaturally, perfectly still, as though he had an itch he was refusing to scratch.

"What about RGP?"

"Who?"

"RGP. It's some rival Buddhist group," I told him, pulling the comforter tight around me. I wished I had the new clothes that were sitting on the floor of the bay in the *Silent Love*. Well, the dry version of them.

"I've never heard of RGP." Everything Marco said still sounded neutral and descriptive—to the point that it was impossible to discern what he thought or felt about any of it.

I paused again and tried to sort through all this, playing catch-up, as always. How many times would I have to endure a sudden wholesale reappraisal of who I was?

"Would you like a beer?" Marco asked.

"Sure. Thank you."

He arose and walked into the house again. I patted the red ski cap down onto my head and slouched farther down in my beach chair. I looked at Lucy, and her eyes swiveled to look back at me. I felt strangely content to just sit there. Perhaps I'd momentarily given up on trying to figure anything out. Obviously, Marco represented a realm far beyond anything I'd ever encountered before. Letting go of trying to make sense gave rise to relief—an unburdening. Fuck sense, Marco had said. As I sat on the patio with my new beagle friend, this sounded like excellent advice.

Marco returned with a bottle in each hand. "Which one would you like?" he asked as he sat.

It seemed like a test—something a Zen master would ask to assess his student's progress. I cocked an eyebrow. He laughed.

"Actually," he said. "They're both bad. It's hard to get good beer here." Now he waved the bottles in the air as if he were hawking them at a baseball game. I flinched momentarily, surprised that this sort of behavior was in his repertoire.

"Here in New Zealand?" I asked. "They have bad beer?"

"Here in my refrigerator. I inherited the beer in it. I'm not much of a drinker." Marco handed me the bottle in his left hand and sat next to me again. He placed his on the top of the cooler that sat between us, unopened. His compact, efficient movements hinted at an athletic background. Even his bottle waving had been strikingly in control and graceful.

I took a swig. "It's fine."

"Great. So what else do you want to know?" He tossed that off as if he were prepared to tell me how to change a tire.

"Who are you?"

"Marco." His face, as usual gave nothing away. I wasn't accustomed to only knowing someone from his bare words.

"I mean, how did you acquire all these special abilities? Are you enlightened? Are you a sorcerer? Are you from the future?" All of this fell out of me in rapid succession without forethought. I guess my subconscious had relapsed into trying to make sense.

"If I have to pick from your list," Marco said, tilting his head, "enlightened is the closest. But it's a misleading term."

"How's that?"

"It isn't what you imagine it to be. Being fully awake is a very matter-of-fact state. There are no fireworks."

"I'd say that reading minds was fairly fireworksy,"

I said with energy. "And making people invisible certainly qualifies."

"There's no one here doing it. Marco is just a construct. You are too, but you don't realize it."

"So you're saying you're enlightened, but you're not here to enjoy it? Should I feel sorry for you?"

He laughed his liquid laugh. "I like that. Yes, let's both have a good cry, Sid. Boo-hoo. I'm so sad. All I know is oneness and love. Poor me." He laughed again. I wanted to say something else ridiculous just to hear him laugh.

"So it's not something to like or dislike?" I asked and sipped my beer. "It just is?"

"Okay, that's fine. Here's the main thing, Sid." He pointed at me, the first time he'd emphasized any of his words with a physical action. "Don't think you know what's going on because you can put a word to it. Enlightenment is just a word."

At that point, he held his hands up at eye level and bent his fingers into odd shapes. It was as though he were making animal shadow puppets. Then he closed his eyes, and a moment later, I felt a tingling surge through my chest. I was alarmed. "What's going on?" I asked. It was similar to Sam's energy but much stronger.

He didn't respond. I began to heat up, the warmth spreading concentrically from the middle of my chest—from my heart. The tingling increased too—becoming a strong buzzing. It was almost overwhelming. And then it *was* overwhelming.

I began to sob as waves of bliss shuddered through me. It was so much more than an orgasm—so much deeper, so much more expansive, so unlimited. All of me was alive with love and joy and boundless energy. I couldn't think. I couldn't talk. I couldn't see. Every cell of me was flooded with love. And the love kept building. I was bursting with it. I kept sobbing. It was so intense, I thought I couldn't bear it. It seared me. And yet it kept building.

I don't know how long I was lost in the experience, but when I eventually became aware of my surroundings again, I found myself on my feet. Marco was hugging me, and it was clear now that he was nothing more than that same energy. It emanated from him, merging with the energy that I had become. It was all the same—all there was. Marco was just a purer, stronger—more concentrated—version of this universal energy.

Eventually, he spoke to me soothingly in soft Italian. Even if he'd spoken English, I probably wouldn't have understood. And if he weren't holding me up, I would've toppled to the ground.

Lovingly, Marco cradled me and guided me down into my beach chair. He returned to his seat, and we sat together again. I cried quietly; the tears leaked out of their own accord. An aliveness settled in me—no longer scouring me. The surge of energy had modified me to be able to hold it—not as intense waves now, but as part of me. I sat in my chair and welcomed the energy home. I felt whole. It was sublime.

After quite some time, Marco spoke. "Things will be different now," he said. He gave me a moment to make sense of the words. It was an effort. "Your heart is open. It won't stay open, but remember this moment. Remember this glimpse of what can be—of what is."

I sat with that. I couldn't really think about it, but I

could hang out with it for a while.

I was completely in my heart, experiencing the world without all my usual mind filters. Colors were brighter, and objects were somehow more three-dimensional. I was more conscious of the space between things, too. Air wasn't the absence of something; it was an invisible bridge between everything. Where I left off and the world began seemed less defined. Sounds, smells, and even the sensation of my body's weight against the fabric seat of the chair were all greatly enhanced as well.

Things were simultaneously more and less real. At the perceptual level, I was so much more in contact with the world, it was ten times more "there" to experience. So it was realer—to me. But I could also sense—in the moment—that it was all just energy. Nothing was solid, really. Nothing was as it seemed to be. I was seeing more clearly, but all there was to see was the massive illusion that energy had conjured.

In that moment, I wasn't interested in why this was so or where the game of life would take me. I was content to be with it as it was—real, unreal, or anything else. I'd never felt so calm, peaceful, and accepting.

As much as I would have liked to remain in that state forever, my mind began to intrude, and my ego gradually slithered its way back into the mix as well. I could hang on to all of what had happened as a vivid memory, but my ongoing experience was devolving into a very dilute version of what Marco had given me.

"Was that what it's like for you all the time?" I asked after a while. I couldn't imagine someone functioning in the world with all that bliss. How could you even pretend to care about ordinary crap?

"Not exactly. I'm always aligned with the energy—doing its bidding—embodying it. But it's integrated in me—or I'm integrated in it, I suppose. So I don't experience it as a feeling or a sensation or something separate. Are you following me?"

I nodded. "My brain is mostly back. Unfortunately."

He smiled. "So as Marco the construct person, I'm in love with everyone and everything. But there's really no 'I' that's experiencing this. It's love experiencing love. There's only love. You understand this now, don't you?"

"Yes. I was love—love energy—and now I'm me again. Sort of. But the love is still there." I paused a moment. "I guess you found love and never went back to being you, right?"

"Yes. If you arrive there on your own, when you're ready, it's abiding," he said, shifting in his seat.

"Abiding?"

"Permanent. Continuous."

I paused again to consider this. "So what was it that you did to me, anyway?" I asked. "How did that work?"

"All I did was send you *chi*—the energy that animates everything. The love. I didn't decide to do it. The energy arranged my hands and sent itself out." He smiled. "I'm chock full of *chi*," he said. "Chubby with *chi*." He laughed his laugh.

"That's all?"

"Yes. A sudden influx of a limited amount of *chi* can work wonders. It activates all sorts of things. The Hindus call it *Shaktipat*."

"Did you say 'limited'? That wasn't the full-bore version?" I was astonished.

"No. So-called individual people are very limited energy containers," Marco said. "Your current internal configuration can only hold a certain amount of life force gracefully. Beyond that, the integrity of the container becomes compromised, and there's permanent damage."

"You can calibrate that?"

Marco nodded.

"This is the Chinese medicine *chi*?"

"Yes. The concept doesn't exist in English."

I was becoming cold again, so I gathered the damp comforter at my feet and pulled it up over me. Our conversation was another thing that was different now. I heard and understood Marco more effortlessly than before, and I had much less of an urge to pick at what he told me. One thing was simply leading to another—more questions from me, mostly—but it wasn't an overly willful chain of events. It just felt like what needed to happen next.

"So I gather you're not a Hindu," I said. "Are you a Buddhist?" That would explain why he knew so much about what Bhante was up to.

"No. I'm nothing. I graduated myself out of everything," Marco replied.

I noticed my beer bottle sitting on the blue cooler beside me and took a sip. It was warm, and the alcohol in it tasted awful. I made a face.

"Go ahead and spit it out," he suggested. "You won't want to drink now." His full bottle sat next to him.

I swallowed and wished I'd spit. "You've ruined my drinking? What else? Will I have to stop beating up old ladies and robbing banks?"

He laughed.

"What about sex?" I asked, thinking about Sam. "Seriously. Will I still enjoy it?"

"Probably more now," Marco said.

I suddenly noticed that Lucy the beagle was gone and asked where she was.

"Lucy is aware that her ability to tolerate *chi* is limited, so when there's energy flying around, she runs off and hides."

He called her name, and she sprinted around the corner of the house, her big ears flopping wildly. Then she jumped up in my lap.

"I told you she'd like you," Marco said.

"You also said she likes everybody."

He smiled. When I tried a few more questions, he just kept smiling, so I sat quietly and watched the bay.

After a while, I scratched an itch on my cheek and was surprised to find I was still crying. Apparently, I'd never stopped.

Chapter Nine

We spent the entire day in our chairs on the patio, with only occasional visits to Marco's outhouse. He brought food and water out twice, but he didn't speak at all. Neither did I.

During the first few hours, I could feel the new energy moving around inside me. Apparently, there was a time lag to Marco's handiwork. Now and then his hands formed odd positions again; I guess he was facilitating the assimilation process. The internal movements were spooky at first—like feeling a critter run up your spine or a Roman candle spitting sparks in your gut. But as the day wore on and the fruits of the energy manifested more strongly, I came to appreciate the software upgrade more and more.

By nightfall, my baseline mental state seemed to be alert, positive, and loving. I was naturally in the moment, but I could retrieve memories or ponder something if I chose to. I wasn't bored for a second, even though all I'd done all day was sit there. I didn't need to say or do anything to become fine. I didn't need to escape or avoid any feelings or thoughts. They just arose, hung around, and then drifted off. Perhaps another one would bubble up, perhaps not. Either way was fine with me.

It was as if I'd made my peace with the entirety of my experience. My judgments about it all seemed meaningless; they were nothing more than self-interested impositions onto life. My role was to cooperate by doing—or refraining from doing—whatever was called for. I knew I didn't have the wisdom to administer this perfectly. That was fine, too.

Finally, Marco announced it was time for bed. I was still ensconced in my brown comforter with Lucy on my lap. The red ski cap was perched on my head. In a lowbrow comedy movie, I'd have been the wacky ethnic neighbor who dropped by and told everyone in horrendous English about an upcoming party where the babes dug happening dudes wearing comforters, ski caps, and beagles.

"Thank you," I told Marco as I rose, shedding Lucy in the process.

"Thank the universe," he said, so I did.

I slept in the "guest shed" on an army cot amidst piles of kites, paint-by-number kits, and antique luggage. Marco told me that these were legacies from the previous owner. He'd bought the island five months earlier. When I asked him why, he said that Lucy liked it, and it was conveniently located to meet me.

I fell asleep immediately and woke up the next morning refreshed, with beagle slobber on my nose and beagle eyes locked on mine. It felt like a warmer day.

Lucy watched me closely as I washed my face in the corner sink—there was running water, at least. And I was able to shave using the toiletry kit that Marco had provided. Most dogs displayed an implicit demand in their eyes first thing in the morning—feed me, walk me, pet me—but Lucy just seemed interested in what I was up to.

Marco had bought "Buddha-sized clothes" some

time ago in anticipation of my arrival. I tried on the clean jeans and purple turtleneck, and they fit me fairly well, although I didn't think Buddha would've been caught dead in a turtleneck.

By the time I'd visited the outhouse again, Marco was back on the patio with a couple of omelets and a pile of toast. "Is there something special about this patio?" I asked. I'd wondered early on why he hadn't invited me into his house.

"Yes. Have some breakfast."

The food was either unusually delicious or my innards had continued to reconfigure during the night. Every bite was a complex and intense experience. The texture of the toast was exquisite. The hot tea was even more sublime than Bhante's, although I could see that it had been brewed from ordinary teabags.

"You'll get used to it," Marco said, watching me chew. "You'll get used to all of it."

"Can I ask more questions?" While I'd been washing my face, I'd concocted some doozies.

"No. We've got to get moving," Marco said. "There's a water taxi coming to pick us up in forty minutes, and then we'll get a car in Paihia and drive to the Auckland airport. We need to be in India by tomorrow."

"Whoa. Hold it. I haven't signed up for anything like that. I appreciate the *chi*, I appreciate the rescue—"

"Don't forget those grilled cheese sandwiches I made yesterday. That was Dijon mustard on those."

"But," I continued, "I'm not ready to go to India with you. I don't have my passport with me, anyway. I couldn't go if I wanted to."

"Chris is bringing it with him. He'll meet us in

124

Auckland," Marco said.

"My Chris? From Santa Cruz?"

"Yes. He's coming to India, too."

I was speechless again for a moment. *Who the fuck is this guy?* Then my new calm settled back in again. *Whatever.* It was all part of the perfect whole, even my shock at hearing Marco's words.

"I called him early yesterday and explained the situation," Marco said. "He was very gracious."

"Chris? Gracious?"

"Well, I needed to demonstrate what I could do first."

"You read his mind?" I asked.

"Better."

"Better?"

"I had his dog spell out 'Help Sid' with pieces of dog food on the carpet while he talked to me."

I burst out laughing. "Oh, I wish I could've seen his face. He was probably right in the middle of giving you shit, wasn't he?"

"Let's just say he was less than gracious at first."

I couldn't stop laughing, and now my laugh sounded like a junior version of Marco's. "Hey, I've got a new laugh," I said.

He smiled.

"Can I ask why you want us to go to India? Or for that matter, what the hell is going on generally? Am I your student now? Are you my guru? Am I enlightened? What about my life—my clients back home? People are counting on me."

"Chris called your answering service, and they're contacting all your patients. You're on an extended personal leave due to unforeseen circumstances."

"They're unforeseen, all right." I paused and realized I was upset. My jaw tightened, and I felt lost in it, and I also watched myself be lost in it. As the undifferentiated feeling coalesced into anger, I found myself resenting this other, more reasonable guy that was now living in my head. I didn't ask for an internal witness. I didn't ask for any of this shit.

I experienced the anger as energy now, too. This was another uninvited alteration. It raced through me with a corrosive tang. It felt wrong. It was driving me to misbehave, but I couldn't respond in the same old way. Had Marco ruined anger, too? Would I always be like this now?

I finally spoke in a much more reasonable tone than I felt. "Isn't this rather high-handed, Marco?"

"Yes."

"You're doing all this behind my back—without my permission. Even the weird hands…"

"Mudras," he said.

"Okay, even the mudras and the *chi* aren't anything I agreed to. There's a lot of presumption here." The angry energy still roiled around, but I found it easy to keep it in check.

"Yes."

"Well, I'm not sure that's okay with me," I said.

"Clearly, it isn't," he replied. "But we have to get ready to go now."

"You already know I'm going, don't you?"

"Yes."

"Fine. Whatever." I threw up my hands as though I were Italian, too.

"You'll need this for our trip," Marco said, handing me a wad of money, which I stuffed into my pocket.

How could I argue with the guy? And although I'd never been to India, I did have an affinity for the place. I'd grown up outside Palo Alto, California, a remarkably international community, due to Stanford University. My parents had befriended several Indians, and my father's college roommate, Charles Singh, was from Kashmir. Growing up, he'd been like an uncle to me.

As I brushed my teeth back in the shed a few minutes later, it occurred to me that between my therapeutic skills and my new *chi*-enhanced operating system, I was now remarkably well equipped to handle whatever came my way. How many people could access the same rarified range of abilities that were available to me? I didn't even know what I was capable of. Maybe I possessed minor-league superpowers now.

Or maybe my ego needs to calm the hell down.

I selected a brown vintage suitcase from the pile of luggage in the shed and placed a change of clothes and the guest toiletries in it. They looked rather pathetic lying there by themselves, and since they'd rattle around in transit, I filled up the space with several paint-by-number kits: a mountain scene, an antique car, and—my favorite—a kangaroo with a pouch full of socket wrenches.

The water taxi appeared on schedule. Apparently, Marco had summoned it to the island before, because the teenage driver moored the small launch where the rowboat had been. Perhaps Marco had moved it up onto the land while I'd slept that morning, although it had appeared to be too heavy for one person to manhandle.

Marco carried Lucy into the boat under one arm. Was she coming too? A white canvas duffel bag was tucked under his other arm.

"Good morning," the teenaged boatman chirped. He was very white and good-looking in a generic sort of way. He had short, curly red hair which was mostly hidden under a huge, beige sunhat. He looked at me even more closely than I was examining him.

"Hey, you're missing," he said.

"What?"

"You've been missing since yesterday morning. They think you drowned. I need to call this in." He reached into his pants pocket, fumbling in his haste.

Marco eased Lucy down onto the deck and placed his hand on the young man's forearm. "Pat, I'd prefer if you'd wait on that."

"Why's that, Mr. Giocassini?"

"Sid here doesn't want to be found just yet. There are people who wish him harm. And I think it was his brother you saw in that photo, anyway. Can you wait until you've dropped us off in Paihia?"

"Well, if you say so. I wouldn't do that for just anyone, Mr. G."

"I appreciate it," Marco said, letting go of the young man's arm. "And say hi to your mom for me."

"Sure thing." He smiled broadly and turned back to the wheel.

We sat behind Pat, Lucy at our feet, as he smoothly pulled out into the bay. During the early part of the trip, heading inland, he chatted with me. We had to speak up to cut through the noisy outboard motor.

"So how do you like the Bay of Islands?" he asked.

"It's beautiful." I liked having a name for where we were. "And it's aptly named. Are you from here?"

"No, no. I came up from Napier. Are you from

India? You have an American accent, but you aren't American, are you?"

"I'm from California."

"Oh. Is someone chasing you? Is that what Mr. G. meant about someone wanting to hurt you?" Pat swiveled his head back and forth from watching where he was going and watching me.

"I'm not sure," I said, which I realized was true. If anything, I knew less about all that than I had before Marco rescued me. Who knew what Tommy T., Bhante, or Jackson were up to? On the other hand, it didn't bother me to be so clueless. *Hell, I don't even know why I'm heading for India, yet here I am en route.*

"How do you know Mr. G.?" Pat asked next. "He's never let anyone else on his island before."

Marco spoke up in his strong baritone voice. "He's my spiritual teacher. He's going to be very famous someday."

"Really? Wow," Pat said. "You know, Mr. G., you're the most spiritual guy I ever met. So if this guy is your teacher, well…wow!"

"Ask him for a blessing," Marco suggested.

"Sure. Great. Can I have a blessing? What's your name anyway?" His guileless face reflected an innocence I didn't see back home.

Marco answered before I could. "They call him Buddha 2.0."

"Cool. Like an upgraded tech product, huh?"

Pat swiveled all the way and faced me—apparently the boat could steer itself for a while. I looked at Marco. He smiled his characteristic enigmatic smile.

So I pointed my right forefinger at Pat's chest. "I hereby bless you," I said. All of a sudden, energy shot out of my finger. Pat was jolted by it—it knocked him back into the steering wheel.

"Whoa!" he said, his eyes wide.

I retracted my finger before he passed out or something. The energy stopped immediately.

Pat seemed dazed. For a few moments, he was immobile, his eyes unfocused. Then he wriggled his torso like a dog flinging water off, nodded furiously several times, and turned excitedly toward Marco. His face was flushed. "I see what you mean about this guy," he said. "That was really something."

"Do you feel more awake?"

"Definitely. It's like five cups of coffee." Pat pivoted and grabbed the wheel again.

I spoke just loud enough for Marco to hear. "What was that all about?"

"Well, it's up to you, Sid," he said. "It could be about becoming a spiritual leader—doing things like that on a grander scale and saving the world. Or it could be a parlor trick you do at cocktail parties back home if you decide to pack it in." His intense gaze bored into me.

"What do you mean, 'save the world'? I thought you didn't agree with Bhante about an apocalypse. Are you saying I need to save people because they're full of sin? You know, like Jesus?"

"No," he said. "There's no such thing as sin. Everyone's perfect just as they are—and there's tremendous room for improvement, too. What I mean is the world's literally going to end soon." His casual tone had returned. This seemed to be his baseline.

"The whole world?" I would've been more alarmed, but it was all too weird to react to in an ordinary way.

"Pretty much. Bhante is right about that, but for the wrong reasons. We've got a few months to keep things going, though." He smiled.

Maybe he doesn't care. This time, the idea alarmed me. I couldn't keep my voice down as I responded. "I'm just me!" I proclaimed. "I don't know anything about all that."

Pat looked back at us. His face was still much more alive than when we'd met.

"He's so humble," Marco said to the teen.

Pat nodded, turned around again, and steered the launch past a buoy.

"I need your help," Marco told me. "We can change things together." He shifted several times in his seat, either belying the calm he was projecting or as a response to physical discomfort—a sore hip? Usually, I could discriminate between two motives—I was a therapist, after all—but in Marco's case, I had no clue.

"Why me? And what are the right reasons if Bhante's are wrong?"

"Who wouldn't listen to Buddha's clone, especially when he'd been certified as being the reincarnated Buddha, too?"

"But you said that wasn't true," I protested.

"These days, who cares?" Marco shrugged. "We need someone who people will listen to. It doesn't matter why or what's true. Whatever works—that's what we have to go with. It isn't unscrupulous to do what's called for in a true crisis, or to put it another way, we don't have the luxury of personal integrity. The stakes are too high."

"So we need to hook up with Bhante's crowd? We

need to let him work his scam? Is that what you mean?"

"More or less. But don't worry. I'll tell you what to do and say. And I'll send energy through you—that's what we set up yesterday. And that's why Pat is a happier man today. Bhante can give you an audience. Together, you and I will transform that audience. If we can't wake up a critical mass of the world's population, the old deal here is doomed. Consciousness will need to build a new game from scratch."

He's got to be delusional. Despite all the phenomena that Marco had generated, this was classic delusional disorder material, grandiose type. Bhante had a religion backing him up, more or less. Marco had come up with this crap on his own. The end of the world. Being its savior. Validating the craziness by signing up helpers. Most systematic delusions are the product of errant biochemistry—schizophrenia or severe bipolar disorder, for example. But occasionally some people simply think their way into crazy.

"I'm not delusional," Marco said. "Remember the ski cap? Remember the limits of logic?"

"You mean the 'fuck sense' teaching?"

He laughed. "Exactly."

I nodded. What else could I do? You can't reason with delusion.

After mulling it over for a while, though, I had to admit that I had yet to encounter some of the core features of a grandiose delusional disorder. Beyond the sheer outrageousness of the ideas Marco had just put forth, for example, there was nothing puffed up or egotistical about him. Perhaps my mind sought the familiarity of diagnosis instead of facing what Marco was telling me.

When I pondered Marco's early logic-defying demonstrations in the rowboat, I felt completely incapable of judging what was possible and what had to be delusional. In my business, we called an idea—and a person—crazy if it didn't make any sense to us. We applied a consensus-based criterion of what sense was. Well, all that was out the window.

So how was I qualified to save the world if, as a therapist, I couldn't even figure out if the concept of world-solving was sane? And if there really was a doomsday looming, I didn't see why the hell I ought to play a major role in any of it. I was just a somewhat spiritual-minded guy who apparently looked like Buddha and had very recently been infused with some sort of esoteric energy by a seemingly enlightened guy.

Actually, that sounded exactly like someone who might be up to his neck in world-saving.

Fuck it. I'll just enjoy the boat ride and my newfound ability to connect to the world. I don't have to decide anything. I'll just let things unfold and see what happens. I was aware that the last time I'd been cavalier about a boat ride, I'd nearly ended up drowning.

My ability to adopt this attitude was a testament to Marco's reconfiguring. Whatever he'd done might've made me a better conduit for directing energy, but it also allowed me to yield more gracefully to the moment—to let go of ideas and just be with my surroundings. The wind in my face was real—well, as real as illusion gets. The water was real, too. The fishy smell was real. The world ending was a science fiction story in Marco's head. For now.

Chapter Ten

Paihia was an unattractive tourist town where the bay ended and the mainland began. We walked the four blocks from the wharf to the car rental storefront past trinket shops and a variety of seafood restaurants. Lucy wasn't leashed, but no one seemed to mind. I saw two people reach for their cell phones when they saw me. I hoped they were spreading the good news that the missing man was alive and kicking. But Tommy, Bhante, or Jackson—whoever that was—might be watching for me too.

Marco didn't seem concerned. When I told him I'd been recognized, he said that everything would work out fine. When I mentioned Jackson as a particular worry, he laughed and wouldn't explain why.

The older Asian woman at Kiwi Rentals greeted me by name—the wrong name. "Mr. Oshin. You're back so soon. Have they found your brother? Did they cancel your flight?"

Marco spoke up. "This *is* the brother. I fished him out of the bay."

"Oh, my goodness. You're a lucky man. Are you twins, then? Is it also Mr. Oshin?"

"He goes by 'B-2,' " Marco told her.

"That's an interesting name. Are you a rapper?" she asked.

"No, I've been healing people," I said. "And now

I'm going to wake them up." She cocked her head like a dog and squinted at me. "I'm sorry," I said. Confusing people certainly wasn't going to help.

"I'll be renting the car today," Marco said. "And we'll turn it in at the airport."

"Okay. Let's get you going, then."

Linda was warm and friendly but not particularly efficient. By the time we got out of there and into our cobalt blue compact, the weather had shifted. And Lucy's mood had, too. She was quite impatient as she leapt inelegantly into the small back seat.

Rain hammered down as Marco pulled out into the left-side-of-the-road traffic and headed south on the motel-lined road.

"I hope we're not being followed," I said.

"We are," Marco said. "There's at least one car—maybe two."

"What'll we do?"

"Drive to the airport." He was completely unconcerned.

I thought about his behavior since we'd docked in town. "You want to be followed, don't you?"

"By Bhante, yes. Or his people. But there might be someone else, too."

"I haven't had a chance to tell you about the attack at the cave or being kidnapped or the guys with guns on the boat," I said. "I think you need to know all that."

"So tell me."

I did, from the very beginning to when I met Marco in the bay. It took a while. Marco listened without interruption as he drove cautiously in the storm, and then sped up to match the light traffic once the sun had broken through. It took us about forty minutes to reach the main highway.

When I finished, Marco was silent. I tried to see which cars might be following us, but it was hard to tell. Even the major north-south New Zealand artery was only two lanes wide, so basically everyone was following everyone else.

"Here are some ideas I have about your story," Marco finally said. "First, I doubt the attack was real. There was probably just one helicopter—the 5:15 commuter flight to Great Barrier Island. They could've timed things to coincide with it flying overhead."

"So who's this Jackson guy, then? Is that just a name they made up?"

"That's me, I think," Marco said.

I stared at him. "You?"

"My last name is Giocassini. How do you think that would sound if it was pronounced in a hurry by a Maori with a New Zealand accent? Something like Jackson, I'd guess. They know I exist, and they know I have an interest in you, so they tried to plant the idea that I was a violent enemy."

"What about Sam? And RGP?"

"Let's stay focused on the parts that relate to our current situation."

"Okay."

"Tommy T. is the head of a major gang in this country. The T stands for Tuttle, by the way, which is why he uses an initial. The primary criminal interest in this matter are the relics, of course," Marco said. "Bones of saints and such are quite precious, although they rarely appear on the open market. And in Buddha's case, there are only a handful of credible known relics in the world—all well guarded. You mentioned cave paintings, too. It wouldn't surprise me if they figured into this as well."

He accelerated hard at this point and began passing other cars rather recklessly. Lucy barked her approval. Apparently, she liked to go fast. I looked behind us. A silver Audi sedan did its best to keep up.

"What are you doing?" I asked.

"Trust me," Marco said. "Don't trust anyone else when they say that, but trust me."

He continued to race ahead, and I endeavored to remain calm. "So why do they want me?" I asked. "I don't have the relics."

"You have value to Bhante's organization, and *they* have the relics. You can be traded for the bones or held for ransom."

"Oh." My stomach tightened, and I frowned.

Suddenly, Marco braked hard and swerved into the parking lot of a car repair shop. Lucy tumbled across the backseat. The Audi followed, fishtailing wildly as it slid to a stop behind us, blocking our exit.

Marco climbed out of the car, and I followed. Lucy barked her displeasure at being left behind. We stood and waited for whoever was behind the Audi's tinted windows to emerge.

It was Sam! She wore light brown yoga pants, a black windbreaker, and a wide smile. She looked as lovely as ever.

"Louise," Marco said.

"Sensei," she replied, bowing briefly before she ran over to hug me fiercely.

"You know each other?" I asked, my voice muffled by Sam's shoulder. I was as confused as I was joyful.

"She was my best student," Marco said.

Sam and I continued to hold each other, more lightly now. "I'm so glad you're alive," she whispered in my ear. "My heart soars."

"This is Sam," I explained. "My Sam." I whispered back to her, "I'm so glad to see you—more than I can say."

"Samavati," she told Marco, finally disengaging to face him again. "I took a spiritual name."

"Namaste, Samavati," he said. "What a curious development. How have you been?"

"Quite well, although things have been a bit hectic lately."

I couldn't muster any words. Confusion now trumped joy. *Could this be a coincidence?* As new Sid, I wasn't sure if I believed in coincidences anymore.

"Let's have lunch," Marco suggested blithely. Once again, he seemed to be completely unflappable.

A bearded guy in gray coveralls emerged from the nearest bay of the repair shop. "Can I help you?" he asked. Like everyone else I'd met in New Zealand who wasn't trying to kill me, he came across as friendly and genuinely interested in helping.

"Do you know a good place to eat near here?" Marco asked.

"Sure."

As the man began to give us complicated directions to a "brilliant" barbecue restaurant, a battered white SUV squealed its way into the parking lot, skidded to a halt, and four large Maori men piled out. I didn't recognize any of them. They carried metal pipes.

The repairman ducked into his shop, presumably to call the police.

"I'll handle this," Marco said, striding forward and

then planting himself in the path of the men.

Sam grabbed my hand. "Watch this," she said. "You've never seen anything like it."

The first of the attackers rushed the older man, his club raised. Marco stood his ground at first and then turned to the side at the last minute. As the Maori man began to hack down with the pipe, Marco snaked out a fist and hit him once on the hip. The bigger man spun and fell. The timing and placement must've been perfect. Not only that, when the Maori man tried to get up, he couldn't.

"My fucking leg won't work," he whined.

"You'll be fine in a few hours," Marco told him. "No worries."

The other three men glanced at one another. Perhaps they thought he'd landed a lucky punch. After all, this was just some old man by the side of the road.

Maori number two moved more cautiously. He held his weapon at his side as he sidled forward. He feinted a punch and tried a kick first. Obviously he'd trained in some type of martial art. And he was quick.

Marco slid to the side again, well before the man's leg reached him.

"It's almost like he can read his opponent's mind," Sam said. "He anticipates so well."

Our protector slapped Number Two's foot as it reached its apex beside his head. The man lost his balance and went down hard, but immediately leapt to his feet.

"Okay," he said. "So it's going to be like that." His voice was deep and resonant.

Marco smiled at him. In that context, it was chilling.

The man suddenly flung the pipe at Marco's midsection and then rushed him with a flurry of punches. Marco caught the spinning metal one-handed and ducked down in a smooth, compact motion. He swept the weapon across the ground beneath the larger man's feet, who tucked both legs up as though he were jumping rope. While the man was still in midair, Marco shot a leg out and tapped him on the side of his knee. When Maori number two came down, that leg crumpled underneath him, and he sprawled onto his back on the asphalt. He couldn't get up either.

Marco hadn't broken a sweat so far; he didn't even seem particularly focused on the task at hand.

"It'll be sore for a few days," he told the second man. "But you'll be fine, too."

The remaining two men suddenly attacked Marco, who leapt free of the fallen Maoris underfoot, landed lithely on the ground, and then sprang up again, his legs shooting out at different angles. He hit one man hard in the collarbone and the other in the solar plexus, and both dropped their weapons and doubled over. Marco landed lightly behind them, poised and balanced. Now he crouched and punched them both simultaneously on the backs of their thighs. They toppled and—no surprise—neither could get up.

Sam was right. I'd never seen anything like this. There was no possibility that any of those men could've touched Marco. As impressive as Sam had been in her fight with Jason, this was on another level entirely. It wasn't even fighting per se; it was a series of purposeful, fight-ending strikes. Nothing more. There was probably no more efficient method of dispatching each of the attackers. It was beautiful.

"Shall we go to lunch?" Marco asked casually.

As sirens sounded on the highway behind us, we pulled out of the parking lot in the two cars. Marco and Lucy led the way in the rented Mazda, and Sam and I followed in the Audi.

"The car repair guy will tell the police what we're driving," I said. "We'd be safer if we got off the main road, don't you think?" As I said this to Sam, Marco exited the highway and headed west down a side road. We followed.

"I wonder why Marco didn't want to wait for the police," Sam said. "We're the victims here."

"Apparently, it's important that we get to India by tomorrow. And you and I are in this country illegally, you know—without passports."

"That's true."

"What happened out on the water?" I asked. "Did they let you go? Did the cops get involved? And how did you end up following us?"

"Wait a minute," she said. "How are you going to get to India without a passport?"

"Marco had mine sent over," I said. "He was your teacher, huh?"

"Yes. He ran a martial arts school in Palo Alto. But it was more than that. Just being around his energy changes you." She swerved to avoid a pothole, and I momentarily lost my balance.

"It sure does," I said, righting myself.

"You're clearer already, aren't you?"

"Yes. You can tell?"

She nodded. "But to answer your question, once you disappeared in the water, there were too many men with guns for us to keep fighting. Frank and a couple of

141

men took off in the speedboat to hunt for you, and Tommy steered the fishing boat toward shore to tend to the man who got shot. I think it was his brother."

"How'd you get away? Do they still have Bhante and Jason and Ram?"

"A cop on the gang's payroll met us at the dock in Paihia. He was okay with the guns, and he had some shady doctor waiting there, but he wouldn't go along with holding Jason Patariki against his will. As far as he was concerned, it was like they'd kidnapped the pope. And Jason insisted that if he was walking away, we were too. Tommy and Frank were furious, but what could they do? The guy was a cop, and I think he was a relative of Tommy and Jason's." Sam sped up to keep up with Marco, who'd pulled ahead of us around a long curve.

"It seems like everybody here is related to everybody else," I said.

This story seemed suspiciously simple. One minute we were all kidnapped and being threatened and beaten up over millions of dollars. Then Sam and the others were free, and here she was sitting next to me. Was that really possible? On the other hand, my narrative was even less likely. I was picked up in a rowboat by Sam's former teacher? In less than one day, he'd completely rearranged me by charging me up with esoteric energy?

"I've missed you," I said. I couldn't think of anything else worth saying.

"I've missed you more," she said. "I thought you were dead."

"Marco came by in a rowboat," I told her.

"What's he doing here?" Sam asked. "The last I heard, he'd retired and was playing golf in Hawaii. His school in Palo Alto is a coffeehouse now called Marco's Not Here Anymore Roasting Company."

"That's a great name. He said he'd won the lottery and bought an island. They've got a lot of them around here, don't they?"

She nodded. "Following you was just luck—if you believe in luck. I was on the road already when I saw you drive by. Bhante lent me his car to shop for clothes and necessities. Paihia is the only town around here with real stores."

"Wait a minute. Bhante drives an Audi?"

"Apparently," Sam said.

By now, Marco had pulled into the back parking lot of a luncheonette where the cars would be out of sight. Rita's Kitchen resembled a 1950s diner. A white Formica counter with round, chromed stools sat across from a row of faded yellow and white vinyl booths. The art on the walls appeared to be paint-by-number scenes, which was an interesting synchronicity. *Apparently, I've traded in the concept of coincidence for synchronicity.* The restaurant was uncrowded and quiet, which suited me.

"So what's RGP?" Marco asked Sam, once we'd sat and given our identical orders—fish and chips.

"It stands for Rakkhaka Guyha Parisa," she told him.

She and I sat on one side of the booth, facing Marco. We held hands under the table.

"My Pali is a bit rusty," Marco said. "In fact, I know about three words."

"Rakkhaka means guarding or protecting—like a servant watching a house. Guyha means that which is hidden by the dress. I don't think I need to get too

143

graphic about that. And Parisa is an assembly of people—the Buddha's order, literally."

"So you're an organization that protects women? Or their virtue? Are you the equivalent of feminist Buddhists?" I asked, turning to face her.

In the filtered light trickling through the dusty lace curtains, her face was softly, achingly beautiful. I was sitting with the two most amazing people I'd ever met. I felt like a fraud. How could I match any of this?

"We're not exactly feminists," Sam answered. "But I've taken a vow not to reveal any more than that." She looked at Marco. "I gather your being here isn't a coincidence," she said.

"No more than it is for you. Sid is at the center of something rather important. A karmic nexus, if you will. I think we both sense that."

"Sid says you're going to India," Sam said to Marco. "Where? Why?"

"Meher Baba's tomb. Near Ahmednagar. Sid needs to continue to experience a progression of energy phenomena to realize his full self—or nonself, I should say."

"Wait a minute," I said. "I've been going through a progression already?"

"Yes. Remember the spark from the handshake with the interviewer at your office? That's where it started."

"Paul," I said. "How do you know about that?"

"I know him," Marco said. "Paul was a terrible martial arts student. But he carries energy from our work together at the dojo."

"He's also my brother," Sam said.

"Paul's your brother?" I said, my surprise evident

in my tone. "Why didn't you say so?"

She shrugged. "It didn't seem important."

I didn't want to forget my original question. I stared at Marco. "You haven't told me how you know about the spark with Paul. Did you pluck that out of my head? If you did, I'd appreciate it if you stayed out of there."

Marco smiled amiably but didn't reply.

I sighed. "Fine. What was the next thing in the energy progression?" I asked.

"Meeting Louise, of course—I mean, Sam," Marco said. "Her heart is very well developed. Then you spent time with Jason Patariki," Marco said. "Cultural icons are invested with very powerful energy, even if they haven't learned to administer it maturely. So each experience has been more intense and transformative—building on the ones that came before. When you were exposed to Bhante and the ancient cave, that combination really amped things up. Then you met me. The work we did on the island took you much further. But it couldn't have happened without what came before."

"Who's Meher Baba?" I asked. "And assuming the progression is supposed to keep getting more intense, does that mean he's above you in the *chi* food chain?"

"He was a lesser-known Indian saint who supposedly said, 'Don't worry. Be happy.' Maybe you've heard the song based on that, which is ironic since he maintained a vow of silence and never spoke. But as you may have gathered from my earlier mention of the word 'tomb,' he's no longer in his body."

"Whose is he in?" I joked.

Marco looked at me closely. "That's a very good

question, but let's not get into that now."

"Didn't Baba do some kind of special energy work in his tomb?" Sam said.

"Yes." He nodded as well, as though to emphasize his agreement.

"What's the point of that?" I asked.

"So people who visited the tomb later could receive help even after he was gone," Marco answered. "It's one of the most powerful places on the planet."

"So I need to hang out there and let it change me more? Why?"

"I told you. We have a mission, and you need to get up to speed to perform your role."

"Which is?" My frustration lurked just below my reasonable tone of voice.

Marco smiled again and didn't answer.

I felt like smacking him. "Will that be the end of it—the last one?" I asked.

"Probably not. We'll see."

I was quiet for some time while Sam and Marco discussed mutual friends.

In the past hour, I'd been handed quite a few answers to the various mysteries I'd encountered. Much as the questions had shown up in too rapid a succession for me to process, now I was experiencing the same thing with the answers.

Perhaps I wouldn't even be Sid by the time Marco was through with me. Was it psychological suicide to agree to have your sense of self obliterated? How would it affect my future with Sam? If Marco was the end result of a similar process...well, it was hard to picture him dating.

I didn't realize I'd turned so far inward until Sam

nudged me with her elbow.

"Hey, no kung fu at the table," I said as I returned to the moment.

"Here's the plan," Marco told me. "We're swapping cars. Sam will return our rental after she drives to the US consulate in Auckland to figure out how to get home. We'll meet her in Santa Cruz when we're back in the States. I'll contact Bhante by phone to give him back his car at the airport since we need to become affiliated with him, and it looks as though his people didn't follow us."

"What if the police stop us?" I asked.

"We won't be the right people for the type of car they're looking for since we switched vehicles," Marco said. "And the man who phoned them can attest that we were the ones who were attacked. I doubt there's a dragnet out for us. If necessary, we'll improvise."

"How do you have Bhante's phone number?" I asked.

"A friend of a friend." He smiled, anticipating my irritation that yet again he was withholding information.

"Would you care to elaborate?"

"No." His noes were absolute. It was clear he couldn't be talked into anything.

When Marco excused himself to use the restroom, I reached for Sam and held on tight. "I could just stay with you," I said.

"If it weren't Marco, I might not let go of you. But Marco is Marco. I've learned not to second-guess him."

"Yeah, I know what you mean." I thought about being out of touch with her, and my gut felt empty. "I wish they hadn't taken our cell phones," I said.

"Oh, I bought another one this morning in Paihia.

Let me see what the number is."

She told me, and I memorized it. "I'll call you when I get one—or if I can borrow one," I told her.

She kissed me, and we held the kiss until Marco returned. I have no idea how long that was. The energy flowing between us was almost as intoxicating as the bliss I'd felt back on Marco's Island. It was different, though—more wild.

"Time to go," Marco said.

When we broke off our kiss, the sudden return to the world was challenging. Then we transferred our stuff from one car to the other, and Sam drove off after another powerful hug.

Marco called Bhante from the driver's seat of the Audi, using the speaker on his cell phone so I could hear too.

"Namaste," he said as we heard Bhante pick up.

"Namaste," Bhante replied. "Who is this, please?"

"Jackson," Marco said, garbling the pronunciation of the name. He pulled out of the restaurant's entrance onto the highway.

There was a pause. "Ah. The fabled Mr. Jackson. What can I do for you?"

"Sid is with me, and he'd like to reunite with you and your organization."

"Then why isn't he the one on the phone?" Bhante asked. "How do I know he's really alive?"

"I'm here," I said. "You're on the speaker."

"Hello, Sid. I'm very gratified you're intact. And I'm so sorry for any danger my actions have spawned."

"Uh, thanks," I said.

"There are some details to work out," Marco said, accelerating to match the light traffic.

"Are you demanding a ransom?"

"No, no," I said. "You've got this all wrong. He's helping me."

"For one thing," Marco continued as if he hadn't been interrupted, "we need to go to India first to continue Sid's spiritual education."

"Very well. But as you may know, there is a certain urgency in this matter. The world needs...well, you either already know or you don't need to."

"I understand," Marco said. "The other thing is we have your car at this point. Can we return it to you at the Auckland airport?"

"Samavati gave you my car?"

"Yes."

"Is she all right? May I speak to her as well?"

"She's fine," I said. "But she's not here." Again, I felt an emptiness inside as I said this.

"I don't have time to explain," Marco said. "We have a flight to catch. Have someone at the information booth at the international terminal at five thirty, and I'll give him your keys. That should give you enough lead time."

"Very well. Perhaps we'll have a chance for a more in-depth conversation another time," Bhante said.

"Yes," Marco replied and hung up.

He started the car, and we zoomed away down the secondary road. "Fire up the GPS," he said. "I have no idea where I'm going."

Chapter Eleven

Once we got on track, Marco requested silence again, so I watched the countryside pass by through the tinted window. I found that, for the most part, I could simply watch and not ruminate about anything.

Sheep littered the very green, gently rolling hills of the central part of the North Island. As we wended our way south toward Auckland, the open spaces between houses began to shrink, and the traffic picked up. More and more businesses and stores lined the highway as it expanded to four lanes and then to six for the final stretch. People drove fairly sensibly, but by the time we reached the airport parking lot, some of the civility had disappeared. Marco had to duel a pickup truck for our spot, and two other cars honked their horns at one another for no discernible reason.

"Where are we meeting Chris?" I asked after we'd parked and grabbed our bags out of the trunk. Lucy leapt out of the car but seemed disappointed to find herself in a parking lot.

"He'll clear customs in about twenty minutes. Then our flight leaves two hours later," Marco said. "Why don't you greet him and tell him whatever you think will help orient him. I have some business here I need to attend to on my own."

"Sure."

"I'll find you when it's time to meet," Marco said.

He attached a leash to Lucy's collar, and the two of them walked away from the terminal. She was in a hurry—probably to pee.

Like everything else I'd encountered in New Zealand, even the largest city's international airport was on a modest scale, with only ten gates. There wasn't the usual level of anxiety in the building, either. The most common phrase I heard around me was "no worries," and I sensed that people meant it. My impression was the culture was markedly less neurotic and paranoid than the States. I wanted to bring a few of my most recalcitrant clients over for psychological rehab.

Chris and his enormous black backpack were the first ones to get through customs. He jogged the last few steps to where I stood and bear-hugged me. I was extremely happy to see him, and I hugged him at least as hard.

"So you're okay?" he asked.

"Yes. Better than ever." I smiled to back up my words.

He stepped back and looked me over. "You do look better," he said. "Did you get a haircut?"

"No."

"Lose weight?"

"No."

"Read a good self-help book?"

"No."

"Did you run off to Bumfuck without telling anyone and join a cult where the guru knows how to make dogs do weird shit?" Chris glared at me, but it might've only been for dramatic effect.

"Pretty much. If you change the 'run off' to 'get kidnapped by a sports hero,' and the 'join a cult' to 'agree to be a fake Buddha.' Turning Karma into a spelling champ is the least of Marco's abilities, by the way."

"One of the letters was kind of misshapen," Chris reported. "I'm signing Karma up for remedial English Composition at the community college."

I smiled at him. "Thanks for coming. I know this is strange and alarming."

"You think?"

"Do you have my passport?" I asked.

"Your passport? Was I supposed to bring that?" He fumbled in his front pocket with a look of confusion on his broad face.

I glared at him, and he whipped it out of his back pocket and handed it over.

"Where is this Marco character, anyway?" Chris asked.

"I have no idea, but he'll be back."

"Would it be fair to say he dances to a different drummer?"

"Oh yeah," I said. "And then some."

"I'm hungry. Do they have pizza here, Mr. Buddha?"

"Probably. Let's go see. I'll fill you in while you eat. And you don't have to call me Mr. Buddha. Sir or Master are fine." I remembered what Marco had said. "Actually, let's go with B-2," I said. "For Buddha 2.0."

"Yeah, right. You're a fucking Buddha now. And like all the spiritual greats, you're named after a software upgrade, and your nickname is a vitamin? Whatever happened to good old Sanskrit? I love all those *K*s and vowels and shit."

"I'm a modern guy," I said. "In the movie of my

life, I'd be played by a former cute-as-a-button child actor—a white guy, of course—who is computer savvy and saves the world by hacking into something or other."

"Gee, that's so original. You should write a screenplay, Sid." He shook his head and grimaced.

Chris was the only black person I saw at the airport, and his Hawaiian shirt was by far the most hideous attire. This one sported big brown cows and even larger pink pigs scattered across a bright yellow background. They looked as though they'd been caught up in Dorothy's Kansas-to-Oz tornado. The skinny, tattooed girl at the pizza parlor said she liked it, but she was obviously lying.

We found seats by an exterior window that overlooked the short-term parking lot. Chris propped his backpack on one of the plastic chairs, and I placed my antique suitcase by my feet. It was a very stylish piece—dark brown leather with a swirled pattern on it. It was small enough to use as a carry-on, too.

I told my story again while Chris ate, forgetting at first that he already knew the beginning of it. He interrupted me repeatedly to ask clarifying questions, which was annoying but likely to be helpful. I knew what mattered to me at this point—what I thought was worth telling. But Chris's perspective might be a valuable reality check. What had I missed? What was worth investigating more deeply?

"Well," Chris said when I'd finished. "I'd like to start by saying I'm totally in favor of saving the world. That's where all the women live, for one thing. Second, if anyone else told me all that, I'd think they were making it up or crazy. But I know you, and you know people. And Karma never spelled out anything before. So my mind is officially blown. I believe you." He twirled a corner of his bushy, black beard and frowned. He rarely engaged in self-soothing, but when he did, it was either his beard or his fingernails.

It hadn't occurred to me that he wouldn't believe me. "So what jumps out at you?" I asked.

"Well, if Bhante could con you, Marco totally could, too." Chris kept twirling his beard, but now his face brightened. God knew why. "I don't know why he'd want to, but obviously he could pull it off pretty easily. If he'd hired Frank and some Maoris, for example, then the invisibility hat deal goes up in smoke. There's an ordinary-world explanation along those lines for almost everything you said. And I've read about gurus that do *Shaktipat*—send energy. There was Muktananda and Baba Neem Karoli, to name a couple. It means they've figured out how to play with energy, but Muktananda liked young girls and Baba Neem Karoli was kinda nuts. So you can have special abilities and still be screwed up. I mean, I haven't met Marco yet. I'm just saying it's possible." His hand was still now. Spinning theories was apparently a more effective soothing strategy.

"Wait until you meet him, then see if that still makes sense to you," I said. A woman brushed my shoulder with her butt as she walked by. I could tell by how squishy it was.

"Sorry," she muttered.

I didn't turn to look, but Chris watched her walk away. "Not bad," he said. "Worth turning around for, bro. Yoga pants."

"I'm kind of focused on this conversation I'm

trying to have with you, Chris."

"Okay, yeah," Chris agreed. "The other thing is all this karate shit. The Jason part I understand. If he's a professional athlete and he works as a bodyguard in a country with strict gun control...well, of course he's gonna know how to fight. That makes sense. But why would a mind-reading guru kick butt? It's anti-spiritual, right? Can you see Mother Teresa squaring off in the ring against the Dalai Lama or Gandhi?"

"She'd knock them both on their asses, I'll bet," I said.

"Yeah, well, what I'm saying is you hear about people getting way spiritual from doing martial arts, but that always seemed like a crock to me." He stared at me expectantly as if my opinion about that mattered more than all the rest.

"What else?" The martial arts piece didn't seem important to me.

"They could all be in this thing together. That's another possibility," Chris said.

"Who?"

"All of them—Bhante, Sam, Marco, Frank, Tommy T., Paul, the supposed clones, the parking lot attackers—the whole cast of characters. That would explain how people seem to know shit they shouldn't know. Suppose everybody's working for some James-Bond-type supervillain?" He grinned. Clearly, he liked this theory best. For Chris, the whole deal was still conceptual. I was the one getting knocked around in the trenches. I thought about sharing this perception, but it wouldn't matter. Chris's brain was a juggernaut.

"Do you mean Ram would be the villain, or are you just playing devil's advocate?" I asked.

"It could be him, but yeah, I'm mostly just brainstorming here. I didn't hear much doubt out of you, so I thought I ought to inject a little into the mix."

"There were times when I was nothing but doubtful and confused," I told him. "But now I seem to be past that. And I can't believe Sam is evil. She's the best part of this whole thing."

"You know that's what's the most unbelievable, right?" Chris said, smirking. I'd never liked his smirk. It was markedly judgmental. "I can entertain the idea that you might be some new messiah or whatever, and maybe Marco has mastered time and space and knocking people down, but a really hot woman falling for you? Come on. Get real. And your feelings for her sound like pure lust, by the way. You don't know her at all."

"Do you think she has an ulterior motive, or are you just trying to insult me?" I knew he was joking, but I still felt hurt. A frown formed, and my gut clenched a bit.

"Well, does it seem likely to you? Why would someone like that have sex right away with *anyone*?"

"I don't know," I said. "We did go through some pretty intense stuff together." I watched Chris finish eating. It wasn't pretty. He was a shoveler. "What do you think of what Marco said about the progression of energy experiences?"

"I guess it makes sense," Chris said. "I dunno. I wonder if some of that energy would do me any good—if I go in the tomb over in India, I mean."

"So you're on board—you're definitely coming with us?" I straightened in my plastic chair and let out a slow breath.

"Oh, yeah. I'm getting in on the ground floor, bro. The first few disciples in successful cults always get to live in the big house in the compound. Plus they get to boss people around and later commit crimes and then cover them up and have lots of sex."

"I think we might try to do things differently," I said.

"Ah, don't tell me that. I just flew a zillion miles and ate bad pizza. I need an incentive. Where's *my* spiritual babe with bare boobs?" He looked around as though she might be lurking nearby. "Hey," he said. "There's a giant Samoan-looking guy out on the sidewalk. Is that Jason?"

I glanced out the window. "Yeah. That's him. He's a specimen, isn't he?"

Jason wore a pinstriped charcoal suit with a light blue shirt and a red tie. He looked as though he might be heading to a photo shoot for a magazine cover. Fortunately, he walked by without spying us.

A moment later one of my brothers strolled by, too.

"Whoa," Chris said. "Look at that. That's surreal."

My doppelgänger spotted us and waved cheerily. We waved back. He kept walking.

"If you think that's weird, just wait ten minutes for the next crazy thing to happen," I told Chris. "Let's see who walks by next. It'll probably be your middle school girlfriend or a Beatle."

It was Marco and Lucy.

"That's him," I said. "That's Marco."

"You're in this country a few days, and now you know everybody that strolls by?"

Marco locked eyes with Chris through the window glass and smiled.

"Whoa," Chris said. "I'm feeling all this shit in my chest."

"Yeah. He does that."

"Whoa," Chris kept repeating every few seconds as Marco did whatever he was doing.

The waitress showed up with our check while he was still at it. "Is he okay?" she asked, gesturing at Chris with ring-laden fingers.

"He's undergoing a spiritual transformation," I told her. "Just ignore him."

"Okay, no worries," she said, ambling away.

By the time I paid with a few of the colorful New Zealand bills that Marco had given me back on the island, our mentor was gone. Chris still had the "whoas," though. I wondered if I should slap him or something. It would have been fun, but he came back to himself before I got around to doing it.

"I feel more alive now," Chris said.

"Yes."

"I like it."

"Yes."

"It's hard to talk."

"Yes."

"What'll we do now?" Chris asked.

"Beats me."

So we sat. Chris was quiet for once in his life. It was five o'clock in the afternoon, and we probably needed to check in for our flight soon. In a half hour, we'd rendezvous with Bhante or his people—probably Jason. I was a bit concerned that my brother had seen us and knew where we were, but it looked as though Marco would join us soon, and he could probably handle whatever arose.

He showed up a few minutes later without his beagle companion and sat down at our table. "Lucy will meet us in India," Marco told me. "I like your backpack," he said to Chris.

"Here's my first question," Chris said, suddenly coming back on line and staring at him. "Which came first—the chicken or the egg?"

"*That's* what you want to know?" I asked. "That's the first thing you want to say?"

"It's a test," Marco said. "He's been saving this up for a long time."

Chris nodded.

"Actually, neither comes first," Marco said. "There is a mutual arising of all so-called events, which only appear to us to be sequential, given our inability to directly perceive the broadband of now in which all illusion emerges. So-called paradoxes and other logical dilemmas are simply particularly challenging iterations of what we are called upon to face in each moment— that there is a transcendental realm beyond our experience in which nothing is pitted against anything else, largely because there are actually no separate parts (or people) to play those roles. So truth embodies paradox. There is no time. There are no chickens. And there is nothing for you to wonder about because there is no you."

After a few beats, while I was still working my way through that, Chris said, "Okay. That totally makes sense to me. Modern physics says just about the same thing, only with a lot more math. What about the meaning of life?"

"The word meaning is, ironically, a meaningless concept when one is attempting to summate that which is meta to the observer."

"Hey, I never got answers like these," I complained. "This is good stuff."

"One size does not fit all," Marcus said.

"Well, in human terms, then," Chris said. "What's the best approximation of the meaning of life?"

"Loving connectedness," Marco said and smiled. "We need to get moving."

There were no nonstops to Mumbai, but Marco had booked us on a flight with a brief layover in Sydney, Australia. We were flying first class, so the young man who checked us in—and almost broke his back dragging Chris's backpack—offered us the refuge of the airline's VIP lounge. It wasn't far, and it was a much more comfortable environment than the airport at large.

"We'll be safer here," Marco said once we'd settled into three adjacent leather armchairs.

"What's the plan for giving the car keys back?" I asked him.

"Chris will meet whoever's at the information desk and say he's me." Aside from his more edifying answers, Marco also spoke with more animation around Chris than he had with me.

"Say what?" Chris said.

"It'll be perfectly safe. I'll be nearby, and I'll intercede if necessary," Marco said. "We can't send Sid out there, or they might grab him again. And they don't need to know who I am. That's our ace in the hole."

"Couldn't they have seen you with us just now?" I asked.

"They didn't," Marco stated matter-of-factly.

"How do you know that?" Chris asked, cocking his

head.

Marco offered up his customary enigmatic smile.

"Okay, whatever," Chris said after a while. "But dude, I can't pull that off. I'm just a chubby nerd. It's true that I now know the answers to all of life's mysteries, but that and a quarter will still get my ass kicked."

"I sent you energy, and you can send it to them," Marco said.

"Really? Cool."

"Aim your right forefinger at whoever's the scariest person you meet at the information booth," Marco said. "Then say 'Marco's energy' to yourself. The rest will take care of itself."

"What'll I say out loud, wordwise, to them?"

"Ask random people in the area if they're from 'Kasriti Sanganika.' Say that back to me."

Chris obliged. It took him three tries to get it right.

"That's the secret name of Bhante's organization," Marco explained. "No one's supposed to know it."

"What does it mean?" I asked. I was dying to know.

"The Secret Path Society."

"Hey, they should write a screenplay, too," Chris said. "That's the lamest secret name I ever heard."

"Have you ever done any improv?" Marco asked.

"Improv comedy?"

"Yes."

"No."

"Pretend you have," Marco said. "Here are the keys. Let's go."

So they left me in the lounge. I would've been nervous in the past, but I was fine. Whatever happened was just the next scene in this quirky movie that my life had become. I was interested in how it turned out, but I wasn't attached to it in the same old way. In fact, I was able to close my eyes and take a nap in my cushy leather chair.

Chris nudged me awake some time later. "Oh man," he said. "That was great. Those fuckers don't know what hit them."

"Where's Marco?"

"In the bathroom."

"Tell me what happened," I said.

"So I got there, and there's Jason and the guy who looks just like you by the kiosk. Jason's got a crowd around him, and he's signing autographs, but the other guy waves to me. I guess he recognized me from through the window of the restaurant. So I start throwing their secret name around, and they rush over. Jason is really fast, isn't he? I wonder how he would've done in his prime in the NFL." He'd been gesturing wildly, but now he held his hands together in his ample lap.

"These musings are not advancing your narrative arc," I pointed out.

"Calm down, bro. We've got nothing to do until the plane takes off, right?"

"We still have to go through security," I said, reaching down to pull up a sock.

"Whatever. So they're really riled up. 'How do you know that name?' Jason asked me. I told him I was Marco, and that I knew everything. 'Everything?' he asks. 'Sure,' I said. 'Ask me something.' "

"Chris, do you really think that was a good idea?"

"You bet. What do you think he asked me?" His

expression was challenging. I needed to guess.

"The egg and the chicken thing?"

"Yes! And I remembered it almost word for word. So there we are in the middle of the airport, and people keep coming up to the guy and asking him for autographs while I'm blowing him away with my metaphysical knowledge. It was perfectly safe, too. It was totally public."

"So you didn't need to send any energy?" I would've liked to hear how that turned out.

"Well, I had to try it out, didn't I? So I aimed it at your brother or whoever the hell he is."

"Let me guess what happened," I said, and then I described Pat the boatman's response to receiving what came out of *my* finger.

"Yup. That's exactly what happened. Then I handed Jason the keys and walked away."

"So it was fun?"

"Oh, yeah."

Marco ambled over and told us it was time to head to the gate, so we grabbed our bags and strode out of the lounge. On the way, I asked for details about Lucy. My understanding was you couldn't just fly dogs across international borders like they were extra luggage.

"She's traveling on her own. We'll see her there," was all I got.

"How did Chris's impersonation help us become more affiliated with Bhante's organization?" I asked next. "Wasn't that the idea? We were supposed to hook up with them so we could use the clone scam to get the word out, right?"

Marco just shrugged. Chris got his questions comprehensively answered in concise, elegant language. I had to make do with shrugs.

The line at security wasn't too long, and it moved along smoothly, but just after I passed through the x-ray machine, an older man in a blue suit told me to wait as the others moved ahead.

"What's the problem?" I asked.

"We'll need to go talk in another room," he said, lifting my bag up off the conveyor belt. He was probably in his fifties, beefy with black curly hair and dark eyes. His badge said that his name was Vlad Goric. His parents could've been Croatian.

"I'm not going anywhere with you unless you explain what's going on," I told him.

"Sir, we believe your suitcase is made from an endangered species. We take that particular crime very seriously here in New Zealand. Please come with me."

Chapter Twelve

A younger, pale-skinned security guard stepped forward and gripped my upper arm. He was built like a swimmer, with big shoulders. The two men marched me toward an unmarked door behind the security machines.

I looked around for Marco and Chris. They stood in the corridor just past us. Chris seemed concerned—his eyes were wide, and he was frowning. Marco's affect was flat and neutral. It would take a lot more than this to erode his poise. As if they'd rehearsed it, Chris shrugged and Marco winked simultaneously. Then my escorts ushered me through the door into a brightly lit, institutional-looking hallway. I could've been in a school or a hospital. As the guard released my arm, and I walked between the two men down the hall, I was struck by how nonsensical the situation was. It just didn't compute.

Why would I have been singled out for some sort of special attention? How could they glance at my antique suitcase and know what it was made of? I asked the older man—Vlad—that question.

"We received an anonymous tip," he said. "And from the looks of this luggage, I'd say that no cows, pigs, or goats were sourced in its manufacture. An official is on his way here to make a final determination."

We reached Vlad's office, and I was surprised to see how cozy it was. There was wall-to-wall light-gray carpeting and incandescent lighting—two torchieres and an old-fashioned green banker's desk lamp. The light blue walls were decorated with framed South Sea island travel posters. And all the modern furniture was unpainted maple—or some New Zealand equivalent. It could've been an upscale therapist's office back in Santa Cruz.

I sat on a plain but elegant chair in front of a huge desk. Vlad parked himself behind it, moved a few things to the side, and placed my suitcase on top. The younger man stood behind me, his arms crossed across his chest.

"Do you really think I'm smuggling a suitcase?" I asked. "Isn't that rather unlikely? People generally smuggle what's *in* suitcases, don't they?"

"Possession of contraband is a class III felony," he told me. "Could I have your passport, please?"

I handed it over, and he typed my information into the black desktop computer that sat just to his right. Then he opened my bag and began sifting through its meager contents. I sat and watched his painstaking search. Eventually, Vlad returned to the computer screen and read whatever was on it. Then he began questioning me.

"Why is it we have no record of you entering this country?" he asked, leaning back.

"I came in on a private jet," I told him, leaning forward.

"To which airport?"

"I don't know."

"You don't know?" He leaned forward.

I shrugged. "It was dark." I leaned back.

"I see." Obviously, he didn't. He stared at me, deadpan, his eyes dull. At least he could've *pretended* to be interested in my answers. "Whose aircraft was this?" he asked woodenly.

"I don't know."

"Where did the flight originate?" he asked.

"I don't know that either. Some island."

He leaned back again and stared at his hands for a moment. They were clasped together, propped on top of my suitcase. As I watched, his grip tightened until the veins on the back of his hands stood out. I'd misunderstood. This guy cared a lot.

"Have you seen police television shows?" he asked, keeping his tone modulated.

"Sure. Lots of them." I didn't have to work at staying calm. I couldn't take any of this seriously enough to get upset.

"This is a bit different—I'm a customs officer—but some of the same principles apply. Giving vague, stupid, or false answers is not in your best interest. If you cooperate with me, we can probably sort things out and get you on your way in short order."

"Even though my suitcase might constitute a felony?"

"I've never seen a case like this prosecuted," he told me. "No pun intended. But we need to find out more about what's going on. Fair enough?" He caught my eye and invited my agreement.

I nodded and considered lying to make my story sound more plausible.

"What is the purpose of your trip to India?" he asked next, fondling my air ticket.

I knew that one. I was pleased. "I'll be hanging out in a saint's tomb, soaking up all the good energy," I said.

"You are a spiritual person?"

"I guess I am."

He stared at his hands again, although they weren't steepled anymore. They weren't his best feature. I liked his dark, curly hair, though, and his teeth. He had very even teeth.

"How does your current behavior square with your spiritual values?" Vlad asked.

"I see where you're going with this," I said. "I should tell you that I'm a psychotherapist. I'm not sure it's worthwhile to try this sort of thing with me."

He looked me squarely in the eye. Now it was obvious that he was an intense guy hiding inside a mellow persona. "I thrive on challenge," he said tersely. "Now tell me about the painting kits."

"They're just to keep the other stuff from rattling around," I said.

"You seem to have packed exceptionally light for an international trip. Why is that?"

"I lost my stuff when I was rescued at sea," I told him. He pursed his lips and turned to his computer screen again. I studied the travel posters. Fiji looked incredibly beautiful, but I was pretty sure I could endure Bora Bora if I had to.

"You're the missing tourist from the Bay of Islands boating accident?"

"Yes."

"And then you were involved in an altercation near Kawakawa?"

"If you say so."

He cocked a bushy black eyebrow.

"I don't know my way around," I said. "Where's Kawakawa?"

"Where a friend of yours disabled four thugs," he said.

"Yeah, I was there. But they attacked us."

"Why?"

"It's a long story."

He cocked his eyebrow again. It was a very expressive eyebrow. And it was about three times the size of mine.

"I guess I'd rather not say," I added. "You wouldn't believe me, anyway."

He sat and stared at me for a very long time— maybe five minutes. I was accustomed to stares and silence in my work. I'd once worked with a plumber who'd sit down and ponder his first sentence for ten or fifteen minutes every session. Perhaps Vlad was employing an airport security technique that had been proven effective with less sophisticated endangered-animal luggage smugglers.

"Do you know when your expert is due?" I finally asked. "I don't want to miss my flight."

"You'll be missing it," Vlad said. "And if I don't get some real answers soon, you're going to be missing a lot of flights, son."

"Oh."

We returned to silence. It was rather restful.

Eventually, someone called Vlad on his anachronistic white desk phone. He listened, grunted, and hung up. "He's here," he announced. "Bob," he said to the security guard. "Would you escort Mr. Frank back to my office? He's at the desk at A-4."

Mr. Frank? Was Tommy T. behind all this? Could it be a coincidence? I couldn't afford to wait to find out. After Bob had been gone long enough to exit the adjacent hallway, I snatched my passport from Vlad's desktop and sprinted out the office door.

"Hey!" he called.

"Sorry!" I called back.

Out in the corridor, I careened in the opposite direction from where they'd detained me. I certainly didn't want to end up back in the security queue. I raced through several crooks and turns, with loud footsteps pounding behind me. Most of the office doors I passed were closed, but I saw several startled faces glance up at me as I whizzed by. After rounding a sharp corner, I saw a dead end looming, so I pushed open an exit door on the side wall and ran through it.

I was in a baggage claim area, near a dormant luggage carousel. Without pausing to think, I dashed up the ramp of the carousel and dove headfirst into the luggage maw. I had no idea what was on the far side of that opening.

I tumbled down another longer rubberized ramp and landed hard on my hip on a poorly lit asphalt lane. I was indoors, but just barely. The building was a giant metal shed with open ends. A tractorish vehicle was pulling a train of flat trailers loaded with bags ahead of me on the narrow roadway. I hoisted myself up and sprinted after it. As I heard a commotion behind me—a high-pitched alarm and lots of yelling—I once again dove headfirst, this time into a moving pile of black bags. I burrowed into the soft luggage and bashed into something much harder—a metal foot locker? It hurt. Then I pulled the bags and suitcases over me. I could only hope I hadn't been spotted and that the tractor driver's big yellow headphones blocked the sound of the alarm.

I poked my head out after a while. The front of the baggage train was just exiting the building, emerging into dimming light. I rolled through the bags and dropped off the side of the trailer, landing on the same hip I'd bruised earlier. I gathered myself as quickly as I could and scuttled outside. The baggage train pulled away without me, picking up speed in the open air. I edged along the exterior of the building, hugging the shadows. I was in luck. The security lights had not come on yet, and no one seemed to be around.

Beyond the corrugated metal buildings that lay across a strip of tarmac, I could see the airport's perimeter fence in the distance. If I could get to that stretch of fencing and then duck behind the last building, I'd be out of sight from any of the main buildings. Maybe I could climb out unnoticed.

The first stretch—out in the open across the asphalt—was the riskiest. I waited until a woman in a hardhat drove by in an orange pickup truck, then I sprinted again, hoping for the best. A moment later, I paused in the relative safety of another shadow, half expecting I'd been discovered. But all was quiet. I continued sidling along the wall of the warehouse.

The cyclone fence at the perimeter was eight feet tall, topped with razor wire. I felt completely stymied, and I hunkered down against the gray metal wall of the building in defeat. *I guess it ends here*.

I decided to wander around and scavenge whatever I could. Perhaps there was something lying around that would help me crawl over the wire. If that didn't work,

I could try to break into the building to see what I could find there.

By a back door, I found five beer cans, a nest of cigarette butts, and several crumpled potato chip bags. I imagined I was a character in a spy movie—one of those MacGyverish improvisers who could think outside the box. What would one of those guys come up with? The beer cans could shield me from the sharp edges of the wire, but holding one in each hand wouldn't get me far. So what could I do? Suppose that I put the cans in the bags and then wrapped all that in my shirt? Wouldn't that be something I could lay on the wire? If I pressed down, the razor edges might pierce the shirt and bags, and catch on the cans, holding the whole mess steady as I crawled over it. It seemed viable enough to give it a try.

I dropped the damned thing twice and had to climb back up again each time. Finally, I had to position the shirt precisely on top of the fence while I hoisted a leg up onto it. Each time I shifted my weight onto my knee, I could get an individual beer can pinned.

The next phase was nastier—inching across it without falling or irreparably slicing myself up. But I managed. Several gashes later, I dropped down onto the far side of the fence. I stood on loose gravel by the side of a deserted road. No one had driven by while I was maneuvering on the fence. It looked as though the lane granted access to a long-term parking lot, but I couldn't tell for sure.

I checked myself out. If nothing became gangrenous, I'd live, but I definitely needed to prioritize getting cleaned up. I pulled the smelly, filthy shirt back on. No one would stop for a shirtless hitchhiker.

I heard a car at that point and spotted headlights to my left, so I stuck out my thumb and pasted a fake smile on my face. The first car sped up instead of stopping, and three more passed by in rapid succession. Finally, an older subcompact pulled over and stopped a good ways from me.

"Are you okay?" a man called out his open window. He was in his mid-forties and spoke with a Chinese accent.

"Not really," I said. "I could use some help."

"I can give you a ride, but that's all," he said. "Are you a Chinese-American? Is that what I see and hear?"

"Nepalese-American, I think," I said.

"Close enough," he answered, gesturing for me to get in the car.

I limped over and clambered into the passenger seat next to him.

"Thank you so much for the ride," I said. "Where are you headed?"

"Howick."

"Where's that?"

"It's twenty minutes northeast. I'm going home after work."

He put the car in gear and pulled out onto the road. He drove quite deliberately.

"My name is Nelson," he said. "My English name, I mean."

"I'm Sid."

His short, black hair sat atop a horse's face—long and square jawed. Perhaps he was some sort of ethnic Chinese. His oversized black and white uniform sported absurdly large epaulets, and he held himself upright in an unusually rigid posture. The car was spotless.

"Where are you going?" he asked.

"You can drop me off at a bus stop in Howick," I told him. "That would be great."

"You know," he said. "Drinking so much that you wake up hurt by the side of the road is not the right way to live."

"I agree," I said, wiping sweat from my face with my hand.

He saw the jagged cuts on my forearm. "Please don't bleed in my car. If you bleed in my car, I'll have to put you out."

"Fair enough."

"You can get free help for your drinking," Nelson said. "And your sinful lifestyle. There's AA, and you're very welcome at my church." He turned left at an intersection and headed out of the airport.

"Thank you."

Nelson was an evangelical, and he told me how Jesus had turned his life around and now he lived the right way and did good works like picking up suspicious strangers. I listened attentively, and soon he was telling me his problems as well. His family—a wife and a fifteen-year-old son—owed money to his uncle back in Shanghai, who was some sort of shady immigration broker.

"We emigrated a year and a half ago," Nelson told me, "and my wife doesn't speak English well enough to work yet. She has not been to university as I have. So we have started a bed and breakfast in our home. My son has made an alluring website with many extremely attractive photographs, and our rates are good, but business has still been slow."

"How much do you charge?" I asked, patting my

back pocket, which was still stuffed with New Zealand dollars.

"Seventy dollars a night. And my wife makes every sort of egg that a guest might require."

"I'd be happy to take one of the rooms for the night," I said. "Do you have a vacancy?"

"Oh yes." His eagerness was obvious.

"Is there a phone?"

"Certainly. We have all the amenities—complimentary soaps, a luxurious white robe, a very fine DVD library. If you enjoy your stay, you'll write a testimonial on our website?"

"Absolutely. What's the name of your place?" I didn't really care, but I owed my rescuer a friendly conversation about whatever was important to him.

"The Chowick Hospitality Suites," he told me. "You see, the local people call Howick Chowick because of all the Chinese immigrants. But our last name is actually Chow, so it's a play on words. My son thought of it. He's a genius. He's going to be a doctor."

Nelson turned off the highway, and we began traversing busy surface streets. This was my first glimpse of ordinary New Zealand, but I couldn't see much in the dark. It looked like a cross between the UK and the US.

"Maybe I can help you think of a name that would work better," I said. "No offense to your son, but if I was back home in California searching the internet for a place to stay, I don't think I'd click on a racist name."

"You think the name is a problem?"

"I do."

"You might be right," Nelson said. "Excuse me. I need to call my wife and tell her I'm bringing home a paying guest."

He held his cell phone up to his ear while he drove with one hand. The conversation was in Cantonese, I think. He spoke rapidly, eyeing me briefly while he talked. Perhaps he was preparing her for the spectacle I'd become.

For the remainder of the trip, Nelson delineated his wildly unrealistic plan to become a day trader, retire early, and "travel internationally in the lap of luxury amongst my true peers."

Lannie, Nelson's wife, met us at the front door of their very ordinary-looking green suburban home. I could tell she immediately sensed I wasn't simply a beer-swilling, bar-fighting hitchhiker, despite my odor and battered countenance. Perhaps she was sensitive to energy or she could read my character on my face.

Lannie's innocent smile highlighted her delicate features. She was so petite and slim, I wondered if she had an eating disorder. Her long, black hair snaked down her back as a thick braid. She must've been ten years younger than her husband. Lannie had obviously dressed up to meet me; she wore a brown tartan business suit with a too short skirt and a taupe scarf. She wobbled unsteadily on her black high heels. I got the impression that welcoming a guest was still a major event in this family's life.

Her English wasn't nearly as bad as advertised. As she bowed to me, she said, "It is an honor," in yet another complicated accent. I don't think she was from Shanghai.

"The honor is mine," I said. "Thank you for the opportunity to enjoy your home."

"We'll need payment in advance," Nelson told me

sternly as we stood in the tiny front vestibule.

"Of course," I said, retrieving my wad of cash and counting out the bills.

"Thank you," he said, clearly relieved that I could pay. "I'll go get my receipt book."

He headed toward the back of the house, and I returned my attention to his wife.

"You know things, don't you?" Lannie asked, peering intently at me. Her accent was thicker now that we were beyond the rehearsed portion of the conversation.

"Yes, I do," I said. "In the morning, we can talk."

"Okay. Thank you," she said. Her smile was achingly sweet.

"I need to make a phone call," I told her. "And I need to get out of these clothes, clean my cuts, and take a shower."

Nelson returned. "Would you like to buy clothes?" he asked. "I could sell you some very nice clothes." He handed me a receipt and tried to smile.

"Nelson!" his wife admonished.

He shot her a glare but then nodded. "Perhaps my son will lend you some," he said. "You're about the same size. He's at badminton practice, but he'll be home soon."

"Thank you. That would be very kind."

Lannie could not stop staring at me. It was a little uncomfortable.

"My wife will show you to your room now," Nelson said.

So I limped up the stairs, averting my eyes from Lannie's revealing skirt. After she'd shown me the compact, nondescript room—plain white walls, twin beds with a table between them, a dresser, a mirror, and a window—she gazed at me with an upturned face and spoke softly, tentatively.

"Just meaning of life? Can you tell now?" she asked.

"Loving connectedness," I said. It fell out of me without thought.

"Connectedness?"

"Connection. Unity," I said.

"Ah. This I believe also."

She smiled a full, radiant smile, transforming herself from merely pretty to quite beautiful. There was light in her; I felt warmed by it.

"Have a good night," I said. I needed to pee.

"On behalf of myself and my family, we wish you a very pleasant stay," she said quite clearly.

"That was terrific," I said. "You're a very special hostess."

She blessed me with another big smile. The room was even brighter now.

"Thank you," she said. Then she bowed again and retreated, closing the door behind her.

I visited the bathroom, peed, and rinsed the blood off my hands, wrists, and ankles. Then I lay on two towels on one of the beds. It was wonderful to be horizontal, although I was thirsty, hungry, and in a fair amount of pain. But I had escaped and I was safe, which amazed me. What were the odds that running out of Vlad's office would lead me to the Chowick Hospitality Suites—or anywhere else? In hindsight, bolting from custody seemed idiotic—guaranteed to make matters worse. But here I was. Apparently, I was poised to perform some sort of karmic function for

Lannie, too. Would even my crassest self-preservation efforts lead to something positive now?

I reached for the cordless phone on the black lacquered bedside table and called Sam. "It's Sid," I told her.

"Oh hi! How's it going? Are you calling from the plane?"

"No. That didn't work out. Now I'm at a B&B just south of Auckland."

"Me too! Are you down the hall from me? What town are you in?"

"Howick. Where are you?" I smoothed down a patch of torn skin on my arm and winced.

"I'm near a harbor at the southern end of Auckland," she said. "It's quite lovely. Why don't you join me?"

"I think I have some spiritual business here. Otherwise, I'd be there in a flash. Can we meet tomorrow?"

"Sure. I have an appointment at ten in the morning to get a temporary passport at the US consulate. Do you want to meet there in the lobby? It's right downtown."

I thought that over. *I'll still be a fugitive tomorrow. But how hard would anyone be looking for me— especially once they realize my suitcase isn't illegal?* At least, I was assuming it wasn't. I suppose it could've been.

"What are you thinking?" Sam asked. "Is the consulate a problem?"

"No, I think it's a good plan. I was just working through how safe it might be for me out in the world."

"Why? What happened?"

"I'll tell you tomorrow," I said.

"Are you with Marco and your friend?"

"No. I don't even know if they're en route to India or still here in New Zealand." I didn't like the sound of that as I said it.

"You want to get off the phone, don't you?"

"Yes. I have some things I need to do. I'm sorry."

"No, it's fine."

We said our goodbyes, which were substantially less romantic this time around, and I headed to the bathroom. After peeling off my disgusting clothes, showering, and drying off, I heard a gentle tap on the bathroom door. By the time I'd fastened a towel around my middle and opened the door, no one was there. But I found a tidy stack of Band-Aids, antibiotic ointment, and handy wipes. A bag of cashews, an orange, and a can of diet iced tea sat in a plastic sack next to those. Lannie had pretty much covered all the bases, bless her heart.

Love welled up within me for Lannie and Nelson. And for that matter, for their son I hadn't met yet. It was a wonderful feeling—a deep, non-personal love. I didn't need to have a relationship with them. I didn't need them to act in any particular way or be anything but themselves. I was just in love with this odd family.

I thought about Chris, and the feeling grew. I felt the same way about him. I thought about various challenging clients, and I loved them. Richard Nixon? The poor man had tried his best. It was an across-the-board attitude more than a feeling, really. It certainly wasn't conditional—if this, then that.

I found myself crying as I began to take care of my wounds. Gradually, this morphed into deep contentment, and then a few minutes later, I felt outrageously happy. The physical pain I was enduring didn't diminish my euphoria at all. It was a concurrent phenomenon—just another event that would eventually give way to something else.

Although it wasn't late by New Zealand time, I was growing sleepy. I found a pen and paper in a drawer in the dresser and jotted down some notes and ideas. It was hard to hold it all in my head, and I'd developed the habit of externalizing thoughts back when I'd tried to be a writer.

Despite my fatigue, I stayed up late journaling about my goals and motives. First and foremost, I needed to find out who the hell I was. I'd been dodging that all of my life. I also needed to sort out who was who in the drama I'd been pulled into. Who could I trust? Who, if anyone, had my best interests at heart? It seemed as if everyone wanted to exploit me to reach *their* goals. What about mine? I vowed to be less passive. I wasn't a follower by nature, I told myself. I was a leader.

What else? I wanted to be in service to the world in whatever way I could. That was why I'd become a therapist. If I could help humanity on a grander scale by sharing my energy or becoming a spiritual teacher, so much the better. And if we really were approaching a global crisis as Bhante and Marco had asserted, I certainly wanted to play my part in resolving it.

I also wanted—no, craved—to continue feeling the bliss and power that Marco had unleashed within me. I was surfing some sort of accelerated spiritual wave. I needed to ride it out. I may have become enlightened back on the island, but as Marco had told me, it wasn't "abiding." I yearned for abiding. I couldn't imagine anyone who wouldn't. My experience had been akin to seeing and hearing after being deaf and blind. Who could be satisfied if they slipped back into the isolation of unawareness? Enlightenment was a benign Pandora's box.

Lastly, I wanted to get to know Sam better. Was the familiarity and closeness I felt with her significant or merely a side effect of all the rest? I felt as though I were in love. Was I?

I should've stopped there and turned in. Instead, I made a list of all the pitfalls and dangers that might lie ahead. At the top of this list was a fear I hadn't faced yet. Was I going crazy? Was all this really happening? What if I were hallucinating or delusional myself?

Chapter Thirteen

In the morning, I stretched my sore muscles and took stock of just how battered I was. Nothing screamed at me. Mostly I'd endured a plethora of cuts and bruises that were perfectly bearable.

I had a feeling there might be something else outside the door, so I took a look. Underwear, socks, a white T-shirt, and a black fleece top sat on a pair of black corduroy pants. A note was taped to the top of the pile.

Dear Mr. Sid. Justin would like you to use these clothing while you are by New Zealand. If possible, return later. Okay to compute on computer in main room. I make breakfast. Look forward to talk. Honored, Lannie.

The clothes fit me perfectly since apparently I had the body of a fifteen-year-old. When I'd been younger and scrawnier, this had spawned a great deal of bullying. It didn't help that I easily fit into my middle school locker once you pulled out all the science fiction paperbacks.

I tiptoed downstairs at five fifteen thanks to my haywire biological clock. I turned on an overhead light and found a desktop Mac on a table in the crowded living room and fired it up. It was time to Google the crap out of everything.

There was no one named Giocassini. Anywhere.

They'd named one of Saturn's moons after a medieval Italian astronomer named Giovanni—Gio—Cassini. Gio Cassini. Did Marco Giocassini combine these names to invent an alias for himself? Or perhaps Marco's powers enabled him to control what showed up in an internet search.

I also couldn't find any record of a martial arts school in Palo Alto that matched Sam's description. On the other hand, there really was a coffeehouse named Marco Isn't Here Anymore.

Next, I looked up all the Bhantes I could find and perused their photos. Mine was Bhante number nine—Supun Wimalaratne. He really was from Kandy, Sri Lanka, about halfway up the west coast of the teardrop-shaped island. The Buddhist temple there housed a tooth that had supposedly been snatched from Buddha's cremation ashes. A succession of kings had guarded it for the last two thousand years, making it a more credible memento than most of the relics in other temples. They kept it in a small gold stupa that looked like a beehive. Once a year, they held a festival and paraded it around on top of an elephant that was lit up with Christmas lights. *Why not?*

Bhante W. had been the abbot of a prestigious, historic monastery up in the mountains east of Kandy until about ten years ago. I found photos of him leading ceremonies in Colombo, the capital city, blessing the UN General Assembly, and standing with several celebrities, including Richard Gere, Martha Stewart, and Jason Patariki. The Maori wore his national team's black jersey and must've just stepped off the rugby field. He dripped sweat down onto Bhante's orange robe.

From what I could gather from perusing websites of other Bhantes, this all fell within the bell curve for a religious leader in his country. But then Bhante disappeared, and Bhantes did not disappear. Nobody had seen him for years, and there were all sorts of rumors on Sri Lankan websites about what might have happened to him.

Jason was exactly as advertised—an international celebrity. He may have been the best rugby player to ever "grace the pitch," as one sportswriter phrased it. And his endorsements had made him extremely wealthy. Apparently, he loved the feel of merino wool against his skin, and he adored using a New Zealand brand of paper towel to capture the "rugged spills" he encountered in his "jet-set lifestyle." He'd appeared in two South African action movies. I saw a trailer for one on YouTube. He was a god-awful actor—maybe the worst I'd ever seen.

There was absolutely nothing about RGP or Kasritri—Bhante's organization—on the internet, no matter how I tried to spell them.

Meher Baba was featured on all kinds of websites. His devotees still adored him even though he'd died in 1969. One look at a photograph of his face told me why. He'd had the sweetest, most soulful dog eyes I'd ever seen on a human. He radiated love at the camera through his eyes. It was like looking at a preternaturally intelligent golden retriever.

His friendly, playful mouth lent him a sense of lightness, whether or not he smiled in his photos. Between those eyes and that mouth was a huge—and I mean truly epic—beak of a nose and a bushy mustache. Meher Baba wasn't handsome.

The overall effect was arresting, though—it stopped the mind cold in its tracks and invoked the heart. Generally, his followers—who called themselves Baba Lovers—were drawn to him simply by seeing his photo. They were, for the most part, very unsophisticated in terms of spiritual or philosophical background. I gathered most of them hadn't even read the handful of books that silent Baba had painstakingly dictated letter by letter on an alphabet board. They just loved him. Deeply. Enough to be transformed by their own love.

Baba—everybody just called him Baba—had been born in India to Persian Zoroastrian parents. He supposedly would break his forty years of silence with "the Word" when the time was ripe for him to usher the world into a new era. Everyone waited around for this, but he never said anything.

Baba really did set out to charge up his tomb, though. He wrote that he worked with "universal energy" to "awaken mankind" on a grander scale than just a student-teacher dyad. So he wasn't really a guru, per se.

Next, I researched the Bay of Islands, which was a major international tourist draw with great fishing, great sailing, and secluded beaches. Rich people with yachts liked to summer there. The internet photos didn't do it justice.

Ram Jessawalla was a reclusive billionaire with a stake in a slew of financial ventures. I found more photos of his (former) yacht than of him, and none of the photos were recent. As a younger man, he seemed to be fond of horses, and he favored a high-rise pomaded hairstyle that made him look like an Indian version of a rockabilly guitarist. As Ram had said, he was frequently vilified online, mostly because his large-scale public works projects changed people's lives in ways they didn't appreciate, such as his building a dam on a Bangladesh river that forced thousands of villagers to relocate.

The US consulate was in downtown Auckland, a block or two off the main shopping street and only a short walk from the water. It would be easy to find. And according to their website, they provided emergency walk-in services for US citizens, including those with legal difficulties.

The Chows' home was also fairly near the sea, according to their very professional-looking website. A commuter ferry departed from Buckland's Beach on the half hour all morning. After a bit of cross-checking, I discovered I could walk a couple of miles to the ferry at this end, and then only four or five blocks to the consulate. It couldn't have been much easier.

Lannie emerged at that point in a shiny red warm-up suit—the kind that fat Mafia bosses wore in 1970s movies. She was even prettier without makeup.

"Good morning," she said. "You sleep well?"

"Yes, thank you. How did you sleep?" I spoke slowly, pronouncing each word as carefully as I could.

"Very different dream. You come with different energy. Different dream now."

"Ah."

She was staring at me again. "Who are you?" she asked.

"That's a good question. I'm not sure," I told her.

"Are you an angel?"

"No."

"A ghost?"

"No."

"A demon?"

"No."

"A guru?"

"No."

"A Buddha?"

"Maybe."

"Ah. Some breakfast?" Lannie smiled and gestured toward the back of the house.

"Sure. Thank you. Can I help?" I felt relief that we'd settled on an identity for me.

"No, no. My job. Poached, scrambled, sunny side up?"

"Scrambled would be great. I don't drink coffee, but I'm growing fond of tea," I said.

"We have tea," she told me.

Her accent charmed me, although I had to work to understand her. "Great."

Lannie scurried away. There was no sign of her husband or son. I remembered that email existed, and I checked mine.

Chris had contacted me a half hour earlier. He owned all the latest gadgets—hell, he'd designed some of them—so it was no surprise that he'd found a way to communicate.

"Bro, we're in the air over the Indian Ocean—our flight was delayed in Sydney. Mumbai in three hours. If you get this, write me back. I didn't want to leave you there, but Marco's driving this bus, and he said they already had Lucy's crate loaded up. I didn't think she'd have much fun in India on her own. I hope you can meet us there. I hope you're okay. Let me know if you need a good lawyer. I did some research online and found some lawyers in Auckland. I also found out some other stuff about all this. Marco says don't forget to change your Band-Aids, whatever that means. Chris."

I wrote him back a quick email outlining recent events, told him that I'd stay in touch as best I could, and logged off.

By now, I could smell toast from the adjacent kitchen, and I headed there. A round table sat in the middle of a very small, clean dining alcove. I was glad the Chows weren't large people or they'd have been banging their elbows on the walls when they wielded their silverware. A bright green tablecloth, an orange placemat, and a red paper napkin greeted me cheerily. Lannie stood by the stovetop.

"Almost ready," she said. "Nelson say I don't sit with guests. I sit with you?"

"I insist."

"Insist?"

"Please sit with me. Where is your husband?"

"Work. Double shifts. Justin sleeps." Most of her attention was on her cooking.

She brought over eggs, toast, and something fried and brown that could have been sausages or potatoes. I could smell the latter, which was a relief. I had no interest in eating meat now. It wasn't that it felt morally wrong; it just didn't seem like food anymore.

Lannie sat down in one smooth motion across from me and watched me eat with a rapt gaze. I focused on my table manners; surely Buddha didn't wolf down his breakfast or spill scrambled eggs onto his borrowed fleece top.

"So how can I help you?" I asked when I was

finished.

"How did you be you?"

I thought it over. "Genetics. Environment. Therapy. Training. And an energy transmission from a spiritual teacher." I tried to keep it simple, but I doubted that she got it all.

"Energy? Can you energy?"

"I'm not sure. I'm new. Shall I try?"

"Yes, please." Lannie sat up straight and closed her eyes. She looked like a little girl—innocent and trusting, expecting something good.

I tried to arrange my fingers to resemble Marco's hands when he'd first worked on me. I felt like a total fraud, but who knew what might happen? Even a placebo transmission might help her. And perhaps Marco would tune in and work through me from his seat in first class.

At first, nothing happened. Then after a few minutes, I felt a great deal of tingling and heat channel between our foreheads just above our eyes. But it moved from Lannie to me! I was the one receiving the energy. My third eye became an expanding vortex—a whirl of energy that grew with each pulse. At first it was dime-sized, then quarter-sized. After five minutes, it was the size of a softball. Eventually, it engulfed my head and stopped spinning. The profound sparkle of the energy was all I could sense. The rest of my body was lost to me. The room was gone. Lannie was gone.

Then I was in a black void, like outer space, but not empty. It was alive and I was it and it was me and I was right there in that moment. I felt as though I had slipped sideways and entered a deeper reality—the one behind the world I usually inhabited. There was nothing there to perceive, yet it all felt hyper-real. I had the notion that I could think of something and it would manifest in that realm. I don't know why. I tried it—imagining Karma the dog visiting me—but nothing happened.

After some time, I became accustomed to not having a body and not being in the world. The awareness that I'd become just rested in the void. I was only the awareness itself.

Time passed. At some point, it made sense to gradually cram as much of my consciousness as I could back into the Sid shell. I had to jettison so much to fit back in; historical Sid enclosed a very confined space. I felt scattered and spacey when I first saw Lannie across the table again, watching me wide-eyed.

What a conceit. I was going to teach her. I was going to play Marco and straighten her out with some buzzing. She was a powerhouse of energy—a wondrous being who had effortlessly provided the next transformative experience I'd needed.

"Thank you," I said.

"Thank *you*," she said.

"What sort of experience did you have?" I asked.

"Energy. Light. Calm. Love," Lannie said. Her English was markedly better now. "Were you in samadhi?"

"I don't know. What's that?"

"Like a trance. In the beyond beyond. No illusion."

"Oh. Yes, I guess I was."

"I am honored," she said, beaming.

"No," I said. "You don't understand. You sent me energy. You put me in samadhi."

"Oh, I don't think so," Lannie protested, shaking her head.

"You have no idea who you are," I told her. "Part of you may live here in this house in Howick, but you are so much more than that. You are a very evolved being. The reason I'm here is to receive your help—not the other way around. Do you understand?"

"Actually, yes," she said. Now her accent was hardly there at all. "I'm understanding much better now," Lannie said. "Perhaps whatever happened, happened to both of us. Perhaps spiritual energy is like a circle—what do you call it? Three hundred degrees?"

"Three hundred and sixty. Yes, I think you're right. It's all-encompassing, isn't it?"

"I'm sorry," she said. "I don't understand that."

"No worries." That was my first "no worries." *What a useful phrase.* "By the way," I said, "thank you for a delicious breakfast. Thank you for welcoming me into your home. Thank you for everything. I love you."

She frowned and looked down.

"I love everybody," I added. "I have a girlfriend."

"Oh, of course. Thank you." She tilted her chin up and smiled radiantly.

How had the universe managed to put us in the same room? I'd been in Santa Cruz the week before. Lannie's husband happened to pick me up hitchhiking. It was impossible to imagine the infinite complexity that could make everyone's life curriculum dovetail with everyone else's. Or at least ours.

I asked her about catching the ferry to downtown Auckland, and she insisted on driving me to the dock. According to Lannie, I'd been in samadhi for an hour and a half. We needed to hurry to catch the ferry that would arrive in the city at nine thirty.

I was getting better at reintegrating after these

energy experiences. I showered again, brushed my teeth, and remembered to change my Band-Aids.

In her neighbor's small station wagon—Nelson had driven the Chows' only car to work—Lannie asked me more questions. It was a short trip to the ferry, but we managed to work our way through a dozen naïve inquiries and their corresponding ill-informed answers. We were so much more than we knew. So much more than our minds. And yet we wanted to know things. Did I know the future? Would Lannie be in samadhi too, someday? Exactly what happened when you died?

I answered as best I could, but it occurred to me that I knew several books that were likely to help her more than I could, so I jotted down the titles. I gave her my email address as well.

"Will you come back? Will I see you again?" she asked as we parted.

"I don't think so," I told her. "But you never know." I felt deep disappointment as I said these words. We'd shared a profound connection.

"I never know?" she said, tilting her head.

"No one ever knows." I hadn't intended this to be a piece of wisdom—it was an idiom, after all. But it was true enough.

It was clear that she wasn't a hugger, so I put out my hand and we shook. Her hand was tiny and hot.

Regretfully, I turned and walked onboard the small ferry. Lannie waved continuously until the boat was out of sight. There she was, this tiny red figure on the shore, waving and waving. I began to cry, and I sobbed until I couldn't see her anymore.

Chapter Fourteen

I rode for thirty-five minutes through the Tamaki estuary to the Hauraki Gulf and then to Auckland. The woman who sold me my ferry ticket gave me a pamphlet that outlined "the wonders of the deceptively mundane voyage from Buckland's Beach to where so many of us find our travail." I didn't find the trip mundane at all.

If New Zealanders used the Bay of Islands as their scenic benchmark, I could understand why they might take the estuary for granted. But from minute to minute, the outrageous beauty of the passing panoramas took my breath away. Thousands of birds dove in the water or glided through the cool, salty air. One green one looked like a giant parrot. It roosted on the ferry's rail and successfully begged for snacks from commuters. There was an intelligence in its eyes that I wasn't accustomed to seeing in a bird. I remembered what Marco had said to me in the rowboat about interspecies contact. That exact moment, the bird swiveled its head, looked me directly in the eye, and nodded.

Life is not only becoming more loving and more beautiful, it's also becoming very trippy. For the rest of the crossing, I avoided eye contact with other creatures and just watched the shoreline.

Skyscrapers and a jumble of office and apartment buildings sat on a series of hills above the Auckland harbor. Below them were berths for ships of all sizes. I felt excitement building in my chest. Whether this was due to the anticipation of visiting a new place, seeing Sam, or attaining some resolution at the consulate, I wasn't sure. It didn't matter much, so I just got on with things.

The sunlit stroll from the dock to the consulate brought me through a large plaza and a crowded shopping street. I enjoyed moving my body—however sore it was—and taking in the sights. I felt incredibly alive and happy by the time I neared the consulate. Apparently, the new me liked walking. I guessed I'd have to settle for that instead of continuous bliss for now.

The US consulate was located on the third floor of an unimpressive-looking office building amidst all sorts of other businesses. It wasn't anything like the stand-alone mansions that I saw on TV when some third-world country destabilized. Maybe that was only embassies.

Sam sat in the spacious, modern waiting room, although I was fifteen minutes early. She looked great. A white mock turtleneck and tan corduroy jeans fit her perfectly. Brand new dark-brown hiking boots and a black fleece beret completed her outfit. She wore her blond hair in a braid.

Sam rose and melted into my arms. "Hey there," she said, hugging me gently. Her shirt was very soft.

"Good morning."

We stood and held each other, and I quickly developed a fierce erection. If I broke our embrace, I might reveal it to the half a dozen other people in the room, so I held on to her. The more I held on, the more stimulated I became. I knew Sam could feel it against her leg.

"It's like I'm in seventh grade," I said. "I'm not sure what to do."

"No one's looking at you," she said. "They're all looking at me."

We stepped apart, and it was true. Everyone was looking at her. "Is this what it's like to go through life as a beautiful woman?" I asked.

"Yes. I'm offered free drinks everywhere too, but I don't drink." We sat close to one another on an upholstered loveseat facing a long, wooden reception counter across the carpeted room. "So what's been going on?" Sam asked. "Why aren't you in India?"

I began to fill her in, but before I got all the way to Howick, a young American man in a gray suit emerged from a doorway and called out a name.

"Louise Arthur?"

"That's me," Sam said and hopped up to take care of her business.

I walked up to the main desk and asked if I could talk to someone, too. The female receptionist was a young New Zealander, which surprised me. In the movies, these places always seemed to be staffed by Americans.

"What would this be about?" she chirped.

"I might be in trouble with the law here," I said.

"Uh oh," she said. "Drugs?"

"Suitcase."

A young man sitting at a desk farther behind the counter glanced up sharply.

"Suitcase?" the woman repeated.

"And I'm in the country illegally," I added.

196

"Uh oh," she said again. "Did you overstay your visa?"

"Not exactly."

"Sid Menk?" the man called. "Are you Mr. Menk?"

"Yes," I said.

"Call Bruce," the man instructed the woman. "He'll want to see him right away."

In fact, Bruce Campbell showed up immediately. A tall, slim African-American, maybe forty-five, he wore a gray suit too. His was more expensive than Sam's guy. I couldn't picture him in any movie, which struck me as odd.

"I'm so glad you're here, Mr. Menk," he said, extending his hand and introducing himself. "Let's talk in my office."

"Sure." I shook his hand and followed him back into a warren of cubicles and offices. A sign on his door told me that he was the vice-consul. A picture window behind his modern desk overlooked a busy street. I sat in a comfortable armchair and waited for him to speak first.

"Well, there's nothing but good news," Bruce said. "You're not a wanted man. Your suitcase is made of embossed water buffalo. When those get endangered, we might as well all move to Mars."

"The women could move to Venus," I suggested.

He showed me his teeth. "Very good. And Mr. Patariki—I believe he's a friend of yours—has stepped forward and told the local authorities that he played a prank on you by bringing you here on his jet. He was at the airport last night and met with customs officials. You committed no crime in Kawakawa—where men attacked you and your companions. You committed no crime on the bay or in Tuaranoa. And we've worked since early this morning to smooth ruffled feathers at the airport. Needless to say, escaping from custody was not very wise. But clearly you were under a lot of stress. You'd almost drowned, you'd been attacked, and now you were being falsely accused. So we called in a favor, and your name has been cleared."

"Just like that? Before I even asked for help? How did you find out about me?"

"The authorities here always contact us if a US national is mixed up in something. And in this case we also received a phone call from a…" He consulted his computer. "Mr. Dante. But the main thing is that we are ruthlessly efficient in my department. I'm on track to be an ambassador in an important country, and that's based on this kind of performance."

"I don't doubt it." I paused and smiled. "I'm thinking Belgium or maybe Austria."

He smirked. "Those would do just fine."

"So my passport's good? I can use it to leave the country?"

"I think I can say in all honesty that New Zealand will be quite happy to see you go. But there is a customs official named Mr. Goric who refuses to return your suitcase unless you personally apologize to him. If it were me, I'd do it, but we're two blocks from Queen Street if you'd rather just go shopping and fill up a new one."

"Is this how it works here? Apologizing to one another for things like this?"

"Yes. It's a lovely country. Inconsequential, but lovely. Everything is less institutional and friendlier."

"Okay. I'll think about it," I said.

"Is there anything else I can help you with?" Bruce asked, spreading his hands as though he were already offering me something.

"I don't think so. You've already done so much," I said.

"In that case, let me ask you this. What's Jason Patariki really like? Is he just a regular guy?"

"How long have you been here?" I asked, surprised by his question. "Are you a rugby fan?"

"Six years. Rugby grows on you. It's like football without all the pads and helmets. You can see the sweat and the blood. I like that." He grinned and showed his teeth again. Apparently, he didn't know how to smile. I wouldn't want to get on this guy's bad side.

"Well, to tell you the truth," I said, "I have mixed feelings about Jason. Sometimes he acts like a colossal jerk, and then other times he does the right thing."

"Like everyone else," Bruce said.

"Yes, like everyone else," I agreed. "We're kind of a messy, bumbling species, aren't we?"

"Amen to that, brother," Bruce said.

When I returned to the waiting room, Sam was waiting. "I'm all set," I told her.

"Me too. Does your 'all set' mean the same thing as mine? Your passport's good? No one wants to arrest you?"

"Yup. It's a miracle." I sat down next to her. "What shall we do now?" I asked. "Head back to California?"

"Let's go to India," Sam said. "I think it's important to spend time in Meher Baba's tomb."

"Okay," I agreed. As soon as I heard her, I knew this was what we needed to do. Don't ask me why.

So we walked to Queen Street, which ran up the hill away from the water, and bought everything we thought we'd need, including an extremely smart phone. Apparently some of the Japanese brands debuted first in the Pacific Rim before they made it to the US. I was able to use my credit card and save Marco's cash. I'd end up in considerable debt after the trip, but that didn't matter.

We also stopped at a cheesy-looking travel agency and Susie—our "personal travel consultant"—cashed in my first-class ticket and booked us two coach tickets from Auckland to Sydney to Mumbai to Pune the following day. Pune was a couple of hours from Meher Baba's pilgrim center outside Ahmednagar.

At the last store, I placed Justin Chow's clothes in a box with two notes, and the clerk promised he'd send it for me. The first note thanked Justin profusely; the second was for his mother. I thought carefully about what to write.

Lannie: don't forget who you are and who you aren't. When you need it, someone or something else will show up in your life, much as I did. Your spiritual momentum is past the point of no return. No worries. Good luck with your new job—go get one. Your English is more than sufficient now. Regards, Sid.

On the bus ride to Sam's B&B, I told her about Lannie and the samadhi experience. Occasionally, I became distracted by Sam's eyes. I remembered them as a darker shade of blue, and several of her blond eyelashes were spiral-shape.

"What do you think about all this stuff that keeps happening to me?" I asked when I was through reporting.

"I think it's an example of the benign conspiracy that underlies our lives. It's always in our best interests, always unfathomable, always transcending all our worldly concerns—whether we realize it or not."

"Yes," I agreed. "That's it."

For the remainder of the ride, Sam surveyed the passing scenery while I considered the upcoming trip. My "okay" to Sam's suggestion that we travel to India had come so easily and felt so right that I hadn't revisited the topic since. Perhaps it had been the same for her.

Sam had traveled to India once before, for which I was grateful. I didn't know what to expect. Beggars with leprosy? Dead animals in the street? Or perhaps I'd meet an amazing array of spiritual beings, unencumbered by materialism or Judeo-Christian conditioning. I discovered that I enjoyed not knowing what might happen, which was something new.

****

We spent the rest of the day and most of the night in bed. Her B&B was as lovely as advertised, but it wouldn't have mattered if it were overrun with rabid hogs.

Our lovemaking was gentler now, with energy and feelings merging in the ever-decreasing space between us. As I gazed into Sam's eyes, love welled up in me, intoxicating me, pulling me into a world of beauty and truth. Her tender gaze melted me—the me I'd known. I not only knew now that I loved her, I loved who I was with her, as well.

At one point, lying in each other's arms, we locked eyes for several minutes, tears streaming down both our faces. The loving feeling kept deepening and deepening until I almost couldn't bear it. In the nick of time, Sam began laughing, and I joined her. We laughed for ten minutes. I don't know why.

For long stretches, we were silent. What was there to say? When we did speak, we shared without any qualms.

I found out that Sam's sister was a psychotherapist in Maryland. Her mother had been an Olympic equestrian. Sam herself had played the clarinet and kept snakes as a child.

"It's a good thing I'm not a Freudian therapist," I told her. "That's a double whammy."

She loved to dance, especially to early rhythm and blues. She'd surfed and played volleyball before becoming interested in martial arts. Marco's school had been based on some obscure Chinese technique that, by tradition, no one ever named. Even the school was nameless, which explained why I couldn't find it in my internet search back in Howick.

She'd traveled extensively, at first with her family, then later as a spiritual seeker. Her favorite foods were pears and water chestnuts, her favorite color was white, and her favorite place was in bed next to me. Or so she said.

I found it odd that the details of Sam's life didn't matter much to me. She could've worked in a sideshow biting the heads off squirrels, and I would've loved her the same. Her disclosures merely satisfied my curiosity.

I told her about myself as well—the parts that she didn't already know. Sam seemed surprised that I'd spent so much time in therapy, which I took as a compliment.

"I was a mess," I told her. "I had low self-esteem.

Dead parents. And I picked really screwed-up partners."

"Let me guess. You tried to fix them."

"Yes. But it was a personnel issue. They weren't fixable. In fact, they were perfectly satisfied being screwed up since I was apparently to blame for all their suffering."

"How did you work your way out of that?" Sam asked.

"I'm not sure I have. How big a mess are you?"

She laughed. "About as much as everyone else." She held up a slender hand when I tried to protest. "It's true, and it's been a problem in relationships. My partners tend to put me up on a pedestal, and then I try to live up to that. It's a lot of pressure. When I can own my humanness—all the nutty stuff—then I'm content. That's hard to do in the midst of a partnership. It has to be safe to be vulnerable like that. If you know someone might use it against you in an argument one day, then you'll keep it to yourself." She smiled. "That's what I'm appreciating about the time I'm spending with you, Sid. I feel safe. When I look at you and sense your energy, I have no doubt that I can trust you."

"Thank you. I feel the same—for the first time in my life." I never thought I'd be able to say that.

"I'd actually given up on relationships," Sam said.

"Really?"

"Yes, until quite recently," Sam said, gazing at me softly. I nodded my acknowledgement of this compliment, and she continued. "It just seemed as though the odds were so low that I'd find anyone who matched up with who I've become, and my role in RGP is very time consuming."

"Is it like a job for you? Do they pay you?"

"Yes."

"Where does the money come from?"

"I'm sorry, Sid. That's all I can say on that topic. I've taken vows."

****

This time around, the airport experience was completely mundane. Our early morning flight was on time. I never saw Vlad Goric or my troublesome suitcase, and we weren't treated any differently than the other travelers.

This pattern continued all the way to Mumbai, where we finally arrived at about nine in the morning—on a different day, I guess. There was something wrong with the gate at the terminal, so we had to disembark via a stairway onto the hot, humid tarmac several hundred yards away. Stepping out of the plane kiboshed the ordinariness of our journey. I was immediately immersed in a high-frequency buzz that transformed everything into a ramped-up version of itself. Basically, India was on acid.

Colors were brighter than anything I'd seen in New Zealand. The sky was bigger. Objects were even more three-dimensional. The steamy air tingled with energy, supercharging everything, imbuing it with life force.

On Marco's island, when he'd sent me energy and my senses had sharpened, it had been a shock—a weird experience that I'd struggled to assimilate. Here in Mumbai, I merrily buzzed along with India's energy. It felt like a power source, not a hindrance.

I realized I was ignoring Sam. As we walked through the shimmering heat toward the terminal building, I turned and glanced at her.

"It was the same for me when I first came," she said, smiling broadly. "It's remarkable, isn't it?"

I nodded.

The airport was chaotic. Mobs of people pushed and shoved just to get to where they'd have to wait in line—which they didn't. There were no lines at all.

"It's not considered rude here," Sam told me. "It's cultural."

Eventually, we found ourselves on the sidewalk, bags in hand, with about an hour to get from the international airport to the domestic one, which was supposed to be no more than twenty minutes away. Our prospective taxi driver spoke to me at the curb in Hindi, assuming I was Indian. Sam answered with a few Hindi phrases and then switched to English.

"You are Americans," the driver said in very fast, accented English. He was a bit shorter than me, with splotchy skin. His head was squarish, and it seemed as though it belonged to a much larger man. He wore a yellow, short-sleeved button-down shirt over light khaki pants, and a navy-blue New York Yankees baseball cap. His brown plastic sandals looked new. He could've played a taxi driver in virtually any movie.

His cab was a small black and yellow box. It did not inspire confidence. While I didn't think I could actually tip it over, I imagined it would fare poorly competing against the bumper cars at the Santa Cruz Boardwalk.

"We're from California," I told him.

"You will find that everyone will wish to steal from you," he said. "You're very lucky I am to be your transport today. I am a religious man. I steal from no man. Or woman."

"That's good," I said.

"Are you a movie star?" he asked.

"No," I answered.

"Not you. Her. You look like a movie star," he said to Sam.

"I am not," she said. "How much to take us to the other airport?"

"Where do you fly?"

"Pune."

"Ah. Beautiful Pune. My brother will drive you there for a fraction of the price. He is almost as safe a driver as myself. And there is a very scenic expressway now. You will see the country and enjoy yourselves. It is much shorter than flying because Pune is only ninety kilometers away. The person that told you to fly there did not know their business."

"Shall we get another taxi?" Sam asked. "Are you refusing to take us?"

"Two hundred rupees to the airport. Door to door. All your luggage, too. No extra charge."

"One hundred rupees," Sam said. "No religious person would try to cheat us this way."

The driver glared at her. "You have been to this country before, haven't you?"

She nodded.

"I swear on Baba's grave I am a religious man," the driver said. "One hundred and twenty rupees."

"Which Baba is this?" I asked, wondering if we had spiritual business with the driver.

"Meher Baba, of course—The Great Awakener."

"That's where we're going," I said. "To Baba's tomb."

He peered at me through half-closed eyelids.

"You're a holy man," he said. "Your kundalini has risen. The snake is awake." He turned to Sam. "And you are most certainly not a movie star," he said. "You are beyond the movies. You are holy too. Your heart is open and pure."

He watched us. Nothing was going to happen until we acknowledged what he said.

"Yeah, okay," I said. "You're right."

"May I have a blessing? The fee now is one hundred and ten rupees and a blessing. Special holy person discount. But you should know that going to Pune does not make sense if you're going to Ahmednagar."

"We have our orders," I said in an effort to curtail the debate.

Sam agreed to the driver's terms, promising to bless him once we'd arrived.

"What's your name?" I asked him.

"Vijay Jayaraman."

"I'm Sid. This is Sam."

"Sam? This is not a woman's name," he said.

"Samavati," she said. "My full name is Samavati."

"You're a Buddhist, then. I know the story of Samavati. Are you really her?"

"Her reincarnation?" I asked.

"Yes, of course."

"Perhaps," Sam answered.

"Good, good. You seek to keep your own counsel about such matters. Who am I to you?"

We piled in and headed out. The other drivers accelerated and swerved as if they were on the way to a hospital emergency room with a woman in labor. At least that's how they drove when an occasional gap in the traffic allowed their frenzy to assert itself. Mostly, the traffic was too dense to be called traffic. Vijay told us not to worry, that the domestic airport was only ten kilometers away, but I still wasn't sure we would make our flight.

After another half mile, in which we saw a low-speed fender bender and a scenario involving a motorcycle and a very agile pedestrian, the traffic cleared a bit and we were able to pick up speed.

A moment later, a delivery truck rammed us from the side and sent us careening off the road into a storefront. I hit my head on something and blacked out.

Chapter Fifteen

I woke up in a pile of brightly colored saris. There was a lot of yelling. And European-style sirens wailed plaintively in the distance.

I was only sort of awake. My senses were operating—I could see and hear—but I couldn't process most of the incoming data. It was all a jumble. And my head hurt like hell above my right ear. It was both a sharp pain and a deep ache; when I lifted my head to look around, it felt a lot worse.

I lay just inside the doorway of an open-air shop. I could only make out chaotic forms and colors outside; I didn't see anyone I recognized. And I couldn't remember much. I knew I was Sid, but I had no recollection of where I was or what had just happened.

"Let me through," a male voice said in Indian-accented English.

My twin brother stood in front of me a moment later. I hadn't remembered I was a twin.

"Come on," he said. "We've got to get out of here." He bent down, grabbed my arm, and pulled me to my feet.

"I believe we should leave him immobile," another man said.

"I am your brother Raj," the first man told me. "It's not safe for you here. They've taken the woman."

"Woman? What woman?" I hurt all over,

especially the side of my head.

"You have amnesia?"

"What's that?"

"Come on," he exhorted, guiding me toward a tiny white van that was parked nearby. I stumbled through a crowd of people, bumping into several, which hurt like hell. One familiar-looking face stood out, and I associated a name with it—Vijay. He called to me as Raj escorted me into the passenger seat of his van and buckled me into the seat belt. I remembered not wearing one in the last car. And then my head throbbed mercilessly, and I closed my eyes.

When I opened them again, we were driving on a modern superhighway in moderate traffic. I didn't seem to have a problem with my memory now.

"Where's Sam?" I asked.

"The woman?"

"Yes." I brushed a lock of hair off my forehead. My hand was bloody. That wasn't good.

"She was injured as well. Not seriously, I think, but several men bundled her into their car and said they were taking her to hospital. I don't believe they were sincere."

"Do you have a phone? Let's call the police," I said, shifting to face him. We needed to do something right away.

"One of the men *was* a policeman," he told me.

"Oh." My heart sank, but my brain must've still been selectively scrambled, because in just a few seconds, I returned to a relatively calm baseline. *Why aren't I panicked about Sam's welfare? The love of my life just survived a serious accident and may have been kidnapped. For God's sake, where's my concern, my fear, and all the rest?*

"There is a great deal of corruption here," Raj said. "I believe these people were watching the airport. And the accident wasn't an accident."

I liked looking at his face. And he seemed to be sincere in his concern for me. "Which 'people' are they?" I asked.

"I need to explain a great deal to you," he said. "You have been laboring under some misimpressions."

"Fine. Go ahead. But first tell me where we're going." The abstract answers could wait. I needed to get oriented in the here and now.

"To Meherabad—your destination. You cannot fly there now. I'll drive you. It'll give us time to talk and get to know one another."

"I don't want to leave without Sam," I said.

"Let me explain, and then you can see what you want," Raj replied. He drove well compared to the alarming antics of the drivers around us. He probably would've only received four or five tickets back home so far.

"Fine. Go ahead."

"Marco is not who he seems to be. He is a very dangerous man. Whatever he has said to you is unlikely to be true. He says what he needs to say to accomplish his own ends. He is convincing. But I learned the hard way who he truly is." He paused and glanced at me to see how I was taking this. It was like me looking at me. I wondered if I'd ever get used to that.

"I'm listening," I said, rubbing my shoulder. I'd have a huge bruise there soon.

"Marco recruited me. He needed a source inside Kasritri Sanganika—Bhante's group—and I was resentful and greedy. He has access to a lot of money. Did he tell you he won the lottery?"

"Yes."

"This is a lie. He has a backer of some sort, and I don't believe this man's money was come by honestly." He shook his head in a way that made me think he was regretful that he even lived in a world where such things were allowed to happen.

"Who's the backer?"

"I don't know." He bowed his head now. "I am ashamed to admit that I took their dirty money."

"Why were you resentful?" I asked. This felt like a therapy session.

"The others from Western backgrounds were favored," Raj said. "And when I heard about you, it was the last straw. You had paid no dues. You were an outsider. Why should you be the one?"

"Wait a minute," I said. "What others? I know we're not clones, Raj."

"How do you know that? From Marco?" He shot me a glance.

"Well, yes. And it's so unlikely, too."

"There are thirty-one of us," Raj said with pride in his voice. "We really are clones made from Buddha's DNA. I seriously doubt that any of us are his reincarnation, but that is a separate matter. Marco has his reasons for wishing you to believe otherwise."

"Have you been in a room with more than two of these so-called clones?" I asked.

"Of course. I've met them all. Well, all the ones who've been found so far."

My gut churned, and a chill ran up my spine. "If Marco is such a bad guy," I asked, "how did he develop all his amazing spiritual powers? How has he helped me become more alive—more open, more loving? And why?"

"You know he lived in Palo Alto?" Raj turned onto another, newer highway, along with a swarm of other unruly drivers.

"Yes." I jammed my foot down onto a nonexistent brake pedal. Merging in India catalyzed basic reflexes.

"He owned a kung fu school there, but mainly he was a Stanford professor. His real name is Bruno Bompiani. He was in the experimental psychology department, and he collaborated with other departments to develop human-potential-enhancing drugs. After some years, he decided to experiment on himself, and he became psychic. He hid this from the others. He also discovered that if he put certain drugs in people's food and drink, they would have internal experiences that mimic legitimate spiritual awakenings. Much as LSD or ecstasy provide intense sensory input and expand one's mind, Marco's new drugs did the same, but even more effectively. If you think back, you'll find that you ate or drank shortly before all your energy experiences. It was that way with me."

I considered this, and as far as I could remember, it did seem to be true. This was the first thing Raj had told me that had substantial traction. I'd been trying to listen open-mindedly, but until this point I guess I'd just been looking for the flaws in his exposition.

"How could you possibly know all this?" I asked as Raj dodged a motorcycle.

"I'll get to that. Just listen. The same drug that enhanced Marco's mind had a side effect of changing his personality. He became grandiose and selfish.

213

Rather than publishing the results of his study, he stole all the medications and the records and disappeared. This was quite a few years ago. He is an even more dangerous man now, unfettered by a sense of right and wrong. Above the law. Above consequences. He seems to use his powers to help people, but this is a trick. It's all about him—his goals and his ambitions. He is the ultimate narcissist—the ultimate sociopath. And he is wrapped in spirit. Hidden in spirit. This is what is so dangerous."

"Why should I believe you?" I asked. Now my hip was killing me. I tried to scoot in the seat to relieve the pain, but nothing helped.

"I am you. Can't you trust yourself?"

"Apparently not." There were a few things that Raj hadn't explained. "What about making people invisible?" I asked.

"Tell me this part of your story," Raj said, so I did.

"Whoever else Frank works for, he also works for Marco," he replied. "When I told Marco I wouldn't help anymore, he signed up Frank. So it was all an act on the rowboat. Of course those people could see you. And Frank kidnapped you because Marco wanted to make sure you came to him in New Zealand. He is persona non grata in the US. If he were to enter the country, he'd risk being arrested."

"What about the attack on the cave—our escape down the cliff?"

"That was Marco's first try at getting hold of you. But Frank didn't know about the back door."

"What about Sam?"

"I don't know about her," Raj said, shaking his head again. He was an expressive head shaker. This time it seemed as though he didn't care that he couldn't answer my question.

"RGP?"

He shook his head again, sending the same message.

"Bhante. What's he up to?" I asked.

"He is a good man who has all of mankind's benefit on his mind. We can trust him."

"This is a lot to sort through, Raj," I said.

"Of course."

I tried to think about what he'd said, but my brain was still sludgy. I watched the scenery for a few minutes instead. We drove by massive gray concrete apartment buildings—dozens of them. There were almost no trees and only an occasional patch of green on the ground, but quite a few residents were growing flowers or vegetables on their small balconies. There weren't sidewalks, but the narrow roadways between the buildings were crowded with bicyclists and walkers. I was reminded of an apiary I once visited outside Washington DC on a school trip.

"You said you'd tell me how you know Marco's backstory," I reminded Raj.

"Yes. There was a man who approached me in Paihia and told me the truth. His name is Paul Arthur. He said he was looking for his sister and that she had been Marco's student."

"That's Sam—the woman in the taxi with me. Was he a blond guy—very handsome?"

"That's him, yes. He showed me various things he'd downloaded from the internet. And I have a confession, Sid."

"What's that?"

"I led him to believe I was you. I learned an American accent in the cave so I could pretend I was Tim—one of the inner circle of clones—to get information for Marco. Then I pretended with Paul as well. I'm sorry." Raj had slowed down while he told me this, and now he sped up again as traffic passed us.

I was beginning to feel very tired. "I'm going to close my eyes again," I said, and I did. In hindsight, it was clear that I'd sustained a serious concussion. I hadn't received any medical care, and I might not have awakened from one of these involuntary naps.

I did wake up, though, when Raj jammed on the brakes and cursed in a language I didn't know.

"What?" I asked.

"There is a taxi in front of us that has suddenly slowed down." He looked to the sides. "There are taxis beside us as well. And one behind us. They're all slowing down."

We had no choice but to decelerate to a crawl and then finally stop. Raj's eyes widened, and his hands tightened on the steering wheel. He locked his door and stared fixedly at the windshield. No one emerged from the cab in front of us.

A moment later, Sam's face appeared at my window. She smiled and beckoned me with a finger, and I reached to open my door to join her.

"Don't go!" Raj shouted. "This is a trap! Marco is behind this!"

Before I could open the door, he stomped on the gas, and the van began to smash its way through a gap between two of the taxis. The crunching and screeching noises sickened me—I think some part of me remembered the sounds of the earlier crash. At first, I wasn't sure we'd break free—we were starting from a dead stop, after all, and our vehicle was hardly a hot rod. But the cabs were very light and flimsy. Raj's van shoved one sideways, and the back corner of another one crumpled as we hit it, scattering bits of cheap metal and plastic all over the road.

I seemed to be locked into a passive state. I hadn't decided to go along for the ride nor was I continuing to try to join Sam. I was just sitting and watching events unfold. My head injury had shut down my initiative.

The engine roared as Raj accelerated over the debris and surged into the open lane ahead of us. The van was actually quite peppy. I turned to look back, which hurt like hell. My head was still very screwed up. The traffic behind us was a chaotic mess, and the taxis were blocked from pursuing us. Raj had made a getaway. I had no idea if this was a good or a bad thing. I couldn't find a way to successfully process what Raj had said, or what was going on now, for that matter. I tried anyway.

Was Sam colluding with an evil version of Marco—Bruno, that is? She had certainly vouched for him. If he was bogus, so was she. Either that, or he'd duped her too—going back years. I knew one thing. Our love was real. That wasn't up for grabs.

Maybe Raj was inventing various plausible fictions to manipulate me—to get me to side with his cause. It came down to a few basic questions. Which was more likely? Clones or Marco's magic? I felt as though I needed to pick one or the other, but in the state I was in, I couldn't.

What I knew for sure in that moment was that I was confused, in great pain, and when I tried to think, my head hurt more. When I stopped thinking and just gazed out the windshield again, my fingers came together in an elaborate, unfamiliar pose. Raj zoomed down the highway, and I applied my hands to my head and relaxed. I could feel cool waves of energy flow through me, and the pain began to recede. Was I a healer now, too? Could a narcissistic maniac bestow that upon someone?

Raj raced on, checking his rearview mirror every few seconds. He exited the freeway after a few miles, and now we were in some sort of high-end suburb, with odd-looking homes—a pastiche of various international styles. Behind high, jagged glass-topped stone walls, I saw the second story of a stuccoed hacienda, a Swiss chalet, and a gothic, church-like stone home.

My head was feeling better and better, thank God. I left my hands where they'd migrated to.

"What are you doing?" Raj asked. He'd been too focused on his breakneck driving to pay attention to me earlier.

"I don't know. Healing myself, maybe."

"Our brother studied Reiki," he said. "But it only works on small problems."

We wound through a more middle-class area now, although if it looked middle-class to me, it was probably very affluent for India.

"Our brother?" I asked.

"Our clone brother, Sid. We call each other brothers."

"Where are we going?" I asked. If we were en route to Meher Baba's place before, we certainly weren't now. It was a testament to my still-untreated head injury that I hadn't questioned this before. Along with alleviating my pain, the energy from my hands seemed to be clearing my mind.

"We have another brother who lives here in Mumbai. The cave wasn't for him. His name is Jal, and his wife is a nurse. He is a very successful entrepreneur."

"Is he expecting us?"

"No, but this is his company car, and he flew me here to help you. He is a very good fellow. He'll want to help. And you can use a nurse, can't you? You are clearly not yourself. I can see that your brain is not right, so going straight to Baba's would be foolish."

I brought my hands down and swiveled my head a bit. No pain.

"How are you feeling?" Raj asked, noticing my movement. "I know it wasn't medically advisable to move you, but I feared more for your safety if you remained prone in that shop."

"I don't know," I said. "I might be fine, or I might drop dead in the next few minutes."

I paused and shifted in my seat, trying to get more comfortable. Now that my head had calmed down, I was aware of several more badly bruised body parts. My shoulder was the worst. And I was still achy from various New Zealand debacles, especially my left hip.

"How far is it to Jal's?" I asked.

"We're almost there."

****

I was able to walk almost normally from the car to Jal's apartment, which was on the ground floor of a three-story wooden building. I felt shaky and weak, but my balance was back.

Jal wasn't home, but we were met at the door by

his wife, Leena, who was a friendly, portly woman in her thirties.

"You are very welcome here," she told me after I was introduced by Raj. "And it's good to see you again, Raj."

She noticed my head. "Oh my," she said. "What happened?"

Raj answered before I could. "Sid has been in a serious automobile accident, and as you can see he has sustained a dangerous head injury."

"He needs to be in hospital," she said.

"Perhaps I could lie down," I said, suddenly feeling dizzy and weak.

"Of course." She escorted me through a small living room to an even smaller bedroom, helping me onto a carved wood queen-sized bed. A pattern of entwined lovers ran across the headboard. The apartment was chock full of overly large, dark wood furniture. It was as if they were afraid of open spaces.

Raj took Leena aside and whispered in her ear for a while. Her eyes widened, and she nodded several times.

She was light-skinned, with black, curly hair that fell to her shoulders. Her glittery sari reminded me of one of Chris's shirts. It was yellow with a horizontal pink pattern that looked like something you'd see on a TV that needed repair. Her face was almost perfectly round with large, mobile features.

I felt better once I'd been horizontal for a minute or two. I could sense my energy gathering itself, beginning to restore my core.

Leena bustled from the room and returned with a flashlight and a wicker basket. She pulled a wooden desk chair next to me. "Let's take a look at you," she said.

While she examined my wound, shone the light into my eyes, and felt my pulse for much longer than an American doctor would, Leena told me about her training. She'd graduated from a medical school in Toronto, Canada, which, ironically, wasn't accredited in India. She had interned in an emergency clinic, where she'd seen her share of urban trauma—gunshots, knife wounds, and vehicular accidents. Once she'd moved back to Mumbai for love, she'd been restricted to nursing.

"You have a concussion, of course," she finally said. "The effects of this are unpredictable. Sometimes when the location is on the side of the head, there is internal swelling and the brain presses against the skull. This can cause damage or even death. But it's not typical."

"How's it look?" I asked. "Am I still bleeding? Is it swollen?"

"You are no longer bleeding. Your wound is shallow. I would guess that you impacted something blunt such as a seat back. As for your swelling, yes, there is swelling, and it concerns me. But as I was saying, in most cases like this, the patient's symptoms will calm down after the first few hours, and then only a headache will persist. Your odds of a full recovery are excellent."

"He has been healing himself," Raj said.

Leena appeared to be skeptical. "Yes, well," she said, before continuing. "Have you suffered any amnesia, blackouts, vomiting, weakness, or scrambly thinking?" she asked.

"Scrambly?" I asked.

She smiled. "Yes. It's a technical term I use with my charges. I work in a pediatric department these days."

"I've experienced everything you mentioned except I haven't thrown up. But I'm feeling much better now."

"In the ordinary course of events," she said, "we would keep you in hospital for twenty-four hours since this is the time period in which something untoward might develop. And your recent symptoms would certainly warrant this precaution. But I understand that you're a sadhu who must reach Baba's tomb. And bad people harbor ill will toward you?"

"I don't know what 'sadhu' means," I said.

"Holy man," Raj said from where he leaned against the doorjamb. It was still very surreal to watch him say and do things in my body, with my face.

"Oh," I said. "Well, yes. I don't know how holy I am, but I do have spiritual business at the tomb. And apparently a hospital might not be safe for me."

"Why don't you lie here and collect yourself?" Leena suggested. "Jal will be home soon. I'll make us all a nice meal, and then I'll assess you again later. If you keep improving, we'll send you on your way."

"Can I ask a question?" I said. "How many people have you met who look exactly like your husband, Raj, and myself?"

"Oh, I'd say a dozen," she replied. "It's a very strange thing, isn't it? Are you new to the idea?"

"Very. And I've had alternative explanations for all of it as well—from someone I have reason to trust."

Raj spoke up. "He means Marco. He is under Marco's spell."

"Have you met him?" I asked Leena.

"No. But my husband has. This Marco, or whatever his name is, must be a very scary fellow. Jal is not a fearful man—far from it—but he was trembling when he returned from his meeting with him. And he would not share any details. This was not like him, either."

"Thank you for everything," I told her. "I'd like to rest, but I'm afraid that if I close my eyes, I may never open them again. Is that a myth, or is that really a risk with this kind of head injury?"

"There are situations where that is so. Not to worry here. Rest up."

She and Raj filed out of the room, and I thought about Sam, deciding that her appearance back when the taxis boxed us in meant she was safe. Then I fell asleep.

I had a dream, or perhaps a vision. I was at the Lincoln Memorial in DC, where I'd once visited in real life as a ten-year-old. Instead of a statue of Lincoln, though, there was a giant marble statue of Lucy the dog. She began talking to me in an Indian man's voice, and I felt Marco-style energy surge through me.

"You don't need to know what you don't need to know," she said. "Don't worry. Be happy."

I remembered that this was Meher Baba's catchphrase. "Are you Baba?" I asked.

"We are all Baba," the voice said. I saw now that the statue's mouth wasn't moving. "And we are all Sid. And we are all Lucy. You know this."

"Who should I believe?" I asked. "Who can I trust?"

"Yourself. And the universe. The universe loves you. Everything that happens serves you. Everything is driven by love."

Chapter Sixteen

I awoke and lay basking in a sublime dream hangover. Eventually, I struggled to my feet to use the bathroom. En route, I checked myself over. I was still in pain, but I'd returned to my current baseline of functioning, whatever that was. I had no idea, really. My sense of self had shifted so dramatically so many times recently, I felt as though a mysterious stranger lived inside me, sharing space with my historical self. This new guy didn't seem to buy into the paradigm that we even existed.

I wandered into the living room after a few minutes. Raj and Jal were meditating, sitting cross-legged side by side on red cushions on the floor against the far wall. Jal wore a charcoal suit with a white shirt and a yellow tie. His feet were bare. I could've distinguished him from Raj even if he'd worn his brother's jeans and green T-shirt. His face—our face—exhibited an arrogance—a haughtiness—that immediately repelled me. He hadn't even opened his mouth yet, and already I disliked him.

"Greetings, my brother," he said, rising and waving his hand jauntily. "I am so glad to meet you." He extended his hand to me, and I moved forward and shook it.

"Let's seat ourselves for lunch and discuss your future," he suggested.

Raj and I followed him into the dining room, which was dominated by a long, glass-topped table. Four places were set, and Leena appeared with a wooden tray as we took our places.

She met my eyes and smiled. "Let's start you with some dahl," she said. "There's chutney on the table. What would you like to drink, Sid?"

"Water is fine."

"Very well," she said and served us, placing the fourth bowl at her place before heading back into the kitchen.

"So Sid," Jal said in fast, heavily accented English. "Raj has informed me that he has illuminated you concerning the man you know as Jackson."

"Marco," Raj said.

"Yes, of course. Marco. Have you had a chance to think over what he told you? May I offer you my computer to research this man? Dr. Bompiani's history at Stanford is well documented. You can email our brothers if you wish for them to share their experiences of this crazy person. Or I can tell you of my own meeting. Just let me know what suits you."

"You're talking very fast and saying a lot," I told him and then took a spoonful of food. He waited impatiently for me to continue, tugging repeatedly on one of his earlobes.

"I listened to Raj," I finally said, "when my mind was clouded. I'll listen to you now with my full awareness. But please, slow down."

Leena came back in the nick of time. The dahl was very spicy; I needed the water she'd brought. It didn't help.

"Certainly, certainly," Jal agreed. "Bompiani is

about power. He has determined that true power—the deepest kind—the ruler of all other powers—must be based on spiritual authority. The material world springs forth from Spirit. If someone can manipulate that realm and convince others to help him, then who knows what he could do?"

If I signed up to believe him about Marco, even temporarily, I'd also have to revert to entertaining the idea that I was a clone. This seemed much more likely in that moment than it had the day before, but it was still a big stretch.

"Can you prove we're clones?" I asked. If this issue were settled, I'd certainly feel more allied with one side or the other.

"Yes, of course. After lunch, I will satisfy you. But let me tell you more about Dr. Bompiani's plan. He tried to recruit me, and he demonstrated his powers to me. I remained stalwart to my truth. So he told me what he had planned, hoping this would entice me into throwing my lot in with him."

He paused and cocked his head. It was a ploy calculated to create suspense.

"So?" I said.

"He wants to be in charge!" he proclaimed.

I laughed. I didn't mean to. It just tickled me—the way he said it. It could've been a line in a Mel Brooks film. "In charge, huh?"

"Yes. This is very serious. What is wrong with you?" he asked.

"I'm sorry. In charge of what?"

"Everything!"

"Oh."

Raj spoke up. "It may sound absurd, Sid, but you

are new to this world of energy and spiritual authority. There is a very real risk that Marco can succeed in ruling the world if you help him. You are Buddha. You are only just stepping into your power." He shook his head slowly. "Make no mistake, Sid, he would be a power-mad ruler. We would all suffer."

"So you're telling me I ought to believe you two and disbelieve Marco? Why should I?" I asked. "It's just words here at this table. Marco backs up his words with energy—and love. He's helped me in amazing ways."

"I could give you a drug," Jal said, "that I guarantee would make you very happy—at least for a while. This means nothing. In fact, it is a problem because there are permanent side effects from this. Our biochemistry and energy fields are meant to be what they are. You will surely suffer from this madman's tampering. We are using words and words alone because words are right and appropriate."

"You realize that I'm a therapist. Don't you think I can tell who's a narcissist or a sociopath? Or who's just annoying?" I said, staring at Jal.

Leena pushed back her chair and returned to the kitchen.

"Perhaps you can know these things when they are the ordinary version," Jal said. "This man is different. Let me ask you this. Did he make you feel special? Did he lie, manipulate, and control you? Is he charismatic and compelling? Does he hide who he is and what he's doing? Aren't these the characteristics of a sociopath? You can say he does all this in pursuit of goodness, but the ends do not justify the means."

Leena returned with more food, which was

alarmingly beige—all of it. I just hoped it wasn't as spicy as the last dish.

"You said you could prove all this after lunch," I said. "What do you mean?"

"I can show you things on the internet," Jal said. "If you saw Stanford faculty photos from years ago and your Marco was there as Bruno Bompiani, what then? And the preliminary findings of the medication study are online—in a reputable journal. You can read that. The human potential movement was very big in those days. We can also show you the DNA testing that has been performed on twenty-seven of us."

"What about Meher Baba?" I asked. "How does he fit into all this?"

Leena spoke up. "Baba is love. He is beyond the beyond, but still he loves. He is watching over all of us. His love guides us. Everyone in the world answers to Baba. He is the guru of gurus. His love is in our hearts. It *is* our hearts."

"Yes, yes," Jal said. "He was a great man. But that is neither here nor there right now."

"Why don't we just enjoy our meal now?" Leena said. "These matters can wait."

"So be it," Jal said, and we ate.

****

After lunch, Leena presented me with tropical-weight clothes—khaki pants, a short-sleeved white shirt, and several other items.

"Obviously, these things of Jal's will fit you perfectly," she said. "He prefers more formal wear, anyway. Your corduroy pants are better suited to Canada and even your socks are a foolish choice for India. We need to keep you all squared away, don't we?"

I thanked her and changed into the new outfit in the bathroom. Then Jal, Raj, and I adjourned to Jal's small office. Our host had bookmarked various websites, which I read as he maneuvered through them one by one. His computer verified everything he'd told me. I felt sick to my stomach. It was clear Marco really was some sort of monster. And the DNA test results from my brothers' blind samples were identical.

There were a variety of other revelatory facts, but by now I was feeling so overwhelmed, the words on the screen just looked like random letters to me. When I tried to focus, I could make out one or two here and there, but otherwise it was as if I had given myself brain damage. I guess I was subconsciously insulating myself from whatever might be too overwhelming. I felt like I was on the brink of a breakdown.

Then denial reared its head. I began working hard to generate less disturbing explanations. Clearly, I couldn't simply believe my senses now that I'd been worked over by all sorts of expert manipulators since I'd left California. My ability to adjudicate what was reality and what was a hoax had been compromised over and over. So I shouldn't just believe what I saw on the computer. And Jal was spoon-feeding me all the information, too. He could've constructed all these websites from scratch. After all, it was far more likely the computer had been tampered with than someone had managed to create human clones decades ago. That was what it came down to.

"You could've preloaded your computer with fake sites," I said. "It all could've been set up ahead of time."

Jal threw his hands in the air. "You're impossible."

Raj spoke up. "What would satisfy you?" he asked.

Then a benign conspiracy asserted itself. The overhead light and the monitor blinked off; the power had failed. It was dim in the room but not dark.

"This is a normal occurrence here," Jal told me. "Please remain calm. I'll go fetch a flashlight. Raj, go get the magazine in my study. We can resume using the flashlight and the article about the drug."

They both trotted off, and the power immediately came back on. Jal's computer must've featured an instant-on capability. His home page stared back at me, and I hurriedly Googled Bruno Bompiani. He was a real person, but not Marco. Bompiani was a six-foot-seven-inch, twenty-two-year-old Italian volleyball player.

I closed the tab and scooted over to a nearby couch. When my brothers—my *triplet* brothers—returned, I was a picture of innocent consternation. "Gosh," I said. "I guess it's all true. I can't deny it, can I?"

"You certainly cannot," Jal said.

"Excuse me," I said. "I need to use the rest room."

They both nodded, and I headed toward the front door, walking as casually as I could. Leena emerged from the kitchen and spotted me just as I reached for the door handle.

"Where you going?" The urgency in her voice betrayed her.

"I'm just going to get a little air," I told her, swinging the heavy wooden door open.

"I don't think that's a good idea," she said. "I haven't re-examined you yet."

"I'll be right back." I kept moving. I was through the door now.

"Jal, Raj!" she called. "He's leaving!"

I bolted. I didn't know the area, but it was unlikely that any of them was in the kind of shape I was in. *Barring any ill effects from the accident, I should be able to easily outdistance them.*

Raj was an athlete. He caught up to me in a couple of blocks. We were running in the street since the narrow sidewalks seethed with pedestrians. Cars honked and bicyclists swore at us as they maneuvered by.

"Stop," he called. "Wait."

Unfortunately, he wasn't the least bit out of breath. I was. He sprinted up alongside me.

"Can't we talk about this, Sid? We'll help you get through it. There's no reason to panic. And this isn't something you can run away from, is it?"

He doesn't understand. He believes I'm spooked by what they'd rigged up on the computer.

"Just let me run it out," I said. "I'll be right back. Exercise helps me cope."

"I'll run with you," Raj said. "You don't know your way."

"Okay," I agreed.

So we continued. I ran 10Ks and trained for a marathon once a year. I'd wear him down, get a lead, and then duck into a store or something.

In two miles or so, most of it on less busy sidewalks, Raj began to slip back. He called to me, imploring me to stop. Instead I focused on my breathing, increased my pace, and took several random turns. The pounding on the uneven concrete accentuated my accumulation of injuries, and my headache was throbbing again.

When I looked back after a while, I couldn't see him anymore. If I were Raj, I'd be calling Jal to drive over and search for me. I needed to get the hell out of there. But where was *there*, anyway? I slowed down and glanced around. I was lost on a busy shopping street somewhere in Mumbai. A motorbike sideswiped me, the boy's knee lightly scraping my hip. Several other people yelled at me to get out of their way.

I knew no one, nor which direction represented escape. What now?

Chapter Seventeen

I found a substantial-looking taxi several streets away. A foot longer than the others, it sported oversized black bumpers. For what was probably a ridiculous amount of money, the dapper driver agreed to take me all the way to Meher Baba's pilgrim center outside Ahmednagar. He'd been there before, he said.

He wore an immaculate, cream-colored, short-sleeved jumpsuit, and he had fastidiously trimmed his black beard. His eyes were a bit dull, as if driving didn't interest him too much, no matter the destination. He was probably my age. The movie he'd appear in would be set in a 1970s disco, and he'd be the guy inappropriately approaching the hottest girl in the place, only to be shot down by a snarky retort.

It seemed like a good idea to get out of town, and my people were probably still at Baba's. I'd call Sam and Chris en route; I could always switch destinations if he and Marco had taken off for somewhere else. Also, I wanted to experience the tomb, even if I had to do it on my own. I was no longer intimidated by its purported energy.

As we climbed in the taxi—I sat in the front passenger seat—the driver told me that his name was Burt.

"Burt?" I asked after introducing myself.

"My parents were Christians, so they liked Burt

Lancaster," he told me.

I nodded my head as though that made sense.

"But they were wrong about being Christians. There is no God," he continued. "And Meher Baba was just a very clever magician. Seeking wisdom from such a man is a waste of time. Especially once he's dead."

"Oh."

Burt explained many more things before we reached the highway heading northeast. Then, mercifully, my disrupted sleep schedule asserted itself, and I conked out. I slept for a couple of hours until Burt took a gas/bathroom/snack break at a modest truck stop—very modest by US standards. Two pumps and a tiny restaurant sat in the middle of a vast dirt parking lot. An ancient man pumped our gas.

"Where are you from?" he asked me in a very thick accent as I climbed out of the car to stretch. Burt had lit out for the men's room after telling me to "exercise vigilance on the vehicle."

"California," I told him.

"Oh yes. My nephew's son owns a motel there—in one of those towns named after a Catholic saint." He studied my face. "You've come a long way. Are you visiting family? No, wait. You're a seeker, aren't you? Are you journeying to Osho's—or perhaps the Ashanti Yoga ashram?"

"Meher Baba's tomb," I told him.

"Very good. You will not be disappointed there. Unless you are trying to stay the same. You cannot stay the same once you go there." He looked me in the eye and smiled. For some reason I really liked this man, and he seemed quite happy.

Perhaps the Indian culture with its historical caste

system helped its members have a more realistic idea about the odds of getting things to go their way. If there was no possibility of doing something grander than pumping gas, maybe it was easier to be content with your life.

"Life is change," I finally said.

"Precisely," he agreed.

When it was my turn to visit the bathroom, I was faced with four holes in the floor with raised tiles beside each to support feet. I was glad that I only needed to pee. Being ethnically Asian hadn't blessed me with an ability to squat particularly well.

I rejoined Burt in the taxi and, for the next hour, watched the scenery and tried to call Chris and Sam on my state-of-the-art cell phone. Apparently, its creators hadn't reckoned on rural India. Burt was mercifully silent.

We passed through small towns every five or six miles. It was hard to distinguish one from another. They were assemblages of small, flat-roofed cinderblock buildings, most of which had been stuccoed over. Sky blue seemed to be the most popular color. Men on elderly green tractors farmed the surrounding farmland. There were virtually no trees.

As the trip continued, I grew stronger and more centered. I was so much more than I'd been a week before. At that moment, in Burt's noisy, bumpy taxi, I felt capable of generating whatever response a given situation might call for.

Of course, I told myself, *somewhere back in here is the usual human idiot mismanaging whatever amazing tools and skills he'd been given. It's only a matter of time before that guy reasserts himself in some spectacularly self-defeating way.*

Finally, with another hour to go on our trip, after failing to reach Sam yet again, I got through to Chris.

"Hi, it's Sid," I told him.

"Bro!" he said. The signal was weak and staticky, but I could hear the excitement in his voice. "Are you okay? Where are you?"

"I'm okay. I'm heading your way—assuming you're at Baba's. But it's been an adventure."

"How so? And yeah, we're at the pilgrim center."

"A truck ran us off the road in Mumbai, and I got a concussion. Then one of the fake clones sort of kidnapped me. Have you heard from Sam? I'm worried about her."

"She's fine. She called Marco a while ago. Major head trauma, huh? It's always something with you, Sid, isn't it? Did you get away, or is this a ransom demand call? I may have money, but you know how cheap I am. Don't embarrass yourself."

"What if I hadn't pulled off a dramatic escape? You'd feel terrible saying something like that, wouldn't you?" I found myself pointing my accusation at the windshield.

"Probably not," Chris admitted.

"What does it take to knock the wiseass out of you, Chris? Do I have to get killed?"

"That might do it. I dunno."

I didn't need this crap right then. "Is Sam due to arrive soon?"

"She's en route," Chris said. "That's all I know. Are you on a bus or something? Sam said the airport wasn't safe."

"I'm in a taxi. Is Marco there? Can I talk to him

236

instead? Really, anyone else would be fine."

"He's doing samadhi. I mean he's sitting right here, but he's totally checked out." Chris's tone was warmer now—evidently he'd sensed my irritation.

"Has he been working you over?" I asked.

"Not too much. He says he needs my brain intact. But we went to two ashrams in Pune before we got here. These gurus knew Marco, and everybody at the ashrams meditated with us. I do feel kinda different since all that."

"Sounds good." Perhaps Marco and a squad of gurus could reform him.

"Plus if the women hadn't been so damned celibate, I think I could've worked the coattail effect and scored big time," Chris added.

"Gee, what a shame."

Then the phone cut out. "Hello? Hello?" I said.

"I'm surprised it worked at all," Burt the driver said. "There are no cell towers here."

"It's a special phone," I said.

"Special or not, it's all the same. No towers. Did I hear you correctly? Were you telling someone about a clone? Are you a science fiction writer?"

"No, I'm not."

"I see," he said. "What are you, then? A software engineer?"

"I'm like a psychologist," I told him.

"This is another ridiculous notion. Psychology!" He was off and running. According to Burt, the entire field was a hoax perpetrated by greedy con men who desired nothing less than to strip mankind of its dignity and make everyone much poorer.

I made an effort to find something positive about

Burt. His syntax tended to be very interesting. And I liked his haircut. It had square notches over his ears and unusually well-defined edges.

"How is it," I asked, "that you developed such a strong negative opinion about both spirituality and psychology?"

"My great-uncle." He stopped, as though that fully answered my question.

"Did someone take advantage of him?"

"Oh no. That's entirely wrong. No one could take advantage of my great-uncle. He was a psychiatrist—the first Indian one in this part of the colony. It was a colony back then. Did you know that we are only a country since 1948?"

"Yes, actually."

Burt ignored that. He seemed to only notice whatever fit his preconceptions. "Well, my uncle had my father locked up. That's one thing. I was very young, but I knew it wasn't right."

"Was he ill?"

"They said he was schizophrenic—that he heard voices. So what? All great men hear voices. This means nothing." He waved the notion away with a grand gesture, swiping his hand across the taxi's headliner.

"I can understand your suspicion."

"Suspicion? Hardly!" He snorted and glared at me. "Then my uncle became involved with your Meher Baba. He would go and stay with him for months on end and talk about him all the time. After that big fraud died, my uncle would bring me to the tomb. He said it was good for me to spend time in it. This was 1970. At first I liked it. I got to be with my rich uncle who was away so much, and, after all, my father wasn't here anymore to take me places. Everyone treated us well because my uncle had been so close to Baba. In fact, Baba secretly spoke to my uncle once, even though he was supposed to never talk. This was very special. My uncle told me all about it when I was eleven. He said he needed someone to tell his secret to in case something happened to him. He said I was like a son to him."

"What did Baba say? I'm imagining it was either something very mundane like 'pass the salt' or something incredibly profound." I smiled at my own notions.

"Well, my uncle told me exactly what it was, but I promised not to say, so I will not say. I am not a man who breaks his promise." Burt stated this forcefully, as though I was about to try to make him tell and he needed to head me off at the pass.

I took a break from talking and gazed out the windshield for a while. The scenery had become less rural now. The towns were much larger, with less space between them, and numerous side streets branched off from the two-lane highway. When I peered down these, I saw tiny, makeshift shacks and storefronts jammed together all the way to the horizon.

"So what eventually soured you on spirituality?" I asked Burt. "I understand why you might feel bitter about psychology, but it sounds as though you had a good time with your great-uncle."

"He abandoned us. One day he was there—well, down the street from us where he lived—and the next day he was gone. No one has seen or heard from him since."

"Could there be some sort of innocent explanation? Maybe he had an accident while he was traveling or something."

"No. He took his clothes and his money. He just left. For months, his crazy patients would come to our door looking for him. One big fellow attacked my mother, and the police had to take him away." He gripped the steering wheel tightly and snorted.

I thought about all this. "So Burt, something *did* happen to your uncle. You said that he told you his secret in case something happened. Doesn't that free you to share what Baba said? I'm sure the world would be very grateful if you did. From what I understand, many people were expecting him to break his silence before he died."

"My uncle only disappeared. He would be very old indeed, but he may still be alive. Because I'm angry at him doesn't mean I can turn him into a dead person in my mind. A promise is a promise. The day after his funeral I will go to the newspapers." He nodded in an exaggerated fashion.

I pondered a bit more. Clearly, Burt wouldn't accept any challenging ideas unless they were phrased diplomatically. "What do you think the odds are that I hailed a cab in Mumbai to go to Meherabad and the driver happened to be the great-nephew of Meher Baba's only confidante?"

"Astronomical, of course. Many things are."

"Do you think that this could be an indication that there's more than meets the eye here—that there's purpose or meaning in the world beyond logic?"

"No." He shook his head vigorously now. I thought his ears might fall off.

"Have you ever experienced spiritual energy?"

"I once believed this, but now I know there is no

such thing," he said.

"Pull over," I said.

"What?"

"Pull over the car. Park. I want to show you something."

"Your tricks will not work on me, but very well." He slowed down and turned into a dirt track between two dark brown fields. No one was around—the first time I'd seen that in India. There were always a ton of people everywhere. "Go ahead," Burt said. "Get this over with. My time is money."

My hands arranged themselves and shot a strong burst of energy to Burt's chest.

His eyes closed, and he began to smile—for the first time. "I know this," he said in a soft, dreamy voice. "I have felt this love before."

Then he passed out and slumped over the steering wheel, honking the taxi's horn. It was the loudest horn I'd ever heard. Oops.

I couldn't rouse him, and I wasn't sure what to do next. I tried calling Sam, but I couldn't get through. With the phone in my hand, it occurred to me that perhaps it had been preloaded with international GPS or some handy map app. At least then I'd know where to go. So I started exploring the touchscreen, which used a different operating system than my old phone. When I pressed the largest icon, which resembled a stylized globe, Marco's face appeared on the small screen, and he began talking.

"Good," he said. "You're on the road to Baba's."

"Sort of," I said.

"Don't bother talking. I prerecorded this back in Paihia," he said and paused to let me digest that.

It didn't make any sense. I'd bought the phone in Auckland after we'd parted company. How could he have recorded anything on it in Paihia the day before?

"Don't worry about the details," he continued. "Remember what I said to you in the rowboat the first day—about things I say not making sense to you sometimes? Just get behind the wheel and keep going the way you were going. When you get to Ahmednagar—there's a sign—take your first right and then ask directions from the oldest person you see."

"Okay," I said to the phone, which had somehow shut itself off.

Chapter Eighteen

Burt was still out. His breathing was regular, though, and when I checked in on him at the energy level, that seemed fine too. On the other hand, I was only a few days into my career as an amateur medical intuitive. What the hell did I know?

Had I inflicted the energy experience on him simply because he'd irritated me? This thought pushed me toward the rather-be-safe-than-sorry option— seeking local medical help (which probably didn't exist).

Marco's message was clear, though, and I ultimately decided to follow his direction. It seemed likely he knew what had happened to Burt. He seemed to be able to use his psychic abilities to track most anything. By inference, then, he was okay with my driver's holiday in blissville.

I managed to lever Burt into the passenger seat after a few false starts. I buckled him in, walked around the taxi, and eased myself behind the wheel. Since they drove on the left side of the road in India—à la England—the manual transmission shifter was on my left instead of my right. Not only would I need to remember which side of the road to drive on, I'd need to train my left hand to operate the gear shift. After adjusting the mirrors, playing with the seat, and fidgeting more than I needed to in a futile effort to postpone my inaugural Indian driving experience, I started the engine and tried to engage the first gear. No matter how I played with the clutch and the black plastic shifter, the transmission would not cooperate. Instead, it made horrible grinding noises, which might've been worth enduring if they'd awakened Burt, but they didn't.

After several frustrating minutes, I sat back in the beige vinyl seat and let out a sigh. My foot was still on the clutch. Along with the sigh, without willing it, I released energy to the car, and the gears meshed without protest. The car was in first now, and it surged forward. I jammed on the brake and put the car back in neutral, avoiding a collision with a slim fencepost.

Apparently, my spiritual superpowers worked on machinery—or at least cars. For some reason, this latest mind-bending weirdness was among the most unsettling so far. How could esoteric energy make gears mesh? Wasn't the energy operating on a nonphysical level? What else might happen without any conscious participation from me?

The next time I tried to put the taxi in first gear, there was no problem at all. I cautiously tooled back to the main road and waited several minutes for a reasonable-by-US-standards gap in the traffic. Then I pulled out and accelerated through the three gears, getting up to speed very gradually in the underpowered vehicle—to the annoyance of everyone behind me.

Driving was even more terrifying than I'd imagined. My Indian counterparts pulled out to pass one another, and then played chicken with oncoming traffic. Most of the time, they veered away at the last possible instant—back into their lane, onto the shoulder, or even off the road entirely. Sometimes cars that had just been leapfrogged passed the cars that had passed them. Other times, it seemed certain that two stubborn chicken participants—vehicles simultaneously passing from each direction—were doomed to die in head-on collisions. But somehow they all managed to stay alive and torment me further. Perhaps there was a sort of traffic-based Darwinism in effect—the less adept practitioners had died off over the years.

Fortunately, it was only a forty-five-minute ride to Ahmednagar's city limits. I just barely recognized the sign I was watching for. It was surrounded by bilingual and trilingual billboards advertising restaurants, hotels, and a "world-class destination grog shop," whatever that was.

I turned right at the designated traffic light onto a busy city street. Now I saw many more bicycles, mopeds, and motorized tricycles than cars. All of these played chicken, too. Why would an elderly woman on a bicycle pit herself against a truck?

Within a couple of blocks, I spied an old man in a blue turban sitting cross-legged by the side of the road. I was watching for one, based on Marco's message. His long white beard was wispy on the ends, and he wore clean black slacks and a light-brown, short-sleeved shirt. His back was up against a low, pale-pink stucco wall, which marked the boundary of a small park. This patch of green was almost completely covered with unsupervised young boys. They careened in waves, knocking each other down, wrestling, and generally raising hell.

Miraculously, I found a parking spot just past this scene, pulled into it, and shut off the engine. I felt a great sense of relief.

I checked on Burt. When I leaned in and drew close, his eyes fluttered. When I touched his shoulder, they opened. His pupils were dilated, and he couldn't seem to focus on me. I watched him try to move, but he couldn't do that either. None of this seemed to alarm him.

"Everything's fine," I told him, hoping this was true. "You just rest."

He closed his eyes again, and his body went slack. He was back asleep—or whatever he'd been doing.

As I approached the elderly man we'd passed up the street, he stared at me with eyes so dark they were nearly black. Despite his white beard, his eyebrows were gray, and the few stray tendrils of hair that escaped his dark blue turban were even blacker than his eyes. His skin was dark leather, with a multitude of deep grooves—they were more pronounced than wrinkles. His nose dominated his face. It was slender and straight, but it ran from above his bushy eyebrows all the way down to his low-slung thin lips.

His gaze was intense. I got the sense that he'd known I was coming—that he knew who I was. The kids behind him in the park continued their wild play. It was distracting.

"Good day," the man said in a crisp high-pitched voice as I drew closer. His English was very English.

I couldn't sense his energy at all, which was strange. "Hello," I said, squatting down beside him.

"Are you Marco's boy?" he asked, swiveling to face me. "You have his energy."

"I guess I am," I said. "You can sense people's energy? I usually can, but you don't seem to have any.

How is that?"

"That's an impertinent question," he replied sharply. "I shall answer the first part as a courtesy, but you are certainly not entitled to know me—to know my energy. Who do you think you are?"

"I'm sorry," I said. "I'm new. I don't know anything." I converted my squatting to sitting. About three feet of distance, fifty years, and a radically different culture separated us.

"I can see that. Here's the answer to your first question. I see auras. These are the visual aspect of personal energy."

"Oh, I see. Thank you. My name is Sid Menk."

He looked up and to the right briefly. "No, it isn't," he said. "My name is Faroud."

"What do you mean?" I asked. "I'm not Sid?"

"No." He peered at me with his liquid, dark eyes. He could've been x-raying me. I could feel his gaze inside me, scanning me. "You'll find out," he said. "It's better to be surprised. Life needs to sneak up on you like a tiger in a river."

"I thought cats hated water," I said.

"Bengali tigers are excellent swimmers," he told me. "This is well known."

"Oh," I said.

A small rock hit me on the back of my shoulder. I pivoted, and a gaggle of boys laughed and pointed at me. All of them were very dark-skinned, more so than anyone I'd seen in India so far. In fact, they were darker than almost any African-Americans I'd ever met. They wore raggedy khaki shorts and various T-shirts with American slogans on them. I saw one that read "Just Do It," and another one proclaimed "Elvis Is Still The

King" in silver glitter. I decided to ignore them.

"I'm supposed to ask you for directions," I told Faroud.

"To anywhere in particular?" His scowl and his glare competed for preeminence.

"I'm sorry. To Meher Baba's pilgrim center—the one near his tomb."

"Ah. Of course. Marco is there. And others," he said. He looked up and away again for a moment. "It will be very interesting for you," he continued. "Difficult, but interesting. Perhaps you would like a blessing?"

"Sure. But first, who are you?"

"I have told you all you need to know in words. My name is Faroud. I am this man you see before you." His gaze was fierce. I got the sense that it always was, whether I was there to annoy him or not.

He ducked, and a pebble whizzed through the space his head had just occupied. He adjusted his blue turban as he sat back up. His facial expression never changed.

"Have they ever managed to hit you?" I asked, turning to watch several boys run away.

"Not so far." He smiled for the first time, revealing brown, broken teeth. "Close your eyes," Faroud said.

I did. He touched me on the forehead—on my third eye—and an incredibly bright white light burst into view. There could be no purer shade of white. I couldn't imagine anything brighter, either. *Would I be blinded by it, even with my eyes closed?*

The experience continued for some time—I had no idea for how long. Eventually, I realized Faroud wasn't sending me the light as some sort of transmission.

Faroud *was* the light. He was revealing himself to me in his own way. The blessing he'd offered was the opportunity to be with his essence—to commune with it, to know it firsthand. The light lived in a Faroud suit.

Then the phenomenon stopped as suddenly as it had begun. I opened my eyes, and the world was more detailed now. The difference was subtle, but noticeable. Who knows what else he had done? I also felt fully rested, as though I'd had a full night's sleep.

"You decided to let me know who you are, after all," I said. "Thank you."

"You're welcome. By the way, small boys have taken all the things out of your pockets," he told me.

"What? Why didn't you stop them?"

"I am not a policeman." He gazed at me evenly, seemingly indifferent to my concern. "Do you want directions or not?" he asked sharply.

I was surprised by his tone. And very annoyed. I understood why he found me impertinent and ignorant at first. But this was different. I was supposed to not care that I'd just been robbed? Who wouldn't care?

"It was a new phone," I said. "A very expensive phone."

"Oh, what good fortune for the boys!" Faroud said, clapping his weathered hands together. "They'll be so happy when they find out how much money they can get."

"Do you know them? Can we get my stuff back?" I asked. I turned and studied the crowd of boys in the park. They ignored me.

"Why are you obsessed by this turn of events?" Faroud asked. "Your things are elsewhere now. Life goes on."

I sighed an ungracious, theatrical sigh. "Fine. I'd love directions, please."

He rattled off a litany of distances and turns based on obscure landmarks. The Chennai Tower? The Aghani mill? The Temple of Satisfactions? I had no hope of following Faroud's directions.

"I can't remember all that," I said.

"You should have written it down," he said. He didn't care at all.

"Maybe you could repeat it more slowly," I suggested. *What will I do if this guy wouldn't help me?*

"No." He smiled again. His ruined teeth were painful to look at.

I stood up and considered my options, patting the travel pouch that was hanging around my neck under my shirt. At least I still had my passport and the credit card I'd managed to hang onto throughout my ordeal. Perhaps I could simply ask someone else how to get to Baba's. After all, how many saints' tombs could there be in Ahmednagar?

"The man in your taxi is coming," Faroud said.

I turned. Burt lurched toward us, so I hurried over and grabbed his arm. "Are you all right?" I asked.

"Oh yes. Very well. Very, very well." He eyed Faroud from several paces away. "Who is this man?" he asked.

"I have no idea, really," I said.

"I am Faroud," Faroud said.

"Namaste," Burt said, shuffling forward and bowing.

"Namaste," the older man returned. "You don't need a blessing today," he added.

"No," Burt agreed.

"Go now," Faroud said.

"Okay."

The old man turned away from us and tilted his face to the clear sky. He closed his eyes and furrowed his brow. It was as if he were tuning into a metaphysical radio station that we couldn't hear.

"I'll drive," Burt said, setting out very deliberately toward the cab. "I'm fine. I know the way."

He was unsteady, but I let him walk on his own as an audition for his return to his role as driver. By the time we'd traversed the half a block to the taxi, his motor skills had markedly improved.

I handed him the keys. All in all, an impaired professional Indian driver was bound to be a safer bet in city driving than I'd be.

"Promise me you'll let me know if you have trouble driving," I said.

"No. I will make no such promise. You may be my spiritual better. You may send energy. You may know everything, and you may be right about everything. I don't know. But you're not my boss. I will do as I choose. If you don't like it, you can get out of my taxi and walk."

He was back, all right. Good old Burt.

****

He maneuvered us through a colorful urban landscape and then down a winding rural road. Chris and Marco stood waiting for us in the pilgrim center's dirt parking lot. The pitted driveway we'd navigated to get there wound through well-tended grounds and gave us a view of the main building, which was a low brick structure with a wraparound, porticoed porch. From the front, it appeared to be about the size of an elementary school in a small town. The energy of the place was strong but not intrusive.

"Did you have a nice adventure?" Marco asked when I'd climbed out of the passenger seat. Burt remained behind the wheel.

"Nice? Was my 'adventure' nice? Sure, let's call it nice," I answered.

He wore one of Chris's less loud Hawaiian shirts. I recognized it—koi swimming in a cloud-strewn blue sky. He also wore a wide-brimmed straw gardener's hat—at least the gardeners in Santa Cruz wore them—and a pair of dark, metal-framed sunglasses. He needed a shave. I was struck by how much he looked like a perfect cross between an Italian and a South American.

"I'm incognito," he said, noticing my attention. He reached out and hugged me, and his energy merged with mine. Chris stood to the side and waited, wearing a plain white T-shirt and baggy, olive-green cargo shorts. Lucy was nowhere to be seen.

Marco's energy was much stronger than mine, of course, but it felt like my own otherwise, which was reassuring. I absorbed it easily and then stepped over to Chris and hugged him, too. I'd forgotten how hard it was to get my arms around him. If anything, he'd gained weight since arriving in New Zealand.

"Hiya, bro," he said. "I'm incognito, too. We're blending."

His black hair was a crinkled mess, and his bushy beard was listing to starboard—no, make that port. His dark skin gleamed from the layer of sweat we all wore. It was probably in the mid-nineties and very humid.

Chris's energy was subtle—I had to hunt for it. It was like a low-pitched, throbby V-8 motor at idle in a garage. It seemed capable of producing power, but only if he figured out how to get the garage door open, put it in gear, and let it loose. He might need the equivalent of a *chi* gas station, too.

"Whoa," Chris said after we'd held each other for a moment. "You're like Marco Junior now, huh? You're vibrating big-time."

"I guess."

"What number am I thinking of?" he asked. He looked upward as though he were having trouble coming up with one.

"How would I know?"

"Six hundred eighty-five," Marco said.

"Long live the King!" Chris proclaimed. "Now let's try Baltic folk songs of the 1950s for $400."

I laughed, let go of him, and stepped back. "I've missed you," I said.

"Of course," he replied. "What's not to miss?"

"Where's Sam?" I asked Marco. "Chris said she was okay. Is she?"

"She's been delayed, but she's fine." He spoke more slowly than I remembered, or maybe he was just tired.

I studied his face and reassured myself that Marco's word on this was sufficient. "And Lucy?"

"She's around here somewhere," Chris said. "Unless villagers have eaten her or sacrificed her to some volcano god."

"I don't think they have volcanoes in India," I said.

"That's because of all the terrific sacrifices people make here. It's the unsuccessful sacrifices that create places with all that lava like Hawaii. Those gods are totally unappeased. They don't want those pigs and goats and hula hoops they get. They want beagles and bassets and corgis."

Marco watched us, a wry smile on his face.

"How did you manage to fly Lucy into the country, anyway?" I asked the older man. "Don't they have regulations against pets because of diseases?"

"Talk about a maestro," Chris answered. "This man could corrupt the Pope. He just bribed everybody. Everywhere. He's slick."

I looked at Marco. He shrugged. "Let's get out of the sun," he suggested.

Burt stumbled out of the taxi at that point. I don't know what he'd been doing in there. Maybe Marco had been holding him in his seat energetically. Maybe he was still dazed. He'd driven just fine, but his walking had devolved—he was shambling again.

"Who are these people?" he asked me.

I introduced everyone.

"I need to go lie down," Burt said. He certainly did. He was swaying and wobbling.

"Perhaps Chris can show you where you can rest," Marco's said. "Chris?"

"Hey," Chris said. "You're not the boss of me." That sounded familiar. Perhaps Chris and Burt would get along just fine.

Marco gazed at him impassively. It was a gentler version of what I'd just experienced with Faroud.

"But maybe you need some time alone with Sid," Chris said to him.

Marco continued to look at him.

"And maybe you're kind of the boss of me," Chris said. He turned to the Indian man. "Come on, Burt. I'll show you where the men's dorm is. You can check in later if you want to stay, but for now there's a spare bed next to mine."

Burt nodded, and they left. Marco pointed to a bench back behind him under an unfamiliar variety of shade tree. It was to the right of the main entrance, away from several groups of people on the long, wide porch. As we walked over to it, I asked him if Chris was driving him crazy.

"Not at all. Sit."

I did. It was much cooler under the tree, and the air was redolent with floral aromas, although I didn't actually see any flowers. The bench itself was very buzzy. Marco noticed me noticing this.

"There are energy hot spots all around the property. That's why we're sitting here. This bench is built out of wood that was salvaged from an outhouse that Meher Baba used for decades."

"Really? It's butt energy?"

"Ridiculous, isn't it?" Marco said.

"But it's real? All this energy stuff is for real?"

"Of course not. None of it's real, Sid. Not even the energy. But energy—consciousness—precedes form. There's a relationship between the two unreal realms— one seems to come first. It's actually an unreal sequence of unreal events, though. There are no gradations of non-reality."

"I think I'll just try to forget I know the word 'real,' " I said.

"That might be more helpful than my explanations, eh?"

"Exactly."

I sat quietly then, content to be with him on the bench. *Why had I ever doubted him so thoroughly?*

When I was with Marco, everything was just fine. When I wasn't with him, though, I only had the concept of Marco to hang onto. This was so outlandish, I was vulnerable to the sort of deception that Raj and Jal had mounted.

A complicating factor was that he wasn't quite likable in the ordinary sense of the word. If he'd been a coworker or neighbor, I'd have described him as arrogant and controlling. I'd seen him demonstrate social graces out in the world, but he didn't hesitate to lie or be rude to me as he saw fit.

Somehow, that was all beside the point when I was with him. The energy that radiated from him rendered the questionable behavior meaningless. Would you care if Jesus' jokes weren't funny? What if Buddha's feet smelled bad? Maybe this was why people kept electing flawed politicians. A given candidate's charisma might convince voters to put aside the messy details of his personhood.

"Tell me who you met after I called New Zealand customs about your luggage," Marco said.

"That was you?" I was astonished.

"Yes."

"Why?"

"To set in motion what needed to happen next," Marco said. "Energetically, I mean. Just because none of it's real, doesn't mean it can't be kickstarted into action."

"You orchestrated all that? You know Lannie?"

"No. All I did was call customs. The universe is self-regulating, and I just gave it its chance to assert itself. That's all."

My face flushed and my fists clenched—who the

hell did he think he was?—followed by a strong rush of gratitude. "Thank you for Lannie," I said.

"I take it he wasn't a government official at the airport," Marco said. "Was Lannie the energy being I sensed somewhere near Auckland?"

"She is. Yes. What do you mean 'energy being'?"

"I'll explain later." He scratched himself on the neck, the first time I'd seen him scratch, sneeze, or burp. "Basically, it's a classification—a rank—in the spiritual hierarchy," he continued. "I need you to tell me about her now. I couldn't approach her myself—our energies are not compatible, for reasons that I won't go into. But I knew you'd find your way to whoever it was if I kept you at the airport. I'll bet she was superficially unremarkable, wasn't she?"

"Yes." It was my turn to scratch. A tiny flying insect circled my head and periodically settled onto one of us.

"Her energy is extraordinary, though, isn't it?" Marco said. "I could feel it all the way from the Bay of Islands." He seemed excited, or some other related emotion I'd never seen him display before.

"Yes. But why would I end up meeting her just because I'd been detained by customs? I don't get that. I get the everything's-connected-and-what-goes-around-comes-around deal. I understand how homeostasis works, too. So I think I generally know what you mean by self-regulation, but why would any of that add up to meeting Lannie?"

"Because the universe needed you to. The more important something is, the more it's governed by meaningful coincidences."

I shook my head. "But suppose I escaped the

airport ten minutes later?"

"You didn't." He gave me the same look he'd given Chris.

"I could've," I said.

He just watched me and smiled.

"Her husband could have kicked me out of his car for bleeding," I added. "Or Vlad could've chased me down outside his office."

Marco waited.

"Or I could have been stymied by the airport fence. I almost was."

"It happened the way it happened," he said. "There are no accidents. You had to find a way over the fence, so you did."

"Okay, fine." I played with my fingers for a moment, tangling and then untangling them.

We sat quietly. Several groups of pilgrims strolled by. Three sturdy-looking young women spoke German to one another and waved merrily to Marco. A couple with two very young children argued in loud Texas accents. And a very short, elderly Indian man walked by holding a trumpet, of all things.

"Perhaps you have questions," Marco said. "Is there anything I can help you with?"

"As a matter of fact, I'd appreciate the opportunity," I said. "I've been stockpiling questions for days."

"Go right ahead." He shifted on the bench and faced me.

A smile began to form on my face, until I remembered how these conversations tended to go. I'd probably end up more ignorant and confused than ever.

"Can you tell me more about how the world might

end if we don't do something heroic? Why do we need to get people to be more conscious?" I asked. "I know I probably didn't have the background to understand before, but now…"

"As I alluded to earlier, illusion—the world as you know it—is a construct that mass consciousness—energy—has created, and now maintains. Very few people need to actively—consciously—participate in maintaining full-scale illusion. That's because almost everyone helps when they're asleep. Have you ever wondered why our brain activity increases instead of subsiding while we sleep?"

"I've read theories," I said. "But none of them are particularly compelling."

"We all participate on an unconscious level at night. We must, or there would be no world."

"And we need the world? We need illusion?" I asked.

"It's plan A—the most elegant vehicle for consciousness to come to know itself. But no. We don't need any particular format or circumstance for the job to get done. On the other hand, it might take a few billion years get something equivalent up and running. And personally, I like it here."

"Sure. So what's the problem? I'm with you so far, but I don't see a problem." I waved the bug away.

"There's an epidemic coming. A virus is loose in sub-Saharan Africa, and there will not be a vaccine."

"So?"

"It's a sleep disorder. The central nervous system can't shut down—rest—the conscious mind once the virus takes over."

"Aha," I said.

"So soon the physical realm will need to be supported by a greater proportion of awakened people to take up the slack from all the non-sleepers—those infected by the virus."

"And very few of us are particularly awake at this point?"

He nodded. "That's by design. Our brain chemistry is configured to block awareness. We're all capable of perceiving and sensing far more than our brains can handle without becoming overloaded. That's why hallucinogenics like LSD are so powerful. They're much more efficient neurotransmitters than the ones we produce ourselves, so they override our built-in filters."

I was happy with this explanation. It was more scientific than usual; it reminded me of the answers that Marco had given Chris.

"Also," Marco continued, "the pieces on a Monopoly board need to remain unaware that they're not a real dog or a real top hat. Otherwise, they can't play their roles properly. The game is ruined if the participants transcend the premise—if they see behind the curtain. Full scale illusion is maintained by a consensus belief in the solidity of the physical world."

"So there needs to be a small percentage of people who are awake—consciously helping to administrate the deal—and a multitude of people who are clueless—lost in the illusion?"

Marco nodded again.

"So how many people will it take?" I asked. "How many need to come on board to keep things going?"

"We'll need to triple the number of conscious humans in a matter of months, or it will all fall apart." As usual, he said this with equanimity.

"What would that look like—if there's nothing here anymore?"

"I don't know. Let's not find out," Marco said.

Lucy ran up at that point and tried to jump into my lap, which was at least a foot higher than the world's most athletic beagle could ever hope to manage. I grabbed her and pulled her up, and she enthusiastically licked my face and wagged herself.

"I love you, too," I told her, and I had a feeling that she understood. She settled down after a while and lay on the bench beside me.

I decided to stop asking questions since the answer to the sole line of inquiry I'd pursued so far was proving to be so challenging. Sleeping wasn't sleeping. An insomnia epidemic was going to wipe out the physical world unless more people became...what? Enlightened?

And how does one go about awakening people on a deadline? I could see how Bhante and his organization could provide us with a platform on a grander scale than we could manage on our own. And obviously I knew how powerful the energy that Marco and I embodied was. *But could it be as simple as that? Will I need to develop a new skill set to persuade skeptical people to believe all the counterintuitive metaphysical teachings that I've been force-fed lately?*

Some time passed while I considered all this. Then I was gradually enticed back into the moment by the combination of an uncomfortably buzzy posterior and an insistent beagle. Lucy had grown bored and was shoving her nose into my hand.

"That's it? No more questions?" Marco finally asked.

"That's it for now," I told him. "I can only assimilate so much in one sitting. Especially if I'm sitting here. Would you mind if we moved?" I asked.

"Let's head up the hill to the tomb," he suggested. "I think it's time."

Chapter Nineteen

I wasn't sure what that meant, but when he rose and began striding toward the driveway, Lucy and I followed. By the time we'd passed the parked taxi and retraced the way up the driveway, she and I had caught up. We walked three abreast to the road. I could see the pilgrim center's grounds in more detail as we marched around several curves.

The flat lawn areas were a bit raggedy, as though the type of grass they were trying to grow wasn't quite suited to the central Indian climate. The earth itself looked very dry, except for a few small puddles in low spots. I got the impression it rained regularly, but most of the ground couldn't hold the water. Stand-alone mature trees bordered various group plantings—mostly flowerbeds and stalky bushes. We walked by one smaller tree that sported purple pinwheel flowers. They smelled like shampoo.

There were birds everywhere. Each tree was full of them, and others roamed the lawn, jabbing their beaks at bugs and worms. I saw several that resembled species I knew—finches, canaries, and wrens. There were also two kinds of beefier black birds, but they weren't crows or ravens.

I could see a larger, more modern building just beyond the pilgrim center. It seemed to share the property, so perhaps it was connected to Meher Baba too. A school? The equivalent of a church headquarters?

We crossed the well-worn asphalt and then stepped across a set of narrow-gauge railroad tracks. A hard-packed path just past them ran straight up a fairly steep hill, and we began climbing it. We strode side by side with Lucy in the middle. Her tongue hung out, dripping saliva, and she panted laboriously.

It must've been in the high nineties now, and the air was so humid, there was nowhere for perspiration to evaporate to. It lay on my arms and brow, turning sticky as more sweat oozed out from under it.

The hill was relatively bare, with scrubby bushes and patches of bare dirt scattered around. There were no birds here, but I saw several lizards scuttle away from our feet, and a brown snake sunned itself on a mini-mesa of limestone.

At one point, I glanced back. The full vista of Baba's property spread out below me. All sorts of small buildings sat behind and to the side of the two I'd seen before. A haphazard array, it looked as though it had developed over time with no particular plan. The land around the compound was being farmed.

After a short but very tiring hike, we reached the tomb. It was at the top of the hill, next to a crude stage and two small houses. There was a 360-degree view from the plateau, and I was struck again by how big the sky looked. I'd never thought of it as something that could embody size, but it seemed to extend itself farther to the sides than back home. And go up higher, as well.

I'd seen a photo of the tomb itself online, but nonetheless I expected something more impressive than what I found. I'd thought it would be constructed on a grander scale—either soaring upward or sprawling horizontally. I guess I was expecting a cross between a Buddhist temple and a miniature Taj Mahal.

The tomb actually resembled a falafel stand or a commercial kiln. It was the size of a large suburban bedroom—a gray stone building with a modest stucco dome affixed to the top. The proportions were skewed. Neither its height, width, roofline, nor window size harmonized with any of the other dimensions. It was an assemblage of spare parts—not quite ugly, but homely, perhaps. And it was unabashedly modest in every respect. I had to remind myself that I was in an impoverished part of the world and the tomb had not been built to inspire awe in someone like me.

Symbols of various religions were painted above the open front door. I recognized most of them. Baba seemed to be an inclusive sort of guy. Back then, this had probably been unusual.

The area radiated unfamiliar energy, but it was too complicated for me to sort through on the fly. It wasn't particularly intense at that point, which surprised me.

Low wooden bleachers—three rows high—sat just to the side of the tomb, surrounding a small brick courtyard covered by a freestanding tin roof. The courtyard was about eight paces across, and a middle-aged Indian man in a black suit, white shirt, and black tie sat on a stool in the middle of it. He faced a dozen Westerners who were scattered across several benches. The man didn't seem to be sweating at all. *How is this possible?*

The pilgrims were mostly white and European-looking, but one couple looked to be Malaysian or Indonesian.

"Come, come," the Indian man said to me in fast, accented English. "Sit. I've just begun the orientation session. Marco, you can take a seat and be patient." He glanced at Lucy, who was snuffling the open-toed sandals of a French-looking woman—small features, odd haircut, and an "I hate NYC" formfitting T-shirt. "Please keep your animal under control," he added.

Marco corralled Lucy, and the two of them ambled to the shade behind the courtyard.

I sat down next to the Malaysian/Indonesian couple and learned that I wasn't to chew gum or spit in the tomb. Women should wear "substantial undergarments" and "button up their other garments to their capacity." Men should be "ever-vigilant concerning the zipper on their pants." This was a holy place, and we should spare no effort to prepare ourselves to properly receive Baba's love.

By the time he was finished, I was wondering just what sort of loutish spiritual pilgrims Meher Baba was attracting these days. Also, I was curious to see if the Frenchwoman would be sent back to the center. In my estimation, her upper undergarment was woefully insubstantial.

Then we had to wait our turn to actually enter the tomb. It was so small on the inside, only a few people could fit around the crypt at any one time.

As soon as I passed through the doorway into the dim light of the tomb, I was hit by a tsunami of energy. I staggered back and might've fallen if Marco hadn't been standing right behind me. He placed his hands on my shoulders and said something, but I was already beyond words—beyond mind.

The energy was indescribable. I became lost in it. It

was both incredibly intense and very, very sweet—a personal love as well as a universal one. Perhaps it was Baba's essence—I don't know. It was by far the most blissful energy I'd ever felt. I was drunk on love. Stoned out of my mind.

I wasn't aware of any further experience, but apparently time passed. Eventually, I found myself sitting cross-legged in the small room. I was alone. My legs were killing me, so I stretched them out and massaged my sore muscles as I looked around.

I was at the foot of a concrete crypt. It was raised about three feet off the stone floor and bedecked with garlands of tropical flowers. Hundreds of brightly-colored blossoms produced an almost overwhelming wave of scent.

The interior walls were gray stone, and every inch of them was covered in amateurishly painted murals of Meher Baba. He was portrayed in a variety of settings—cradling a lamb in his arms, sitting on a wooden throne, walking through a meadow. They had all been painted by the same artist.

I now felt no esoteric energy at all—either from the tomb or from inside myself. I missed it. It was as though I'd been living in a symphony hall, enjoying the constant companionship of the music, and then I'd woken up deaf one day.

Eventually, I clambered to my feet and stretched in the empty tomb. Where were all the pilgrims? Was Marco out front waving them off? Was it dinnertime by now?

I wandered out of the building. Bhante stood waiting. Jason, Chris, and my two brothers—Raj and Jal—sat on bleacher seats behind him. The tomb keeper was gone. There was no sign of Marco or Lucy, either.

The older Sri Lankan stepped forward and hugged me. I could sense my heart send him something; it didn't feel like anything special, but there'd been a lot of inflation in that realm lately.

Bhante was jolted. I had to hold him up briefly before he was able to step back and stand on his own.

"Oh my goodness," he said. "Who are you? How could this be?"

"I've been through some transformative experiences lately," I told him.

"I can feel this. I did not know such a thing was possible," Bhante said. He looked stricken. Maybe it was humbling to realize that there were still things he didn't understand.

I shrugged. What did it matter? Here I was.

"Thank you for your blessing," he said. "Will you join us?"

"Sure."

Jason stood up and extended his hand as I moved forward. I shook it. A burst of energy shot out to him, and he fell back onto his seat, dazed. The bleacher shook, and the wooden bench made a cracking noise under him. It gave way a moment later, and he lodged in the vee of the tilted halves of the broken slat.

Obviously, the energy still resided in me and was available to others. *Why am I blocked from my internal experience of it?*

My brothers exchanged puzzled glances. This wasn't the Sid they knew.

I turned to the nearest one. "Raj?" I asked.

"I'm Tom," he said in an American accent.

"I'm Charles," the other one said in an Australian

one.

"Whatever," I said. I looked at Chris. "I assume everyone here has met my friend." I didn't know what name he was using since he'd impersonated Jackson at the Auckland airport.

"Yes," Bhante responded. "We have been chatting while we waited for you."

"I told them some of my best jokes," Chris said. "And then I had to explain them. This is a tough crowd."

"Are you here all week?" I asked.

"Yes. Don't forget to tip your waitress," he said.

Bhante watched us with a gentle smile. My brothers looked confused. Jason was still out of it in his wooden roost. I was surprised that no one had made an effort to rescue him, although it probably would have taken at least three strong men to pull him out.

I sat down next to Chris and faced the Kasriti Sanganika contingent.

"You're glowing," Chris whispered to me. "Don't be touching me too. Did you get bitten by a radioactive spider?"

"So what's the plan?" I asked Bhante. "What happens next?"

"First of all," the robe-clad older man said, "congratulations, Sid. Clearly, you are the one we have all been waiting for. Your current energy signature validates our earlier confidence in you."

"Thank you." I didn't much care what he thought, but I didn't need to be rude.

"We will introduce you to the world at the tooth festival," he added.

"The tooth festival?" Chris asked.

"In Kandy, Sri Lanka," Bhante told Chris. "It's a sacred event for Therevada Buddhists. Think of it. Buddha's tooth." He pivoted to face me. "Sid, perhaps you will be able to demonstrate your energy abilities during the relic parade. The world's eyes will be on us."

I had no idea if I could summon and release energy on a grand enough scale to impress serious Buddhists. Bhante was still studying me, awaiting a response, so I shrugged.

Bhante continued talking. "Or perhaps I'll simply vouch for you as Buddha's clone. I am well known in my homeland, although I have not been there for many years. My appearance alone will garner attention. The unveiling of Buddha's toe bone—the source of your birth—will ensure that your introduction to the Theravadan community will not pass unnoticed. Our irrefutable provenance all the way back to his son—this cannot be denied. Thus, our movement will be launched one way or another."

I nodded, but the idea that you could prove the origin of something that was 2500 years old sounded ridiculous to me.

"These are exciting times," the Sri Lankan added.

I nodded again. I don't think I was excited enough to suit Bhante. "That sounds good," I tried. He perked up a bit.

"Tom has been to film school," Bhante said.

"UCLA," Tom said. I felt like asking him to sing his alma mater or tell me who the quarterback was.

"So he'll videotape the proceedings and post them on YouTube and other sites," Bhante said.

"Great idea!" Chris said. "I can do the voiceover narration. I'm really good at faking sincerity and authenticity. And it might be fun if I used a Bugs Bunny voice."

Once again, Chris's sense of humor missed the mark with his target audience. I wished I could yell, "Cut!" and we could re-film Chris's takes.

"Would you be willing to entertain questions?" Bhante asked me.

"Sure," I said.

"What is the nature of your relationship with Jackson?" He leaned forward in anticipation.

I looked at Chris, who pointed to himself. He was still passing himself off as Jackson.

"We're like brothers," I told Bhante. "We're very close." I'm not sure why I settled on this characterization.

"How is this so?" Bhante asked. "Didn't you just meet?"

I shrugged again.

Bhante addressed another question to me. "Who is the older man who was with you in New Zealand? Is *that* Mr. Jackson?"

I pondered how to respond. I felt like confessing at this point, but I decided to just let things unfold.

Bhante leaned back and watched my face. "That's fine. I'm certainly not entitled to know anything you don't care to share."

"True dat," Chris said.

"But I think perhaps the other man is Marco—who also uses the name Jackson. Why do we need to deceive each other?" Bhante asked.

This pissed me off. Who the hell was he to talk about integrity? "That's a good question," I said with heat. "Tell me why you misrepresented my birth brothers as clones. That's clearly a much bigger lie."

"They *are* clones!" Jason bellowed. He started to rise from his broken bench slat, his fists clenched.

Bhante held his hand up to the giant Maori, and Jason calmed down. It was a bit like a dog trainer employing a hand signal to control a pit bull.

"Perhaps it's time to reveal our deception," Bhante said to me. "You're right. There are no clones. You and Jal and Raj are triplets. We believed you needed to think you were a physical copy of the Buddha or you wouldn't be willing to accept your calling. Our understanding was that if we went ahead and represented you as a world teacher to the media, you would be loath to cooperate unless you yourself had already accepted this as the truth. So we employed an elaborate ruse to convince you of your special status. There was no time to take a gradual approach to help you let go of your old ideas about yourself. The festival is almost upon us."

I frowned and worked to control my anger. "That doesn't compute. There's got to be more to it than that. Look at how elaborate all this has been. No one goes to this much trouble and spends this much money just to convince one person that something is so."

"They do if they're religious fanatics," Chris said. "Trust me, these people are. They think you're going to be the next Jesus. It's a whatever-it-takes-to-get-the-job-done deal, bro."

My eyes hadn't strayed from Bhante's. "And the raid on the cave?" I asked. "Did you lie about that as well?"

Bhante nodded. "Please forgive me if this was a misjudgment that has caused you suffering, Sid. We felt it was important to create a bonding experience. Working as a team on a dangerous task is an excellent method to achieve this."

"A ropes course," Chris said. "Without the ropes."

"We could've been killed," I pointed out.

Bhante nodded, conceding the point.

"Do you realize how traumatic these experiences have been?" I asked in a loud voice. I'm sure my anger was evident now. "You kidnapped me, for God's sake. And a bystander too. And you attacked the core of my personal identity. Forget the cliff. Do you have any idea how harrowing this shit is? *Do you*?" Now I was shouting.

Bhante leaned away from me and nodded. I didn't see any remorse on his face, but at least he wasn't trying to justify his behavior now.

I continued, with more heat than ever. "You launched a series of other painful events, as well. I was held at gunpoint, I almost drowned, and I was attacked by thugs several days later. All of this stemmed from your decision to use me for your organization's own ends—however noble or ignoble they might be. I think you've betrayed the Buddhist values that the title 'Bhante' stands for. I think you deserve no respect or cooperation whatsoever." I paused for breath and assessed Bhante's reaction.

He'd leaned back, and he held his face rigid except for his eyebrows, which must've been up at the top of their range when he froze. *Probably no one has spoken to him like this in a long time.*

"Nevertheless," I said a bit more calmly, "I *will* work with you—on my terms. But if there's any more deception or violence, I'm out. If Jason loses his temper again, I'm out. If 'Tom' and 'Charles' don't start acting like Raj and Jal—or whoever they really are—I'm out. If you piss me off with another smarmy, self-serving rationalization, I'm out. My cooperation is conditional. Do you understand?"

"Yes," Bhante said in a small voice, looking over my shoulder into space.

We sat there in pause mode for a while. I think I'd released energy as well as words, but I still wasn't directly experiencing anything in that realm. The absence of energy phenomenon was like a deep ache.

"Who's your boss?" Chris finally asked Bhante. "Who really runs the show?"

"I cannot say," Bhante replied to me, as if I'd asked. "I have taken a sacred vow."

I cocked an eyebrow, and he flinched as though I'd raised a fist.

"I agree to the end of deception," he said hurriedly, "but I cannot tell you everything you would like to know. This would represent a betrayal that would serve none of us."

"What's your interest in RGP?" I asked.

"Again, it would not be wise to reveal this. Let's just say that Samavati was swept up in events."

I stood up. "Let's just say that you're screwing around again. This is your last warning. Shall I walk away right now?"

"Point taken," Bhante said. "I actually don't know the answer to your question. We may or may not have an interest in Samavati and RGP."

I turned and began to walk away.

"Wait! Wait!" Bhante called. "It's true. I'm just accustomed to…well, sounding wise. It's hard for me to say, 'I don't know.' But in this case, I truly don't."

I could sense that he was telling the truth now. I strode back and sat down.

"So let's talk about logistics," I said. "Are you providing transportation and housing for myself and my contingent—to Sri Lanka, I mean?"

"We get huffy when he calls us his entourage," Chris said.

"Are we including the real Marco as well?" Bhante asked.

"I don't know," I said. "I think so. And maybe a nice beagle."

"A nice one?" Jason asked. His voice was uncharacteristically gentle.

"Let me see what I can do," Bhante said. "We'll need to leave in three days' time in any case."

"All right," I said. "Now I think I need a bathroom. Right away. Is there an Indian version of Montezuma's Revenge?" I asked.

"Oh yes. We call it Delhi Belly," Raj/Tom answered. "You haven't been drinking beverages with ice cubes in them, have you? People forget about that."

"As a matter of fact, I have."

He pointed to a nearby building. I sprinted to the bathroom and almost made it in time.

Chapter Twenty

I became very familiar with the—thank God—Western-style toilets at the pilgrim center. The next morning, while other visitors toured the Baba-significant sites in the area—his home across town, his favorite meditation spot, the Meher Baba Trust library in the city—I lay on my cot, visited the bathroom, and made minor forays around the grounds.

I didn't feel as deathly ill as when I'd suffered food poisoning a few years earlier, but whatever the bacteria were up to was a lot worse than ordinary diarrhea. When Marco returned from wherever he had been, he told me he could cure me, but that instead I needed to crap out toxins and release non-spiritual energy. I'd be much better off after I'd gone through it, he said. Apparently, my physical system was undergoing an updating to become better able to house and support the new energy. Intestines 2.0—the sequel.

Anyway, Marco disappeared after telling me that. Chris reported he'd taken a taxi to run errands in the city, but neither of us knew exactly what that meant.

Bhante and his people took off shortly after our meeting, precluding my getting to know my brothers for who they really were. I'd been looking forward to that. Raj—who said he really was named Raj—said that he'd email Chris our trip itinerary to Kandy once he'd made the arrangements from the Sri Lankan end. Jal—

who *was* Jal—shook my hand and told me that I was a trouper and a good sport. Jason apologized for his latest outburst before he left with the others. It was obvious that his energy had shifted in response to what I'd sent when we shook hands.

I didn't see Burt, but I heard he'd decided to stay at the center for a while. He was reputed to be very grateful for my energetic help.

The men's dorm, a long, narrow room with two rows of mosquito-netted cots, was basic, but given that we were paying the equivalent of eighteen dollars a night, I could hardly complain. A row of small, high windows on one wall faced a series of black and white photos of Baba on the opposite wall. He'd sported various looks through the years—he'd been fairly dashing in the 1930s, for example.

There were a few simple pieces of wooden furniture, most notably a foot locker at the foot of each bed. The lighting was adequate. The temperature? Very hot.

That afternoon, I was able to sit on a bench in the square courtyard in the middle of the center and carry on a conversation with Chris. It was a well-tended garden area, with brick walkways, several small shade trees, and a pergola covered with passionflower vines. We sat under it, but it was still hot enough that most everyone else chose to lounge on the big porch in front of the building or sack out in their dorm rooms.

"So how are you doing?" I asked Chris after I'd filled him in on my recent adventures. "Is all this okay with you?"

"Sure. I'm flexible. I miss Karma, though."

"Do you think she'd like it here?" I hadn't thought

about Chris's dog for quite a while.

"Naw. It's too hot here." He shook his big head, flicking sweat onto my cheek.

"What do you make of Marco, Chris?" I asked.

"I dunno. He's got all these powers and he's kind of a fun guy, but there's something off about him."

"What do you mean?"

"Well, I'm in no position to judge him. Don't get me wrong. But sometimes I get this vibe that the whole thing's a performance—a way he's decided to act—for whatever reason somebody like Marco does things. I mean, I'm grateful for how he's helped me—between answering questions and sending me energy, I'm certainly way cooler now—but I'm still wondering how it's all going to turn out."

"Me too," I said. I adjusted my position to get the glare from a window out of my face. It was an effort.

"I don't mean in terms of what'll happen overall," Chris clarified. "I mean in terms of who Marco turns out to be—what he'll do. Most people, I know what to expect. I trust them, or I don't. I can count on them, or I can't. I guess I'm operating strictly from a working hypothesis with Marco. There's enough circumstantial evidence to assume he's the real deal, so I keep going with that. But there's no absolute proof, and maybe there can't be. I dunno. The jury's still out. And he hasn't really told me what my role is supposed to be. Why drag me all the way here?" He paused and looked me in the eye. "What about you?"

"As things have unfolded, I've had to go back and forth a few times about Marco," I said. "Lately," I continued, "I feel confident Marco is a good guy. In my case, he's been orchestrating all kinds of wonderful, heart-opening experiences. How can I look *that* gift horse in the mouth? And without Marco, there would be no Lannie or Faroud or all the rest. Basically, I'd still be a schmo therapist thinking that spiritual energy was a New-Age conceit."

What little of my energy was left ebbed away as I spoke. I was groggy, and I could barely focus my vision. I needed to get back in bed; Chris walked me back, and I fell asleep on my bed in about two seconds.

I woke up to find Sam standing beside my cot. "You're here!" I croaked. "You're really okay."

Before she could reply, a tall male wearing a doctor's white coat stepped in front of her, nodded to me curtly, and turned his back to speak to Sam and Marco. In his late fifties, he looked a bit like an Indian Richard Gere—if Richard Gere had just been told that his dog had died. His face seemed to be set in a permanently mournful expression.

"Where is the record of Mr. Menk's vaccinations?"

I resented his intrusion into our reunion, but I was too weak to protest, having expended all my available energy on my first words.

"We didn't get any," Sam told him. She stepped to the side and beamed at me. My heart lightened as though I'd shed some encrusted casing.

Sam wore a plain white T-shirt, khaki shorts, and flip-flops. She'd tied her hair back into a ponytail, and without framing, her bone structure stood out. I loved her high cheekbones. I loved the way her face gleamed with an inner light. My freed heart throbbed with love, almost painfully.

"Why didn't you get vaccinations?" the doctor asked. "This is very foolish. We have cholera, yellow fever, typhoid. And for malaria, all you need are inexpensive pills. Why wouldn't you do these simple things?"

Sam's kind, loving expression didn't change. "Our travel agent didn't mention it, and we never planned to be overseas, anyway."

"This is confusing nonsense," the doctor said. He turned to Marco. "What do you have to say?"

"I think we need to focus on the here and now," Marco said, "not what wasn't done in the past. Can you help him?"

"Oh, I very much doubt it."

"Why not?" I asked, more loudly than I intended to.

"Ah, good," the doctor said, pivoting to face me. "You're gathering strength. My name is Dr. Kadam. I'm the Trust physician."

"Why can't you help me? Do I have one of those horrible diseases? Am I going to die?"

I felt feverish, and the turn the conversation had taken catalyzed all sorts of emotions that competed with love. One second, my gut clenched in fear. Then angry energy shot up from my chest into my head. Then I loved everybody.

"I can't help you," the doctor said, "because you aren't ill—you don't have any of those diseases. But you should've gotten your shots. I must insist on administering them as soon as you are well enough to tolerate them."

"So it's kundalini?" Marco asked.

"Yes," the doctor replied. "The sudden release of kundalini energy plays havoc on the G.I. tract. We see this here frequently. Baba's tomb awakens the serpent that lies asleep at the base of the spine. Then it travels upward, and we have this. The diarrhea and fever usually last a day or two, and then things calm down."

"So I'm okay?" I asked.

"Tip-top," Dr. Kadam said. "It's just too much for your system at first. But it's a blessing—Baba's blessing."

"Is there anything we can do to help him suffer less?" Sam asked.

The doctor clasped his hands together and placed them in front of his chest. Then he just stood there facing her. He closed his eyes and rocked back and forth for a few seconds.

"I think you know what to do, don't you?" he said. "Although you have masked yourself, your kundalini was activated a long time ago, wasn't it?"

Sam nodded.

"Why don't we leave you two?" he said, looking at Marco. Then he gestured toward the door, and the two men left.

"How are you?" I asked Sam. She gazed down at me, tears in her eyes, and my heart opened even more to her.

"Shh," she murmured, moving closer and placing a hand on my abdomen.

"Okay," I said.

Sam gently moved her hand around and then settled on a particularly sore spot just below my navel. She closed her eyes, and a moment later, cool waves of something flowed through me, soothing and relaxing me. Then I slept again.

The next time I woke up, Chris was there. He was back to wearing a hideous shirt. This one was light yellow with multicolored birds on it. Most of them looked like they were having a hard day.

The travel alarm clock on my bedside table said it was eight in the evening—I'd been asleep for several more hours. I felt much better.

"Hey, Chris," I said. "I think my fever's gone."

"Great."

"But can you help me to the bathroom?"

"Sure."

"Hurry!" I called a second later.

I endured yet another twenty-minute session of gut-emptying torture, but then I felt even better.

Chris and I sat on either end of my cot, and he said, "Hey, I heard Sam healed you or something. Is that true?"

"I think so," I said. "I didn't know she had any energy tricks up her sleeve. I may have been underestimating her in that department."

"Maybe she's just not a big braggy show-off like some nouveau superhero types I could name. What's your special ability again? Crapping?"

"No. Vomiting," I said. "Crapping is just a sideline. I moonlight as Crapman when Vomitman's on vacation."

Chris laughed. "So anyway, welcome back," he said. "Fever Sid was useless. I couldn't understand half of what he was saying. But *this* guy can keep up with me and even give it back a little. I'm digging it, bro."

"Thanks. But let me ask you this, Chris. Do you know much about kundalini?"

"I do now. I've been researching it online. The good news is I concur with the doctor, although he's kind of a jerk. Your symptoms are classic kundalini, and it's a real thing, but the bad news is I think he's full of shit when he says it'll all be over in a day or two. There are people who have problems their whole lives from a sudden onset of kundalini energy."

"Maybe the Baba-generated version is more benign than the online version," I said, rocking back and forth. It felt soothing.

"Maybe. I hope so." He looked doubtful.

"Have you spent time in the tomb?" I asked.

"Yeah, but I can't feel much of anything happening in there. I try to go in when this Swiss girl who wears these baggy shorts is meditating. She sits cross-legged, she closes her eyes, and she doesn't wear any underwear. I've decided to go after a different kind of peek experience than the other seekers—one that's spelled with two *E*s."

It took me a moment to get this, and he saw that on my face. "Never mind," he said. "You look tired. Are you ready to go to sleep for the night? Do you want some rice or something?"

"God, no. More water," I said. "And then more sleep. Thanks."

"No worries, mate," he said in a terrible New Zealand accent.

Chapter Twenty-One

I felt substantially improved in the morning, having slept the whole night through, despite a nearby pilgrim's merciless snoring. A water shortage dictated that we could only shower every three days, so I used my shower credit and cleaned up. It felt great to shave, too.

I still couldn't feel any spiritual energy. *Perhaps the tomb knew I'd be overwhelmed by whatever it had done—whatever is currently going on inside me.* I noticed my thoughts—"perhaps the tomb knew." Really?

My intestines settled as I walked to the dining hall. Almost everyone I passed greeted me by name and asked solicitous questions. By the time I arrived, I almost felt normal. I was shaky, certainly, and ill-equipped to handle more stress. But I was in the ballpark of low-end normal—as if I were hungover.

The dining hall was bigger than it needed to be, with an altar just inside the entrance. Yet another photo of Baba sat on it, surrounded by large-petaled, red flowers I didn't recognize. It was old Baba this time—shortly before his death. His eyes seemed to see exactly who I was and love me anyway. How could a photograph love someone? Did Baba look at people through the eyes in his portraits—from Baba heaven?

It smelled wonderful in there, which I took as a

sign that I might be ready to eat again. I smelled eggs and a multitude of spices. I also caught a whiff of fruit or fruit juice. Mango? Guava? Something tropical.

The walls of the rectangular room were whitewashed and bare. The floor was smooth concrete that had been painted light brown. The simple wooden tables and chairs were arrayed in long rows and looked sturdy, but also uncomfortable. It was well-lit, with surprisingly modern track lighting suspended from the high ceiling, and a row of clerestory windows.

The spartan room looked even more so because it was relatively empty. There were only ten minutes left before the volunteer staff shut down the buffet; most pilgrims had already come and gone.

I spied Marco sitting by himself in the back corner, near the array of tin trays that constituted the modest buffet. He wore a brown T-shirt and tan shorts, and he needed a shave. His muscular legs reminded me of a cyclist friend. He waved me over.

"Good morning," he said. "How are you feeling?"

"Much, much better. I think I can eat now."

"Great. Try the things that look like pancakes." He pointed at the remnants of his on the tin plate in front of him. "And I think the rice dish would work out for you, too."

"Okay."

I sidled over and put together a plate of lumpy not-pancakes and rice with indeterminate red and brown specks. There was a glass pitcher of purified ice water and a ceramic pot of tea. I brought over a cup of both as well and sat down next to Marco.

"Eat," he said. "I want to tell you some important things."

I nodded my assent and tried the pancake-ish things. Were they made out of turnips? Parsnips? It was definitely a root. I had to press down hard with my fork to make inroads.

"When Baba died," Marco said, "his spiritual position—his job, if you will—fell to someone else. Not me. At any given time, there are various qualified candidates—advanced souls who are capable of regulating universal energy." He watched me closely. Was he about to tell me even more intense things?

"I don't know what that means," I said. "Did Buddha do that, too? Is it something that comes with being enlightened?"

"I don't know Buddha's deal. Just being enlightened doesn't necessarily mean you're capable of running things at the core level. There are thousands of fully awake beings, but only a handful of spiritual administrators."

"And you're not one of them." I shoveled food in my mouth and chewed self-consciously.

"No." Marco shook his head and smiled. "They have too much overtime."

I nodded. "They probably need a union," I said, "but if *they're* not management, I guess nobody is."

"That's certainly true," Marco agreed, smiling. "So Baba had a successor—someone who stepped in and seamlessly filled that role. But in the meantime, the actual Baba reincarnated again."

"Wait a minute," I said. "If Baba was enlightened—and then some—why would he need to come back? Didn't he work through all of his—what do you call them—samskaras? The karmic gunk?"

"Yes. Good question." Marco leaned back in his

chair. "Sometimes enlightened souls come back purely to be in service—to help the world—not because they have any personal business."

"Is that what they call a bodhisattva?" I asked. I tried the rice dish. It wasn't bad.

"Exactly," Marco said. "But the energy in Buddha or Jesus or Baba is something different than an ordinary bodhisattva's. These incarnations only show up every eight hundred years or so to help keep things on track. None of these avatars has ever reincarnated right away before."

"Hey, is it you? Are *you* Baba?"

"No, I'm too old. Baba's reincarnation is forty-two."

"Okay," I said. "I'm following you so far."

"So the problem is now we have the Baba position-holder and Baba himself—in a new body—living concurrently. As I said, this isn't how it usually works." Marco swatted away a bug. I had the fleeting thought that it was the same one following him around for days.

"So are they working as a team? Are we better off because we've got both of them?"

By now, we were the only breakfasters left in the sweltering dining room. The heat had ramped up while we were speaking, and it was quite uncomfortable. Kitchen workers hauled buffet items out of the room, and one of them came by and took our empty plates and silverware.

"Next time," the young African-American woman told me with a glare, "bring your shit up to the window."

"Sure."

Marco began speaking again. "You'd think the two

could get along—that their teamwork would benefit us. But as it happens, the successor and the incarnation are in bitter disagreement over who should perform which function, and what should be done about the state of the world."

"Really?" That didn't make much sense to me.

"Have you noticed how chaotic the world has become? How we seem to be veering toward self-destruction as a species?"

"Well, sure."

"That's the result of two different hands on the world's helm. Both of them have their own ideas about how to create and maintain the energy templates that precede physical manifestation. Are you familiar with these concepts?"

"Not really, but let me get the rest of this straight," I said. "You're saying that one guy does one thing and the other one undoes it or does something else entirely?" I wiped the sweat from my brow and then wiped my hand on the front of my shirt.

"Yes. They ought to be beyond this sort of behavior, but technically they're still people. And they emerged from two different traditions, as well— Hinduism and Buddhism. That doesn't help."

"Is this why that new disease is out of control?" I asked.

"Not exactly," Marco replied. "But life on this planet is not a viable system as it stands. All sorts of cataclysmic problems will keep arising if you and I don't intercede."

"Hold it," I said. "It's one thing to fight thugs or oppose crackpot religious groups. This sounds like something on an entirely different level. These guys are like demigods or something, right?"

He nodded. "But that's not really the problem," he said. "Don't sell yourself short in the energy department, and I'd advise you to never underestimate me." He turned to face me; his gaze was a laser.

I didn't need a warning; I would certainly never underestimate him. "Okay," I said, since he seemed to be waiting for a response before he'd continue.

"The problem is," he said, "there isn't a pre-existing energy template for this eventuality—for our intervention. We'll need to generate it from scratch—out of basic, undifferentiated energy—and this is much more difficult. We'll be working against the flow—against karma."

"So we'll be up against two spiritual heavy hitters *and* the resting inertia of the entire universe?"

"That's right, Sid."

I tried to mimic a movie trailer for some lame action flick. "And the fate of the world hangs in the balance?" I said in a booming announcer's voice.

Marco took me literally, which scared me. "Yes," he said.

I paused and thought for a moment. "And in the meantime," I said, "we have to awaken people's consciousness because the insomnia epidemic means that too few people will be sleeping to support illusion?"

"Right." Marco smiled. "You can see why I need a partner. And it's a good thing that Chris and perhaps Sam will be on board, too."

"It sounds to me like we need a whole army."

"You may be right. I'm sorry I couldn't level with you sooner, but imagine how this conversation would've gone back on my island."

"Even now, it sounds totally crazy."

"It's ironic that you're a psychotherapist, isn't it?" He tilted his chin up and watched me through half-closed eyes.

"Very." I mulled over what he'd said. "I have a question," I told him.

"Go ahead."

"I've been thinking that this was all about Buddha, with a side trip to Baba's tomb to get infused with energy. Now it sounds like it's really about Meher Baba—or his legacy, I guess. Is Bhante full of crap? Are the Buddhists wrong about things? How do I reconcile all the competing points of view I've encountered so far? And how do I commit to whatever you and I are supposed to be doing if I can't?"

"That's up to you," Marco said. "You have to sort through that for yourself. If something makes sense to you and it fits your experience, hang onto it. If not..." He waved his hand.

I saw the Italian in him in that moment. He could've been the ringmaster in a Fellini film or maybe a relatively benign Mafia boss in a Scorsese movie.

Marco continued. "Perhaps what I'm saying now makes sense to you. Perhaps it doesn't. This is an example of what I mean. My role is to say things to you. You make of them what you will. I'm not here to argue, play salesman, or prove anything to you. There is a way to hold all this without experiencing its diversity as mutually exclusive or adversarial, but if you decide to walk away, there's probably another way to save the world. If not, we'll all just reincarnate on some other planet—in some other type of body."

"Really? How many other inhabitable planets are there?" I asked him.

"About eighteen thousand in this universe."

"How could you possibly know that? And what do you mean, 'in *this* universe'?"

"Modern physics is right about the multiverse. There are an infinite number of universes, Sid."

"My head hurts," I reported.

"I assume you've been in samadhi by now?"

"Yes."

"Do it some more. You'll see for yourself," he said.

I thought things over. Breakfast had gone down smoothly, and I could practically feel the calories firing up my brain cells. After a few minutes, I was just about ready to formally throw my hat into Marco's ring. Then Chris careened into the room.

"Guys!" he called. "I've got news. That really old man with Burt is his great-uncle, and he's some kind of spiritual capo, and he's in the tomb. Even I could feel his vibe from way across the plateau, and there's weird light leaking out from the windows. You don't want to miss this."

I looked at Marco.

"He's the position holder," he said. "Baba's successor."

"Really?"

"Yes. And the reincarnated Baba is here, too," Marco added.

"So the shit's going to hit the fan?" Chris asked.

Marco smiled. "It will be lively. Very lively."

Chapter Twenty-Two

We headed back up to the tomb. With each step, the energy phenomenon that awaited us throbbed more strongly. It was a lot like the outhouse bench energy, but amplified a hundred times. When we climbed high enough, I saw a purple aura soaring skyward from the tomb. I'd never seen anything like it before.

Surprisingly, I didn't feel panicked. If I'd been on my own, I'd have been more concerned. But energy didn't intimidate me now that I felt whole, and I walked and sweated with Marco and Chris by my side. We were a team. I guess I'd signed up after all.

Burt stood by the front door. His dark beard wasn't as perfectly trimmed now, and he sported a multi-colored bruise on his forehead. I didn't see the tomb keeper or any pilgrims.

"You can't go in," he said. "It's a high-level meeting. My uncle has returned."

"My friend is at that level, too," I said, gesturing at Marco.

"Oh, I doubt that," Burt said. "He is obviously an ordinary fellow. He is nothing like my uncle or the other man."

Marco pointed a finger at Burt, and sparks flew out of his fingertips. It reminded me of my handshake with Paul back in Santa Cruz. Then he told Burt that he knew his favorite number—twenty-seven—and that

Burt had wet his pants when he'd become lost in a crowd when he was six.

The Indian man's eyes widened.

"And what about *this*?" Chris said, dancing around and snapping his fingers like an idiot.

"That I am very much unimpressed by," Burt said. "But perhaps Sid and his friend should go in. The African man can wait out here with me."

Marco went in first, and I followed. We dispensed with the traditional bowing.

A very old Indian man sat cross-legged against a side wall, his eyes closed. He reminded me of Ram—the yacht owner—but he was lighter skinned and more wrinkled. Also, he had hair—Ram had been completely bald. His nose and ears drooped as if gravity were getting the best of him.

He was moving his hands in complex, ever-shifting mudras, creating the purple-tinted energy that we'd spied from the hill. It bounced around the room, but it didn't feel harmful. I sensed the visible component of his effort was just a side effect of what he was really doing.

Across the room sat a Tibetan-looking man in a maroon robe. He was in his early forties, and his round face exhibited a curious combination of compassion and despair, as though he'd started with one and then developed the other one later. I couldn't say which came first.

His hands were apart on his lap—he held them still—and a ball of golden energy gathered between them. A moment later, he released the bright orb into the tomb. The new force reminded me of Bhante's energy field, but it was much stronger.

The two men's energies didn't meld at all; the phenomenon was intense and chaotic in the enclosed space. One rebounded off the other, whirling and dancing and splitting into weird energy shards. It was difficult to bear.

I gathered myself and held firm against this onslaught. Perhaps if it had been aimed directly at me, I couldn't have managed.

"Let's talk," Marco called.

Both men looked up, and the energy instantly stopped. It was an amazing contrast. One second all hell was breaking loose, and the next, the tomb was exquisitely peaceful.

"Marco," the Tibetan man said in a thick accent. His voice was low and raspy.

"Marco," the older man acknowledged. He spoke with an upper-class English accent. His voice was soft and tired-sounding.

"Hello, Rinpoche," Marco said to the Tibetan. "Hello, Ram," he said to the Indian man.

I looked closer. It *was* Ram. Billionaire Ram. Without the purple haze in the air, bare of whatever makeup and disguise he'd employed when we first met on his boat, it was clearly Ram.

"Hello, Sid," he said. "I'm sorry for my deception in New Zealand. It was necessary."

"That's what people keep saying," I replied.

"Who are you?" Rinpoche asked me.

"That's a good question," I said. "I wish I knew."

He laughed uproariously—a deep, throaty belly laugh. "Very good. Good answer," he said. "Sit. Please, sit. Both of you."

"Sid is Bhante's find, and I've been working with

him," Marco told the man as we hunkered down, our backs against Baba's crypt.

"You've finally taken a student? Good for you. It's about time," Rinpoche said.

"Is it appropriate that Sid be here?" Ram asked. "How much does he know?"

"Most of it," Marco said. "And you might want to take a moment and sense his energy."

There was a pause while they both checked me out. I felt it as tendrils snaking through my torso. Then both of them nodded. I guess they weren't doling out compliments or handing out grades, but I still felt disappointed neither one said something along the lines of "Holy shit!" or "That's some terrific energy you've got, stud!" Especially since I was still unable to feel it myself.

"To answer your question more directly, Ram," Marco said, "it *is* important that he sit in at our meeting. I think you'll see why, presently." Again, both of the other men nodded.

"I'll just bring Sid up to speed on a few things, and then we can proceed," Marco said.

"Very well," Ram said.

Marco spoke to me next. "Ram really is Burt's great-uncle. He's also Bhante's boss, even though he's not a Buddhist. He was a psychiatrist, then Meher Baba's confidant, and now he's a billionaire."

Ram nodded as I glanced at him.

"Bhante left traditional Buddhism behind to work with Ram, who is Baba's successor in the spiritual hierarchy," Marco continued.

"But Bhante presented himself as such a staunch Buddhist traditionalist," I protested. "He even said that non-Theravadan Buddhism was crap—well, he used a nicer word, of course."

"Overcompensation," Ram said. "Guilt. All that psychological mumbo-jumbo I used to peddle."

Marco spoke to me again. "When Baba passed the baton on to Ram, he kept it a secret so Ram could carry out his duties without interference or distraction."

"Baba regretted becoming a public figure," Ram said. "He told me to drop out of sight—to use my abilities to build a life that afforded me anonymous freedom. I settled on the lifestyle of a reclusive rich man."

"Why are we wasting time?" Rinpoche said. "Hand him your résumé, Ram. Let's be done with this."

Marco held up his hand. "Bear with me," he said.

Rinpoche nodded again.

"May I ask a question?" I asked.

"Certainly," Ram answered.

"What did Baba say to you when he finally broke his silence?"

"Ah, Burt told you about that. Well, there's no harm in revealing it now. He said, 'All craving is a devaluation of the present moment. If you can be in love with each moment—with exactly how things are— then you shall not know suffering.' "

Rinpoche spoke up. "Amen, as they say in your country, Sid."

I nodded my agreement. There it was in a nutshell—a recipe for happiness.

"Now, this other gentleman," Marco said, gesturing at the Tibetan, "is a bit of an enigma."

Rinpoche smiled. "I prefer to think of myself as a riddle," he said.

"So I can't tell you much about him. He started out as a monk, and he's still pretending to be one. He doesn't like me. He doesn't like Ram. I don't know what he likes. But Baba is definitely the soul inside him. See if you can sense that, Sid. He is the reincarnated avatar."

I closed my eyes and gave it a try. I could not. I opened my eyes and shook my head.

"In the interest of fairness," Rinpoche said in his thick accent, "I wish to tell you more about your teacher."

"Sure. Go ahead," I said.

"He has acquired his power in illicit ways."

I looked at the others. Ram nodded his agreement. Marco watched the Tibetan impassively.

Rinpoche continued. "He is exploiting you as he has exploited others. His ambition always steers him away from proper behavior. He has no place in the spiritual hierarchy because of this, yet his energy and power keep him knocking on our door, threatening to knock it down someday—which he may. One of us needs to direct universal energy on this plane, but we should all pray it isn't Bruno."

I looked at Marco, who still looked serene and untroubled.

"Wait a minute," I said. "*Bruno*. You're calling him *Bruno* now?"

Rinpoche smiled.

"He's screwing with you," Marco said.

Rinpoche continued to smile and then spoke again. I enjoyed hearing his beautiful, low-pitched voice and his odd accent. I'd never met a Tibetan before. It was a shame he was saying such disturbing things.

"I can sense now you will be an important teacher, Sid," he said. "So you need to be properly trained. No one will follow you, and you can share no wisdom with the world unless you are charismatic and command respect. You are not these things now, are you?"

"No, and I'm not saying I am. But why don't you do all of this yourself? Why me? And who *would* be the best trainer if it's not Marco? You?"

Rinpoche smiled and wouldn't answer. Mr. Enigma—aka Mr. Annoying.

Marco turned to Ram. "Is there anything you'd like to add?"

"I have had a different experience of you," he said. "I have seen a mixture of problematic and salutary qualities. I would tell Sid to keep his mind open about all of this. Answers emerge when we're ready."

Ram looked at me and smiled. I glanced at Rinpoche and Marco. They were both smiling, too. I was sick of smiling. It was as if I had to pick which smile I liked the best, but I didn't like any of them. They were all scary smiles, fraught with hidden meaning and vast power.

I just sat. I was in way over my head with this crowd, and I had no idea what to do. So I just sat. Maybe answers would emerge. Maybe they'd tear me limb from limb. Maybe I'd wake up and all this would be a dream.

"Let's get started," Marco said to the others. "Thank you both for agreeing to this meeting."

The two men nodded again. I was sick of that, too. It was all nods and smiles with these guys.

"So what can we do to settle this?" Marco asked. "We can't go on this way."

"Agreed," Ram said.

"I'm listening," Rinpoche said.

"I have several ideas," Marco said. "And I'm open to hearing yours. We could share power, with clearly defined boundaries and no overlap. Or we could hold some sort of contest to see who's the most capable, although I can't imagine what that would look like."

"Neither can I," Rinpoche said.

"We could also flip a coin," Marco continued. "Or whatever else we could devise that would mimic chance."

"There is no such thing as chance," Ram said.

"Of course not," Marco agreed. "Another option, we could fight an all-out war and see who's left standing."

"That is not an option," Rinpoche said. "We would destroy that which we seek to preserve."

"Agreed," Ram said.

These people had no idea how brainstorming worked. Let the man finish. Then I understood what Marco was doing. He was presenting all the unpalatable possibilities first so when he presented them with the one he wanted, they'd appreciate it more.

That's exactly what he offered next. "Or we could agree to a neutral third party who could do the job for us," he said. "Someone we could all agree to work with. Someone with the requisite energy configuration. Someone free from the constraints of a religious tradition or the bias of any spiritual background."

There was a pause. Then they all looked at me. I felt my guts tighten. My head hurt, too.

"I've already got a job," I said. "And I'm not neutral. At the moment, I'm terrified of all of you, especially Rinpoche because of his creepy smile."

He laughed again. "Very good. 'Creepy smile.' Excellent."

"And I'm mad at Ram for lying to me. And Marco has been both very annoying and very helpful ever since I met him, so I don't know what to think. Let's say I'm ambivalent about him. You need someone who's never met any of you—somebody new."

"It's an interesting idea," Ram said, completely ignoring me. "Instead of using Sid as a proxy as my organization had planned, we could actually show him how to do the work and leave him to it. And clearly, Marco, you've been moving him along splendidly. Rinpoche, what do you think?"

"I gather, until quite recently, this man was rather ordinary, wasn't he? We're not on Broadway here. This is not *My Fair Lady*. It could take years to develop him properly."

"So?" Marco said. "Suppose we declared a truce in the meantime. Suppose we joined forces to train him for a few years."

"It could work," Ram said. "I won't be around much longer, anyway. I don't wish to waste my remaining years squabbling. Nor do I want to hand things over to either of you." He glared at the two other men.

"I can't work with Marco," Rinpoche said. "But otherwise, the concept is sound. Unprecedented, but sound. The way around any impasse is sideways, after all."

The others nodded. I cleared my throat. "Once again," I said. "I'm not interested in the job. This won't work if I'm a draftee instead of a volunteer, will it?" I tried to keep my voice steady, but my pitch rose and I spoke hurriedly. I could feel panic welling up. There was only so much I could take.

They all ignored me.

"Look at the Vietnam war," I added. "Our draftee army was a bunch of dope-smoking slackers."

Rinpoche laughed. "That war was Ram's mess," he said.

"Baba's," Ram insisted.

God, they were a cold, ruthless trio. This was all about power, not love or compassion.

"Sid has a point," Marco said.

"Yes, I do," I said, "And furthermore—"

Rinpoche waved a hand at me, and my vocal cords tightened. I couldn't speak at all. Now I felt full-blown panic, but I couldn't do anything about it.

"If we agree to this idea in principle," Ram said, continuing to speak as if Rinpoche's striking someone mute was nothing special, "then we can look at how to take care of that aspect later. We are all creative. I have no doubt that if we need to, we can surmount these sorts of obstacles."

"True," Marco said.

"Here is my objection," Rinpoche said. "I don't know this man." He surveyed me for a moment, and his gaze was intense. "Yes, I can see that Sid's energy is remarkable. But you two have already formed relationships with him. Marco has been infusing him with his own energy. Others have as well—I can feel this. And Ram has been using him in various ways. I cannot agree to anything without the opportunity to familiarize myself with this man—to form my own relationship."

"Fair enough," Marco said.

"Agreed," Ram said.

"I am not fond of any of the other ideas on Marco's list of solutions," Rinpoche added. "Nor do I have new ideas."

"I feel the same," Ram said. "Sharing won't work. And we cannot divide the indivisible."

"Does anyone know of a better candidate than Sid?" Marco asked.

How the hell had Rinpoche paralyzed me?

"More advanced? Certainly," Rinpoche said. "Wiser and more grounded? Of course," he added. "But these elements emerge from an association with institutions that preclude true neutrality. A Buddhist would favor one of us. A Hindu another. And so forth. Sid does seem to be a nothing—a blank slate. This sets him apart."

"Yes," Marco said. "Ram, why don't we give Rinpoche and Sid a chance to meet properly?"

"Certainly."

As the two men got to their feet, I tried to leave, too. Nothing happened. It was as if the signals from my brain had been blocked and couldn't get to my legs. A maelstrom of emotions and adrenal responses swirled within me. Marco and Ram left the tomb. Rinpoche waved his hand and released me from his control. I massaged my neck and coughed. It seemed as if he'd reduced my panic, too.

"Sid," he said, "tell me about yourself."

He sounded as though he worked in HR for a big Tibetan corporation—although there probably weren't any. This was an interview I needed to screw up royally—an anti-interview, if you will. My goal was to convince him I was wholly unsuited to the job. On the other hand, he'd probably know if I lied or otherwise tried to fool him.

"I'm a psychotherapist. I'm single. I was adopted by rich, white parents. They're dead. My best friend is named Chris. Perhaps you've met him. He's at the pilgrim center. He's the African American who wears those horrible Hawaiian shirts."

I wasn't finding a way to act like a jerk yet, but maybe having a wise-ass friend would help tarnish me.

"Oh yes," Rinpoche said. "A delightful fellow. Very fun."

"Where are you from?" I tried. Maybe he'd allow me to engage him in a dialogue. Then I could mess with whatever he said.

"I am Tibetan by birth, but I was raised in Ladakh, India, in a refugee community. Shall we take turns asking questions?"

"Sure."

"How do you tolerate Marco—Bruno? He is controlling and arrogant and outrageous. He is what you call a 'loose cannon'—yes?"

"Certainly, but who can I compare him to? My only other experience of people like him includes a guy who paralyzes people when he doesn't like what they're saying. And *he* laughs about a war that killed hundreds of thousands of people, too. Then there's this other guy who lies and gives money to a secret organization that kidnaps people. So what do I know?"

He laughed again. He was far too entertained by me.

"You're just as arrogant as the others," I told him.

"I suppose so," he said. "Your turn to ask a

question."

"Why don't you just let Ram run things until he dies and then take over and do it yourself?" I asked.

"Good question," he said.

Damn. I hadn't meant to ask anything that reflected well on me.

"If Ram were to be the sole administrator at his age, it would only be a matter of time before Marco could oust him and seize power. This would be a disaster. Like you, Marco arrived at his status in an unorthodox fashion—he had no teacher, he used drugs, and he has absorbed others' energies. Unlike you, he has always wished to wield absolute power. The fact that you don't want to is in your favor. Second, Ram could choose to continue his role even after he no longer has a body. He would be even less competent in that case. Neither of these situations would allow us—myself and the residual Baba within me—to help the world get through this difficult era. I know that we are the right men for the job."

This was eminently diagnosable stuff, or it would be back in California, at least. He thought he was Baba and Rinpoche, all in the one body.

"Then why would you ever agree to have me do it?" I asked. "How could I possibly perform as well as you and Baba, or you *as* Baba, I suppose?"

"It's not your turn," he said. "You already asked your question."

"So what?" I said. "I don't give a shit whose turn it is, you fat prick."

He laughed. "Nice try. Here's my question. What is love?"

"What?"

"What is love?"

"Uh…it's all there is, isn't it? It's another name for life-force energy—for the consciousness that brings forth the physical world. It's the same as beauty or truth or a million other things. It's all love. I love you," I said.

He'd done something to rob me of my ability to answer dishonestly. "Hey!" I said. "Stop that."

He smiled.

"My turn," I said. "Are you seriously saying that Marco is Bruno Bompiani? That he was a rogue Stanford researcher?"

"It doesn't matter," he answered. "But I'll tell you this. There is more than one spelling of that name."

"It matters to me. Are you saying I googled the wrong guy back in Mumbai?"

"When behavior is dangerous or abusive, what matters is the net effect of the behavior, not its origins." Rinpoche shifted his position, winced, and rolled his neck for a moment. "A car accident," he said. He paused and then spoke again when he saw I wasn't satisfied with his explanation. "Suppose I got up and kicked you in the shin," he said. "Maybe I'm schizophrenic and a voice in my head told me to do it. Maybe it's a new type of therapy I'm testing on you. Maybe I'm mean and vengeful. What does it matter? You were kicked in any case, and it hurts exactly the same, no matter the reason. Would you come back for more kicking if my reason was good enough?"

"I understand. You're saying I should respond to Marco based on the not-okayness of his current behavior, not on the back story of how he developed the bad behavior."

"Is that a question?" he asked.

"Let's pretend my voice went up at the end of that sentence," I said.

"Sorry, it's not your turn." He laughed. "This is fun," he added. "I like you."

I was screwing up my screw-up. "Wait a minute," I said. "How long are we going to do this? I have to go to the bathroom."

He closed his eyes, grimaced, and then opened them again. "No, you don't," he said. "Not anymore."

He was right. "That didn't count as a question, by the way," I said. "It's still my turn."

"No, it isn't."

Surely Rinpoche couldn't be fond of this kind of arguing. Wasn't I demonstrating another ordinary human foible?

He continued. "Let's let Baba's old body decide," he said. He turned to the crypt behind me. "Baba? If that wasn't a question, speak up. If it was, stay silent like usual."

He held up a hand and cocked his ear. Then he tried to throw his voice like a ventriloquist. He wasn't very good at it. "Let the kid have another one," he said, pretending to be Baba.

I felt a chill run up my spine. The voice he used was identical to the one in my Baba dream. That was exactly how he'd sounded, which no one but Ram could have known, since Baba had never talked to anyone else. It was eerie.

"Do you experience Baba as a separate person inside of you?" I asked. "Reincarnation doesn't work that way, does it?"

"It doesn't usually. And that's not the best

characterization. But we have an arrangement. These things are possible—they're just rarely called for."

The two others came back into the tomb, Marco leading the way.

"So how's it going?" he asked.

"Sid is acceptable to me," Rinpoche said. "His energy remained strong and pure throughout the conversation."

I leapt to my feet and sprinted out of the tomb, knocking Ram to the side as I passed him. I'd had enough. More than enough. They could all go fuck themselves.

Chapter Twenty-Three

My mind was now officially, totally blown. All the previous mind-blowing had been nothing compared to this. At the tomb, I'd been keeping it together to make my case. Now the crazy reality was asserting itself.

I was going to run the planet? Administer mystery energy? And this trio of power-hungry maniacs was going to mess with me against my will—rearrange me even more?

I kept running beyond the tomb complex. Really running. I was bathed in sweat after a few dozen yards. I headed down the far side of the hill, away from the pilgrim center, where I discovered a rough path heading toward some sort of stone ruin across a wide, plowed field. A human projectile, I hurtled down the rugged hill, one misstep away from a broken leg. I didn't really think I could escape from Marco and the others, but I needed to try. Enough was enough.

I was so weak, I could only jog shortly after joining the path. By the time I reached the low stone wall at the end of the field, I was reduced to walking fast. And when I reached the doorway of the old stone building, I collapsed to my knees and gasped for air. I felt much the way I had after swimming away from Tommy T.'s fishing boat. And about as wet. *But here, no one can save me the way Marco had in his rowboat. How could I be rescued when all the qualified rescuers are the ones plotting against me? No ordinary person can stand against them.*

And what ordinary person would empathize with my frantic attempts to evade enlightenment, oneness, and power? These are universally valued across all cultures. Don't we all yearn for these?

I decided I didn't care about any of that. I was sick and tired of the whole deal. Thinking about it was just renting out space in my head to these people—or whatever they were. *Fuck them. Fuck them all.*

I wished Sam was with me. For days now, events had conspired to keep us apart—to keep me from discussing ongoing developments with her, to limit her loving presence and healing energy. Here I was, on my own, forced to handle—or not handle—the craziest part of the whole insane thriller plot that had become my life. It wasn't just unfair. It was wrong. Deeply wrong. I craved a connection with Sam in that moment. She could've been my cable back to my essence, my truth. Without them, I was lost.

I crawled into the ruined building. There was no ceiling, and the black, sooty floor immediately caked on my knees. More soot stained the simple limestone walls, and various animal droppings decorated most of the site. But somebody had swept a corner of the ruin recently, and there was no trash or graffiti.

I sat down and began to lose consciousness, sprawling across the filthy floor. *Holy shit. Is this a remote attack by Marco or Rinpoche? Am I still sick with kundalini?*

Then I dreamt. I was alone in a temple—the building I was in. It had been a temple. But it was new in the dream. Brass lanterns hung along the light-pink side walls. Brightly painted statues of Hindu gods and goddesses soared larger than life on a gray stone altar, which sat on a beautiful, green marble floor. I stood still, looking at the statues. I felt peaceful.

"Hello, Sid," a deep voice said from behind me.

I turned around. It was Meher Baba. He wore a navy-blue doorman's uniform with red trim, and he smoked a huge cigar.

"Whimsical, aren't I?" he said. He had a Brooklyn accent.

"I guess so," I said. "Aren't you dead?"

"Not necessarily," he said.

His accent was gone, and now he wore an LA Lakers basketball uniform with the infinity symbol on it. He stood about eight feet tall.

"I'll bet you're a handful to cover in the pivot," I said.

"I don't know what that means," he said.

Now he wore an orange robe and munched on a jelly doughnut. There was no transition between personas. "Here's the main thing," he said. "The others are all crazy. You can be spiritual and crazy. It's a common combination. So you really do need to be the one to run this world."

"Seriously? Me?"

"Yes. It's not as simple as it sounds, though."

"Believe me, it doesn't sound simple at all," I said.

He smiled. "It's not my old job you'd be doing, you see, and it's not exactly you who would be doing it—not *this* you. You'll see."

"When? When will I see?"

"Soon." Now he looked exactly like the black-and-white photo of him that hung in the reception area of the pilgrim center.

"Why me?" I asked.

"You're the reincarnation of Buddha's son," he said. "And you were my father."

Whoa. Could that be true? "Tell me what to do," I said.

"Just love," he said, gazing at me with his compelling, loving brown eyes. "Love and then love more. Love everybody and everything. Love all the time. Love, love, love."

Then he vanished, and I woke up. Five dogs lay with me, surrounding me in a circle. There was an exact distance between each of them—about a foot. They were all skinny and black, with various white patches.

Chris called my name. The dogs growled. I reached over and patted the nearest one. They stopped growling, and I sat up. All of the dogs sat up, too.

"Whoa," Chris said, ambling into the ruins. "Cool building. Cool dogs."

I watched him. It was difficult to reenter the ordinary world after the dream—or the vision, I guess. And I certainly hadn't had an opportunity to assimilate the sudden appearance of the nearly identical dogs. Talking to a person was more than I could manage. I did feel much calmer after the conversation with Baba, though.

Chris sat down beside one of the black and white dogs and patted its head. Then he looked at his hand. "I've probably got rabies now, or maybe some parasite that eats your brain," he said.

"Probably," I parroted.

"You know," he continued, edging away from the nearest dog, "the whole point of staying on the grounds of the pilgrim center is it's safe there. There are a lot of bad stories about people who wandered away. This isn't movie India. This isn't a big city with lots of tourists. Come on back with me, Sid."

Three of the dogs cocked their heads and listened to him. The two nearest me continued to watch me intently. They all seemed unusually aware for dogs.

"Did Marco send you?" I asked.

"Yeah. He said you were wigging out. Since I'm so gentle and soothing, of course he thought of me. So get your ugly, dopey ass moving, Sid. I don't know what happened in the tomb while I was chanting with fucking Nana and some old lady from Missouri, but you're not accomplishing anything by sitting here with these mangy triplet dogs—who smell awful, by the way. Why the hell did I ever touch one of them?"

It wasn't like Chris to miscount anything—there were five dogs—but I let that pass. I was more focused on integrating the information Baba had shared in my vision. In essence, he'd told me to go back to the others—or at least to accept the position I'd been offered. But he also said that the reason I needed to cooperate was that the others were crazy. That certainly didn't bode well.

Maybe I'd manufactured the dream experience. Although it had felt like I really had met Baba, the subconscious is capable of amazing things.

"I needed some time to process things," I finally told Chris, mustering some cognition. "And it feels safe in here. This was a temple."

"How do you know that? It's just a bunch of messed-up walls. Every ruin isn't a sacred site, you know. Some of them used to be slaughterhouses or whorehouses." He swept his arm across the room, such as it was.

"That doesn't matter, Chris. The thing is, I won't be ready to go back until I figure some stuff out. You have no idea what they're asking me to do."

"Who? Marco and the uncle?"

"There was a Rinpoche in there, too—a Tibetan guy. Actually, I think you've met him."

"Sure. That guy is a blast," Chris said. "Have you heard him laugh? He laughs at everything. So what do they want you to do?"

"Pretty much run the world, I gather. Or be one of the people that does, anyway."

"Well, this planet is shit out of luck, then, isn't it?" Chris said. "No offense, Sid, but that doesn't make a lot of sense."

"Exactly," I said. "So how about you go away and come back in a while after I've had a chance to sort things out. I've got all these dogs here, too. I'll be safe. Who'd mess with a holy man surrounded by big dogs?"

"All right," Chris said. "Marco's not going to be thrilled about this, but that's his problem."

"Thanks," I said.

"Take care," Chris said as he got to his feet and padded away.

I tried to think clearly about my situation, but that wasn't in the cards just yet. Instead, after a few minutes of muddled not-thinking, I decided to go ahead and feel whatever feelings were lying in wait.

They rushed in and flooded me, but without the usual physical expressions—at first, anyway. Nothing clenched, nor could I detect any fight or flight response. My mind took the brunt of the feelings in a way that I couldn't explain. *Aren't minds precluded from directly experiencing emotions?*

I still fumed, but my fear was preeminent. And I was quite bewildered. These formed a stew of sorts, with even more emotions embedded in it, like chunks of meat.

I explored each of these, finding more and more, realizing I was simultaneously feeling every emotion I knew. Some were specific and situational. Others were more global. I now felt terrified of Marco, for example. And my endocrine system was back online. When I thought about him, my entire lower body clenched and my heart started pounding. I also felt disheartened—a lead weight squatted on my head and shoulders. Everything was such a mess, with maniacs running the show.

But I was thankful to be alive and healthy. I felt dread, I felt trapped, I felt repulsed, I felt outraged. But I was happy the planet was so beautiful. And I also felt longing, tenderness, reverence, and a new appreciation of the absurd. After a while, the strongest emotion became a surprising love for the dogs who still encircled me.

All five held themselves perfectly still as I jumped back up into my head. I couldn't afford the luxury of exploring all this. A single emotion might've been helpful—a guide of sorts. Angry? Go change something. Fearful? Run away. Tuning into the full range of emotions? Useless.

Unfortunately, I still couldn't think very well. I decided to meditate. In the past, I'd felt energized and sharper after sitting—like pressing a Sid restart button.

When I shifted position to begin, the same three

dogs that had listened so attentively to Chris jumped up and trotted away. The other two continued to lie at my feet.

In seconds, I was in samadhi again, and this time there was absolutely no experience to have and no one there to experience anything, anyway. Everything just went blank.

I wasn't asleep or unconscious, and the blankness wasn't onerous or boring. There wasn't an I, in fact, and the blankness wasn't the absence of something. It was more like being in contact with something realer than anything I'd ever known—something so real, there was nothing to know about it. It had no attributes or qualities, nor did it have an absence of these. It was transcendent of the realm in which anything existed. It just *was*.

I don't know how long I stayed in this mode, but I woke up from it when the remaining dogs started barking. Or so it seemed. When I opened my eyes, the dogs were on their feet and their mouths were moving, but no sound came out.

"Hello?" a voice called through the doorway. "Are you in there, Sid?"

It was an oddly familiar voice—a voice from the past.

A moment later, a sixty-year-old white man ambled into the ruined temple, accompanied by the other three dogs.

Then I saw who the man was. It was my father. My dead father.

Chapter Twenty-Four

"I realize this must be a shock," he said.

Alan Menk—my adopted father—was a relatively short man with a wide face that somehow managed to look proportionate to the rest of him and render a captain-of-industry bearing. On this occasion, he wore wraparound sunglasses, which seemed odd. Other than being fifteen years older since the last time I'd seen him, he looked like himself, all the way down to his pressed khaki pants, white shirt, and black shoes. My mother had called this "the uniform." I suddenly wondered if she was alive, too.

Before I could respond, my father approached me and continued talking. "Your mother and I faked our deaths because we had to. I know it was hard on you."

He stumbled momentarily on the uneven floor, but the dog walking beside him provided an inadvertent hip-check, and he righted himself. Then he lowered himself to the ground and sat across from me with his legs stretched out in front of him, leaving all of six inches of space between us. The three dogs spread out, and the five of them formed another uncannily perfect ring—this time around both of us.

"Wow," was all I could say. Both my mind and body felt numb and useless. I felt like a zombie instead of a grateful son who was joyous to see his father alive.

"The thing is," he continued, "your mother's been

running RGP for many years—with my help. Before we took charge, it was a cult, basically—an eddy in the stream of consciousness."

As usual, Father never missed a chance to inject what he considered to be a clever phrase into a conversation.

"Now, the organization is in a position to transform the world," he continued. "And you're part of that. But we have rivals—bitter rivals. If they knew your mother and I were alive, we wouldn't be for long."

I nodded. I just couldn't muster words. *Mom's alive, too. What the hell!*

"It's fine if you just want to listen," he said. "I need to tell you quite a few things." He drew several labored breaths before speaking again—was he asthmatic now? "You've probably noticed that your life and Shakyamuni Buddha's share many parallels. This was not by accident. Your mother and I raised you to become a Perfect Master—a fully realized soul—a modern Buddha—a…"

"Yeah," I interrupted with an edge to my voice. "I get it."

He laughed quietly, a careful, small laugh. "Sid's still in there, isn't he? Your energy is impressive, and our people have been reporting your meteoric rise, but that was a classic Sid-ism, wasn't it?"

"Why don't you just keep telling me things?" I wasn't in a rush to restart a personal relationship with this resurrected ghost. I didn't like that this was my reaction, but it was what it was.

"Certainly," he said. "Our disappearance was part of your preparation. It's important that you understand that. You needed to experience loss and suffering on a grand scale. You also needed to live a more ascetic life—without the benefit of the family money."

"Is that why you left me practically nothing at all in your wills—why everything went to a foundation?" I asked.

I'm sure my resentment was evident in my tone. I was surprising myself with my immaturity. I thought I was beyond this sort of behavior.

"Partly, yes. But that foundation *is* RGP, and we've always been acting in your best interests all these years—from behind the scenes, of course. Remember that scholarship that came through when you were ready to drop out of graduate school? That was us—the foundation—RGP. And when you needed to fix up that horrible old Jaguar of yours to commute to your first real job? Did you ever wonder why that mechanic charged you so little to fix so much?"

"No," I said.

"He replaced the engine and transmission, and you never even noticed," my father said. "I painted black smudges and grease marks on the new parts myself."

"This is creepy shit, Dad. Did you ever stop to consider that?" Heat rushed into my cheeks, and I shook my fist for emphasis. "Did you know I was treated for paranoia when I was twenty-four? I saw people following me. I was convinced I was being monitored by someone or something."

"Of course we knew that because we were the ones following you. We were also the ones who spoke to your therapist to make sure your psych record didn't include a diagnosis of psychosis or anything else that could be damaging to your future."

"Jesus Christ, what is wrong with you people?" I

said. "You fake your deaths, you leave me nothing, you spy on me, you interfere, you try to manipulate me into becoming who you think I ought to be. This is like anti-parenting. This is crazy. You're both crazy."

"It was absolutely necessary," my father said.

"In *your* opinion," I said. "I am so sick and tired of hearing that. Do know how many times I've heard that lately?"

He started to answer.

"Oh, shut up," I told him. "You waltz in here as the biggest, most ridiculous non sequitur ever. What the hell? What do you think you're doing? Where did you come from? How the hell did you find me here? This is ridiculous. Why should I believe anything you say?"

My father grimaced and gathered his breath again before he spoke. "Your mother said you'd react this way. I said no, he'd be reasonable. He's spiritually evolved now, Andrea, I told her. Look at it this way, Sid. We've given you the best chance to develop into someone similar to your namesake. And it's worked! That's the most important thing—it's worked. We're very proud of you."

I was enraged. Marco's high-handedness was bad enough. This was beyond the most draconian Skinnerism I'd ever heard of. It felt like something the Nazis might have tried if they'd been Buddhists. Well, evil Buddhists. My parents had been entrusted to care for me—nurture me—to support my dreams. That certainly didn't include sacrificing my autonomy for their cause. What sort of life could I have had if they hadn't made me an orphan at twenty-one, for God's sake? Obviously, RGP was still a cult. Who were they kidding? These were fanatics.

Perhaps my father could read my expression. "It's not that different from what happens in other families. Parents want the best for their children. Maybe they steer them toward a medical degree or an arranged marriage. We just had loftier ambitions for you, Sid. And the world needs for us to have them—don't forget that part. It's been a Viennese waltz with destiny taking the lead and—"

"Okay, I get it," I said.

A cascade of arguments bubbled up. There were so many obvious differences between what my parents had done and what normal parents did to guide their offspring that I didn't even know where to begin. My father's pretty speeches were just dressed up, weak-assed excuses.

What I did know was that there was no point in arguing with him. There never had been and there never would be. Although my mother wore the pants in the family—my father was content to follow and not lead—once he'd settled on a point of view, he was remarkably rigid and stubborn. When I was growing up, at least these fixed opinions weren't generally ill-informed or self-centered. Early on, I learned to differentiate between the value of a given opinion and the way someone held it. My father consistently role-modeled how not to hold one.

How quickly and thoroughly I'd been sucked back into our family dynamic. For all the progress I'd made as an adult—in therapy, as a grad student in psychology, and for that matter, as Marco's protégé—apparently I was still easily triggered by my father simply being my father—doing what he always did.

In this case, there were plenty of other topics to

focus on and a host of questions I needed to ask. But here I was, shoving everything I'd learned to the side, ignoring the loving energy that I knew I truly was, readying myself to tear the guy a new one if he said one more irritating thing.

I decided to ask a question before he had the chance to set me off again. "So are you aware of Marco's plan for me?" I said.

"The infamous Dr. Bompiani," he said.

Really? We were back to that? I peered at him intently. I wished I could've seen his eyes behind the sunglasses. I once trusted this man sitting across from me. Could I trust him again now that he'd resurrected himself and was supposedly leveling with me?

"You're saying that Marco is Bompiani?" I asked. "You know that for sure?"

"Of course. Your mother taught with him at Stanford. He's been over to our house, to departmental parties—you probably met him years ago. You just don't remember. He looked a lot different back then."

I was flabbergasted. I just couldn't reconcile this with my hard-earned who-was-really-who experience. And I wasn't capable at that moment of reviewing all the Marco/Bompiani evidence yet again. But this was my own father—well, adopted father. I couldn't simply dismiss what he said, either.

"Where's Mom?" I asked. This was the next question on the list in my head. A better son would've asked it first.

"Well," he said. "That's the thing. That's why I'm here." He took a deep, raspy breath. "Your mother's been kidnapped."

Chapter Twenty-Five

"You might have mentioned this right away," I said.

Once again, I felt more annoyed at my father's modus operandi than alarmed by his news. I wasn't proud of that. Maybe it was because until a few minutes ago, I'd thought my mother was dead, anyway. Or perhaps I'd been through so much trauma lately, a kidnapping no longer registered as a bona fide crisis on my internal Richter scale.

"Yes, I probably should've told you sooner," my father said. "Now we're in a bit of a rush. But I wanted to be sensitive to your position—to truly—"

"Who has her?" I interrupted. "What do we need to do?"

"It's a New Zealand gangster. And we need to go—to get out of here."

"Okay."

I struggled to my feet. I felt weak and spacey—probably from not having eaten much for the last couple of days.

All the dogs sprang to their feet, too. I didn't know what their deal was, but they moved in unison, with an unearthly surety—as though they already knew what was about to happen. *These are not ordinary dogs.* And why hadn't my father commented on them? Were they his?

Three of them—the same trio that had split off before—moved forward and assembled around my father as he began to walk ahead of me toward the doorway of the old temple. One led the way and the others trotted along beside him. I followed.

I looked behind me to see what the remaining two dogs were up to. They'd vanished. Was there another way out?

My father escorted me around the outside of the roofless stone building. In the dimming light, an overgrown trail led away from the back of the ruin. India's version of overgrown was beyond anything I'd experienced before. But someone had hacked a slim avenue between a wild array of flowering bushes, tall grasses, and vines, and we walked on spongy, dark green ground cover. Again, my father almost fell, and the proximity of a dog helped right him.

A short walk brought us to a crude dirt road. A dusty silver BMW sports car—a Z4—was parked there. Sam sat in the driver's seat.

"Get in," she said. "Hurry!"

I was at another crossroad. Who should I trust? What should I do? Although I'd yearned to be with Sam scant minutes before, I felt so unsure of myself that even this option confused me.

"You really do need to go," my father told me. "I'll stay here and clean things up."

I had no idea what that meant, but with Sam and my parents—the RGP contingent—representing the get-in-the-sports-car-with-the-beautiful-woman-who-seems-to-love-you choice, and Marco and company offering the scary-puppetmaster-version-of-being-groomed-to-rule-the-world...well, I hopped into the

BMW.

I never seemed to have enough time to properly consider what would later turn out to be a pivotal choice. I kept getting blindsided. And tricked. And hurried. Would I regret this latest decision down the road—literally, in this case? After all, I was leaving Chris behind. Could he hold his own with Marco and the others if they came after him? I knew he couldn't, but I didn't see why they'd harm him. And my father—how in the world could he "clean things up"? What did that even mean?

Sam's proximity pulled me back into the moment. She wore an emerald-green scoop-neck top and a white baseball cap. Her blond ponytail snaked its way out the back of the cap. She was sweating; it reminded me of our nights together. I felt a rush of lust, followed by an even bigger rush of love.

"Take care," my father said, waving goodbye with his idiosyncratic wave. It was a cross between a beauty queen's and a little kid's. I was moved; tears filled my eyes. He looked so old and out of place, and I loved him. I guess there was something about people waving goodbye that summoned my heart. I remembered Lannie in her shiny red warm-up suit at the dock near Howick. Then I began to sob. Sometimes it felt as though life was nothing but a series of losses—an incessant tearing away of whatever seemed to matter.

The dogs howled. It was an eerie sound and very loud. As Sam put the convertible in gear and accelerated hard, they switched to barking. I would miss them too. I didn't know why.

Sam focused on her driving. The narrow track ended at a paved country road, and she zoomed onto it, dodging several bicyclists. She snuck a look at me as she expertly played chicken—at much higher speeds than her competition. "Are you okay?"

"Yes. Just sad. But I'm enjoying it." I felt energized and grateful that I could still zero in on a particular emotion—still be human. But in that moment, I also missed the bliss of spiritual energy. I'd been awash in it the last time I'd seen Sam.

Sam concentrated on driving for a while before she spoke again. "I'm sorry I couldn't tell you about your parents or Bompiani sooner."

"He really *is* Bompiani, then?"

"Yes, but he's not evil, as some people would have you believe—just misguided."

"So does he have all sorts of powers, or is he conning me like my brothers said?"

"Both. He has abilities, yes. But he's also bankrolled a team of tech people, private investigators, and actors to pursue his goals."

"Which are?"

"You probably have a better idea of that than I do."

That was no help. *Is it possible that someone else could be more clueless than yours truly?*

The road had become relatively curvy, and Sam's breakneck driving was very distracting. Fortunately, the traffic was relatively light by Indian standards.

"I can say this," Sam continued. "Marco has an amazing mind. Between his psychic abilities, his ability to charm and impress, and the fact that he was a genius professor of psychology even before his enhancement meds, he's capable of enacting remarkable plans."

"And apparently he can talk squadrons of people into helping him, too."

"He pays well."

"Let me get this straight. So I *am* a clone?"

"No, you're not. Bhante's people have been running a hoax about that right from the start. That's one reason this has been so confusing. Nobody's been completely aboveboard. Not even us, I'm afraid. Your mother can explain our motivation to you better than I can."

"I saw DNA tests online."

"Think about it. How could you be a clone? It's ridiculous. They probably rigged data on fake websites."

"If you knew all along," I asked, heating up, "why did you go along with Marco's bullshit? And why lie to me? I've been developing a fantasy of being in a relationship with you someday, but without trust, what's the point?"

"I can't explain all that now. It was your mother's idea—part of the plan. I didn't choose to withhold information. It wasn't personal. And I share your fantasy, Sid. There's something that's been pulling me toward you all along—something more than ordinary attraction—more than ordinary love."

I loved hearing this, and I knew it to be true. "How *is* my mom?" I asked. "Aside from being kidnapped, I mean. What's she like now? My dad seems about the same, except for some health problems."

"She's a lovely woman. A dedicated woman. A role model for me—an inspiration. And very down to earth."

In the dark, we approached a highway. A surprisingly well-lit gas station sat at the upcoming corner, and three good-sized, bright-yellow motorcycles were parked in front of it. The riders sat on their bikes—helmetless—and watched us approach. They weren't Indian. They were Maori.

We turned the corner and roared away. The bikers did too. I turned to look. The three men were chasing us. Maoris. In India. Did Tommy T.'s empire extend across the Indian Ocean? Had someone with vast resources hired them? Ram?

"Did you see—?"

"Yes. I don't know if we can outrun them," she said. "But I'll try."

A long straightaway stretched ahead of us, and the traffic was still light. Maybe it was dinnertime for decent, law-abiding folks. For a while, we pulled away. We had a head start, and the Z4 had more low-end torque than the crotch-rockets did. But gradually they gained on us.

The taillights of a bus loomed ahead in our headlights, moving half our speed. Sam pulled out to pass, but a steady stream of oncoming cars kept us trapped.

One of the bikes accelerated up beside us, and a man I recognized from Tommy T's fishing boat gestured with a pistol for us to pull over. In the open-air car, in the narrow Indian lane, I could practically reach across Sam and knock the gun out of his hand, or at least shove him. Maybe he'd lose his balance. Maybe I'd lose mine.

Before I could act, Sam swerved out into the traffic and floored the accelerator. We were about to play super-chicken. In the dark. With gun-toting bikers chasing us.

I closed my eyes as we approached the first tiny car

in the oncoming lane. *I don't need to see my death coming. I'll just go ahead and die. I'll be okay. I'll just be dead.* Adrenaline surged through me again, mimicking the spiritual energy I was missing.

Everyone honked. I heard a gunshot. We swerved hard to the right and then to the left. Both times, I thought we'd roll over. How could a car stay upright in the midst of this?

I opened my eyes. We were doing about a hundred and ten on a stretch of open road. If an animal wandered onto the road, we'd die. If we hit a major pothole, we'd die. My adrenals got to work again, and I shivered. I decided not to catalog all the potentially fatal outcomes.

I turned to look at our noisy pursuers. All three bikes were right on our tail; their headlights formed an even row.

After another quarter mile, Sam called to me over the racket. "I'm up to a hundred and twenty. I don't think we can outrun them. And we'll come up on traffic again soon. I can't keep taking crazy chances. Sooner or later, the odds will catch up with us. Do you want to surrender?"

"Not especially," I shouted back. My courage—or perhaps foolishness—surprised me.

"Okay, then," Sam said. "Hang on tight."

She immediately jammed on the antilock brakes. We didn't skid, but we came close. The smell of burning rubber was pungent, and the car's suspension screamed in protest.

Two of the bikes shot past us—one on either side. The third one crashed into our back bumper, and a skinny New Zealander flew over us. His trailing foot nicked my ear, and then he landed on the front edge of the hood just before we came to a stop. He slid to the pavement and lay inert.

Sam hurriedly backed up, turned around, and burned rubber again, zooming up to speed. I watched the other two bikes reverse course as well. They were quite a way behind us now but would soon catch up again. Being faster was a much more advantageous attribute in this race than being able to stop sooner.

"What should we do now?" Sam asked. She was weaving and dodging cars with the accelerator floored again.

"Would we have an advantage off-road?" I asked.

"No."

"On a different kind of road?"

"No."

"What are the odds you'd win in a fight against opponents with guns?"

"Not good."

"Let me think," I said.

Instead of thinking, something else happened. All the metabolic energy that had been simmering in me suddenly came to a boil. The intense sensation triggered the return of my ability to directly experience my own spiritual energy, and this gave me an idea.

"Let them get closer," I said.

"Are you sure?"

"No. This might not work."

"That's good enough for me," Sam said, forcing a grin.

Part of me was amazed. How could she smile? The other part was continuing to gather energy.

Sam stopped passing cars and let the bikers catch

up. They'd put away their guns to drive at high speeds, but now one of them reached for his again.

I unbuckled my seat belt and swiveled all the way around in my seat. My hands moved themselves into position, and then I shot out a powerful energy beam. It was a relief to release all the pent-up power; it was much more than I could comfortably hold.

Both of the Maoris veered off the road. They gradually slowed and then fell over in an adjacent field. One of their headlights illuminated the other biker's face. He was smiling broadly and looked stunned.

"I blissed 'em," I said. I felt empty, but not in a bad way.

Sam turned onto a side road as sirens sounded behind us.

"Where are we going?" I asked.

"Elsewhere," Sam replied.

"Excellent."

Chapter Twenty-Six

Sam drove for a half hour before we found a gas station, where we purchased a map from a girl who must've been eleven or twelve. We had no idea where we were. The absence of street lights—and any electricity at all for some stretches—kept the night landscape hidden. And the place names on road signs meant nothing to us.

Map in hand, I nonetheless felt completely lost on a variety of deeper levels. I simply couldn't swap perspectives fast enough to keep up with the shifting sand under my feet. Who was I? Who was Sam? And what was the deal with my not-dead parents? Some of the recent craziness was conceptual—weird ideas I had to either accept or reject. But my father had sat right across from me. I couldn't pretend he hadn't been there.

So apparently, Marco definitely was Bompiani. This was another disorienting factor. I'd gone back and forth so many times on this one, it didn't seem to matter anymore. But not-mattering on that scale felt scary. I was in unfamiliar territory. Could I accommodate the temporary nature of everything I thought I knew? One minute, any given fact was there in front of me and I was grasping onto it for dear life. Then it morphed into something else. Or it oscillated back and forth. Or somebody else knew the score but wouldn't tell me what it was. It was as if none of what happened to me was *ever* real—just an aspect of a process that was always en route to the next thing it *seemed* to be. I was forced to immerse myself in a quagmire of meaning and identity. I didn't like it.

Fortunately, Sam was willing to chat and answer questions as she drove. The nearest big city that was likely to have an airport was Aurangabad, a three-hour drive. As time passed and we talked, I began to feel marginally better. I could also feel my energy regenerating, continuing to heal and transform me. I could rest in the warm, loving buzz.

According to Sam, that energy was the main reason that RGP had allowed Marco to recruit and control me. "He embodies extraordinary energy," she said. "The drugs he took could've revolutionized the world if they hadn't generated such dangerous side effects on his personality. And of course, if Marco hadn't run off with them. Did you know your mother began the drug trial alongside him? Just as the benefits started to kick in, off he went with the rest of the trial meds. But that's one reason she is who she is—her having tried the drug for several weeks."

"I had no idea," I said.

"Marco has never expressed an interest in sharing or transmitting his energy before—until now."

"Until me?"

"Until you," Sam agreed. "And unless he did, no one could possibly stand up to him. But whoever he shared it with could become his first real peer—the only person capable of successfully opposing him."

"That's more ironic than usual, isn't it?" I said.

"Yes, it certainly is. So we made sure people like Bhante knew all about you. You weren't effective bait unless an organization that Marco respected validated your status." She downshifted and passed a minivan.

"Bait?"

"A poor choice of words. I'm tired. Let me put it this way. We helped Marco decide to send you the energy. Any regrets about that, Sid?"

"No. But let me point out that your methods, Kasriti's methods, and Marco's methods are all pretty much the same. Tommy T.'s may be more violent, but at least he never tried to con me." I thought things over for a while. "Even with all my energy and new insights about the world," I finally said, "Marco has always been a dozen steps ahead of me. I'll never be a match for him."

Sam nodded. "He understands people. He always has. That's what made him such an outstanding martial arts instructor."

"Was he a professor back then—when you knew him?" I asked.

"He must've been, but we just knew him as Sensei Marco. It's his middle name, actually."

"So RGP wanted him to give me his energy so I'd be rearranged by it and have it on tap to use against him?"

"Not necessarily to attack him, Sid. Just to be able to hold out against him as necessary. Suppose he decided to use energy to wipe out my brain? Wouldn't you want to be able to push back with your own?"

"Of course," I said.

"A major component of the plan was your buying into Marco's story—becoming truly convinced. If you weren't—if you were privy to what we knew—then he might read your mind and know that. For him to proceed with his plan for you—including the full energy transfer—he had to be sure that he had you under his thumb. You can see why I couldn't tell you much."

"Yes. You set him up to create Buddha 2.0, and now you're stealing me back."

"That's one way to look at it." Sam also told me my mother had developed a psychic-blocking technique so Marco couldn't read their minds. He couldn't read everyone's mind, anyway, so this didn't arouse his suspicion.

As we continued to drive—I took a turn at the wheel—I filled her in on the events she'd missed since we'd parted in Mumbai, including the recent scenarios in the tomb and the temple.

"What they told you in the tomb isn't true," Sam said. "They may think they're running things and that they could train you to, but that's not so. And Marco rented a laser light show from a disco in Pune to generate the light show."

"You're kidding. *That's* what the purple light was? But I could feel the energy, too."

"Marco can split his energy off and implant it—do all kinds of tricks—like an energy ventriloquist."

"So all that stuff about Baba's reincarnation and spiritual office-holding is just bullshit?" I asked.

"Well, I wouldn't put it that way. It may be a religious belief of theirs, and who am I to call someone else's beliefs bullshit? But although Meher Baba announced at one point that he was an Avatar—a Buddha, if you will—this wasn't the case. I suspect Marco is using Baba's benign legacy, as well as Ram and Rinpoche's beliefs, for his own purposes. He likes to usurp existing infrastructure. Why invent something when there's already something in place that he could just subvert?"

"Are there other people in charge of the spiritual realm—just not them?" I asked.

"No, it doesn't work that way. The system is profoundly impersonal. We're all tiny cogs in a vast karmic machine. There's no hierarchy. Just teachers. Great teachers show up periodically. Energy workers show up. That's it. These are just jobs that need doing—the same as bricklayers or doctors or hockey players. Nobody is more important than anyone else."

"But some people are more directly involved, right? More aware? Don't they have a greater responsibility to get things to work out?" I gasped as a car nearly rammed us as it turned from a side road.

"What's 'working out?' That's just an idea you have about how things should be." Sam was unfazed by the other driver. "Look at it this way," she said. "At any given moment, there are people of all different ages in the world."

"So?" I had no idea what she was driving at.

"So is an eight-year-old less evolved then a thirty-year-old? No. He's doing developmentally appropriate things—eight-year-old things—just the way he's supposed to. Comparing and ranking them is ridiculous."

"Ah, I think I see," I said. "So if you accept the idea of multiple lifetimes, then we're all at various stages—various levels of development in various lifetimes—and that's like being at different chronological ages."

"Exactly." Sam glanced at me and smiled.

"How can you say all this so authoritatively? How can anyone know things like this for sure?"

"RGP is the keeper of lost Buddhist truths, including what is possibly the biggest secret in the world," Sam said.

"*And*?"

"And I think your mother would want to tell you about it," Sam said.

"How about a hint?" I asked. "A clue? You can't tease me this way." I tried to look adorable to ensure her cooperation.

She pursed her lips. "All right," she said after a bit. "We owe you that, don't we?"

"*And*?"

"Who says Buddha was a man?"

Chapter Twenty-Seven

That was all she would say. So apparently, RGP was privy to some insider knowledge about Buddha having been a woman. I tried to remember what the letters RGP stood for. It was composed of Pali words that meant something like "the organization that keeps secrets about what's under dresses."

This was a revolutionary idea that no one would accept without incontrovertible proof. And how could there be any after thousands of years? It was like saying that Jesus was…what? A midget? From Mars? I really couldn't think of anything equivalent. Could an entire religion be built on an overt deception?

After some time, as we continued driving, I realized I had failed to express ordinary concern about my mother, and worse yet, I didn't feel particularly worried. I asked Sam to tell me more about her situation to assuage the mild guilt I felt.

Sam told me that Tommy T. and whoever was bankrolling him wanted to swap her for me. "They haven't threatened to harm her, though. It's not an 'or else' situation, as far as we can tell."

"Why do they want me so badly? What's your take on that?" I asked.

"I don't know. It might be about the relics, or it could be a bounty from an extremist religious group that found out about you."

We rode in silence for a while, then I finally asked her if she had a plan, and if it included rescuing Chris from Marco's clutches.

"One thing at a time," Sam replied. "Chris is safe for now." She turned and looked me in the eye. "Truly." In a moment, she spoke again. "We'll fly to RGP headquarters—well, it's like a headquarters."

"Where's that?"

She turned to me again and smiled. "Santa Cruz, actually."

It began to rain. Hard. Sam pulled over, and we tried to put the top up on the convertible, but it got stuck partway and wouldn't budge in either direction. The passing cars and trucks seemed unsympathetic to our plight. No one stopped to offer us rain gear, a nice hot cup of tea, or any comforting words. Perhaps they suspected us of being upscale bandits trying to prey on good Samaritans—or whatever ancient ethnic group had demonstrated altruism in India.

"Whose car is this, anyway?" I asked. "What's a BMW doing here?"

"I have no idea. Your father just gave me the keys and told me where to find it."

We were getting drenched as we stood beside the car, which Sam had parked next to a rock-strewn field. Her very wet green top was becoming transparent, and I could see the outline of her nipples. It was raining so hard, only seconds later I could see the nipples themselves, stiff and straining against the thin fabric that was plastered against them.

"So it's his, then?" I asked, returning my gaze to her eyes.

"Oh no. How could it be his?"

"What do you mean?"

"Well, of course your father doesn't drive, Sid."

"Why not?"

She stared at me. I took the opportunity to scan her breasts again. They were lovely.

"He's blind," Sam said. "You didn't notice he's blind?" She saw the shocked expression on my face. "I'm sorry, Sid. It's macular degeneration. He's been completely blind for about two years. But he's got the dogs."

"The black and white hounds? Those are his?"

"Yes. They're not trained seeing-eye dogs, but somehow all three of them manage to get the job done. They're remarkable creatures—not like any other dogs I've ever known. They were given to him by some mystery woman who showed up one day in a pickup truck."

"There are five of them," I said.

"No—three."

I was much too tired to argue. Maybe the five dogs rotated duties so only three were on the job at any given time. Still, the whole thing seemed extremely unlikely. The dogs hadn't even worn collars, let alone guide-dog harnesses.

"You're saying my father is using untrained dogs to help him get around—that he maneuvered around the temple with their help? Really?"

"Your father and the dogs—Manny, Moe, and Jack—have some sort of special relationship," she said. "They're his eyes."

Water streamed down my face. "On a more mundane level," I said, "I'm very wet. And the leather seats are getting soaked, too. Do you think there's a

BMW mechanic nearby?"

"Do you?" she responded with an edge to her voice.

I'd been joking, of course. I think her wherewithal had about run out. "Why don't we try driving the car anyway, even with the top stuck partway up," I suggested. "What's the worst thing that could happen? We're talking about German craftsmanship here."

"The top could fly off."

We were getting wetter by the second. "Oh, I don't think that's too likely," I said.

She paused and gathered herself. After a few deep breaths—her wet breasts rising and falling—she nodded her assent, and we climbed back into the car.

When she started driving again, the top promptly fell off, clattering on the pavement behind us. We both started laughing and couldn't stop. Sam pulled over to the side of the road again.

"So much for craftsmanship," I finally managed to say.

"The world's going to hell in a handbasket," Sam added between peals of laughter.

"I like the last time you lost your top better," I told her. "I mean on the cliff."

"I want you to know I don't do that all the time. It just seemed to be called for under the circumstances."

"So what percentage of the time do you take your shirt off if it's not all the time?"

"Oh, only about 92.4 percent. You know, whenever any problem needs solving."

I laughed. I was relieved that the tension that had been there two minutes ago had morphed into comedy. We were exhausted and soaked, our future was wildly uncertain, and we were in the process of trashing someone's expensive sports car. But I, for one, felt extremely happy.

"Come here," I said. "Give Daddy some sugar."

Sam laughed, scooted over the gear shift, and climbed onto my wet lap. The rain was lighter now. We held a passionate kiss. Our energies danced, and my heart soared. Her essence was pure light like Faroud's, strong and fiery like Marco's, and as sweet as anything I'd ever tasted. It was sublime. I *loved* this woman.

Sam's lips were soft and hot, and she simply held them against mine and let the energy build. In a minute, our hands began roaming. Mine held her exquisite breasts, and hers stroked my back. Neither of us was in a rush. The longer we waited for the fireworks, the better they'd be.

Her right hand reached down into my pants and tickled my erect cock with a callused finger. I slid a hand down and pressed it flat against Sam's belly, pushing her down onto the gearshift. I'd forgotten we were in a car.

Sam laughed. "I don't think this is going to work."

"No, I guess not. We'd probably get arrested even if you survived being impaled by the shifter."

Chapter Twenty-Eight

The domestic airport in Aurangabad didn't inspire confidence, but the airline employee who helped us plan our trip did. She booked us from Aurangabad to Calcutta—Kolkata now—to Singapore to Honolulu to San Francisco. Sam charged the tickets to an RGP credit card, which I found amusing. It was a beautiful card, though, with a silver logo incorporating the organization's three letters superimposed over a photo of a gold, reclining statue of Buddha—a very indeterminately gendered Buddha.

We left the car in the airport parking lot, and God knew what happened to it.

The trip seemed interminable. Halfway through, I felt utterly depleted and indescribably uncomfortable. My aches and pains and each airline seat were incompatible bedfellows. Even Sam's company couldn't make the trip fun. Fortunately, I was able to sleep on the Singapore to Honolulu leg, laying my head on Sam's lap and my feet on an empty seat. When I was falling asleep, I had a feeling that I'd have a big dream, but if I did, I didn't remember it.

Before the final leg, during a three-hour layover in Honolulu, I bought—once again—a change of clothes, a bag of toiletries, and a backpack to put them in. It wouldn't be safe to stop at my apartment in Santa Cruz to pick up my own things. For the hell of it, I added a red Hawaiian shirt that displayed African-American hula girls dancing on surfboards. Who in their right mind would make such a shirt? Chris would be jealous.

After shopping, I sat in the airport while Sam stretched her legs outside in the sun. I would've enjoyed walking, but returning to California was starting to feel real, and I needed to think about that prospect on my own.

On a bench in a large atrium in the airport, I wondered what it would be like to be in my hometown after everything that had happened. How were my clients faring? What had my suitemates made of the wreckage in the waiting room? Were all my houseplants dead—well, the three that had survived my last breakup?

How long had I been gone? It felt like three months. I counted the days; it had only been twelve. Could anyone have been through more in less time?

Then another thought bubbled up. Like everyone else I knew, I'd been outright delusional most of my life. The things I'd believed to be the most real were actually the least. I had consistently, willfully ignored or misinterpreted my own experience in order to hang onto culturally sanctioned ideas about the world. Any clear-eyed eight-year-old could see that these were a crock. I was so grateful I'd been pummeled by all the recent confounding, paradigm-busting experiences.

The flight to San Francisco was uneventful, unless you counted a very fat man falling over a crouched air hostess as an event.

Sam had made a series of phone calls from various airports. We were met in the baggage claim area by a hefty African-American woman who warily eyed the

Hawaiian shirt I was wearing.

"I'm sorry," I said.

She wore a plain brown dress and red running shoes. She had freckles on her cheeks, which I've always liked on African-Americans. Otherwise, there was nothing particularly attractive about her. She could've been a character actor in a '70s sitcom.

She handed me a business card. It read "I'm resting my voice."

"Is this a spiritual thing?" I asked.

She nodded.

I nodded back and felt energy fall out of the top of my head. It was a very odd sensation which only lasted for a few seconds.

The woman registered receiving it without a fuss. Perhaps it wasn't her first experience of this phenomenon.

She mouthed the words, "Thank you," which seemed like cheating to me if you were supposed to be silent.

Sam hugged her. "This is Anne," she told me. "Anne, this is B-2—Andrea's son."

Anne clasped her hands together and bowed. I bowed back.

After an unusually short wait at the baggage carousel, Anne drove us for an hour and a quarter in a small station wagon to an upscale home on Escalona Drive on the west side of Santa Cruz. It was prime real estate, up a long driveway between two oversized Tudor-style homes, and halfway up the hill to the university, with spectacular bay and ocean views.

The gleaming white house sprawled across the ample property in a single-story design, reminiscent of both Japanese and Danish architecture. A creek ran down the steep hillside alongside it. It was dammed at the top, forming a pond that turned out to hold koi. At the bottom, speckled trout swam in another pond under an arching wooden bridge that connected the carport to the house. Between the two, the creek fell over a series of steep, man-made waterfalls, lined with ferns and small ornamental trees. Japanese-style gardens filled in all the open spaces on the property, except for a small side lawn that overlooked the koi pond. A Mexican-style string hammock hung between two wooden posts across part of the lawn. It looked like a great spot for an afternoon nap.

All in all, it was spectacular, one of the most beautiful homes and settings I'd ever seen. And from the street, no one would even know it was there.

"Headquarters?" I asked. "This is quite a headquarters."

"A wealthy donor willed it to us," Sam said. "We'll be safe here."

After we'd carried our bags across the bridge and followed Anne up the stone walkway, my mother met us at the front door.

"You're free!" I said, hugging her enthusiastically. "I thought I might lose you again." I felt joy, mixed with the remnants of the trepidation I'd been holding at bay while she'd been kidnapped.

She looked much older than I remembered. And much more awake. My mother wasn't particularly good-looking, but she'd never scared any babies, either. Her brown eyes were deep set in her long face, above a snub nose that didn't go with the rest of her. Her white hair was cropped short. She wore a plain gray top over a long multicolored skirt. As usual, her oversized feet overflowed her black flip-flops.

Her striking energy felt like a cross between Sam's and Bhante's, but milder, with more structure. I didn't really have a vocabulary for all this.

"I just got here," my mother said when I let her go. "Your dad negotiated a deal. They were happy to take money instead of you, as it turned out. These are gangsters, after all."

"Were you mistreated?" Sam asked.

"Far from it," my mother said. "There was one Caucasian man and two Maoris—what a beautiful people they are. I could look at them all day long. When the Caucasian pushed me once—I guess I was moving too slowly to suit him—one of the Maoris knocked him flat and the other one sat on him. It was quite comical. They said I reminded them of their auntie."

"Did the white guy look like a rat?" I asked.

"Very much so. Do you know him?" she asked.

"Only too well," I told her. "He seems to be quite fond of kidnapping people."

"He was with Jason Patariki back at Sid's office," Sam explained.

"Ah. The infamous Frank. Come in, come in." She gestured to the doorway behind her, and then to Anne, as though her acolyte's silence meant she needed a separate invitation. "Can I get you anything to drink? Are you hungry?" She had switched to Mom mode; this was who I knew.

The house was sparsely but elegantly decorated with Southeast Asian antiques. The ceilings were unusually high with an assortment of skylights, and each room was on a slightly different level. The white walls contrasted with the reddish-brown hardwood floors. It wasn't a type of wood I'd ever seen before.

As we settled into the spacious living room, with a view of the bay and the boardwalk down the hill, I asked my mother if we could talk in private.

"Of course. Anne, could you check on our other guest? Sam, make yourself at home."

They both nodded their assents and departed quietly.

I sat on a tufted red loveseat, and my mother—Andrea—sat across from me in a low rosewood chair. A black silk rug lay between us, and a white porcelain statue of a prone dog lay on that. The dog seemed to be laughing—or at least very happy.

On the plane, I'd planned what I intended to say when I saw my mother, but instead I blurted out, "What the fuck?" And then I repeated it.

"In hindsight," she said, "we could have done things differently. But if you feel like a pawn in a chess game, welcome to the club. Welcome to reality. We're all pawns in a chess game. And your father and I have suffered from losing you, too."

I shook my head. "I doubt that very much. At least you knew I was alive—that you'd see me again someday. And you instigated the suffering."

"Of course. You're right, dear," my mother conceded, waving her hand in a characteristic gesture. Growing up, it had meant, "Yes, yes, whatever. Let's get on with things."

"Our behavior is indefensible," she continued. "You have logic and the moral high ground here. But try to put yourself in our shoes. Is our family more important than the entire planet? Suppose we would have been ceding this world—this plane of existence—to Marco or someone like him if we proceeded in a normal, straightforward way. What then?"

"That's a lot of supposing, Mom. I'll grant you there are always situations that call for an outside-the-box response. But who doesn't have a bias when they try to determine if that's the case? How could you be so sure of yourselves? By definition, it's arrogant to act in a drastic fashion when it's not possible to be sure about something."

My mother nodded. "Good point," she said. "I can't argue successfully with you about this, Sid. If we reduce the situation down to mere words, its essence is lost. All I can do is apologize. I'm sorry we felt it was necessary to put you through this. I love you very much."

"You say you're sorry, but I'd be willing to bet you'd do the same thing over again. You think you're right. You think you've got Buddha on your side or something, don't you? I don't hear what you said as a real apology. That's what people say to appease someone." I said this with some heat. "By the way," I continued, "I love you, too, of course—and I mean more than I love Joe Q. Public, since I seem to love the whole damned world now." I said this with an attitude. My tone certainly didn't reflect much love.

She smiled. Although my mother didn't show her teeth when she smiled—it looked like a smirk in photographs—it was still a warm expression—a soft offering.

"I imagine it's all still new and hard to get used to," she said. "But let's go back sixteen years. You were twenty-one—and a young twenty-one, I think you'd admit—when we needed to act. You lacked the maturity to handle the truth."

"I'll certainly agree that I was an even bigger idiot sixteen years ago," I said.

My mother held up her hand. "That's not my word, Sid. You were just young. Imagine us trying to have a conversation like this back then. You weren't even around enough for us to be in the same room, were you?"

"No, you're right about that," I said.

I watched her for a moment. Her head cocked to the side just a bit and her posture in the wooden chair was erect, but relaxed. She could've been chatting about what color hat to buy. This was not the same matriarch who had run our family on caffeine, nervous energy, and family therapy textbooks.

"You look great," she said to me, "except for that shirt. That's the most horrible shirt I've ever seen. I don't know what you were thinking. But otherwise, you look just like Buddha might have looked if she'd been a man."

There it was. It hung in the air between us for a while. "Was she a lesbian, at least?" I asked.

My mother laughed. "Maybe."

"How is it that the whole world is sure he was a man?" I asked.

"They don't have access to the same information we do. We have Buddha's diary."

This was getting weirder every second. I pictured a thirteen-year-old Asian girl in an orange robe lying on a floral bedspread in her girlie bedroom, scribbling in a pink vinyl diary.

Dear Diary, today I meditated for twelve hours and discovered impermanence. Also, I think Jimmy is way cute, but Suzy likes him, too.

"Come on," I said. "Buddha lived in 500 BC or something. How could anything like that still be around?"

"Do we have plays and philosophical tracts from the ancient Greeks?" She asked.

"Sure."

"Why is that, do you suppose?"

"Did they write on stone?" I asked. "Did the Romans pass it all on? I don't know. But I get your point. The Greeks were BC folks, too, so I guess it's possible for written material to survive that long."

"Yes. The main thing with surviving classical literature is that throughout history someone always valued it enough to recopy it—keep it alive—and even make it a part of their culture."

"But how do you keep something like that secret for so long? Isn't the fact that something *isn't* secret the very reason it stays alive? Isn't that what you just said? People know about some text, so they kept passing it on. For that matter, why hide the truth in the first place? Did Buddha pretend to be a man when he—or she— was alive? Or did other people change the story afterward? The whole thing is crazy, Mom—and I know crazy. At this point, if anyone knows crazy, it's me."

"Let's go back to Buddha's time," she said.

This reminded me of Bhante in the New Zealand cave library. It was time for a history lesson again. Oh boy.

"It was, of course, a patriarchal world. Women

were convenient receptacles. I know that's a vulgarity, but it's true. We were property. Baby makers. Now suppose you were a woman who became enlightened on her own. A woman who could teach the world how to suffer less—how to live. What would you do?"

"Well, obviously you're pulling for me to say, 'Pretend to be a man,' but I've also become an expert at how unspiritual means don't justify a spiritual end. How could Buddha turn people on to the truth by role-modeling deception? How can you start a religion on a lie? Buddhism is about Buddha being Buddha—how any of us can be like him—or her—if we just see reality exactly as it is. Am I right? So if Buddha's a fraud, the whole thing's a house of cards, isn't it?"

"Sid, all religions are based on withholding information from the general public. Most people aren't in a position to understand the core of a new philosophy or belief system. That doesn't mean that a given message is any less true. Buddha *was* enlightened, *and* she really could tell others how she attained this—how they could get there, too. Jesus *was* a peace-loving man who knew a better way to live. Does it matter that he was just passing on things he learned in India? For that matter, when he spoke in metaphors and parables, was he lying? Do you think he's really living in the house of his father now that he's dead? It's the same in all religions. Ironically, the Truth with a capital T needs to be disseminated by employing minor untruths. That's just how it works. A female Buddha would have been ignored—or worse."

"Okay," I said, "let's assume that an androgynous-looking woman could pass for a man. Then what would be the point of writing a diary that might expose the impersonation?"

"Buddha set up RGP and asked them to caretake the diary—which was written on hardened clay tablets, by the way. She told us that when her prophecies came true, we would need to reveal it. That time is almost here, Sid. You're the first man to know Buddha's secret. And we need your help to change the world—to create a level playing field for everyone."

"Mom, I've heard that rationale a lot lately."

"Listen, Sid. Here are the nuts and bolts. Until women gained sufficient equality—under the law and across a critical mass of cultures—the diary couldn't tip the scales and create true, equal empowerment. But Buddha knew there would be a time when the irrefutable revelation of her gender could change everything. And she detailed what that era would look like." My mother gazed calmly into my eyes. "It looks like this, Sid. Exactly like this."

"I don't buy it," I said. "Men will never hand over the reins to women based on an ancient artifact. It doesn't matter what it is. Greed, power, and control drive inequality—not an incorrect reckoning of historical facts. If you prove the Buddha was a woman, all you'd do is destabilize various institutions— Buddhist ones, for the most part. And those are much more on your side in the first place."

"There's more to the plan," my mother said. "Don't you think others have addressed all these concerns over the years? But I think it's time for dinner. Why don't you go wash up? I'll show you your room. I think you'll like it."

"Yeah, okay. I'm sorry about my hissy fit before. It's really not like me," I said.

"I know, dear. Don't worry."

Chapter Twenty-Nine

Twenty minutes later, I was the last to convene in a colorfully tiled dining room, which overlooked the property's upper pond—the koi pond. Floor-to-ceiling windows afforded a view of a dozen multicolored fish, swimming in remarkably distinct phalanxes.

The other houseguest turned out to be Paul Arthur—Sam's brother, who had interviewed me in my office.

Side by side at the white linen-covered table, Paul and his sister's resemblance was obvious. His face was slimmer than I remembered, and his eyes were a different shade of blue from Sam's. But they both embodied the Nordic bone structure and facial features that I associated with Vikings and blond supermodels.

Paul stood and greeted me warmly, offering his hand. I reached across the table to shake it and felt the same spark I'd been disconcerted by when I'd met him. Now, I could recognize that it was simply a poorly boundaried charge that Paul carried and didn't know about. He had a fair amount of potential—energetically—but he hadn't developed it much.

"Paul's here to stay safe, as well," Sam said, once I'd seated myself between Anne and my mother, across the table from the siblings.

"We'll talk about all that after we eat," my mother said.

Instead, while we ate, my mother peppered me with questions. Why hadn't things worked out with my last girlfriend Susan? Did I enjoy my work? How had I met Chris?

"Here's where I see myself ten years from now," I finally reported after ten minutes of this. "And if I were an animal, I'd like to be a fuzzy little kitten. And I think I could be an asset to this company because I'm so damned cooperative when I'm being interrogated."

There was silence at the table.

"I'm sorry," I said. "I guess I'm uncomfortable being the center of attention." And I'd never liked the controlling side of my mother, either. Who knows what might've emerged out of a free exchange of ideas between us? She was substituting what she wanted instead.

"I know I'm your mother and I push your buttons, Sid. But you'd better get used to the attention part. You'll be the center of all kinds of scrutiny soon."

The food was simple, vegetarian, and plentiful. Apparently, Anne had cooked, and now she served us, too. We drank water, not having been offered anything else.

Sam picked up the conversational slack after I'd derailed my mother. While I scarfed down a roasted eggplant and kale salad—it was awful—she told the others about the cliff descent (the PG-rated version—sans toplessness), the parking lot fracas, the Mumbai taxi wreck, and the motorcycle chase. Strung together, her narration sounded like an action movie trailer.

When the last bite had been eaten, I turned to Paul. "So why do you need a safe haven?" I asked.

"RGP hired me again—this time to deliver the

ransom money for Andrea to Tommy T.'s men. It didn't go as smoothly as it could've," he said. His voice was much more familiar to me than it should've been. I briefly wondered what that was about.

"What do you mean?" Sam asked. I'd assumed she'd had a chance to talk to Paul, but perhaps she hadn't.

"It might have turned very ugly," he said. "The kidnappers were trying to intimidate me, and I wasn't armed. My martial arts skills are nothing like Sam's."

"Marco said you were a bad student," I told him.

He laughed. "I probably was, but he was a very impatient teacher, too."

I glanced at Sam. She nodded and smiled back.

"This was out at the end of the city wharf," Paul continued, "just past those nooks where all the sea lions congregate."

"I love the word 'nook,' " Anne said and then immediately clapped a hand over her mouth.

My mother raised an eyebrow; Anne lowered her head.

"I like the word 'congregate,' " I said, smiling at Anne, who looked up and brightened a bit.

"So you were in the midst of all the tourists?" I asked Paul.

"Yes. They were all freezing, as usual, in their shorts and T-shirts. The fog was in. So basically, four Maori men were about to take the bag of money away from me, with no guarantee that we'd see your mother again."

"Yikes," Anne said. This time she shook her head ruefully, pushed back her chair, bowed, and left the room.

"It's only her second day of silence," my mother explained.

"So what happened?" Sam asked Paul.

"Jason Patariki happened. He showed up at full speed from out of nowhere and threw two of the guys over the railing into the bay. That guy is amazingly strong. These weren't small people. Anyway, after that, we followed the protocol we'd agreed on."

"Were the tourists freaked out?" I asked.

"Some of them," Paul said. "But for most, it was like we were putting on a show. I think the sea lions were more upset, all in all. They certainly raised a ruckus."

"Did you know Jason already?" I asked.

"No, no. I mean, I sat with him in your waiting room that one time—you don't forget a guy who looks like that—but I just thought he was part of a gay couple waiting for therapy."

I laughed. "Jason and the rat-faced guy? They would have been a wildly unlikely couple if they were gay, wouldn't they?"

"Well, my gaydar told me about Jason—I'm gay myself. I don't think he's out, but he's totally gay. Anyway, I only knew his name out on the wharf because he introduced himself right before the sirens chased us all off."

"Ah," I said. After a brief silence, while everyone digested Paul's news, I turned to my mother. "Did they have you in the back of a van or something?"

"Are you picturing a white Econoline like your uncle had when you were a kid—that one that smelled like hay inside?"

"Actually, I was. They always use something like

that in the movies."

"Sorry to disappoint you, Sid. First, they kept me at a rather nice B&B by Neary's Lagoon, and then during the exchange on the wharf, I was stationed on a bench by the surf museum on West Cliff Drive—with a minder, of course."

"You don't seem too shaken up by your experience," I said.

"What's the worst thing that could have happened?" she said. "I'd die? I'm looking forward to finding out what's next. Also, the bench was a great spot—very scenic, with scads of darling dogs passing by. And the Maori man who sat with me—I think it was Tommy T.—does he wear cowboy clothes?"

I nodded.

"Well," she continued, "he told me a fascinating story about how his first marriage ended. Did you know that some women are addicted to enemas?"

"I did not," I said.

"Me neither," Sam said.

These kidnappers didn't sound much like the thugs I'd escaped from in the Bay of Islands. Maybe Tommy T.'s overseas crew was more reasonable or he was hesitant to screw around in a country where he didn't have cops on his payroll. More likely, my mother's ability to get along with anyone had prevailed. It was one of the reasons she'd been such a successful therapist and teacher.

"It takes all kinds, said the lady as she kissed the cow," Paul said. "Our mother used to say that."

"Boy, *there's* an idiom from a more innocent era," I said. "Nowadays, there's probably a cow-kissing porn website."

I was struck by how ordinary the tone of our conversation was. We could've all been cousins at a family reunion or work colleagues discussing a clueless boss. Perhaps everyone at the table was either sufficiently evolved or had been desensitized to the point that life or death outcomes—whether for an individual or an entire world—constituted casual topics.

I decided to ask a few direct questions and get as-direct-as-possible answers. My mother could fill in a lot of blanks if she was willing.

"So is it up to me to save the world?" I asked her. "People have been telling me that."

She laughed. "We're a little full of ourselves, aren't we?"

"But isn't the world in crisis?" I said doggedly. "I understand I can help improve things—and I won't go into the details with Paul here—but don't we need to do something special to keep it all going?"

"Now isn't the best time to go into that, Sid—as you said. You and I will have to have another private chat soon."

"What about Bhante's relics?" I asked next.

"What about them?" She seemed irritated by my question.

"Do they exist? Are they really Buddha's remains?"

"I believe so," my mother said. "Are you double-checking on things that Dr. Bompiani told you?"

"And Bhante," I said. "I guess I should've done this before. Here's another question. Do you know if I'm the reincarnation of somebody?"

"You definitely are," Sam said.

"Who?"

"Whoever you were before."

"I agree," my mother said.

"Me too," Paul added.

"Thanks," I said. "You're a very helpful group. Paul, here's a question for you. Was all that just a song and dance back in my office? If my parents are such an important part of RGP, why did you need to go through all that 'testing' to 'discover' me? Didn't everyone already know who I was?"

My mother answered for him. "The members of RGP didn't care to take it on faith about you. We needed to satisfy everyone that we weren't acting out of nepotism—that you were legitimately who we told them you were. We're a democratic organization at heart, despite our need for hierarchy. We don't proceed without a consensus."

Paul spoke up. "I certainly wouldn't want my sister risking her life on your behalf if you were just the fantasy of proud, deluded parents."

I turned to my mother again. "What about Dad? Where is he?"

"On his way," she answered, "with your friend Chris, whom I'm looking forward to finally meeting."

I took a sip of water, which prompted Sam and my mother to drink as well.

"Dad's really blind, huh?" I asked.

"Oh yes," my mother answered.

"And those dogs really help him?"

"Yes, I don't know what he'd do without them."

"And you see three of them?" I asked.

My mother cocked her head in a characteristic manner. This was her what-are-you-getting-at expression. I got this a lot when I'd start to work my parents for permission to pursue dubious activities.

"Yes," she said. "How many do you see, Sid?"

"Five, actually. I see five."

"That's interesting," she said, leaning forward to peer at me more intently. "What did the extra two do? Did they act different than the other three? Was there anything remarkable about them?"

"Yes. The extra two suddenly disappeared when Dad and I left the old temple in India. And of course, it's odd no one else sees them. Why do you ask?"

"I don't think they're regular dogs," my mother said. "I think they're spirit dogs, Sid. One is probably your father's and one is yours."

"Come on," I said, "that's ridiculous."

"I have a spirit animal," Sam said.

"Really?" I asked. I'd never believed in anything along those lines.

"Yes. I could sense she was with us on the cliff in New Zealand."

"Isn't that a Native American thing?" Paul asked.

Sam nodded. "But it's real."

"Sid, look around," my mother said. "If I'm right, and you have the ability to see the spirit world, you'll see your dog here. Our spirit animals follow us—guide us—protect us. They're always with us. It's nothing spooky. They're just beings without bodies—beings that embody certain qualities that we might need. And particular animals represent various human attributes—courage, loyalty, or whatever—so those are the guises that these beings use."

"What's your animal?" I asked her.

"It's a red-winged blackbird," my mother said. "I met her in a vision—on a retreat in Santa Fe."

"And yours?" I asked Sam.

"A jaguar. I call her Maria."

"All right," I said. "I'll give it a try. I'll look for my dog."

"Use more than your eyes," my mother suggested.

I tried it. At first, all I saw was the room, the koi pond outside, and all the rest of ordinary reality. Then I unfocused myself—tried to sense instead of just seeing. Perhaps I could open up to receiving whatever was out there.

I saw the dog. He gradually materialized outside—on a flat gray rock next to the pond. He was plowing his nose into the water and snuffling, trying to catch a fish.

It was definitely one of the two that had disappeared in the ruined temple—this one had lain just to my right on the dirt floor. He was a medium-sized hound mix, jet black with three vaguely diamond-shaped patches of white.

"Holy shit," I said. "Sorry, Mom. He's right over there." I pointed.

Everyone looked and then shook their heads.

"We can't see him," Sam said.

"I don't think he knows he's a spirit," I said. "He's trying to eat the koi." Just then the dog sat up, swiveled his head, and winked at me. "No, wait," I said. "He does know."

Chapter Thirty

When we all finally pushed our chairs back and stood, the spirit dog raced across the lawn and leapt through a closed window. The glass didn't break, and he wasn't hurt. He was just inside now. He looked quite pleased with himself.

The dog trotted beside me back to my room, where I'd planned to check my email. When I reached down to pat him, my hand went through the image I saw. He wasn't there enough to touch. But I was sure that I'd patted him at the Temple—not one of the three real dogs, but this one.

I settled into a modern office chair behind a red Chinese-style desk. The dog padded past me and lay down on the bed.

I decided to name him "Spot." Why not?

"Hi, Spot," I said, turning to see his reaction. There was none. He gazed at me evenly from across whatever was between his realm and mine. Distance? Time? Probably it was something more incomprehensible.

I decided to just go ahead and turn the computer on. I couldn't pet Spot, feed him, or take him for a walk. So I might as well go about my business as though he wasn't there. Which he wasn't, of course.

For a moment, I noticed how easily I'd accommodated this latest weirdness. It didn't seem worth thinking about further, though.

I'd received dozens of emails from friends and extended family, all wondering where the hell I was. I sent out a group reply that attested to my current well-being, but I didn't attempt to describe any of my recent adventures. How could I possibly explain any of it in a paragraph or two?

I'd also received emails from Chris, Lannie, Bhante, and Marco. I'd given my address to Lannie back at the family's bed and breakfast in Howick, New Zealand. I don't know how the two older men got hold of it—maybe from Chris.

Chris's email read "Marco turned out to be a dick. He's definitely way spiritual, but he's still a dick. Your dad—if that's who he is—persuaded me to go with him and his cool not-quite-seeing-eye dogs to wherever you are. He won't tell me where. See you soon, unless this guy is really a serial killer who had plastic surgery to resemble the guy in your old family photos. Love and kisses. Yer pal, Chris. PS: Your dad/the serial killer is phenomenal at bribing people to let him take his dogs places that don't allow dogs. The man's an artist. Right up there with Marco."

Lannie's email was several days old. It read "I continue to grow. Thank you for your help. I need to tell you about a vision I had this morning. I think it's real. An old Indian man with a big nose and a funny mustache floated up in the air in front of me while I was making eggs for a nice woman from Canada. He spoke my dialect of Cantonese, and he said you could trust the diamond dog and that this dog has been helping you all along. Who is this diamond dog? Are you okay? Where are you? Warm regards, Lannie."

The one from Bhante was shorter: "We are still

hoping to work with you to help the world awaken. Please reply as soon as possible. Your servant, Bhante Wimalaratne."

Marco had an interesting email address: marcoisbompiani@neededtofoolyou.com. His message read "Remember in the beginning—when what I said didn't make sense to you, and I told you to ignore that and pay attention to how things turned out? Remember who you were then and who you are now? Remember how you experienced yourself when you were with me? It's all unfolding just the way it needs to. All is well— doubts and all. Love rules. See you soon. M."

The "see you soon" concerned me, but I decided to put that aside and answer Chris and Lannie.

I reassured Chris that my dad was my dad since I wasn't sure if he'd been joking or not. And I validated his perspective on Marco, employing more elegant, non-dick language. I decided not to risk telling him where I was, but I did tell him I thought he'd like it here. I finished by describing my Hawaiian shirt and telling him that I had an invisible dog now.

I thanked Lannie for helping me at her house and in the email. I told her that the man who had appeared in her kitchen had been Meher Baba, even though he was dead. I also told her that I was safe and the diamond dog lay near me as I wrote. By the end of this short reply, I was crying again. I felt profoundly connected to Lannie, although I'd probably never see her again. Just thinking about her made me cry.

I decided not to contact Bhante or Marco. Exposing myself to another round of their cleverly packaged words might lead to backsliding and signing up for further manipulation. It had been hard enough to escape their clutches before. In fact, I'd never truly escaped anything. I had either been rescued or had foolishly jumped from the frying pan into the fire.

Alone in my room—except for Spot—my internal energy began to assert itself again. No longer supported by the intense energy field of India and no longer drawing on anyone else's, as it had with Marco, I sensed that for the first time, I was experiencing it—and myself—in an unadulterated way, just as it was.

Purer and clearer than before, it was like an accomplished soprano's voice, projecting only the exact pitch of a given note, with no added texture or overtones. The energy was also slightly less strong than I remembered, and distinctly less buzzy. I felt calm and poised as it coursed through me. I was aware that immense power was on tap—that what I was experiencing in that moment was just the tip of an iceberg. The episode with the motorcycle-riding Maoris had opened my eyes to both my ability to draw on the energy, and the versatility of it. Apparently, it could heal, awaken, or stun as the situation called for. At some point, I'd been affected by it in all those ways myself.

Sam stopped by to let me know we couldn't sleep together under RGP's roof. She stood in the doorway and looked great in worn jeans, a gray sweatshirt, and a pair of my mother's flip-flops. Her long blond hair trailed across her shoulders. She also looked tired; I could see lines at the corners of her eyes that I'd never noticed before. But she was still grounded. There was a solidity to her that never seemed to falter.

"Okay," I said. "No sex."

"Well, you could act a tiny bit disappointed, Sid."

"Sorry. I guess just looking at you seems sufficient."

"That's sort of sweet. I give it a B plus."

"I didn't know I was going to be graded," I said. "I thought this was a pass or fail deal. I firmly believe grades are overrated. I think what really counts are all my extracurricular activities." I raised my eyebrows and tried to leer at her.

"I do too," Sam said. "Very much. But those activities are exactly what's *not* happening tonight."

I felt relaxed and playful with her, and I liked it. I had an urge to show her Marco's email, so I did. "Do you find that last line alarming?" I asked when Sam was done.

" 'See you soon'? I suppose so—a little. But what was he supposed to write? Good luck to you in your hidden location where I can't screw with you? That lacks Marco's customary panache, don't you think?"

"Good point. I'm just aware of who we're dealing with here. He's capable of amazing things."

She took my hand and held it gently. We sat side by side in chairs in front of the desk. Spot seemed to be asleep on the bed.

"Let's take a look at that—what Marco can and can't do," Sam said. "I think I know a little more about it than you do. What have you observed about him that seems remarkable?"

"Well, he's psychic, right? And not like anyone else I've ever heard of. He's not guessing the gender of an unborn baby or which playing card you're holding. He's plucking exact numbers and thoughts out of people's heads."

"A real psychic can predict the future," Sam said.

"Marco just reads minds and makes inspired guesses about the future—and only sometimes, and only with some people. It's random snippets—nothing all that useful. Sure, it's amazing at first. But it's not a reliable tool he can use against anyone. It's just not as powerful as he wants you to think it is. And it's only a side effect from taking drugs. Marco didn't advance himself on a spiritual path and earn this ability. He *is* very developed spiritually—I'm not saying he isn't. But the mind reading is all about enhanced brain chemistry. Anyone who took the same pill for long enough would be able to do it, too."

"Like my mother?" I asked.

"She didn't get to finish the med trial, so no. Otherwise, yes—that's what I mean."

"How do you know all this?" I asked. "I've spent more time with Marco than you have."

"Your mother. Andrea knows a great deal about how he operates. Otherwise, you wouldn't be sitting here now. She says he was arrogant, elitist, and controlling before the med trial, and that now he's still all those things. And all that's overshadowed by the much more dangerous personality changes the drug cocktail triggered."

"I'll ask her about all that tomorrow," I said.

Sam took her hand back. "My elbow hurts," she said.

"You're such a complainer," I said, shaking my head. "First it was…well, I can't think of anything else. And now it's this whining about your elbow."

"What else?" Sam said.

"What else have you complained about? I told you—I can't remember."

"No, Sid. What else have you noticed about Marco?"

"Oh. Well, I gather I don't know anything for sure." I thought for a moment. "He can't make people invisible, can he?"

"No."

"Can he transfer his energy at will?"

"We don't know," Sam said. "It's possible. Basically, if *you* can do something, he probably can, too. So look to yourself for answers about that. But you're the only one who Marco has deemed worthy of receiving any of his energy so far. So it's hard to say." She smiled wanly. "I need to sleep."

"Me too."

We stood, hugged, and then kissed relatively chastely. Sam turned to go. I remembered one last thing I needed to ask.

"So I guess there isn't really an insomnia epidemic looming, huh? Some weird disease that'll keep sleepers from maintaining illusion?"

She faced me from the doorway. "As a matter of fact, I've heard rumors about that. If there really is such a disease, we're going to have a very big problem. The idea that sleeping minds keep the physical realm afloat is correct." She yawned.

"Would the world—the universe—just disappear?" I asked.

"If there's not a critical mass of consciousness supporting it, there's no illusion. I don't know if it would disappear or blow up or just never have existed in the first place. I don't know, Sid. Can we talk about this in the morning?"

"Of course. Goodnight."

"Goodnight, my love," Sam said.

When she'd left and shut the bedroom door behind her, I pivoted and spoke to Spot.

"She called me 'her love,' " I told him. "Her love."

My spirit guide glanced up and listened attentively. I could sense that he understood me. Then he winked again.

I winked back. Things were looking up. I had a mother and father again, a girlfriend of sorts, a dog of sorts, and assorted spiritual superpowers. No one was currently trying to kidnap me, kill me, or drive me crazy. My best friend was on his way here with my father. I was in a beautiful house with a belly full of healthy food.

I fell asleep compiling a gratefulness list. Of course, I didn't know how many wild events I'd be ungrateful for the next day. If I had, I might not have fallen asleep so easily.

Chapter Thirty-One

I awoke the next morning to find Spot trying to lick my face, but I couldn't feel it.

"Good morning, Spot," I said.

He pantomimed a bark—or maybe he really barked back in Spiritland or wherever most of him was. At any rate, I couldn't hear him.

Why was he attempting to wake me up? I watched him for a moment through sleepy eyes. He might've been a cross between a skinny black lab and something houndish with longer legs. Another breed had contributed the white spots to his fur. His ears were oversized and hung down alongside his handsome face. One of them was mostly white, the other mostly black. Spot was very muscular. If he'd been a real dog, he'd have been a handful to manage on a leash.

I peered past him. *Uh oh.* This wasn't the same room I'd fallen asleep in. It wasn't even the same house.

I sat up and looked closer. Was I dreaming? I found myself reclining on a cushy duvet on a queen-sized bed in a hotel room. There was another bed across a narrow aisle and a blanket-covered figure lay in it, turned away from me. The room was so generically decorated, it could've been anywhere. Everything was beige or taupe or cream-colored. Heavy, patterned drapes covered most of the windows.

Had I been kidnapped again? Drugged and taken?

I looked down to see what I was wearing—was it the same T-shirt and boxer shorts I'd had on when I fell asleep? It was, but my body was only a blurred image now. I wasn't solid; I could see through me. I wasn't even as solid as Spot had been. I looked around for him—to compare our images—but he was gone.

I began to freak out. It certainly didn't feel like a dream. It was some sort of waking nightmare.

Then Spot was there. He suddenly appeared beside me and tried to lick my face again. This time I felt his tongue and saliva. He was completely solid-looking, too. Was I on his turf? How else could I feel him? Had he led me somehow into the spirit world? Was it comprised of mid-priced motel rooms?

"Hey!" I called to whoever was asleep in the other bed. As soon as I spoke, Spot ran off. "Hey!" I called again.

The man turned over and faced me. It was Rinpoche—the Tibetan from Baba's tomb.

"Hello, Sid," he said. "So you're astral traveling now. Good for you."

"Not on purpose," I said. "What is it, anyway? I've heard of remote viewing—like in a near-death experience—is it something like that?"

"Sure. Same kind of thing. Your consciousness is wandering around outside your body. It's fun, isn't it?"

"Terrifying," I said, although I was feeling calmer now that he'd provided an explanation. It was a spooky explanation, but it was better than some of the alternatives I hadn't been willing to explore—such as being dead.

"Well, it has no context for you, does it?"

Rinpoche said. "You haven't come out of any tradition. This is unusual." He smiled his weird smile. "But terror can be fun," he added.

"What do you mean?" I asked.

"Never mind," he said. "What can I do for you?"

"What do you mean?"

"You're visiting me, Sid. You woke me up. What do you want?"

"I don't know." I thought for a moment. "How about this? Should I be worried about Marco?"

"Oh yes. Don't underestimate him."

"And you really think this plan to put me in charge of the world makes sense?" I asked.

"No, I don't. I was just agreeing to it to stay alive. Marco was planning to kill us if we didn't agree."

"Yikes. So I'm in danger, too?" I asked.

"Absolutely. But Sid, my sources tell me you're involved in something bigger."

"What could be bigger? What sources?"

"I don't know exactly what your destiny is," Rinpoche said, "but it transcends all this tomfoolery. And I know this because I'm in contact with energy beings."

"People without bodies?"

He nodded. "Not people. But something like what you mean. They visit me at night like you're doing now."

"Are they like a spirit dog? Did a spirit dog tell you?"

He laughed his wild laugh. "I enjoy you, Sid. You are a fun person. And you can tell your dog to come out from the bathroom."

I turned to look that way, and Spot ran into the

room and barked. I could hear him clearly. It was a deep, growly bark—a bark that said, "Don't fuck with my owner, Bucko!"

"Oh my!" Rinpoche squealed in a silly falsetto voice. "I'm so scared. Save me from the scary spirit dog." Then he laughed again, this time throwing his head back and really letting loose.

Spot stood beside my bed. I think his dignity had been compromised.

"So is this it?" I asked. "This is what astral traveling is? Talking to some joker in a hotel room?"

"For you, I guess," he said. "Perhaps your subconscious is guiding you and it operates on a more mundane plane than you'd like to think. Personally, I like to explore the galaxy—visit other worlds."

"That sounds a lot more fulfilling. Will you teach me how to do it?"

"No," he said, rolling over in the bed to face away from me. "Leave me alone. I'm tired. I'm going back to sleep. You don't know what the hell you're doing."

Spot barked again, and suddenly I was back in my body in the house in Santa Cruz, panting for breath. I was awake and by myself. I was also sweating and shaking. I checked the clock; it was after five in the morning, but it was still dark.

Wow. That had been real—well, not a dream, anyway. Real had become a very relative term with diminishing value. What realm was the real one? Or a better question might be: were any of them any realer than the others?

Generating new, unanswerable questions was not helpful. I decided to go for a run. I was wide awake, and I'd had no legitimate exercise in quite some time. If a bike had been handy, that would've suited me best, but running would be the next best thing.

I peed and splashed water on my face. The guy in the bathroom mirror was more Indian-looking than I remembered. And older—much older. I didn't identify with my face the way I had before. It happened to be the way I looked. It wasn't who I was.

I got dressed and then, as quietly as I could, made my way through the dark house to the front door. It was a cool morning, but if I kept moving, I'd be fine in my T-shirt and pants. I built a rhythm down the long driveway and then turned onto Escalona. The street was quite dark, except for the limited range of a few orangey streetlights. A small dog yipped. I ran.

After a block or two, I heard footsteps behind me. My first thought was *Oh good, here's someone to run with.* I swiveled my head to see who it was. Jason Patariki.

"Don't blast me," he called. "I come in peace."

I sped up, but a moment later he pulled up next to me, and we kept running. I fantasized about sprinting away or ducking between houses, but who was I kidding? I had about as much chance of that as beating him at arm wrestling.

"What do you want?" I asked. "You're not my favorite person."

"First, I wanted to thank you," he said in his rich baritone voice. His New Zealand accent was especially pronounced. "The energy you sent me in India—outside the tomb—it's changed my life."

I turned to look at him for a moment as we ran. He smiled his million-dollar smile. Jason truly was a beautiful man. All his features were large, and of course, his body was huge, but somehow the arrangement was all of a piece—harmonious. He wore what looked like the same khaki shorts and black polo shirt I'd first seen him in, along with a brand-new pair of purple running shoes.

"Really," he said, seeing the skepticism on my face. "First, it just knocked me on my ass. And I was angry when I gathered myself. But there was a time lag. Over the next few days, my heart opened. I love you, Sid."

I glanced over at him again. He was crying.

"So thank you so much," Jason said. "*You* are my teacher now."

"What about Bhante?" I asked.

I slowed down a little, and he matched my pace. I was starting to breathe hard and break a sweat. Jason wasn't.

"I've left Kasriti. I can't be involved with those people."

"Why should I believe you?" I asked.

"Don't you have special powers? Can't you tell when someone is lying?"

"Maybe," I said. I shifted laterally in my mind and opened up to his energy. It was relatively easy to do now. Jason's *chi* was very strong, but disorganized. It was like discordant music. Each discrete note was pure; things just didn't fit together quite right. Clearly, there were no false notes or creepy energy. He was telling the truth.

"Whoa," he said from alongside me. "Can you turn the volume down, Sid?"

"What? Oh, sorry." I'd been inadvertently radiating energy beyond my physical body. The boundary between inside and outside was a lot vaguer now. My edges were softening. I willed the phenomenon to stop, and it did.

"Thank you, teacher," he said.

"Let's stick with Sid," I suggested.

"Sure. No worries."

We ran a bit more, and then I turned a corner, planning to return on a street three blocks down the hill. Jason effortlessly kept up with me.

"Let me be your bodyguard," he said. "You need one."

"I have Sam," I told him.

"Look at you right now," he said. "You're out alone in the dark. Where's Sam? What if I hadn't been me? What if people like Frank are hiding right now behind all these trees? Plus, I want to be near you. I want to learn. I need more help. You're the man, Sid. You're the real deal."

"I have another protector, too, Jason. He's always with me." I glanced around for Spot, but I couldn't see him.

"Where?"

"He's invisible. He's a spirit dog."

"That's wonderful," Jason said. "I have a spirit animal, too. It's a Maori thing. But they can only help in certain ways. There are rules. And a dog isn't a proper spirit animal, anyway—it has to be a wild animal."

Just then, Jason tripped and almost fell. I looked down in time to see Spot dart away from between the big man's legs.

"Spot doesn't like that kind of talk," I said.

"Okay, okay. Sorry, Spot," he said.

I considered Jason's offer. "It's not really up to me," I said. "I'm staying with the RGP people—with my mother. They might not want you in the house."

"They would if you told them you needed me there. Please let me help. If you don't want a bodyguard, maybe there's something else I can do. I'm rich. I'm famous. That could be helpful. The world needs you. The world needs your energy. Let me make sure the world gets what it needs."

His heart was in the right place. Jason truly did love the world and want the best for it. I could sense that. "How did you find me, anyway?" I asked, postponing a response to his request. Every breath hurt now, and my calves ached.

"It's a long story," he said, "but basically, various people followed various people."

We weren't far from the house now, but the last three blocks back were steeply uphill. "All right," I gasped. "Let's try it. I'm sure Sam has better things to do than babysit me all the time. And I have no idea what Spot can do."

"Great!" he said, slapping me on the back so hard that I almost fell forward onto my face. Maybe I needed a bodyguard to protect me from my bodyguard.

We ran in silence for a while. I was a bit surprised by what I'd just said. Apparently, I trusted my newfound ability to read energy more than I distrusted someone who'd played a distinctly negative role in my recent personal history.

When we were within sight of the RGP driveway—it was becoming lighter by the minute—one of the parked cars facing us on Escalona Street turned on its headlights. The glare was right in our eyes.

Somebody goes to work early. But a moment later, four men piled out of the car and spread across the asphalt in front of us. Silhouetted against the lights, I couldn't see who they were. I turned around. Could we run? The same scene was unfolding behind us, but it was at least six men in that direction. I could see them clearly. Maoris.

"I'd say, 'Let's try running,' " I said, panting, "but I'm just about out of gas."

"I can see that," Jason said. "But I don't know if I can fight them all off."

"Should we try?"

"I think we have to. They may want to kill you."

Chapter Thirty-Two

"Really?" I asked. Surprisingly, I didn't feel much of anything. *I need to keep feeling,* I told myself. *I need to stay human.*

"Really. Can you shoot your energy at them? Can Spot help? Do you have a phone with you?"

Before I could answer, the men behind us charged. We sprinted toward the ones in front.

Jason waded in and started kicking in crisp, wide arcs. Three men fell, and only one got up. The fourth one facing us came at me, and I sent a burst of energy his way. He staggered back, with an incongruous, sweet smile on his face.

In the meantime, someone grabbed me from behind and pinned my arms. With a roar, Jason plucked him off me and hurled him into a short, goateed guy. Someone else landed a punch to the side of Jason's head—just above his ear. He didn't seem to notice. Two more men came at me—there were just so many of them.

I sent out more energy, and this time a delayed release of adrenaline turbocharged it. I could feel the shift in intensity, and the gangbanger beside me certainly could, too. He went stiff and then toppled over.

Another guy seemed unaffected, though. He launched himself into the air, his right leg extended. His foot was on a trajectory to smash into my nose.

Then Spot intervened. He leapt in the air and met the guy at the peak of his jump. He bit his ankle through his black warm-up pants. I don't think the attacker felt it as a bite, but he lost his balance nonetheless and veered off course, landing hard on the pavement next to me.

Another younger man took his place. Some of the attackers who Jason had felled had recovered. I blasted this latest guy, and he was only mildly affected. It seemed to distract him and slow him down, but otherwise he remained intact.

I took a moment to look around at the full-scale melee. We were ridiculously outmanned, especially since I didn't know how to fight, and the effect of my energy on our adversaries seemed to vary tremendously.

I could see Jason fighting two men to my right. Several others circled them, cheering on their compatriots.

The Maori men that Jason fought were obviously accomplished martial artists themselves. One of them seemed to be even quicker than Jason, and the other one fought dirty—throwing powder from his pocket at Jason's eyes and aiming most of his kicks at his crotch.

As the stunned man in front of me regained his senses and others joined him, Spot continued to bite, trip, and harass whoever tried to hurt me, but his influence was limited. He could get underfoot and interfere with an attacker's balance and timing, but that was about it.

I let loose multiple energy bursts; some of my targets seemed to be temporarily incapacitated, while others were merely confused. Mostly, they paused, shook themselves, and then kept coming at me.

After a few more minutes of this, it was clear that we were screwed. Jason was being held at bay within a circle of attackers—and several of them held chains or clubs.

Then a big guy wearing a straw fedora hefted a metal baseball bat as he eyed me from about eight feet away. When I glanced behind me to see if I could try running from him, I saw two more men standing with their arms crossed. One of them blew me a kiss.

Spot stood by my side, but even he looked worn out. His tongue hung out of his mouth, dripping spirit saliva, and he was breathing harder than any of our attackers.

The gang member with the bat moved forward cautiously. He'd seen what I'd done to some of the others. I zapped him with all I had left. No effect. Either I was out of juice for now, or he was immune to my energy.

He raised the bat, and I readied myself to dodge his blow. Spot inserted himself between us, but as the bat lashed out, it went through his spirit form unimpeded.

The guy anticipated which way I'd move, and in a millisecond, I was going to have a seriously smashed shoulder.

Then I heard an unearthly high-pitched shriek, which seemed to freeze the action. To my eyes, it was as if everything had slipped into super slow-motion. I could see the bat, and I could see my shoulder, and I could see the air between them. I could see everything with complete clarity.

A foot flew through the air directly in front of me.

It was the only thing that moved in real-time, making it appear incredibly fast. The foot drove into the side of the bat, and then everything sped up again.

The bat clattered onto the street, and a moment later, Sam landed next to it and punched the big guy who'd been wielding it. He sank to the ground. Then she raced around me and came after the other two.

I pivoted to watch. She was a marvel. It was like a dance, really—a violent dance.

After Sam dispatched the men behind me with a series of kicks and strikes, she moved on to several more who were en route to where Jason was trapped. One of these guys—a slim, older man—put up a pretty good fight, but Sam prevailed when she swept his feet out from under him and then kicked him in the head.

Next, she began attacking the men surrounding Jason. The big Maori joined in with renewed vigor, and it wasn't long before all the attackers were either lying on the ground or fleeing.

I just watched, and Spot watched me watch. I had no idea how much he understood. Was he like a regular dog without a real body, or was he able to think like a person? Either way, it felt good to have him by my side.

We walked over to where Sam and Jason stood, catching their breath and smiling at one another.

"We'd better get out of here," Jason said. "They know where you are now. We can take my rental."

"What do you mean 'we'?" Sam asked, frowning. "Just because you fought on the right side for once doesn't mean—"

"Let's go," I said. "I'll explain later. We don't have time for this."

Sam raised an eyebrow. It had specks of blood on

it.

"Jason is with me now," I said. "It's okay."

Sam nodded warily. We followed the big man to his silver SUV and piled in. Spot had disappeared again. Jason slalomed through the obstacle course of downed men as we heard sirens approaching.

I saw Paul and my mother standing at the foot of the driveway as we zoomed by. I waved and tried to smile. I didn't want them to think we were leaving against our will.

"Where to, boss?" Jason asked.

"I don't know," I answered.

I thought about it as he drove expertly out of the neighborhood. Everywhere I could think of seemed too risky. If they could find me at the RGP house, they could certainly find me at my apartment, my office, Chris's house, or any of the motels and hotels in the area.

"Any ideas, Sam?" I asked.

"My place in Los Gatos won't be safe," she said. "But perhaps we could stay at my best friend's house. Jason, do you think it's likely anyone's done that level of homework—that they know who my friends are?"

"Probably not," he said. "But maybe."

We'd reached the intersection at Mission Street— the commercial stretch of Highway One—and I directed him to turn left. I don't know why.

"How about some place farther over the hill?" I suggested. "A motel in San Jose or up the peninsula in Palo Alto."

"Wait a minute," Sam said. "I know the perfect place. Take another left at the next light, Jason. And will someone please tell me why we're suddenly trusting this guy?"

I filled her in as we drove seven or eight miles inland—into the redwoods. I wanted to ask about the slowing-down-time trick back on the street—had that been her or me?—but I hesitated to bring it up in front of Jason. Since I also wanted to ask Sam where we were going, I did that instead.

"My cousin lives off the grid," she said.

"Where's that?" Jason asked.

"It's not a where," I explained. "It's a what—a house without any public utilities."

"Oh, out in the bush," he said.

"Exactly," Sam agreed.

We headed up the San Lorenzo River Valley toward Felton, the first of a series of small, funky towns along Highway Nine in the Santa Cruz Mountains. A lot of folks up there grew pot, owned guns, and drove pickup trucks with their choice of pit bulls or Rottweilers in the back. Their neighbors were just as likely, though, to be high-tech engineers, commuting to Silicon Valley in leased German cars.

It was a beautiful drive. The steep road wound through a redwood forest that was only occasionally interrupted by a meadow or small home. Coastal redwoods weren't as massive as the sequoias that thrived farther inland in the Sierras, but they still soared majestically several hundred feet in the air.

The trees filtered the light, so it was dimmer than back in town. A few other cars on the road used their headlights, but it wasn't really necessary. We also passed several packs of serious cyclists making the climb. It was a dangerously narrow road for them to be riding two or three abreast, but they were.

A mile or two before we would've reached Felton, Sam directed Jason to slow down and turn into an overgrown dirt track on our left. It was between a second-growth redwood and a sprawling bay tree, and he would never have seen it if he hadn't been alerted.

After a few hundred yards, we turned again, this time nosing the SUV between two more trees where there wasn't a road at all. Sam pointed to more gaps in the redwoods and Jason maneuvered through them until we finally had to stop.

"We need to walk in from here," Sam said.

"Will my rental be safe?" Jason asked.

"No," she replied.

We climbed out, and Sam led the way. Beyond the first uneven row of redwoods, a path of sorts led into the darker interior of the forest. A complex pattern of fallen redwood needles littered the ground, and a huge banana slug tried to slime its way through them.

The trees themselves exhibited personality. Some sent out huge roots that snaked along the ground like partially submerged sea monsters. Others were twins or triplets—multiple trunks shooting up from common bases. And some of the redwoods' bark was ridged in regular, vertical rows, while other trees displayed wild swirls, burls, or tree carbuncles.

I'd been picturing Sam's cousin's place as a handcrafted cabin surrounded by vegetable gardens and docile livestock. That seemed very unlikely now. I was glad I trusted Sam or I might've had to start visualizing an abandoned quarry with a pile of bodies at the bottom.

We hiked in silence for perhaps a quarter mile and then a loud, hoarse voice shouted at us from somewhere out of sight. "Who the fuck are y'all?"

"It's Sam. Eric's cousin. Is that Bobby?"

"Whose cousin?" The voice was nearby, but its owner remained tucked out of sight.

"Spink. Spink's cousin," she called.

"What about the guy who looks like a cop?" the voice called. I think he was hiding behind a tree.

I looked at Jason, and he looked back at me.

"It's not me," I told the voice. "I look like a middle-school science-fair winner."

"Yeah, you do," the voice said.

"Well, fuck if I look like one," Jason said. Apparently, he had strong feelings about this.

"Hey, is that an Australian accent?" the voice called.

"Bobby!" Sam said. "I know that's you. Why don't you come out and talk to us?"

"Okay," he said and then stepped out from behind a redwood and strode forward. He was an overweight, fortyish white guy with bad skin. His black, stringy hair looked unnaturally shiny, and Bobby's nondescript face could've earned him a job as an extra in a movie. His torn, stained clothes fit him poorly. His shirt was way too tight while his voluminous jeans dragged on the forest ground.

"I guess there aren't any Aussie cops around here," he said, staring at Jason. "Unless you're using a fake accent?"

"I'm a Kiwi, mate," Jason told him. "Don't ever call me an Aussie again."

"Okay, okay," Bobby said, backing away a step. "No offense, big guy. Geez, you *are* big, aren't you? What do you weigh, anyway?"

"So do you remember me, Bobby?" Sam asked.

He turned and looked at her. "Sure, I remember you. You used to bring us blankets and shit, didn't you?"

He was homeless. We were heading for a homeless encampment.

"Yes," Sam said. "I know it gets cold up here at night."

"Well, it's good to see you," he said. "You're about the prettiest woman I ever saw. What's your bra size, anyway?"

Sam shook her head.

"Spink's not here, though," Bobby continued. "Did you bring us anything?"

"No. We're here because we need help—a place to stay where no one can find us. Do you think anyone would mind?"

"Earl might. I dunno. Let's go ask him."

Now Bobby led the way. He walked with a limp, but he wasn't especially slow. Sam followed directly behind him, and I followed her. Jason brought up the rear. In short order, we'd ventured off the path, around a rock outcropping, and then through a small circle of adolescent redwoods. Finally, we passed under a drooping tree branch and entered a large clearing within a partial ring of much older trees.

Bobby kept walking, but the rest of us stood shoulder to shoulder and paused to survey the scene. It was definitely a homeless encampment. Khaki tents and blue tarps were scattered around, and a fire blazed away in a square pit in the middle of the open area. Half a dozen raggedy-looking men and two big dogs sat around the fire. Everyone but the dogs seemed to be arguing.

Maybe that's why the dogs noticed us first. They lunged to their feet, barked fiercely, and then raced toward us. Bobby jumped to the side to give them a clear path.

As the first dog neared me on a dead run, his teeth bared, his tail started wagging and he began squeaking like a mouse. He skidded to a halt and rolled onto his belly at my feet. The second one—an older, bushier mixed breed—arrived a moment later. She pushed her nose into my hand and began licking furiously. She had to step onto the first dog to reach me, but he didn't seem to mind. His eyes rolled up in his head, and his squeaking changed to moaning.

"Holy shit!" a rough voice exclaimed. One of the men jogged toward us from the campfire.

Tall and wiry, with a long, multicolored beard that thinned out at the bottom, he was probably a well-worn fifty. He'd tied his thinning gray hair back in a ponytail. The man's dark eyes sat above a crooked, large-pored nose, set so deeply, it was hard to see them until he drew close.

"Hi, Earl," Sam said.

"Who's this guy?" he asked her, gesturing at me with a dirty thumb.

"Buddha 2.0," Sam said.

"Two point what? Why are the dogs acting like that? They don't like anyone."

Earl stood directly in front of us now, studying the behavior of the two dogs. He didn't acknowledge Jason at all. I'm not sure he noticed him.

The younger dog—some kind of shepherd—purred like an overgrown cat. He had quite a repertoire of undoglike noises. The furrier, older one was still licking like mad.

I was reminded of being awakened by Spot during the night. I looked around for him, and there he was, sitting in the middle of the fire. He bit the flames.

"2.0 is a spiritual leader," Sam said.

The other homeless men had made their way over by now. One of them—an older Asian guy—stared fixedly at Sam's chest. Another one—just a kid, really—held his head low and slumped so much, I wondered if he'd fall over.

"Who cares about leaders?" a third man said. "Leaders suck." He wore army fatigues and a remarkably sour expression.

Sam ignored him and stayed focused on Earl. "A bunch of thugs are after us, and we need sanctuary."

"Can he talk?" Earl asked, cocking his thumb at me again.

Bobby pushed through the others and stood next to Earl, gawking at the dogs. It was the most classic gawk I'd ever seen—no other word could describe it.

"Call me Sid," I said, extending my hand to Earl.

"I've got HIV," he told me, his eyes locked on mine.

"So?"

He grinned and gripped my hand. Energy surged through my fingers into his.

"What the fuck!" He pulled his hand away. "What the *fuck* was that?"

"Love," Jason told him. "It's pure love. This is an amazing dude. You could be healed now."

"No shit? From HIV?" Earl studied him. "Hey, I know you. The rugby World Cup—2003. You were on the New Zealand All Blacks. You scored more touchdowns or whatever the fuck they call them than anybody but that Welsh guy—the one with the weird hair."

"That's right."

"Don't tell me your name. I know your name. Jonah?"

"No."

"Joshua?"

"No."

"January?"

"No."

"Geronimo?"

"No."

"Vestibule?"

"No."

"Eddie Stoat?"

"No."

"Earl!" Sam said. "His name is Jason Patariki. Can we stay here for a while?"

"Of course. Have you had breakfast?"

"We have not," I said.

"It's doughnut day," Earl said. "We've got doughnuts. Just don't eat the bear claws. I love bear claws."

So we all trooped to seats around the fire. The dogs were hesitant to move at first but then happily followed me. When I sat, both of them tried to climb onto my lap; they each had to settle for cuddling up against a hip. They were very smelly, but I preferred their odor to that of the man sitting next to me.

The men passed around a black plastic garbage bag filled with stale doughnuts. I took two.

"We always keep the fire going," a young, extremely skinny guy sitting near me said. His skin was pasty white, as though he'd never been in the sun.

"Why's that?" Sam asked.

"It's symbolic," another man said. He could've been a barista at one of the self-consciously hip coffeehouses back in Santa Cruz. His clothes were almost clean.

"Symbolic of what?" Jason asked, a doughnut in each huge hand.

"Well, it's more of a tradition," another man answered. It was the Asian starer. He'd stopped staring at Sam; now he stared into the fire.

"It's a symbol!" the first man insisted. "It's a symbol of—"

"Fires!" Bobby shouted. "The fire is a symbol of fires." He began laughing.

"It's a tradition, God dammit!" the Asian man shouted.

"A symbol!" the first one shouted back.

"I vote for Bobby," the young, shy man said. It was the first time he'd spoken. When we looked at him, he covered his face with his hands and began rocking side to side.

"Shut up," Earl said. "Everybody shut up. This is stupid."

It was becoming clear to me that some of our hosts had issues.

"We're a colorful group, all right," the one camper we hadn't heard from said in an improbably high voice.

I looked closer. A woman with a narrow, grimy face hid in a voluminous gray overcoat, her unfocused blue eyes and blond rat's nest hair the only evidence that the coat was inhabited.

She spoke up again. "We'd all be good character actors if we knew how to act. We could be in one of those movies where left-handed people play the piano or they hide Jesus from the Romans." She looked at me, her eyes focusing for a moment. "Are you Jesus? You smell like Jesus."

"He's the next best thing," Jason told her.

She stared at him for a long time, trying to focus again. I think she was overmedicated. "You're really big," she said.

"Yes, I am," he agreed.

The doughnut sack had made the rounds and was back again. I thought about taking a bear claw but decided not to risk it. I settled on a frosted cruller. It was crusty, but delicious.

"So where's Spink?" Sam asked. "I was hoping to see him."

"He's in jail again," Earl told her. "But he gets out tomorrow."

"What was it this time?" she asked.

"The usual," he told her. "So what brings you up here? Did I ask you that already? I don't have such a good memory." One of his eyes twitched, and he rubbed it.

"It's a long story," Sam said. "I'm not sure we have time for it."

"Are you shitting me?" Bobby said. "All we got up here is time. And anyway, whose fault is it if there isn't enough? You could've come yesterday. You'd have had plenty of time if you came yesterday."

"Well, I'll tell you what," Sam said. "As a way to repay you for letting us stay, I'll go ahead and tell our story. Then you'll see why we came today and not yesterday."

"Cool."

So she did—a very abridged version of events that was still completely unbelievable. It took her about twenty minutes.

"Okay," Earl said when she'd finished.

"Makes sense to me," Bobby said.

I looked around. Almost everyone was nodding his head.

"Great story," the very skinny guy said.

"Three stars," someone else added. "It could've had more sex, though."

There hadn't been any at all in Sam's version.

"I agree," I said, glancing at Sam. "Lots more."

Chapter Thirty-Three

Sam was able to charm the "Fire Is a Symbol!" guy into lending her his cell phone. It was a duplicate of the supposedly cutting-edge smartphone that I'd purchased at great expense in Auckland.

"I'm not entirely the original owner," he told us. We did not investigate this further.

I wouldn't have thought there'd be any signal in the middle of the forest, but there was—just barely.

"The park's wired," the man told us.

"Park?" Sam asked.

"We're in Henry Cowell State Park. Why do you think it's all trees and shit up here instead of bowling alleys?"

"Andrea?" Sam said into the phone. "It's Sam. We're okay. Are you?"

As she listened, she nodded to me and then strode away to talk in private. I hoped she was trying to keep our hosts from eavesdropping—not me.

They were much more interested in getting healed. Once Earl told everyone how great he felt from our handshake—although he added that it may have been the bear claws—everyone lined up to get a jolt. I probably didn't need to shake their hands to get the job done, but since their unspoken leader had gotten his treatment that way, that's what they wanted. It was interesting to see how varied the energy transmissions were. They ranged from a mild tingle to a full-blown blast—to the woman, as it happened. She weathered it well.

Did the energy know how to distribute itself? Did it embody some sort of wisdom? Was it routing through me from somewhere else? I still knew next to nothing about how it all worked.

It was easy to see why real yogis brought their students along gradually, revamping their energy systems over time. If I hadn't been a therapist, I might've slipped into psychosis by now. Perhaps Marco—or his energy—knew how much I could handle.

Jason stood at the end of the treatment line. "Me too," he said. Then he added—in a convincing Cockney accent—"More please, sir?"

I cocked my head.

"I played Oliver in *Oliver Twist* in acting school," he told me. "Our teacher had a warped sense of humor."

"I saw the trailer for one of your South African movies," I told him, shaking my head.

"Hey, those are still big hits in Indonesia and the Philippines. I made a lot of money doing those films." He looked at me and gestured at my hands. "So are we doing this? Do you mind?"

I reached out to shake his hand, and he stepped forward and engulfed me in a massive hug. Energy immediately shot out from my heart to his. His grip on me loosened, and his muscular body relaxed.

While the energy flowed, I thought about Paul's assertion that Jason was gay, and the Maori's declaration of love for me. Was our loving embrace something personal? He knew I was straight.

After a minute or two, the energy faded, and we were simply hugging. "It's time to let go, Jason," I said.

Eventually, he did. I could see how hard it was for him; he was getting hooked on bliss. With Marco, I'd also had a strong urge to lose myself in his energy—to submerge my identity and melt into it. But my desire to abdicate personhood always felt selfish—an escape from whatever I was here to do.

As I sat back down and waited for Sam to return from her long phone conversation on the other side of the clearing, I patted the dogs—Magoo and Miss Jessie. They were incapacitated by bliss. Perhaps I needed to learn how to consciously shield my energy. Marco was clearly working undercover in the world—a secret agent for...whatever the hell he was up to. Maybe I needed a lower profile, too—at least energetically.

Sam started back toward me. A young African-American man I hadn't seen before burst into the clearing behind her.

"It's the cops!" he called. "The cops are here!"

The campers jumped to their feet and scattered in pairs. Both dogs followed Earl, who took off with Bobby to our right. The woman and the skinny guy ran to the left. Obviously, this wasn't the first time they'd been raided.

"We don't need to get arrested for illegal camping," I said to Sam, clambering to my feet.

"You can't sleep outdoors in this country?" Jason asked. This was the first time he'd spoken since our hug.

"Not around here," Sam said. "Let's go."

We ran in the opposite direction from the lookout, which, unfortunately, was also in the opposite direction from where our car was parked. I figured we'd be able to loop around and find our way back to it eventually.

Jason led the way, setting a moderate pace on the narrow path. I heard rustling noises behind us at one point, and I pictured a phalanx of cops spread out in a line, methodically marching forward.

In short order, though, we came to another, smaller clearing. They were waiting for us there; we'd been herded.

"Hold it!" a woman's voice called.

So we did.

Two female park rangers in crisp brown uniforms stood before us. They looked to be about twenty years old—maybe they were interns. They weren't armed.

"Good morning," one of them chirped.

"Uh, good morning," I said.

The one who had spoken was slightly built and wore glasses. She was very attractive, but had taken pains to disguise herself as plain. The black plastic glasses, her blond hair hanging down her forehead in uneven bangs, and the way she held herself all seemed to be designed to fool the eye. "Don't look at me, don't desire me"—that was the message.

The other one's black curly hair sat atop a tall, beefy frame. Her very smooth and rosy complexion reminded me of a farm girl in an Irish movie. She smiled with her mouth, but frowned with her eyes, an interesting combination.

"We really prefer that you not camp in the park," the tall one said. "It creates all sorts of problems."

"You're not cops?" Jason asked.

"Oh no," the first one answered. "We're the new park liaison team. We'll be interfacing between campers and the staff. I'm Julie, and this is Theresa."

"Well, it's nice to meet you. My name is Jason, and this is Sid and Sam."

"What a delightful accent," Theresa said to Jason. "Where are you from?"

"New Zealand. What about you?" He smiled his million-dollar smile.

"Watsonville—right down the road. I've always wanted to go to New Zealand. Is it as pretty as they say?"

"Well, Theresa, I don't know what they say about it in Watsonville, but it's the most beautiful place I've ever seen. And I've been all around the world."

"So you're backpackers?" Julie asked. "You're traveling internationally? You know, whether you're homeless or tourists looking for a free place to stay, the rules are still the same."

"We are going to have to ask you to leave," Theresa added. "I'm sorry."

"You know," I said, "I appreciate the way you're dealing with us, but I've met some of the campers up here. I can't imagine your approach is going to be effective with them."

"Well, we'll see," Julie said. "It's a pilot program. And it's only our third day."

"What should we be doing differently?" Theresa asked. "Help us out."

"I think you need to be a bit firmer," Jason suggested.

"Oh, okay," Teresa said. She frowned, looked him up and down, and then lowered the pitch of her voice. "All right, you big galoot," she said. "Get a move on. Don't make me use this whistle."

"Very good," I said. "That should do the trick."

"What's a galoot?" Jason asked. "For that matter, what's interfacing?"

Julie spoke up. "Seriously, though, are you guys going to leave now? We can't stand here chitchatting. We've got other illegal campers to round up."

"Of course we'll go," Sam said, who'd been observing all this with a smile. "Which way is Highway Nine?"

When we got back to the car, there was no car. No one bothered to voice a theory about what might have happened to it. Jason did swear a few times.

"What now?" I asked Sam. "Did you make plans with my mother? Do you still have the phone?"

"The so-called owner of the phone came and reclaimed it right before everyone took off," Sam said. "And the plan we made depended on our having wheels."

"Let's walk down to the highway and hitch," Jason suggested. "Everyone wants to pick up a beautiful woman."

"Thank you, Jason," Sam said. "I guess we'd better. You can hide behind Sid so you don't scare people away."

He looked confused. "Since he's smaller than me, how could I hide behind him?"

"You can't. It's a joke," I told him.

We made our way out of the big trees, down the dirt road, and assembled in a driver-friendly formation by the side of the narrow highway. Sam stood with her lovely thumb out, while Jason and I sat on the ground ten feet behind her, minimizing Jason's bulk. There was a fair amount of traffic, but no one stopped.

Finally, a blue Volvo with tinted windows pulled over onto the gravel shoulder just ahead of us. The driver climbed out as we scrambled toward it. It was Paul, Sam's brother.

"Hi," he said rather matter-of-factly. "I'm glad I found you."

"How the hell did you?" Jason asked.

"Well, I knew where our cousin camps, and even though Sam told Andrea you were safe and sound, I don't trust Earl or Bobby at all. So I thought I'd drive up and see if you needed help."

"Do you think those two stole my rental?" Jason asked.

"Probably," Paul said. "Bobby stole Spink's car once, although he gave it back later. And Earl is very erratic. I think he's bipolar, but he won't take any meds."

He looked at Sam as we stood beside the car in front of a particularly large redwood. "I can understand why you decided to come here," Paul added. "But it wasn't a good idea."

"Well, we're here anyway," I said, "whether it was a good idea or not. Let's make the best of it."

"Of course," Paul said. "Hop in, everyone."

"You're such a big brother," Sam said, giving Paul a hug and a peck on the cheek before the two siblings climbed into the Volvo's front seats.

"It's my job," he told her.

Jason and I squeezed into the back. Although it was a full-sized sedan, Jason's shoulders barely fit through the door and he filled two-thirds of the bench seat. I imagined the headline of my obituary after Paul took a corner too fast and the Maori spilled onto my side of the car. "Behemoth Flattens Area Therapist." Or maybe "Rugby Great Crushes Wannabe Messiah."

Paul, however, drove quite deliberately, and we wended our way back toward the coast safely. It was relaxing to just sit and not need to deal with any weirdness for a while. I felt as though I'd been listening, talking, and processing more in the last couple of weeks than in all my years as a therapist.

Once we reached Santa Cruz, Paul turned south onto Highway One, and we began retracing the first part of the route Jason and Frank had taken when they shanghaied Sam and me to the Monterey airport.

I caught Sam's eye when she turned her head to look at an art car in the lane beside us—it had doll heads glued to every square inch of its surface.

"Only in Santa Cruz," Paul said.

"So where are we headed?" I asked her. "What's the plan?"

"We're meeting Andrea, your dad Allen, and Chris at the Seascape Golf Club down in Aptos," Sam told me.

"Why there?" I asked. It seemed like an odd choice. I'd never been to the course itself, but I knew Aptos fairly well. My ex-girlfriend, Susan, and her three flatulent cats had lived there. It was only ten miles as the crow flies from Santa Cruz, but it was on another planet culturally—more like Southern California. You were likely to spot the stereotypical resident in the upscale wine section of the local grocery store—a fifty-two-year-old, tanned, blond, tennis-playing woman.

"It was your dad's idea," Paul said. "He went to college with the general manager there—Charles Somebody."

"Singh?" I asked. "Charles Singh?"

"Yes, that's him. And who'd look for you at a golf course? It's not exactly a gang hangout. Even most law-abiding people don't know they have a restaurant there. Andrea says the food's pretty good, too."

I hadn't seen my father's roommate—Charles—in years. We'd kept up for a while after my parents had supposedly died. God, it was strange they were back. Wondrous, really. But eventually Charles had taken a new job somewhere else, and I'd gotten involved with friends of my own.

Seascape was tucked away in a ritzy residential neighborhood—Rio Del Mar—about a quarter of a mile inland. The course wasn't easy to find; I pictured would-be golfers wandering door to door in the suburban maze, looking for where to go to scratch their golf itch.

The parking lot was a third full. By now it was late morning. The fog in Aptos hadn't dissipated yet—some days it never did. I'm convinced this was one of the reasons Susan had been depressed, although I couldn't blame any climatic factors for her infidelity.

The clubhouse was a long, nondescript building painted dark green. It blocked us from seeing the course itself from the parking lot. Several exhaust fans on the roof of the building screeched at us as we headed for a pair of glass doors.

We entered a square dining area with a bar on the left. The decor had probably been classy in the 1940s. There were exposed beams and dark wood wainscoting. The walls were covered with black and white photographs of other, more famous golf courses. The room looked like an expanded version of my grandparent's lake house. We'd summered there when I was quite young.

Two red-faced older men sat on upholstered stools at the bar next to the almost empty dining room, and a foursome of women wearing various shades of red were arranged around a table near a dormant big screen TV.

There was no sign of our people, but Paul walked through the room and we followed. The pro shop loomed ahead of us in a glassed-in area. Racks of golf shirts and sweaters crowded out a few sets of clubs.

To our left was another larger dining area, and Paul led us there. This one overlooked the golf course, and beyond that, Monterey Bay.

I was hungry again when I smelled someone's french fries. As it turned out, they were Chris's.

"Yo!" he called from a circular table across the room. "Over here!"

He sat between my parents, facing the interior of the room despite the picture window that soared behind them. They'd saved us seats with a view; this was undoubtedly my mother's doing.

Chris's mouth was full of fries. I think he would've remained seated, stuffing more into his mouth, but when my parents stood, he was shamed into doing it too. Well, Chris's version of shame. Whatever he did, he never seemed too upset with himself.

"Isn't it beautiful here?" my father said, still wearing his dark glasses.

"It certainly is," Sam said. "It's like a park out there, isn't it?" She gestured at the course below us.

"Hello, Sid," my mother said. "You're looking well."

I nodded my acknowledgment.

"I've been hearing all about how cute you were as a baby," Chris said to me.

I looked at my mother, who shook her head.

Chris continued. "And now I know all your embarrassing moments like when you threw up on your prom date and that time you invaded Poland."

"Your friend is quite a character," my mother said. "He's kept us amused while we waited for you. Did you have trouble finding the place?"

Sam spoke up. "There was a problem up in Felton. Paul ended up bringing us down—he knew the way."

"Oh dear," my mother said. "Is everyone all right?"

We nodded. I found it hard to think of Andrea as the leader of a spiritual organization. She was such a mom.

Jason coughed loudly, as though he were in a high school play and hadn't properly calibrated the volume of a real cough.

"Oh, I'm sorry," I said. "This is Jason Patariki. He's going to be helping to protect me. Jason, these are my not-so-dead parents—Andrea and Allen Menk."

"Pleased to meet you," Jason said, reaching his hand out to my father. "Where I come from, we introduce each other first thing."

My mother had to prompt my father to offer his hand. I'd completely forgotten that he was blind! What a thing to forget.

While they shook, my mother spoke to Jason. "We introduce one another here, as well. I raised a barbarian." She smiled at me lovingly, negating the sting of her comment.

"Well," Sam said, "at this point, he's a bit more enlightened than your average barbarian."

I liked that she was sticking up for me.

"I dunno," Chris said, reseating himself. We all followed suit as he continued talking. "I'll bet Attila and Genghis Khan never abandoned their friends in germ-infested countries on the other side of the planet, leaving them in the clutches of power-mad, mind-reading sorcerers. Your son is a brute," he told my mother.

"Are you hungry?" she asked me, ignoring Chris.

"Starving. Man does not live by doughnuts alone."

"I'm not sure what you mean by that," she said, "but the veggie burgers are very good here."

"Mom, I'm perfectly capable of choosing my own food."

"Don't take it personally," my father said. "She does that with everyone."

We were right back at the family dinner table, circa 2002. Apparently, I remained a slave to the old family dynamic. "Sorry, Mom," I said. "I'll try the burger."

"No, no. You have whatever you want, Sid."

This was round two. Since I knew where we were going with this, I headed it off at the pass by changing the subject.

"So Charles Singh runs this place?" I asked my father.

"Yes. I asked him to join us in a while."

"Why is that?"

"You'll see." He seemed to be having trouble breathing again—as he had in India.

The lunch conversation stayed light. Chris provided his usual outrageous counterpoint to whatever real topic someone was attempting to discuss. Jason charmed my parents with anecdotes about fellow

406

celebrities. And Sam and I sat quietly while my parents played their roles as host and hostess. It was their party, it seemed.

Charles joined us just as we finished eating. We all rose again to greet him.

He was a middle-aged, non-practicing Sikh, from Kashmir originally. But he was very American in manner and outlook. He'd been an exchange student in high school and had never returned home. I'd known him my whole life.

He was about my height and coloring, but his hawk nose was much bigger and more chiseled than mine. In photos, he looked fierce, as though he were about to pull out a ceremonial dagger and carve someone up for eyeballing him. But in person he emanated a warmth and bonhomie that overrode all that.

That day, he wore a pink golf shirt and dark khaki pants. He looked very out of place at the golf course, but then again, he'd looked equally out of place at the luxury hotel he'd managed when I was a boy. This was my sense of him throughout my childhood. From his name—Charles—to his house, his friends, and his career, he'd always seemed like a fish out of water.

Charles hugged me. "Damn, it's good to see you, Sid. Why did we ever lose touch?"

I shrugged. Then my father introduced everyone.

"*The* Jason Patariki?" Charles asked, shaking the Maori's hand.

"The one and only."

"What an honor. My brother was a rugger, but it was too rough for me. I played once, and then I ran back to the cricket pitch."

Charles reached out then and pulled my father's

hand off the table to shake it, reminding me again of his sightlessness.

"Where are the dogs?" I asked my dad.

"Charles said it would be better if we left them in the car," my mother said.

"He's a heartless bastard," my father added, grinning.

The Sikh laughed. I'd forgotten his laugh; it was more of a bray.

I thought of Spot. I'd forgotten about him, too. What was going on with me? The more I learned to live in the moment, the less I seemed capable of hanging onto the immediate past. Where would it end? Would everything not in plain sight in a given moment cease to exist for me?

Spot appeared by my side and then immediately disappeared again. Maybe I could summon him by thinking about him, or perhaps he knew from his end when I needed a reminder.

"Sid?" Charles said. "Could I speak to you alone in my office?"

"Sure. Excuse us, all."

Chapter Thirty-Four

I followed him out a side door, down an external flight of stairs, and into a dark room under the dining room.

"Sit, sit," he said, gesturing at a well-worn office chair in front of a battered metal desk. I'd have thought that the general manager of a golf course would've had a nicer office than, say, an Auckland customs official. But this space was nothing more than a storage area with some old furniture in it.

I'd assumed Charles wanted to talk to me about my dad—about his health, more specifically. But instead he began rather obliquely.

"You know, Sid," he said, "I've been a good friend of your family for a long time. And it was very hard to see you suffer when I knew perfectly well Allen and Andrea hadn't died in a plane wreck."

"Uh huh."

"And I wanted to step in and rescue you from your suffering—to tell you about them, and also a few other things that might've helped you get through that difficult time."

I wasn't sure where we were going with this. Was he apologizing—working off his guilt? Did he have something else on his mind?

"Now it's time to tell you," he said and then stopped.

Apparently, it wasn't time quite yet. But I knew from my work that if I waited, it would come. Charles wanted to tell me something, and he was getting ready to do it. I watched his face. He seemed to morph from fear to sadness to shame to anger—at himself? He was all over the map. What could arouse this particular constellation of strong emotions? I had no idea.

"So it's time," he said again.

"Please," I said. "Go ahead."

"I wanted to tell you before, but Andrea said it would impede your progress."

I waited.

"So the thing is, Sid…" He took a deep breath and looked me in the eye.

Then his phone rang. *God dammit. Give me a break.*

Charles gathered himself again, relieved to be interrupted. He picked up the phone, said, "Yes?" and then listened for a while. "Okay," he said, "I'll be right there." He hung up and turned back to me. "I'm sorry, Sid. This'll only take a minute. Can you wait here for me?"

"Why don't you tell me what you need to tell me first?" I suggested. "You'll feel better, and you'll probably be able to handle your business better, too."

"It's an emergency," Charles said. "The computers are down, so the registers aren't operating."

He pushed his chair back and strode out, leaving me alone and frustrated in his crappy office. I decided to meditate for a few minutes to re-center myself. If Charles wasn't back soon, I'd wait for him upstairs with the others.

Just as I closed my eyes, though, I heard my name

called. I looked around. There was no one in the room.

"Sid! Over here!"

The voice was coming from across the desk, but no one was there. I got up and walked over. Marco's face was on the computer monitor. He winked at me.

"Hi, Sid," he said. "I'm sorry I can't be there in person. Let's talk."

I fell down onto Charles's desk chair. "I think that's the first time I ever heard you say you're sorry about anything," I told him. I was really just stalling to regain my composure.

"It's just a figure of speech," he said. "I'm not actually apologizing."

"No, of course not. That's not in the evil genius handbook, is it?"

He smiled. It was probably impossible to hurt his feelings, assuming he had any. I felt very unintimidated by Marco, though—free to say whatever I pleased.

"I need to tell you some things," he said.

"Of course you do. Everyone needs to tell me things."

"Are you willing to listen?"

"Maybe—for a minute," I said. "I'm in the middle of something here. But go ahead—I'm listening."

"People have started dying," Marco said.

"What?"

"Let me explain. You've reached a certain status spiritually, so whoever has tried to harm you is now facing a karmic reckoning."

"They're being punished?"

"Not exactly. That makes it sound personal. It's just how the universe works. It balances itself. Do you imagine that Judas or Pilate had fun lives after Jesus was killed?"

"I suppose not. But how do we know it's some instant karma deal? Maybe they're just dying for the usual reasons."

"It's the way it happens. Take Frank, for example—your Rat-Face. He returned to his scam in LA yesterday—driving around a fake paper-shredding truck and then selling people's financial information to criminal gangs."

"That's a creative crime," I said.

Marco nodded. "Frank was on the 405 heading south when a truck in front of him lost a crate of chickens from its load. He jammed on his brakes, skidded, and banged into a guardrail."

"So far, that's only a little weird—LA weird."

"Frank had just taken off his sunglasses, and he had them on a lanyard around his neck. Can you guess why?"

"It got cloudy? The sun set? Does it matter?"

"There was a partial solar eclipse down there," Marco said.

"All right. We're getting pretty random here," I admitted.

"They were sunglasses he'd stolen from a department store. They weren't shatterproof. When the airbag in his truck inflated, it broke the frame of the glasses, and a metal piece drove a shard of glass into his heart."

"Ugh."

"The vehicle behind them happened to be an ambulance, and they could've saved his life, but earlier that morning a former employee had stolen a key piece of medical equipment."

"Okay. I see what you mean."

"Frank's dead. Tommy T. is dead. Bhante's been diagnosed with a rare type of blood cancer. One of your brothers fell in a sink hole and broke his hip. The other one is in jail for a crime he didn't commit."

"What about you?" I asked.

"I'm just fine," he said. "I've never been your enemy."

"So you say."

"I do. Now Jason is a bit of a special case, but be aware that if you're standing next to him, you need to stay alert. Keep your eye out for falling pianos. Or escaped lions. Regardless of what you currently think about me, the world truly does need you. Be careful, Sid."

"I will. But let me ask you this," I said. "You say you're not my enemy, but you lied to me, manipulated me, and put me through all kinds of psychological hell—not to mention you probably dosed me with an illegal drug."

"And are you the better for it?" Marco asked. "Have all these things been in your best long-term interest?"

"The way I understand life now, everything is always in my best long-term interest. That doesn't differentiate what you've done from anything else that happens. I know you're an ends-justifies-the-means kind of guy, Marco. You told me that early on. But I'm not. And if we're looking for harm that's been done, what about that list of dead people you just told me about? Haven't your actions led these people to their doom?"

"Certainly not. Everyone determines his own

karma. You're still hung up on cultural and moral norms," Marco said. "These things don't matter. Not for you and me. Our evolution—our energy—has freed us from these human constraints. Now, each event that comes our way is a unique instance for which there is no textbook response. A skillful behavior will always fall out of us because of who we've become. We're off the map. Surely you've noticed that your previous set of human responses are obsolete now?"

"Well, my emotional responses certainly seem to be beside the point, and I've definitely become far less judgmental," I said. "But I don't know about the I'm-an-exception-to-the-rules part. That sounds like what you hear from a newcomer at an AA meeting."

"The man you were with—Charles Singh—is about to tell you something extremely repugnant, according to our cultural norms. Will you be repulsed? No. You will love him and hug him. You will heal him. This will be what is called for. So it is with me. I've done what was called for with you. I have no regrets."

"I've had enough," I said. "I'm still vulnerable to this kind of talk. I need to protect myself. Goodbye, Marco."

I shut down the computer and the monitor, returned to the chair in front of the desk, and pondered Marco's pronouncements.

If it was true that fate was targeting my enemies, what did that mean? That karma was a mean son of a bitch? That I was responsible for a succession of bizarre tragedies? Perhaps Marco was killing people and framing Fate. Rinpoche had feared for his life. Should I?

Charles returned. Presumably, Marco's tech guys

had screwed with the Seascape computers and had now released them back to the golf course's control.

Would Marco's predictions turn out to be true? How could he know what Charles would do?

"Thirty-eight years ago," the Sikh began, "I was a very different man. It was because of what happened that I became the man you see now. Some things are sobering and make you realize that you must change your ways."

He paused and gave me a chance to respond. I did not.

He looked down. "This is very hard for me," he said. "I have lived with so much shame all these years, and now my shame is here in the room with us."

I waited.

Charles took a deep breath and glanced up at me. "I'm not sure I can say this," he told me. Tears welled up in his eyes. He looked down again.

"Do you want to write it down?" I asked. "You could write it on a piece of paper and give it to me."

"Yes. This is a good plan," he said.

He scribbled on a notepad, tore off a sheet, and then slid it across the desk to me. His hand was trembling.

The note read "I impregnated my own niece when her parents trusted me to watch over her in the States. She was only fourteen. She died in childbirth. I killed her with my penis."

Jesus. I looked across the desk at Charles. His head was bowed, and he was sobbing.

"Why are you telling me this?" I asked. My tone was sharper than I'd intended. Charles was an incestuous pedophile, my mind told me. But my heart urged me to ease his suffering. "It's the distant past," I told him before he had a chance to answer. "Let it go. Forgive yourself."

"You don't understand," he said. He stopped crying and looked me squarely in the eye. "You don't understand what I'm trying to tell you."

I waited again. This was getting annoying. *Tell me, or don't tell me.* Charles finally got it out.

"I'm your father," he said.

Chapter Thirty-Five

So there it was. My lifelong quest to know my birth parents was finally over. Now I knew who I was—or who I had been, I guess. I felt surprisingly unsatisfied. I'd much preferred the born-in-Nepal version that Marco had fed me back on his island.

I could never meet my birth mother. I only existed because of a statutory rape. And I wasn't about to drop everything to go on a fishing trip to get to know my new dad.

I felt angry, but I also felt very sad. That poor girl. She'd never even had a chance to meet me—or my brothers. And for some reason, Charles felt he couldn't be a father to any of us. Why had my parents kept his secret? Was it part of the give-Sid-a-childhood-exactly-like-the-Buddha's plan? What about the other two babies? Were their fates simply subordinate to mine?

Charles had reverted to sobbing again. Periodically, he tried to force out words, but his grief overwhelmed him. Finally, he managed to say, "I'm so sorry, Sid. I'm so sorry."

"Why?" I asked. "Why give us all away? We were triplets, right?"

He nodded. "Yes. I couldn't cope—not with three infants. I was a selfish alcoholic. And I had a family already—a wife and a daughter. Andrea and Allen were happy to take you—it was their idea—but they insisted the other two boys be sent overseas for adoption. That was their offer, and they wouldn't say why until just last week." He paused and watched my face.

"Did you give them the pick of the litter?"

"What?"

"Never mind."

Charles was still studying me intently. I became aware he'd been waiting for decades to find out how I was going to react to his news. So far, I'd asked questions and confused him with inappropriate humor. I needed to do better. After all, he was a fellow being who was suffering intensely—whatever he had or hadn't done. When I realized this, love filled me.

"I forgive you," I said. "I love you." And I did. My desire for more answers—more explanations—was swept away by the waves of energy that cascaded inside me. For a moment, I remembered Marco had predicted all of this, but then that was gone, too.

I walked around the desk, pulled Charles out of his chair, and hugged the crap out of him. What else was there to do? Only love could heal something like this.

My energy surged out to him, bathing him, washing away his guilt and shame. What little of these I had left markedly diminished as well. For the first time, I understood that whenever my energy benefited someone, it blessed me, too—in exactly the same way.

I had to hold Charles up after a moment. He made gurgling noises at first, and then he began humming— kind of like a cell phone set on vibrate. Once the energy settled down, I lowered him back onto his chair. He was still humming, but it wasn't as loud now. His eyes were closed, and his face at peace. He wasn't asleep, but he wasn't awake.

As I stood beside Charles, I felt the new energy in him—what I'd sent—connecting to his own, merging into something more. I could sense that he'd be fine—he'd thrive, in fact. But I could also tell that if he were awake during the ongoing reconfiguring process, he'd get in his own way.

I moved over to the other side of the desk again and sat down. I was in no hurry to get back upstairs. Once again, things were coming at me much faster than I could process them.

I considered what Marco had told me first. Suddenly, people were dying. Or getting cancer. Or falling down. I'd never thought of karma as something so negative—so punitive. Despite Marco's explanation, it still felt counterintuitive that the universe would dole out instant, drastic payback to anyone. And all of this was supposed to be because of me? Because of who I had become?

Of course, Marco could be fabricating the whole thing. But why would he? His goal seemed to be to warn me—to get me to be vigilant around Jason. Did he need to lie so outrageously to motivate me to stay safe? It didn't seem like it. It had also felt true as he was telling me.

So how can I protect people from this phenomenon? Should I tell everyone not to cross me? Maybe I can figure out how to settle disputes faster than the universe can nail my adversaries. But would that really be for the best? Who was I to second-guess karma? I know what alarms me—what feels wrong— but what does that have to do with the price of bananas?

I tried to think about being Charles Singh's son—

making me a Sikh by birth, I guess—but this went nowhere. I simply couldn't get my mind in gear about it. Was it too much to absorb? Too irrelevant now? Perhaps I just wasn't in charge of my mind anymore. Maybe the energy or karma or whatever it was didn't think it was a good idea for me to ruminate on the subject. I didn't know.

Once I understood I couldn't think about it, I walked out of the office and back up the stairs to the dining room. It was empty; everyone was gone.

The bartender strolled over, an older woman dripping with Native American silver jewelry—rings, earrings, and noisy bracelets.

"Are you looking for your friends?" she asked in a gravelly smoker's voice.

"Yes."

"They went out on the terrace to have dessert. Would you like anything?"

"Sure. Pie?"

She rattled off a long list of choices. Were golfers big pie eaters? I settled on blackberry.

"There he is," Jason called as I stepped onto the expansive back deck of the clubhouse. Spot sat upright in the Maori's voluminous lap. Jason didn't seem to be aware of him.

"It's about time," Chris said. "What did the guy want? Did he offer you a job as the beverage cart girl?"

"That's right," I said. "It took a while to fill out all the paperwork and sign up for the gender reassignment surgery."

The table hugged a railing overlooking a two-tiered golf green, with three golfers just walking off it. Two of them swore; the third one shook his head.

420

My mother caught my eye as I sat down between Sam and Jason. She obviously knew what Charles had been planning to tell me.

"I'm fine," I told her.

"Oh, good," she responded. "I thought you would be."

I heard a loud cracking sound, and I glanced to my right. A huge oak tree on the edge of the course split in two just above its base. My first thought was, "Here we go—karma's coming after Jason." But I could see that both halves would fall at angles that would spare us. One headed for a small herd of golf carts by the back door of the building. The other would end up on the course itself, alongside the green.

As we all watched the slow-motion tree suicide, Spot suddenly jumped up on the table in front of me and began silent, frantic barking. Almost simultaneously, I heard a golf ball being struck on the fairway below us. I dove at Jason, and as we tumbled forward, the ball headed to our right.

False alarm, again.

But the hard-hit ball caromed off a branch of the falling tree with a solid *thunk* and then whizzed through the space where Jason's head had been a moment earlier. We lay sprawled on the wooden deck as the ball rocketed into the shingled wall behind us, bounced off, and then hit Jason on the temple where he lay.

"Shit," he said, and then he passed out.

Karma had found its target anyway, co-opting me to help get the job done.

"What's going on?" my father asked.

"Jason's been hit on the temple by a golf ball," Sam told him.

"Call 911," he said. "That's the one place you can die from."

****

I rode in the ambulance with Jason. By now he was awake, but groggy.

The male EMT, a surfer type, told us that Jason's vital signs were good and he'd probably be fine.

"Shut up," the female EMT told him. "You know we're not supposed to say things like that."

"Lighten up, Monica," he said.

Monica looked like a weight lifter, which was handy, given how much Jason weighed.

She looked at me. "I can tell you this. So far, no individual has ever died from a collision between a sports ball and a cranium on *my* watch."

I found both of these commentaries to be only marginally reassuring. I had tried to send Jason healing energy back at the golf course, but nothing had happened. I found this disturbing. Could the universe have the power—and inclination—to shut me down when it had revenge on its mind?

The emergency room at St. Domnio's Hospital was remarkably unchaotic, given the number of people crammed into it. Every seat was either taken by someone in pain or by a suitably anxious companion.

They parked Jason's gurney in a hallway by a row of scary-looking medical equipment. A beautiful, overweight RN told us that he'd be given "top-of-the-line priority" due to his "as-yet-untreated head trauma," but even this "privilege" "might entail a distressful waiting period." We were to "remain quite calm" and "report any new, untoward symptomatology."

"Were you an English major in college?" I asked.

"No. And I'm a busy nurse now, so please excuse me."

As I stood next to Jason, who remained quite calm, I was finally able to send him a steady stream of low-level energy.

"That feels great, Sid," he said. Jason brightened considerably, and after a minute or two, when the energy subsided, he once again told me that he loved me.

"I think you just love what I can do," I said. "You're a bliss hound."

"Can I help?" a melodious woman's voice said from behind me. I turned around, ready to smile and say no thanks.

A very short and very slight fiftyish Asian woman with a gray buzz cut and a chaplain's collar smiled at me. She may have had the most radiant, loving smile I'd ever seen. I could immediately sense this was not an ordinary person. Her energy was incredibly smooth and intoxicating—like a single malt whiskey taken intravenously. I felt drunk—well, more than drunk. Energy drunk. I struggled to maintain my poise.

Her badge said her name was Lanai Tu. Perhaps she was a Vietnamese-American whose parents had liked Hawaiian porches.

"Hi," I managed to say. "I'm Sid, and this is Jason. And you seem to be love and joy and beauty all rolled into one."

"Does that line work on many women, Sid?" Before I could answer, she spoke again. "I'm sorry. Force of habit. Let me start over: right back at you, Sid. Who are you? I've never felt energy like yours before."

"He's my spiritual teacher," Jason told her. "He

just healed me. I'm fine now."

He sat up and swung his massive legs off the side of the gurney.

"Let's let the doctor decide that," she suggested. "I understand you probably have a concussion, and there can be a variety of complications from that."

"Are you a priest?" Jason asked. "We don't have a lot of women priests in New Zealand."

"Where are my manners?" she said. "My name is Lanai. I'm an interfaith chaplain here at the hospital."

"You're really a Buddhist, though, aren't you?" Jason asked, swinging his legs and stretching his muscular arms.

"How did you know that?" she asked.

"Your haircut. That's a Buddhist haircut." He jumped down onto the floor, which shook.

"Goodness," Lanai said. "Are you a professional football player?"

"Rugby. Retired. Now I help Sid save the world."

"Good for you," she said.

Since Lanai had arrived, I'd been feeling my energy gathering itself. Now I felt a major maelstrom ramping up. It was going to be epic. I only hoped that Lanai could safely handle it.

Before mine could send itself out, the chaplain's energy shot forward and penetrated me, flooding my heart. It joined with my own revved-up *chi*, and this potent combination spread throughout me. It was as if an energy bomb had been detonated in my chest, and now energy shrapnel was shooting everywhere. I couldn't have stood it long, but I didn't have to. I was immediately launched into samadhi again.

The black void wasn't as black this time. And it

wasn't exactly a void, either. It was undifferentiated possibility. There was a hint of everything in it, although there was also nothing.

My samadhi self was also subtly different now. I wasn't me. I wasn't an individual. But I also didn't lose awareness and simply disappear into the void that wasn't a void. As the pure awareness that I'd become, I remained an intact entity of sorts—just not anything like before.

As I had the first time I visited this realm, I had the strong sense that I could conjure up reality, but this time I didn't try. It didn't feel right. What did feel right was to just be present—to just hang out and let Spirit do whatever it wanted. I was in complete surrender. If I never returned to being Sid, so be it.

I had no idea how long I was in that state or what spiritual work I might be accomplishing. I woke up in a hospital bed in a well-lit white room. The first thing I saw was the faded outline where a large cross had once hung on the wall facing me. Perhaps St. Domnio's Hospital had decided to become less aggressively Catholic.

I felt alert. I wondered if you could get the spiritual bends from shooting to the surface too fast.

Jason lay on the bed next to me. His eyes were closed. Sam was asleep in a black armchair. She wore a white tunic over turquoise pants and looked more beautiful than ever. Chris was asleep on a yellow, egg-crate pad on the floor next to her.

I wished Chris were awake to explain what had happened. And then suddenly he was. That was interesting.

"Yo, bro," he said. "You're back. They said you

might not make it."

I wished the others would stay asleep. They stayed asleep.

"Why not?" I asked. "I'm fine."

He got up, ambled over, and perched on the side of my bed. I sat up and stretched. Everything hurt. A lot. Maybe I was less fine than I thought. I also noticed a series of punctures and bruises on my arms. Had the hospital been working me over with injections and IVs?

"Well," Chris said, "your heart rate was down to twenty-eight beats a minute, and you had virtually no brain activity. For some reason, people who work in a place like this get concerned about that kind of thing."

"So your point is I should've become comatose somewhere else?"

"Well, first of all, they said it wasn't a coma, even though they didn't know what it was instead. But otherwise, yeah, you could've picked somewhere else more convenient—where people wouldn't kick up such a fuss over you. Do you know how hard it was for Sam and Andrea to get you out of intensive care—off all those machines?"

I looked at the massive figure on the other bed. "Did Jason have a bad concussion after all?" I asked. "Is that why he's here?"

"Yeah, but he's fine. He just commandeered the other bed because he's selfish."

"Then why is he wearing a hospital gown?"

"Well, a bunch of weird shit keeps happening to him. It's like he's cursed," Chris said.

"Wait a minute," I said. "How long have I been here?"

"Three days."

I was taken aback. *Three days?*

"Hey," Chris continued. "How come we haven't woken anyone up? Sam always goes to full alert whenever a nurse even walks by the door. She thinks she's your bodyguard since Jason got all cut up."

"What do you mean, 'all cut up'?"

"Well, the latest thing was when he was standing over there." He gestured to the corner of the room by the window. "That's not safety glass."

"Let me guess," I said. "A crazed pigeon flew in after it got drunk because a meteor knocked over a wine bottle."

"Meteorite," Chris said.

"Otherwise I nailed it?"

"I'm just saying it's a meteor up in space and a meteorite if it gets all the way here. And yes, it *was* a bird—good guess. A big-ass pelican, actually, even though we're a mile or two inland. If the bird hadn't died after it flew through the window and speared Jason in the shoulder, we could have asked it for its full back story. As it is, we'll never know if it was drunk."

I paused and thought for a moment. "I've been in samadhi," I told Chris. "Do you know what that is?"

"Sure. The beyond-beyond deal—like Marco and Sam."

"Sam goes into samadhi, too?" I asked.

"Geez, bro. She's *your* girlfriend." Chris carefully studied Sam and Jason. "You're doing something to them, aren't you? Some energy thing that's keeping them zonked out?"

"I think so."

"You don't even know what you're doing?" His tone was incredulous.

"No. Every time I visit samadhi, I come back a little different. I'm always more in some ways and a whole lot less in some others."

"In other words," Chris said, "you have no idea what the fuck you're doing. At best, you're a subconscious shaman."

"That's about right," I said. "Isn't it lucky I have you around to keep me humble?"

"Damned straight."

A young Filipina nurse scuttled in. "You're awake!" she chirped. She was very happy. "I'll just check your vitals."

I wished she would leave.

"On second thought," she said, "I'll go and tell your doctor the good news." She turned on her heels and ran off.

"Nice butt," Chris said. "Hey, that was you, wasn't it—getting her to take off like that?"

I nodded.

"Are you going to become power-mad and enslave all the regular people except for me?"

"Sure," I said. "That sounds good, except for the 'except me' part."

Chris was silent for a moment. When he spoke again, it was with an uncharacteristically sober tone. "Seriously, bro, what are you going to do? It's tremendous overkill if all you ever do is zap people, boss them around with your mind, and then maybe space out for days on end—you know, your current repertoire."

"I agree, but I'm still not sure what's going on— what I need to do," I told him. "Everyone I meet has a plan for me, and I've heard all these crazy ideas about who I'm supposed to be. So far, though, all I've managed to do is narrow down who I can trust. That doesn't tell me much. Just because someone's trustworthy doesn't mean they know what's going on."

"That's true." He pursed his lips while he paused. "So what's common to all the feedback you've gotten? Where do the ideas overlap?"

"Have you heard about the insomnia disease?" I asked. "That's one thing I've heard from several sources."

"Yeah, I did some research on that after your mom mentioned it," Chris said. "By the way, I really like her—you know, as far as moms go—but it's hard to see her as some big-time spiritual leader."

"I agree. So what did you find out about the disease?"

"It turns out it's bullshit," Chris said. "As of last week, that is. Before that, it seemed for real."

"Oh?"

"Yeah. The insomnia is actually an early symptom of something that messes up your blood sugar for a while. It's not a big deal. At first, they thought it would be because it was something new that was coming out of Africa. Let's face it, white people are still scared of us."

"You Africans?"

"That's right." He smirked.

"Okay," I said. "Let's brainstorm a little. If I'm not here to head off a metaphysical disaster due to an epidemic, and we're no longer buying into Marco and Bhante's agendas, then what's left? Should I be doing what famous gurus do—write books, give talks, lead meditations at the UN?"

"Dude, you have to actually *know* something to do that shit. You don't know your ass from your elbow—we've already established that. And for that matter, you don't know how to teach anything, either."

"Let's not get carried away with the humbling thing, Chris." I wagged my finger at him, and he wagged his back, mocking me.

"You know I'm right," he said. "Anyway, those famous gurus are the uncool guys that still have tons of ego left. They're ambitious, right? They want to be on TV. They want to control people. That's not for you, even if you could pull it off, which you can't."

"Do you think the most evolved people stay undercover—work anonymously?"

Chris shrugged. "Probably."

"How's the patient?" A man's voice boomed from the doorway. The voice was familiar. I turned my head to see who was striding toward us. It was Marco.

Chapter Thirty-Six

"I thought we could continue our conversation, Sid," he said.

Marco stood at the foot of the bed. He wore a white medical coat and his badge identified him as Dr. Sid's Friend, Department of Mind, Body, and Spirit.

"A badge doesn't make you a friend, dude," Chris said.

"Maybe it would be better if we met alone," Marcus said to me. "Why don't you wake up the others and ask everyone to give us a few minutes?"

"I don't think so," I said. "In fact..." I wished he would leave.

Marco turned, took a step toward the door, and then stopped. With an effort, he pivoted and came back. "A new power," he said, surprise on his face. "Fascinating. But it won't work on me."

"You're not so tough," Chris said.

"Yes, I am," Marco said.

"Well, okay, maybe you are, but my point is we're not intimidated. Sid has superpowers up the wazoo now."

Marco laughed. "That's a good place for them, isn't it? Who would look there?"

"Good point," Chris said. "You can be such a fun guy, Marco. Why do you act like a dick so much? What's the point, really?" He stared at him with defiance.

Marco ignored him and addressed me. "Your energy is remarkable now, Sid. I don't know where it came from—samadhi alone doesn't explain it. And it's beyond the scope of my own in several respects. I want to acknowledge that. But you haven't outgrown your need for a mentor. Without guidance from someone more experienced at managing energy, you will perish. And there will be collateral damage."

While he was talking, I did more wishing. I directed Jason's cuts and bruises to heal. I wished that, when I snapped my fingers, both Sam and Jason would become fully alert, ready to fight if necessary. I also tried to radiate a general stay-away vibe to keep any real doctors or nurses from wandering in.

"I appreciate your concern," I said. I could sense that whatever other motives Marco had, he also did care about my welfare, and he sincerely believed he could help me. Of course, Marco's version of sincere was more complex than Joe Q. Average's. When I continued to scan him, pushing past whatever defenses had shielded him in the past, I was startled to see how conflicted he was. There was no aspect of his psyche that didn't embody a healthy percentage of its opposite. And all of it was relatively extreme. He was very compassionate, for example. This was an authentic, hard-earned aspect of his outlook and behavior. But simultaneously—they didn't take turns—Marco was also incredibly angry. The two elements didn't mix, temper one another, or interact in any way that I could sense. They were just both there.

My rational mind couldn't make any more sense of it than that. It didn't feel wrong, though—as though he were broken and needed fixing. Marco was exactly who he should be—like everyone else.

I also understood now who Marco was in a more global sense. He wasn't the monster that others had depicted—he wasn't a sociopath. But he certainly wasn't fully enlightened. His energy and knowledge base were on a par with that status, but his inner chaos bespoke the work that still lay ahead of him. Psychologically and emotionally, he was a well-managed mess. Much of what he said or did was for effect—a performance designed to manipulate people. Even now, in the hospital room, he was posturing and choosing his words with a cunning that undermined his purported spiritual evolution.

"Get out of my head," Marco said tersely.

I nodded and stopped probing.

"I am who I am," he said, looking at me intently. "Whether you knew what this was before or you know it now or you wonder about it, I'm still *this*. Whether we call me Marco or Bruno or a dick"—he nodded to Chris—"I'm *this*—that which stands before you. Like you and everyone else, I'm ever-changing, but right now, as always, I'm *this*. Good or bad. Like it or not. All I can be is *this*."

"That's a load of self-serving crap," Chris said.

Marco glared at him and lost his poise. Perhaps my intrusion into his psyche had been destabilizing.

Energy shot from Marco's right hand. I could actually see it now as a dark, surging ray in the air. I didn't wait to see what effect it would have on my best friend. My own energy burst out of me and met Marco's—blocking and disrupting the visible wave pattern. His energy dissipated harmlessly after a second

433

or two.

"Don't do that again," I told Marco.

"What? What do you think I did?"

"Perhaps it wasn't conscious," I said. "But you'd better keep your energy under control."

"Or?" His face was tight and his eyes were fierce.

"Or we'll end up in some kind of energy war," I said. "And I don't think we want that."

"I might," Marco said. "If you're determined to be my enemy, why should I let you continue to develop and perhaps become my equal—or superior?"

"I have no ill will toward you, Marco. I thank you from the bottom of my heart for all your help. You have nothing to fear from me."

"I wish I could believe that," he said. "But you have no idea what it's going to be like to hold so much power. Power really does corrupt. It would be irresponsible of me to allow someone I've imbued with this much spiritual energy to administer it without supervision. Would you train a young therapist for a week and then step away and let him screw up clients on his own?"

"Of course not. But that's an invalid comparison. In your case, we're talking about involuntary supervision, while my trainees have asked for help. And when I'm working with interns, I don't sit in the therapy room with them and direct their actions. They approach me for anything they think they need. They set the agenda. Unsolicited help is interference. Give me your cell phone number, and I'll call you with any questions I have."

Marco waved his arm in the air. "Words. It's all just words," he said. "You talk for a living, Sid. Of course you have words for everything."

I softened my voice. "I listen for a living," I said. "And I'm hearing your concerns. What do you need from me to keep this from getting ugly?"

"Uglier," Chris said.

"Let me in," Marco said. "Open up and let me in your head the way you were in mine. I'll take it from there."

"I can't do that," I told him.

He shook his head slowly and then raised his hands in front of his chest. "I'm sorry, Sid," he said. Then he blasted me with an intense wave of high-pitched energy. I was rocked.

I felt a burning sensation in my chest, and all the muscles in my torso and neck tightened painfully. My head felt as though someone were sticking needles in it. I didn't know what to do.

"What's going on?" I heard Chris ask. It sounded as if he were a hundred yards away.

The energy took me over. A frenzied buzzing spun in my gut. Marco's attack was activating a resonance, and my own energy was being co-opted—used against me. I could barely think or act.

I held up a hand, hoping that something would happen—that my energy would know how to defend itself.

White light shot from my fingertips toward Marco. As it met the dark waves he was directing my way, the two energies merged and morphed into a supercharged field that filled the room with pinpoints of sparkling gold light.

"Hey!" Chris said. "What the fuck!"

Marco switched to another wavelength with a

tighter, faster pattern. Despite my best efforts to protect myself, the new energy blasted me again. It was an assault on every level—energetic, of course, but also physical, emotional, and mental. The intense, grinding pain drained my defenses.

Marco knew how to fight this way. I didn't.

I improvised, radiating a force field of sorts around me. It seemed to help for a time—only a muted version of Marco's energy penetrated it. But his battering gradually wore me down. I tried to counterattack, but all I could send at that point was intense love.

"That feels great," Marco said. "Send me more love, Sid."

I checked on Chris. He was asleep or passed out beside me.

I redoubled my efforts to hold off Marco, and it worked for a while. But I could sense that he expended far less effort generating and sending his energy than I used to defend myself against it. Sooner or later, this equation would tip in his favor.

I snapped my fingers to activate the others. To do so, I had to relinquish my first line of defense—the energy in my hands. An almost unbearable vibration blitzed me—an oscillating, destructive wave. It was going to tear me apart.

Then I heard a shriek, and I refocused on the scene in front of me. The awful energy relented as Sam kicked Marco in the side of the head. Jason rushed the older man from the other side. Marco blocked a follow-up punch from Sam and slid sideways. Just as the Maori began a backhand fist strike, Marco leapt in the air and kicked both of them simultaneously. It was an impossible move—especially in the close quarters of the hospital room.

Sam sprawled onto the floor after taking a blow to the solar plexus. Jason staggered back, having been kicked in the upper thigh, but kept his feet. If Marco had been aiming for his groin, he'd just missed.

I crawled out of bed as Marco came at Jason. The big man surprised him by initiating a quick leg sweep. I don't think Marco was reading his mind. But he backed away from Jason in time, and a millisecond later, he lashed out a leg of his own to topple him. Jason managed to fall onto the other bed instead of the floor. He was unhurt. Unbelievably quick for someone his size, he scrambled back up.

I looked around for some sort of weapon. All this kung fu was wonderfully cinematic, but a stainless steel bedpan to the back of Marco's head seemed like a more practical solution.

The fight raged on behind me as I scavenged. God, I was stiff and sore. Out of the corner of my eye, I saw Sam rush Marco with a series of punches, each of which he blocked with his forearm. As Jason engaged him simultaneously from the other side, Marco casually flicked away the Maori's powerful fists with the side of his own. It all looked so effortless. It was hard to imagine Marco could lose this fight.

I couldn't find anything that would serve as an effective weapon—not even a bed pan. I stood in the corner of the room under the TV and tried to send energy. If I could time it just right, maybe I could throw Marco off-balance and give Sam or Jason an opening. But my energy was weak and diffuse now. I couldn't target it at all, and as I tried, I felt myself becoming dangerously depleted.

Then I remembered my new ability to influence people—to alter reality, perhaps. Surely I could use that in some way that would influence the outcome of the fight. Suppose I told the TV to jump off its mount and land on Marco's head? I reached out my will and tested those waters. The TV didn't budge. Then I thought of something else; I could call in the cavalry.

Sam and Jason held their own for another minute or two, and then I heard footsteps pounding in the hallway outside the room. Three burly security guards burst in. One even held a gun—well, a stun gun.

"All right!" the gun wielder called. "That's enough!"

Everyone froze, except Chris, who decided to wake up at that point.

"What the fuck?" he said, sitting up.

The spokesperson, flanked by his two colleagues, swiveled and aimed his weapon at Chris.

"Shut up," he said. "Who's the perp?"

We all pointed at Marco.

"He impersonated a doctor and broke into our room," I said. "Be careful. He's a martial arts master."

The guard waved his stun gun. "Don't worry. I've got Suzie here, and she doesn't take any shit from anybody. I don't care if he's Mohammed Fucking Ali."

Marco immediately kicked the gun out of the man's hand and launched himself in the air. As the guard stood there wondering what had just happened, Marco planted his hands on the man's shoulders and vaulted over him. He tucked his body into a graceful somersault, landed on his feet, and sprinted away.

After a moment's hesitation, the three men turned and ran after him. I had no doubt he would escape their clutches.

"Well," Chris said, "he really stuck the landing. I'm giving him a 9.6."

Chapter Thirty-Seven

Once Jason and I found our clothes, the four of us took off before the police arrived. My interview with the customs official back in Auckland had convinced me no one in a position of authority was likely to believe any of my story. And the current saga was about a hundred times crazier than the one I'd unsuccessfully told two weeks before.

I had to use my "wishing" several times for us to get past nurses and orderlies as we negotiated the maze of the hospital's hallways.

"The building's on lockdown," a uniformed man told us when we reached the front door. I wished he'd make an exception for us.

"But of course I'll make an exception for the four of you," he said. "Out of the way, people," he told the other would-be exiters. "We've got exceptions coming through."

In the parking lot, as police sirens wailed, we headed for Chris's car, which he'd parked at the far end of the lot under a stand of trees.

"What's up, Sid?" Sam asked. "Are you controlling these people somehow? I'm not sure I'm comfortable with that."

"Yeah, I know. It turns out that since I woke up, everything I wish for comes true—at least in terms of other people's behaviors. Oh, and I think I healed

Jason, too."

The big man confirmed this. "I don't think it's a bad thing, though," Jason added. "Did you want to stay there, Sam, and talk to the police for the next few hours?"

"It's definitely practical," Chris said. "I'm sure we can all agree on that. But let's face it, if this weren't Sid, I for one would be totally freaking out. I mean, some other guy might make me bark like a chicken."

"Chickens don't bark," Jason pointed out.

"Just ignore him when he says things like that," I advised.

"Hey, that's why it would be so freaky," Chris protested. "Anyone can bark like a dog."

At the car—Chris drove a hybrid—Sam called my mother to let her know I was okay. She listened for a while as well and then answered yes several times.

Chris pulled out of the parking lot onto Soquel Avenue—one of the only continuous north-south thoroughfares in town.

Sam hung up and spoke to me. "Your parents would like us to meet them at the boardwalk. They're on an outing with some of our newer acolytes. Is that okay with you?"

"I guess," I said.

"I love the boardwalk," Chris said. "They have deep-fried everything."

"Do they have carnival games?" Jason asked. "I always win at carnival games."

"What are you, twelve?" Chris said. "It's all about the crap food, bro. That, and all the trashy women in tank tops and halter tops and bikini tops and—"

"Yeah, okay," I said. "We get it. You like tops."

"And bottoms," Chris said.

I was conscious of Jason's unacknowledged gayness—according to Paul, anyway. *Is he comfortable with this sort of talk?*

A long strip of old-fashioned rides, games, souvenir shops, and fast-food kiosks that hugged the main beach, the Santa Cruz Beach Boardwalk was tourist central in the summer. All the roads leading to it would soon be hopelessly clogged with families from San Jose, Salinas, and points north. This time of year, though—early May—it was only open on the weekends.

"What day is it?" I asked.

"Saturday," Sam answered.

"Tops galore!" Chris proclaimed.

"Are you really all sorted, Sid?" Jason asked. "It didn't look good back there. The doctor said you might be a vegetable."

"I was rooting for a rutabaga," Chris said.

"Is he always like this?" Sam asked.

"Pretty much," I told her. "Sometimes he's worse."

"If you really loved me," Chris said, "you wouldn't say shit like that. I bring peppy, irreverent sunshine to your dreary life, Sid. At least, it used to be dreary back when all you did was sit in a room all day with crazy people."

It was only a few miles to the boardwalk parking lot, which was in the middle of the worst neighborhood in town. Chris and Jason argued about a variety of inane topics on the way there. I got the feeling this was how they'd passed the time in the hospital while I was in samadhi.

The lot was about two-thirds full, with a

disproportionate number of minivans, SUVs, and RVs. As we climbed out and began walking toward the boardwalk, I felt a childlike excitement. This always happened to me—ever since my first visit as a kid.

Sam held my hand as we led the others across the street, over the tourist train tracks, and under a colorful archway. We entered the amusement park through a small plaza next to a historic carousel. The boardwalk proper was just ahead.

"So where are we meeting?" I asked.

A sea of people stopped and stared at Jason. I don't think they were rugby fans. He was just a spectacularly well-put-together, giant man. For that matter, Sam was drawing her share of attention too.

"By the log flume ride," Sam told me. "Wherever that is."

"To our left," I said. "Past the big roller coaster."

The carousel blared a calliope tune, tattooed parents shouted at their hyperactive kids, and I could hear crashing waves from the contiguous beach. The aromas of suntan lotion, popcorn, hot dogs, pizza, and the tang of the salty bay water sickened me a bit.

I'd seen it much more crowded, but as we tried to make our way down the long, asphalt concourse, we still had to dodge packs of attention-seeking teenage girls (wearing Chris-pleasing tops), families with baby strollers, and squads of self-absorbed college students. After a block or two, we also encountered an oncoming gang of young Hispanic men, although gangs were supposedly barred by the boardwalk. Usually I saw quite a few security guards when I was there, as well as an occasional police officer. But there were none in sight.

The gang—if they were a gang—walked four abreast. There were two rows of them. Their heads were shaved down to black stubble, and they all wore black jeans and white dress shirts buttoned up at the neck.

Ahead of us, everyone sidled to the edges of the wooden promenade to let them pass. Several of the men walked with their elbows extended, picking off whoever hadn't yielded thoroughly enough.

As Sam and I stepped to the side, by a chocolate-covered frozen banana stand, Chris headed to the counter.

"I'll just be a minute," he told us.

I turned to see where Jason was. He stood in the middle of the walkway, his feet planted. He smiled at the oncoming squad of young men. He'd decided not to yield.

"Jason!" I called. "No."

Grudgingly, he sidled over to where we stood. "I have no patience with that," Jason said. "In New Zealand, I lost too many friends to that bullshit."

My parents sat at a wooden picnic table just shy of the flume ride. They were surrounded by women in white dresses. Four sat at the table with them, and another dozen congregated behind them. They were all sizes, shapes, ages, and ethnicities. They seem to be very alert—even excited.

"RGP novices!" my mother called. "Meet Sid!"

The women that were sitting stood, and then all of them bowed in unison. I could see down most of their dresses, which was distracting. Several of them were quite busy.

"Hi," I said.

"Perhaps you could give us all a blessing," my father said.

"Sure."

I held up my hand and stopped thinking. Energy surged out, and all the women staggered. I enlisted my mind again and wished that everyone could handle the energy gracefully. Then they were standing at ease again. I wished that they were happy and healed and as awake as they needed to be to navigate their lives effectively. Everyone smiled.

"My goodness," my mother said. "That was far more than a blessing, Sid. Where did you learn to do that? That was an extraordinary transmission."

"It's an artifact from wherever I was when my body was lying in the hospital. A chaplain sent me energy in the emergency room and got it started."

"They don't have chaplains at St. Domnio's anymore," my mother told me.

"Well, Lanai was one—right, Jason?"

"I'm sorry, Sid. I don't remember a chaplain."

Chris tried out *his* stage cough at that point.

"I'm sorry," my mother said. "Where are my manners? RGP, this is Sid's friend Chris on my right and Jason Patariki on my left, and of course you all know Sam."

They all bowed again. I swear that one of them—a young African-American woman with tight cornrows—shimmied a little as Chris ogled her breasts.

My mother gestured to the empty seats on the benches, and the four of us replaced the women who'd been sitting there.

"Would anyone like any food or drink?" my mother asked.

"Yes," Chris and Jason answered simultaneously.

"Anything crappy," Chris added, with a half-eaten frozen banana in his hand. My father laughed.

The white-dressed women drifted away, breaking into pairs as they moved down the boardwalk.

Once again, my father's dogs weren't with him. For that matter, where had Spot gotten to?

I wished he were here with us, and suddenly he was lying on the table in front of me, blocking my view of my mother. I wished he'd move, and he did. Spot now perched on my mother's lap. He lowered his head and glowered at me, his ears back. I don't think he liked being bossed around.

Sam spoke up for the first time since we joined my parents. "Sid seems to be perfectly fine," she reported. "We're ready to move forward with the plan."

"After we eat, dear," my mother said. "Chris, would you mind being our waiter? I need to talk over some things with the others, and this way you can pick out whatever you deem to be the most delightfully crappy menu items."

"That's a compelling argument," Chris replied. "But I'm disappointed that you used the word 'crappy.' Don't stoop to my level, Mrs. M."

My mother ignored this. Chris took our orders and wandered off.

"Jason," my mother said. "I'm not sure I'm comfortable with you hearing what I have to say, either."

"That's fine," he said. "I can sit across the way there." He gestured to a bench across the boardwalk that abutted a ring toss game.

"Or you could just play the game while you're over

there," I suggested.

"Really?"

"Sure, why not?"

He jumped up and jogged into the stream of tourists. Sam, my parents, and I sat quietly and watched the parade of people for a few moments.

"So what's on your mind?" I asked my mother.

Her phone rang. She picked it up and mouthed, "It's Paul." Then she stepped away to talk. In just a few seconds, she rushed back.

"The Maoris are headed here," she said, her voice raising in pitch. "Paul's been serving as a lookout. They're on the boardwalk."

"I guess we'd better go," I said. "Should we split up?"

"That's a good idea. Your father and I will stay," my mother said. "We need to look out for our novices, and I don't think they'll try anything here in public. At least, not with us."

"Are you sure?" Sam asked.

"Yes, yes. Hurry, dear. We'll call you when things settle down."

I noticed several of the RGP women trailing Chris as he headed back to the table with a heaping cardboard tray of food. I hoped the others were safe.

"Chris! Jason!" I called. "We need to go!"

"I'm bringing the food with us," Chris announced. "I don't care if it's the fucking apocalypse."

Chapter Thirty-Eight

I led the way toward the south end of the amusement park, where a railroad trestle bridge spanned the mouth of the San Lorenzo River. Once we got across that—there was a narrow, enclosed walkway alongside the rarely used tracks—we'd be home free, just blocks from Chris's house in the Seabright neighborhood.

After a few hundred yards, we ran out of boardwalk and began striding up the concrete pathway that led to the bridge. I felt as though I were leading a small parade—as though we were celebrating some sort of unlikely holiday.

Local people often used the bridge to walk to the boardwalk after they'd parked for free in Chris's neighborhood, but there was no one on the rickety-looking wooden structure when we got there.

I decided Jason should traverse first—we needed fighters at both ends. On a bridge, those were the only places we'd be vulnerable. The boards beside the tracks protested the imposition of his weight with disturbing creaks and squeaks. Chris ran onto the bridge next. I followed him—more cautiously—and Sam brought up the rear.

A wire fence ran along our right shoulders, keeping any daredevil bridge-crossers from the railroad track itself, which had gaping holes between its ties. On the water side, a waist-high wooden railing protected us from falling into the river.

It was a lovely view inland over the rail. The river was peppered with water birds, and it wound snakelike up toward the mountains. It smelled pretty bad, though. That time of year, the San Lorenzo was still swollen from the rainy season, but didn't have enough current to fight its way through the sandy beach to the bay.

When Sam and I were about halfway across, Marco suddenly dropped down from the bridge's superstructure and stood in front of me, holding a pistol. On the far side of him, Chris and Jason were almost across. Sam was trapped behind me on the single-file walkway.

"Hello, Sid," he said, smiling his creepiest smile.

"A gun?" I said. "Really? I thought martial artists were against guns."

"Your thoughts have never been your best ally, have they?" he said. "Why do you still believe any of them? Have I taught you nothing?"

By now, all the others had noticed him. I wished everyone ahead of me to keep moving; there was no reason they should be in jeopardy. Marco wanted *me*— or wanted me dead, more likely.

"Marco!" Sam called from behind me. "Put the gun down. The police are right behind us. This is something we can work out."

"I'm going to kill Sid," he told her. "But you can live if you stay out of it."

I watched him. He looked five years older than when I had first met him. And there was a hint of something in his dark eyes that hadn't been there before. Fear? Desperation?

I felt none of them, just an interest in how this would turn out.

"How about this?" Sam said. "You and I fight for Sid. If you win, you go ahead and kill him. If I win, you let him go."

"Why would I agree to that?"

"It appeals to your sense of fun."

"That's true."

"And we both know who'll win, don't we?"

"Yes. You have no chance." He paused and thought a moment. "So this isn't really about Sid living or dying, is it?"

"No."

"It's about how you're going to live with yourself after he's gone. You'll feel better if you had an opportunity to try to save him."

"Yes," she said.

"Give her that," I said. "Kill me, but let her fight. Come on, Marco."

"All right." He turned to look behind him.

The others stood on the far side of the water. Jason was straining to return and fight, but my will held him off.

"Sid, you need to keep the others there and make sure that the police stay away, too. Or it's no deal."

"Agreed," I said. "How shall we do this?"

I couldn't picture how the two of them could fight on the narrow walkway, and I was standing between them, too.

"You crouch down," Marco said, "and let Louise step over you. I'm putting the pistol in my waistband. I won't use it until after we've finished fighting. Agreed?"

"Sure."

"Thank you," Sam said.

As she climbed over me, Sam whispered something in my ear that gave me hope. Then she attacked.

The action was furious. In the confined space, with a mesh fence on one side and the railing on the other, there was no room for anything exotic. Both performed a series of straight-ahead punches, blocks, and feints. Neither landed a significant blow for the first thirty seconds.

Marco smiled continuously. Clearly, he *was* having fun as he toyed with his former student.

Sam tried a few snap-kicks, aiming them at Marco's legs. He evaded them easily and countered with a similar kick that would've landed much higher on Sam's body if she hadn't backed away. All of this was happening more quickly that I could clearly see, and Sam blocked my view of most of Marco's moves.

When she crouched and swept a leg forward to trip Marco, though, I could see that he was waiting for this. He cocked his left leg, and then paused to savor the moment before he kicked her in the head.

"Watch out!" I called.

She lurched to the side, below the wooden railing, and then shouted, "Now!" to me.

We both grabbed the railing, swung ourselves over, and jumped off the bridge. It was probably sixty feet down to the San Lorenzo River.

I didn't know if it would be deep enough to absorb our plunge, and perhaps Marco could pick us off from above before we could swim out of range. But all that seemed less risky than remaining on the bridge.

I hit the water feet first, and I thought my ankles would break. But they didn't. The river was very cold and also very dirty. As I surfaced and looked for Sam, I heard the pistol and saw splashes nearby. Sam burst to the surface a moment later, gasping for breath.

"Stay under," she gasped. "Swim underwater—that way!"

We both dove again, heading inland, away from the river mouth.

Could I wish anything for myself? Could I hold my breath for fifteen minutes if I willed it? Swim like an Olympian? Maybe I could wish that someone would rescue us—haul us out of the polluted water into a boat or something.

When I needed to come to the surface, I heard the gun again. But it was definitely farther away now, and I didn't see any splashes this time.

"Here I am, Sid!" Sam called from behind me.

I turned around to see her, and damned if there wasn't a boat in the water behind her.

"Look," I said, pointing.

It was a good-sized motorboat, and it was towing two inner tubes—empty inner tubes. Had I wished this? From the water line, I couldn't see who was steering the boat. Maybe I'd influenced a random fisherman to help us.

We both swam frantically toward the inner tubes, reaching for them before the boat zoomed past us. Sam grabbed hers first. I didn't think I'd get to mine in time, but the boat slowed down a tick—just as much as it needed to—and then I snared the other tube. I locked onto it with both arms up to my armpits, and then the boat sped up again.

Several more shots rang out. I kept my head ducked down and hung on as the boat accelerated. On another day, if the water were cleaner, it might have been fun to be towed up the river. As it was, I just focused on holding on tight, periodically checking on Sam.

After a few hundred yards, she smiled from her perch alongside me in the boat's wake. "I love you," she mouthed.

"I love you, too," I mouthed back.

Ten minutes later, after we'd been pulled through several bends in the river, the driver of the boat slowed and then stopped.

I sat up on my tube, and Sam did the same. Did whoever it was even know we were back there? A moment later, a slight figure appeared at the bow. The sunlight was behind whoever it was—we could only see a stark silhouette at first. Then she moved to the side.

It was Lannie. Lannie Chow from Howick, New Zealand.

"Hello, Sid," she said. "Hello, Samavati."

Chapter Thirty-Nine

I didn't know I was still capable of being surprised on a grand scale, but I was.

Lannie's accent was completely gone now. She spoke flawless American English. And she looked even more beautiful than I remembered. She wore her shiny red warm-up suit, and now she stood self-assured and confident in it. Her porcelain-white skin gleamed in the sun, and her very black hair hung long and loose.

"Who are you?" Sam called from her tube. "How do you know our names?"

"Sid knows me as Lannie Chow," she said. "We met at a bed and breakfast of sorts in New Zealand."

"And you just happened to be driving by in a boat towing two tires?" Sam asked.

Lannie began hauling us in, a hand on each of the thick ropes that held the tubes. It didn't seem as though she'd be strong enough to manage this, but she quickly reeled us in with no visible effort.

Her dark eyes were incredibly present. She was right there—with no part of her held in reserve or split off on another interior task. As much as Marco had been in the moment—and *his* eyes reflected a remarkable ability to pay attention, too—Lannie was light years beyond him. It would've been alarming if I hadn't already met her—albeit as Lannie 1.0, not this new improved version.

We struggled onto the boat's slippery white fiberglass deck and stood, wet and cold. Both of us towered over Lannie. She was even smaller than I remembered.

She fetched us each a beach towel from a bin behind her, and we wrapped ourselves in the towels and sat on damp plastic seats.

Lannie stood in front of us, her arms at her sides, a gentle half smile on her face. She waited for one of us to speak first.

"Let's get back to the 'who are you?' question," I said. "And then I'd like to know exactly what's going on. How did you find us? Why are you here?"

"I'm here to wake you up," she said. "Both of you. All the way awake." Her smile widened; it was so contagious, I smiled too, despite my misgivings.

"I don't understand," I said.

Lannie put her finger to her lips to silence me. Then she began humming.

At first, it was a normal sound—just one soothing note. The pitch was slightly lower than I would've thought she could manage. Gradually, though, the humming grew louder, and then even louder, and then impossibly loud. How could anyone produce a sound like that?

Then Lannie lowered the pitch even more, and I could feel something in my gut resonate with the wall of sound. The humming grew more complex—it was a wider band of tones now, and I could feel various parts of me vibrating along with it, especially the top of my head.

Spot appeared on the deck in front of me, sitting up, watching me closely.

"Where did that dog come from?" Sam shouted.

I looked more closely. Spot was completely solid now—the way I'd seen him in India.

The humming increased in volume again. It hurt. It permeated every cell in me. It was almost too intense to bear.

Spot's eyes rolled up in his head, and he passed out, pitching forward. I grabbed him and held him tight. He was very warm, very dirty, and heavier than he looked.

The humming became a roar and then a crescendo of every sound I'd ever heard—all of it at once. It was *the* sound, I suddenly realized—the root vibration of the universe. I was experiencing Om—the Big Bang's impetus to explode into creation. It was an extraordinary epiphany; I had no doubt about what I now knew.

I felt overwhelmed and panicky for a few seconds. My eyes closed involuntarily, and all the muscles in my abdomen clenched. I concentrated on holding Spot—it helped me center myself.

Then I began to feel the intense raw love that was embodied in the sound. The root vibration *was* love. Love was behind it all.

I'd only experienced dilute versions of this before, but now I was in direct contact with the unadulterated searing heat of cosmic love.

It burned away my ego—my remaining sense of self. As all of me vibrated along with the love, there was no one left to do anything else. There was no part of me that wasn't also the vibration itself.

And then there was no vibration, either. The energy was there, but there was no consequence driven by its presence—no cause and effect. It just *was*. Nothing else was real.

An instant later, I found myself in the blackness of samadhi again. It was absolutely quiet and still and blank. I was awareness again—not as any sort of "I," but as an energy form—the consciousness that I now knew myself to be. I was capable of perception and thought—or something analogous to these, I guessed. But this iteration was something new and more profound—way beyond what I'd experienced in previous visits to samadhi.

I wondered how Sam was faring—how the Om was affecting her.

Then she was there, suspended in the void. She wore a low-cut wedding gown. Her blond hair splashed down over her milky shoulders onto cleavage that seemed to be more substantial than I remembered. Her face displayed surprise—not delighted surprise, not shocked surprise. Just surprise.

She looked down at herself. *Is this how you usually picture me?* she thought. I could hear her thoughts as readily as I once heard her voice.

I pictured her in a black bikini, and now she wore that. There was no transition between the two realities; one moment Sam was in a dress and the next she was in a bikini.

I'm not a dress-up doll.

Sorry, I thought.

I didn't know if she could read my mind in return—or for that matter if this was really Sam. But when I tried to physically say I was sorry, there was no physical me to do it. The urge to talk expressed itself as a projected thought.

I created an image in which this Sam wore the same clothes she was wearing back on the boat—if anyone was still sitting there. Now she was in her white tunic over her turquoise pants. Unfortunately, they were soaking wet.

Thanks a lot. Let me try.

Sam manifested an imperfect, but dry version of the same outfit. The seams of her top were inside out, and her pants were too short.

I didn't mean to communicate this perception, but apparently she heard it.

Hey, that was just a first try, Sam thought, and now her clothes were just right. *Wow*. She surveyed herself. *That was fun. Let me try something more ambitious.*

She thought a mountain into existence, and now we sat on its peak—side by side on a flat, wide rock. As I watched, Sam manifested several other slightly lower mountains around us. They were all remarkably similar—not what you'd find in nature. And while the other mountains were snowcapped, our higher peak was not.

As I noticed these things, they morphed into a more realistic, logically-consistent version of the original scene. Had Sam heard my thoughts and edited her work, or had my attention to them transformed them directly?

Beats me, Sam thought.

I noticed her thoughts were more colloquial than her spoken words. I also noticed she'd forgotten to create a sky, so I transformed the dark backdrop into an azure expanse with a few puffy clouds.

Sam reshaped the clouds into barnyard animals. Then she made them wave to me. I waved back.

The distant landscape, however, remained out of focus. It was a gray, undefined haze. I imagined an even more ambitious mountain range that stretched to the horizon in every direction. And it was there. I added several lakes and a vast forest that covered the lower altitudes of the mountains. For good measure, I created a few hawks in the air just below us.

Sam added a Disneyesque castle on top of a nearby peak. She made it turquoise—to match her pants, I guessed.

I imagined a fleet of impossibly long silver zeppelins and a red suspension bridge that spanned a wide valley to our right. I sketched in quite a few details, but the creation still resembled a thrift store painting more than an actual place.

Is all this real? Sam asked.

Before I could formulate a thought in response, Lannie was standing in front of us. Her samadhi persona was exactly the same as she had appeared in the boat. I hadn't conjured her as far as I knew, so perhaps she was the one manifesting her image. If so, she was clearly better at this than I was. Every detail was sharp. And she'd portrayed the interplay of light and shadow on her skin to render her image more three-dimensional than ours.

I can answer your question, Sam, Lannie thought. *Yes, this is real. It's a new world that you're bringing into being with your thoughts that aren't thoughts.*

What are they, then? I thought.

Where is your mind? she asked. *Here? In this space? And who would be thinking these thoughts? The Sid and Sam you no longer are? Energy is expressing itself through you. You are administering power that is beyond individual mind. Thoughts are stories we tell ourselves about the world—about ourselves. They embody far too low a reality quotient to generate any traction with the elemental aspects of existence.*

I considered this—apparently not with my mind, although it felt like it. I guess Sam thought a question I hadn't heard, because Lannie looked at her and spoke again.

Yes, this is how worlds are made—how illusion comes to be. It's all completely real to those hawks— and it would be to any beings in those aircraft if Sid had created pilots or crews. She gestured at the zeppelins in the sky. Several of them were ramming into one another.

Oops, I thought.

Your consciousness is now aligned with the universe as a whole, Lannie thought. *The energy fields that constitute so-called matter will dance to whatever tune you hum.*

Are we humming now and we don't know it? Sam thought.

Exactly. Let me help you sense it. She raised an eyebrow, and then I could hear a symphony of humming—all sorts of tones and textures. Some of it was coming from me.

It's vibration that animates matter, isn't it? Sam asked.

Yes, of course.

Clearly, Sam had more background in all this than I did. That insight would never have occurred to me.

What feels like thought now, Lannie projected, *is really a refashioning of Om energy—sound, vibration— whatever word you like. None of them do the phenomenon justice, of course. So it's a kind of internal humming that's responsible for the grunt work of creation.*

But we were just playing, I thought.

That's all it ever is, Lannie thought. *It's just play.*

She looked down at herself and imagined black velvet overalls and a yellow satin shirt. Her hair was in a thick braid now that was tucked into the pocket of her overalls.

I wondered what I was wearing. I hadn't thought to look—or whatever the eyeless equivalent of looking was. It turned out I was nude.

I wasn't about to say anything, Sam thought. *I've been enjoying this.*

I manifested jeans and a white T-shirt.

Lannie manifested a chair-shaped rock in front of us and sat on it. Her attention to detail created a remarkable contrast between her hyper-real rock and our pallid mountaintop. If something could be more than lifelike, that's what her creation was.

You have more questions, she thought to Sam.

Yes. Who are you?

This one will not be easy for you to hear, Lannie began. *Much as you are the energy beings who have created these mountains—this partial world—I am the being that created yours. For billions of years, I've been tending to it, nurturing your kind, and all the other creatures on it.*

So you're God? I asked. I felt a wave of awe. It wasn't an emotion. It was a realization that I was about an inch tall and I sat across from the infinite.

Call me that if you wish, Lannie thought. *But it's only the illusion of time that sets me apart from you or anyone else. I unfolded from my constricted sense of self into the energy I really am on a very different time line. That's all. Five billion years ago, I sat on my proverbial mountaintop as another energy being explained all this to me. Eventually—or at least it seems as if it's eventual since constricted beings believe in events and time—everyone graduates from the physical realm.*

This is hard to absorb, Sam thought.

Yes, Lannie/God agreed. *Even when we cease to believe in our tiny, false selves, we're still resistant to the notion that our true nature is god-like. We're afraid of owning our own magnificence. But when events force us to question what's real—and if anything is—then we're drawn to the truth.* She looked at us with loving eyes as she thought this.

I love you, I thought.

I love you, too, God thought. *We are love. All of us. But we need more than an intellectual recognition of this. At some point, we need to develop an abiding, full awareness of the love in each moment, and most of us also need to receive energy transmissions to complete our work here. Then we cross from the mundane world to the energy realm. There are various ways this can happen. Sam's path has been traditional; Sid's has been unique. But sooner or later, all of this comes to pass for everyone—or will come to pass—or did come to pass. Language is inadequate in these matters.*

So everyone becomes a creator? Sam asked.

Yes.

I was having no personal reaction to any of this now. Unlike Sam, I wasn't finding it hard to absorb. On the contrary, it was deeply satisfying to hear—more like the experience of snapping down the final, missing jigsaw puzzle piece of a seemingly unsolvable puzzle. And I knew—absolutely knew—that Lannie *was* God and God was speaking the truth. Her thoughts perfectly explained why my life had unfolded the way that it had—why the psychological rug kept being pulled out from under me. It had simply been necessary— preparation for something else. Something more. This.

None of us projected any thoughts for several minutes.

I realized that the mythology of being a person— living in a body—created a tyranny of continuity. When we believe that we inhabit a solid, real context, subject to time and the "laws" of physics, we stay trapped in an absurdly finite realm, where suffering rules.

I sat in this new world we'd begun to make, and I felt a freedom unlike anything I could've ever imagined. I was now a peaceful, limitless expanse of love energy, One with everyone and everything. Consciousness was infinitely variable. I was consciousness. I was free.

I completely opened up my mind—or whatever it was—and Sam heard it all and then shared her experience with me. It was almost exactly the same.

Why me? I thought to God. *I'm not surprised that Sam is ready to move on. But why me? Aren't there people who are far more worthy—who wouldn't have needed so many weird events and energy transmissions to be here with you?*

Of course, Lannie thought. *But I was Charles Singh's niece.*

What?

I was your mother, Sid. In my last body. I was a

girl named Amrita—Charles Singh's niece.

Oh. I'm sorry.

She waved her small, graceful hand in the air. *Your karma has always been unusual,* she told me, *even compared to your two brothers.*

I don't understand, Sam thought.

I opened up and filled her in on what I'd learned about my birth in Charles's office at the golf course.

Sam turned to God. *So you incarnate in bodies like the rest of us?*

Yes. I've lived for over three decades as Lannie Chow, running things from that body, waiting for you both to develop. More recently, I was temporarily Lanai Tu, as well—"Lannie, too," Sid. I thought you might get that one. Wasn't that hospital chaplain's energy familiar?

Now that you mention it, yes.

Sam thought something next. *Who else have you been? How much have you participated in human history?*

It's a common misperception that I incarnate as headliners. I wasn't Buddha or Jesus or Mohammed. I wasn't even a world-changing figure like Alexander the Great or Lincoln. I'm usually behind the scenes— operating without public scrutiny.

But you've been involved in my life all along, haven't you? I thought.

Yes. I worked with your parents quite a bit throughout your childhood. As a therapist, you know that it all starts there. I also helped shape Marco, Bhante, and several others so they could play their roles. You needed Marco's inimitable head-on teaching style to confound your mind and help you find your heart. You've been trapped in your head for many years. Meher Baba played an essential role, as well.

Even though he's been dead for decades? I thought.

Yes. That doesn't matter. I also fed energy to various other people so they could pass it on to both of you.

Andrea talks about feeling guided, Sam thought. *And I've often felt energy routing through her that she seemed unaware of. For that matter, I'd never even have met Sid if another member of RGP hadn't been so ill the morning after Paul's appointment.*

God smiled. *Bad yogurt. Bacteria hardly need any nudging at all.*

So do you intercede in human affairs quite a bit? Sam asked.

Not really, God thought. *Most of what you're wondering about is simply generated by the natural flow of energy. If you were to keep creating this world we're visiting—and this is not your destiny—you'd see how much illusion simply flows once you've applied a gentle push. Those hawks below us, for example—good job on those, Sid—will mate and make more hawks. Over time, their species will evolve, and then someday a new type of creature will supplant them. There's a great deal of turnover in the animal kingdom.*

That sounds like a major personnel issue, I thought.

God laughed. *Yes, of course. But remember, none of this requires effort or magic tricks. Life unfolds. It's much the same with both your spiritual paths. One thing has led to another, for the most part. If you have a role to play, events will maneuver you into that role.*

I thought another question. *So when people tried to kill us, the universe didn't let them?*

That's right. You're both part of a higher spiritual priority. Unfortunately, a side effect of this phenomenon is that the hostile energy directed at you comes back onto your aggressors.

So what Marco said about Frank and the others is true?

Yes.

What's the deal with all these enemies, anyway? I continued. *Why do gangs, terrorists, and cults all want me dead?*

There are real mystics in the world, God thought. *And real psychics, real prophets, and quite a few very good guessers. Your existence, Sid—your energy, your upcoming role—these have been accurately envisioned by a host of people. It's hard to stay sane when you have these abilities and you live in a logic-driven culture, so many of these people are also somewhat crazy. Hence, their irrational, violent approach to what they consider to be a threat to the spiritual status quo. They have no reason to trust someone like you—an outsider with alarming spiritual power.*

So getting back to your role, Sam thought, *if all that's so, then why have you helped us so much? Why didn't you just let nature—karma—run its course? Sooner or later, someone else would've ended up here in samadhi with you, right?*

Is it because the universe needs new worlds? I added.

There's no such thing as need, God said. *That's just a human construct—a projection of your psychology. No, the reason I've stepped in is I'm ready to merge into diffuse consciousness—into Love. It's time to abdicate my role here as creator and maintainer.*

Do you get a good retirement package? I asked.

God smiled. *I knew Chris would be a bad influence on you.*

I laughed.

So what does that have to do with us? Sam thought.

You two will be my successor.

You mean, successors, right? I asked.

No. I'll explain in a moment.

One of the zeppelins veered toward us, and I waved it away. Then I manifested a robot pilot in each of the aircraft's cockpits. Another zeppelin immediately steered clear of Sam's turquoise castle.

Typically, God began, *the evolution of creator beings does follow a more gradual, natural course. Souls are ready when they're ready, which isn't very often. The average soul incarnates eight and a half million times.*

Yikes, I thought. *Are there enough human bodies for that?*

Your species has always been so human-centric. There are rocks, bugs, lizards, other mammals—they're all imbued with various levels of consciousness. And that's just on Earth. It's always the same energy everywhere—this energy—organized into various patterns—some simple, some more complex.

Oh.

So I'm not in the habit of directly accelerating anyone's spiritual growth. But even my energy isn't limitless or permanent. It's winding down, and it has been for centuries. I'm no longer able to do my job in the manner I'm accustomed to. I don't believe this world will thrive if my hand remains on the helm.

And that's where we come in? I asked.

Yes. I couldn't afford to wait until a suitable candidate evolved. So I created one—or two, as it happens.

Sam projected a thought. *So if we've gone through an anomalous process—an acceleration—what does that say about us? Are we different from other energy beings—other creators? Will we still be able to do what you do?*

No, accelerated souls are not capable of creating viable worlds. Look around you. Of course it was only your first effort, but this is a completely derivative reality. There is nothing original here. Even if you became more creative, you wouldn't be capable of manifesting what you imagine—only what you already know.

I've never seen a zeppelin before, I thought.

You've seen photographs. You just made yours longer and sillier-looking than the ones in the photographs. And by the way, your robot pilots are very unhappy.

I took a moment to improve their mood.

Do you see what I mean? God thought. *Do you really think your attention to detail is sufficient to construct an entire world?*

No, I guess not.

Sam thought, *So are you saying that as a team we could maintain the Earth even if we couldn't create it? Is that what you mean?*

Yes. Together, you can. You'll need to remain human on the surface. You'll eat, sleep, have a job, and all that. While we're in bodies, we have ordinary business to attend to. You'll perform most of your spiritual work at night. While others sleep, you'll enter a different samadhi—a particularized creation state. Unlike here on this mountain—and I will erase this soon—the equivalent realm back on Earth is not a blank canvas. It's already populated with my work. You'll see.

So how would this work? Sam asked. *Would we divvy up the maintenance responsibilities—I'll take Asia, Sid takes South America?*

No.

We could take turns, I suggested.

I'm sorry, God thought. *I'm afraid there's only one way this can work. You must cohabit one body— literally merge—or the world will be lost.*

Holy shit, I thought.

Ditto, Sam thought.

Which one? I asked. *Sam's or mine?*

Sam's. Her body is fitter than yours, and her heart is stronger. It will last fourteen years longer.

Oh.

Sid's body will have to die so both of you can live in Sam's. Again, I'm sorry.

So if you were God, you'd draw up a very different blueprint...oh wait, I interjected.

There's that inner Chris acting out again, God thought.

Why aren't we freaking out? I asked. *I don't seem to have any emotions anymore.*

No, God agreed. *They're gone. But you can have them back if you want to—once you're in charge. It's always a balancing act between personhood and godhood.*

So it's my call? I thought. *About feelings and all the other details?*

Our call, Sam corrected.

Lannie nodded.

Is there any demigod couples' counseling we can do? I asked. *We're already disagreeing on pronouns. And something tells me that if we take any internal votes, we might end up deadlocked.*

I'm sure you'll work things out, God said, smiling again. It was an achingly sweet smile. *But here's the real question*, she continued. *Are you ready to sign up? Do both of you agree to this?*

Do we really have a choice? Sam asked.

Yes. Truly. If it feels as though it's a sacrifice, please say no, because that would indicate you still have too much ego in you to do the job properly.

I looked at Sam lovingly, and she returned the look. I could feel her love bathing me with blissful energy. We mutually decided to merge our minds—just long enough to think *We agree,* in unison.

It was an odd sensation. Perhaps it would feel more natural once we were physically united.

Good, God thought. *So here's what comes next. Both of you will wake up in Sam's body in the boat, next to Sid's corpse. This will be a shock. Remember, though, that there was never really a Sid in the first place. We are energy, not matter.*

What did I die of? I asked.

What would you prefer?

An aneurysm?

We can do that, God thought. *In fact, you can do it yourself if you like. Just wish it right before you go back.*

Will you be there? Sam asked.

On the boat, no. I've been seen in two places at once before. It's messy to clean up. I'll be back in New Zealand finishing out Lannie's brief life. The aneurysm idea is appealing, Sid, but I think I'll fall off something. I've ended some of my favorite lives that way.

So how will we know what to do? Sam asked. *Don't we need guidance—training? I'm imagining it will be very challenging at first.*

Yes. Go stay with Chris. I'll help you integrate, and then I'll teach you how to run things. I'll be working through Karma the dog.

Really? I thought. *Karma the dog?*

Yes. Spot isn't bright enough. Karma was originally a spirit dog, too, but she's much more now. How do you think she wrote a message to Chris using pieces of dog food? Do you really think Marco could manage that? She's been helping you for years, Sid.

Oh. I'd forgotten about the dog food, even though it had seemed to be the most amazing of all of Marco's early feats.

What about Marco and the others? Sam asked.

That's another reason that your body is preferable, Sam. With Sid out of the picture, most of the melodrama will fade away. Together, you'll have no problem handling what doesn't. None of these people will seem as formidable now.

We all paused, and I consulted my laundry list of unresolved questions and mysteries that I'd compiled over the last few weeks. Some of them were still pending, and it seemed as though this might be my last opportunity to get them answered.

Do you mind if I ask more questions about what's happened to me? I thought.

Go ahead, God thought. *Satisfy your curiosity if it helps you let go of it all.*

Marco's psychic powers and all that showy stuff back on his island. Was it real?

First of all, it wasn't his island. And as you surmised, he is, in fact, somewhat psychic. But the rest was trickery. Frank was on Marco's payroll at that time, as was one of your brothers. And so forth.

So meeting Marco on the water wasn't a magically arranged synchronicity, either?

No. He bribed two of Tommy T.'s men to let you escape. And he knows those waters well.

Did he really win the lottery? I asked. *Is that how he can afford all this?*

No. His father died and left him money.

At this rate, slogging through every weird event in chronological order would take forever. I decided to streamline our conversation. *Do I have an accurate idea of who Marco, Bhante, Jason, and my brothers are?*

Yes, God thought.

And my parents were being straight with me since we reconnected?

Yes, although their understanding is, of course, incomplete.

Was Buddha really a woman? Sam asked.

That Buddha was—Shakyamuni Buddha. Usually they're a man. RGP really is in possession of her fired-clay diary, by the way.

Who is Faroud—the old man with the turban I met on the street in Ahmednagar?

Like Rinpoche, he's an advanced soul. Both of them contributed their energy to creating you as you are now. Faroud believes he's helping people lose their attachment to material things when he steals from them.

It wasn't those boys who emptied my pockets?

No.

Is Rinpoche Baba's reincarnation?

No, but his belief that he is represents a garbled intuition of what the world needs—two souls in one body.

Is Ram Baba's successor?

No. The role is self-appointed.

Here's something else, I thought. *I had a dream where Baba told me I had been Buddha's son. Is that true?*

Yes. That was Baba, and he spoke the truth. You were Rahula and Samavati was Mahapajapati Gotami—Buddha's aunt—who raised him when his mother died a week after his birth.

So Sam didn't just happen to get dragged into my drama, did she? We have an ages-old connection that we sensed when we met, right?

Yes. Your attraction to one another is both historical and a reflection of your upcoming symbiosis. You really are two halves of a whole.

I realized that I didn't need more answers. I was content to know that it all *could* be explained. My curiosity was clearly irrelevant to the matters at hand.

Hey, I thought. *My first name is Sid and Sam's last name is Arthur, so together we're Sid and Arthur— Siddhartha.*

God shrugged. *So sue me. I like a good pun.*

Epilogue

So that's how Sam and I came to run the world. If you notice a cataclysm begins to develop—a world war, an epidemic, a rogue asteroid en route to Rhode Island—*but then it doesn't happen*—that's us. Of course it goes both ways. We certainly don't withhold a modest disaster or hardship if that's what you need. We love you too much to cheat you out of any essential human experience.

Sam and I merged seamlessly. There just wasn't that much individuality left in us after meeting Lannie/God.

The smallest things trip us up the most. Should we order a burrito or an enchilada at the taqueria (where everyone stares at our boobs no matter what we wear)? And which ghost-self gets to select the next US ambassador to France?

I want to acknowledge that I've changed most of the names, places, and other identifying features to create this so-called novel. I've also omitted some of what happened to limit the length of the book, create a more coherent narrative flow, and—believe it or not—make my story more credible.

In terms of metaphysical content, I've taken the precaution of including several spiritual red herrings to prevent readers from becoming inadvertently accelerated in their march toward enlightenment. If you were a recalcitrant jar—and the analogy is apt—would you rather be battered against the edge of a countertop or run under hot water for a few minutes? I'm picking the hot water for you.

Finally, I've selected a likely impostor and convinced him he's the author of this book. Obviously, our work would be compromised if our identity was known.

It turns out that it's quite easy to foster this sort of grandiose delusion in a writer's mind. They're all a little full of themselves, aren't they?

A word about the author...

Verlin Darrow is currently a psychotherapist who lives with his psychotherapist wife in the woods near the Monterey Bay in northern California. They diagnose each other as necessary. Verlin is a former professional volleyball player, country-western singer/songwriter, import store owner, and assistant guru in a small, benign cult, from which he graduated everyone when he left.

Before bowing to the need for higher education, a much younger Verlin ran a punch press in a sheetmetal factory, drove a taxi, worked as a night janitor, shoveled asphalt on a road crew, and installed wood floors. He barely missed being blown up by Mt. St. Helens, survived the 1985 Mexico City earthquake, and (so far) he's successfully weathered his own internal disasters.

Verlin is also the author of a psycho-spiritual mystery: *Blood and Wisdom*. He encourages readers to visit his website or email him to find out more.

verlindarrow.com
verlindarrow@gmail.com

Thank you for purchasing
this publication of The Wild Rose Press, Inc.

For questions or more information
contact us at
info@thewildrosepress.com.

The Wild Rose Press, Inc.
www.thewildrosepress.com

To visit with authors of
The Wild Rose Press, Inc.
join our yahoo loop at
http://groups.yahoo.com/group/thewildrosepress/